VAGABOND

BOOK TWO OF THE HIGH REALM CHRONICLES

James Robert Wright

First published in November 2020

ISBN 9798-568491309

For Mother and Father

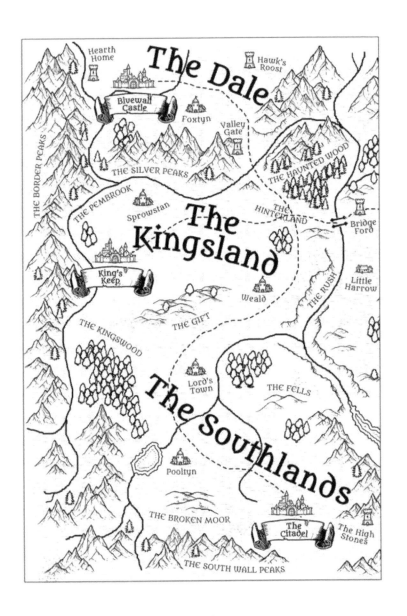

THE STORM MOUNTAINS

Storm Hall

Rosewood

The Head

Porby

Domadge Bartyn

Oaktyn

Eaglestone

Lynport

THE VIELDING

THE GREENWOOD

Eagle Mount

THE PINK HILLS

THE EASTERN DOWNS

Ashbee Castle

Elderwyne

Ruins of Ryding

THE SHATTERED CLIFFS

High Realm

THE GRANITE MOUNTAINS

Prologue

Deakon rushed from the barracks that had been his home ever since he had arrived at the castle, buttoning his jerkin as he ran. He snatched up a spear from the rack beside the door, testing the weight and balance as he did so. He had been a soldier for many years, and such rituals were automatic to him. He had lost friends to poor quality weapons in the past, and he did not intend to join them any time soon.

'What's happening?' he called across to one of his fellow soldiers as they emerged into the castle courtyard.

The other simply shrugged.

'No idea,' he replied.

'Enough of your jabbering!' the serjeant barked, overhearing them. 'Jump to it!'

More and more soldiers spilled out of the barracks, their white shields flashing in the afternoon sun.

'Where are we going, serjeant?' Deakon called.

The serjeant ignored him, and led his men towards the keep of the castle that lay a couple of hundred paces away.

'It's probably just the wedding getting out of hand,' Deakon muttered to his friend, who sniggered in reply.

Catching another glance from their serjeant, the two soldiers stopped their chuckling and ran in silence. The air was filled with the sound of boots pounding the flagstones beneath their feet and their belts and chain mail jangling.

A sudden shout from up ahead drew Deakon's attention, and he saw some of their fellow soldiers edging backwards out of the keep. Some of them were injured, clutching at their wounds, and all of them were looking fearfully at something that Deakon could not see.

The source of their fear soon became clear, when other figures followed the soldiers out of the keep. They were a filthy, ragtag group. They looked to be the prisoners from the dungeons, deep down in the bowels of the castle. But how they had gotten free of their cells, or where they had found weapons, Deakon could not have guessed. Two huge men, just as filthy and mangey as the others, led the rest of the prisoners down the steps from the castle keep in pursuit of the defeated-looking soldiers.

'Quickly boys!' the serjeant shouted.

Deakon and his fellow soldiers dashed forward, joining with more of their number who were spilling through the gates from the town beyond. They reached the soldiers who had been pursued, battered and beaten, from the keep. They looked relieved at the sight of reinforcements.

'Hey, you! What's going on?' Deakon asked one of them, who was cradling an injured arm.

'He's dead!' the soldier said, looking wildly at him.

'Who is?'

'Sir Rayden! The boy killed him.'

Deakon frowned, sure that the soldier was mistaken. The filthy prisoners were gathered in front of the keep, swords and spears and axes in their hands, looking defiantly at Deakon and the other soldiers. The dirty, rough-looking prisoners were outnumbered, but this seemed to do little to discourage them. The two huge prisoners had blood on their weapons, and appeared eager for more.

There was muttering all around Deakon as word spread that Sir Rayden had fallen. He could not believe it. Sir Rayden was the greatest swordsman in The Southstones, and it had been his wedding day. How in the Mother's name could he be dead? Surely he could not be killed by these prisoners who resembled little more than a band of ruffians.

And then the two huge men parted and a single figure appeared amongst the filthy prisoners. He was young, little more than a boy, but he carried a beautiful sword in his hand. He looked out across at the mass of soldiers that were stood in a semi-circle around his grimy band of convicts, waiting to kill him and the others who had somehow escaped from the dungeons of Eagle Mount.

Now, the boy was speaking to the motley bunch of prisoners. Deakon was too far away to hear the words, but he seemed to speak to them as though he was their leader.

A boy, giving inspiring words to grown men?

It was something Deakon never thought he would see. But it mattered little. Whatever the boy had been hoping to achieve would end here; he would die on the tip of a spear, and it would give Deakon no greater pleasure than to be the one to do it. He pushed his way to the very front rank, in the hopes of being the first one to reach the enemy. If Sir Rayden had indeed be killed, then Deakon would avenge him.

Archers levelled their crossbows at the boy and his band of miscreants, and Deakon smirked beneath his helmet. These prisoners would pay for what they had done. He waited expectantly to see the looks of horror pass over their faces.

And then something altogether unexpected happened. The escaped prisoners were cheering! Deakon had been expecting screams, and begs for mercy, and cries for forgiveness. But they were actually *cheering*.

'For Lord Roberd!' the boy yelled.

Deakon's mouth dropped open slightly in surprise, and he felt something he had not felt in a long time.

Fear.

Then the prisoners were charging directly towards him, with those two huge men at the front. And Deakon knew, in that moment, that he was in trouble.

CHAPTER ONE

For honour

Lord Warner Camoren paced restlessly up and down the study, his hands clasped firmly behind his back. He was an early riser, usually waking long before the cockerels announced the dawn, and that morning had been no different. After checking that no message had arrived during the night, he had hidden himself away in the study, ignoring the sounds of the castle waking around him. From the study window, he had watched the sun rise in the west, the inky blue sky fading into pale orange, before pacing impatiently up and down the chamber, scowling at his surroundings.

The study that he had taken over in this dingy castle was much smaller than that in his own home of Pooltyn Castle, back in The Southstones, where he was the baron. The walls were bare of ornaments and the fixtures were basic. The rest of the castle was no better; the hallways were draughty and in places the outer walls were in need of repair. The Leclarc family, who had called the castle home before Lord Warner had taken it for himself, were an old noble family of respected heritage, but they were not rich. The nobility of The Southstones would never have allowed themselves to fall into poverty as the Leclarcs had done, and Lord Warner had felt little sympathy for them when he had forced them into their own dungeon. He had not cared that it was the family's generous, charitable nature towards the folk who lived in the surrounding villages that had caused Sir Jay Leclarc to give away most of their gold, and if anything this had actually lowered Lord Warner's opinion of them. Common folk should respect and fear their noble masters, in his opinion. The Leclarcs were soft-hearted and weak, and their miserable castle was evidence of that.

It was fair to say that Lord Warner had enjoyed little of his time in Hightop Castle.

However, the basicness of his current lodgings was not his primary concern at that moment, and was not the reason for his restless pacing. It had been over a week since he had received his last communication from Sir Rayden Monfort. Lord Warner had little love for Lord Aric Monfort's son, but the silence did concern him.

Soon after Lord Aric had removed the Jacelyn family from power and seized the castle of Eagle Mount for himself, he had tasked Lord Warner and his men with capturing Hightop Castle. The home of the Leclarc family lay just a day's ride to the north of Eagle Mount, and offered spectacular views of the surrounding land. Lord Aric believed that some of the noble families in the north of The Head might not bow so readily to Monfort rule, and so, as Lord Aric's most trusted friend and baron, Lord Warner had been ordered to take Hightop Castle and keep watch for any signs of aggression from the north.

Lord Warner had easily taken the castle from the Leclarc family. He kept only a handful of soldiers to guard his castle, and they were quickly overpowered by Lord Warner's much larger force. Sir Jay Leclarc had refused to bow down to Lord Aric's rule, and so Lord Warner had taken great pleasure in imprisoning him, his family and his handful of soldiers in the castle's dungeons. As he shut and locked the dungeon door, plunging them into darkness, Lord Warner had told them that they ought to get used to their new Monfort masters, as they were there to stay.

True to his duke's command, Lord Warner had taken up residence of the small castle on its lonely hill and kept a watchful eye to the north. While he expected that most of The Head's nobility had no love for their new Monfort rulers, they had clearly decided that it would be foolish to attempt to fight back, and so had wisely behaved themselves. No sign of aggression or opposition to Monfort rule had appeared from the north, or from any direction for that matter, and Lord Warner had quickly grown restless and frustrated by the lack of action. This guard duty seemed below the Baron of Pooltyn, and the task should instead have fallen to one of the many lesser lords or knights that Lord Aric had at his disposal.

Lord Aric had kept Lord Warner well informed of the progress they were making in establishing Monfort control over The Head, and he had received almost daily messages from him. This went some way to helping to remove Lord Warner's feeling that he had been forgotten out there in his isolated castle. When he had learned that the boy who had been Lord Roberd Jacelyn's ward was continuing to evade capture, he had offered to send some of his own men to aid in the search. Lord Aric had declined the offer, not wanting to weaken the garrison of Hightop Castle.

Then, a little over a week ago, Lord Warner had received a letter, this time from Sir Rayden Monfort, his duke's son. The letter was brief and unfriendly, saying merely that Lord Aric was returning to The Southstones and that Rayden himself was now in charge of The Head. Lord Warner had not been surprised to learn that Lord Aric was not remaining in The Head, but a part of him regretted that he himself had not gone with him. Lord Warner had long been a close friend to the duke for many long years, and his counsel had always been considered welcome. Sir Rayden, on the other hand, thought little of Lord Warner. The two had butted heads on several occasions, no doubt triggered by Sir Rayden's jealousy of Lord Warner's close relationship with his father. It was no secret that Lord Aric despised his son.

Shortly after Lord Aric's departure, another letter had arrived from Sir Rayden, just as short and curt as the last one, telling Lord Warner that it was not necessary for him to travel back to Eagle Mount for his wedding to Sophya Jacelyn. Lord Warner had thrown that letter straight into the fire. He had harboured no intention of attending anyway. He had never enjoyed feasts and banquets and had no interest in watching the peacock Rayden flaunting himself. Especially not when the Monfort family was on the cusp of achieving greatness. Other things were more important

But since then, there had been nothing but silence from Eagle Mount. No letters at all. And this is what now concerned him, and was the reason for Lord Warner's unsettled pacing up and down the study.

Perhaps this was just Rayden being Rayden, he thought. He was certainly not his father, and maybe he did not place as much value in the loyal and honourable barons of The Southstones as Lord Aric did, and as such did not think it necessary to write to Lord Warner and keep him updated. He shuddered at the thought of what the Monfort family would become in future years, when Lord Aric would no longer be there to lead them.

He paused his pacing and glanced at the blank piece of parchment lying on the desk. Several times over the past few days he had been tempted to pick up his quill and write a letter to Sir Rayden himself, demanding an update on the current situation. But each time he had felt this urge he had instead shaken his head and resisted the temptation. Afterall, he did not want to look like some insecure maiden, unsettled by a lack of attention. Likewise, he did not want to write directly to Lord Aric himself. He knew that the duke had no love for his son, but Lord Warner was well aware that even his friendship with Lord Aric would not protect him if he openly criticised his son. An insult to a member of the Monfort family was unforgivable, regardless of how deserving of criticism that particular Monfort was.

The sun had fully risen by now, and Lord Warner let out a gruff sigh. He should not dwell on the silence coming from Eagle Mount, and would instead need to focus on the coming day.

He gave a sudden start when there came a swift knock on the door. He wrenched it open immediately, alarming the soldier on the other side whose fist was still raised in a knocking motion.

'What is it?' Lord Warner demanded. 'A letter?'

'No, my lord,' the soldier said, stepping backwards at the thunderous expression on his baron's face. 'Horsemen are approaching the castle. We're not sure who they are.'

Lord Warner seized his sword from beside the door and marched out of the study. He made his way out onto the castle walls and paced around to where another of his soldiers waved an arm at him. Reaching the man, Lord Warner put his hands against the stone parapets and peered over the battlements, staring in the direction that the soldier was pointing.

There were four horsemen approaching from the south-east, galloping up the hill towards the castle's closed gates. They looked to be nervous and skittish, and were glancing over their shoulders as though the very hounds of hell gave chase. Lord Warner peered beyond the riders but saw no sign of pursuers in the morning sun.

'Can you make out who they are?' Lord Warner asked the soldier who had spotted them.

The soldier shook his head, looking warily at his baron. Lord Warner was prone to fits of rage, and would regularly take his anger out on those nearby.

'Sorry, my lord. Not at this distance I can't.'

Lord Warner glanced across at the man, and saw the state of the soldier's blue jerkin. Muck was smeared across the Camoren family's symbol of the swan on his breast.

'You are filthy,' he said in disgust. 'Get out of my sight.'

While the soldier hurried away, Lord Warner shielded his eyes with his hand and squinted at the horsemen. However, if the soldier's young eyes could not make out who they were then he had no hope. He was in his sixtieth year, and while he preferred his head to be shaved like an egg, his white beard betrayed his age. But if anyone thought that this made him less formidable then it was a mistake they only made once. Many had seen him use his fists to punish those who displeased him, even if their crime was little more than having a dirty uniform.

Lord Warner continued gazing intently towards the four figures who were still riding hard towards the castle. Were they friend or foe? He could not tell, but he would not take any chances. He turned to the soldiers who had begun to gather on the walls, looking interestedly at the approaching riders. Over their heads two banners flapped from the poles above the gate. One carried the black marching knight symbol of the Monforts, while the other bore the swan symbol of the Camorens.

'Archers!' Lord Warner barked at them.

The archers among the soldiers jumped at his loud voice, and hurried to obey. They notched arrows to their bow strings, and aimed down at the approaching horsemen, ready to let loose at their baron's command.

'Stop right there!' Lord Warner bellowed, when the four figures had ridden within shouting distance. 'You have a dozen arrows aimed right at you.'

The horsemen reined in sharply and looked up at Lord Warner high above them on top of the wall. Their horses shifted nervously, their hooves tapping restlessly on the grass.

'Lord Warner Camoren? We're friends!' shouted their leader.

'You must consider me a fool if you think I would simply take your word for it. Who are you?' Lord Warner demanded.

18

'My name is Sir Edmon Crafter,' came the reply. 'I bring ill tidings, my lord, which do not cause me joy to carry.'

'Crafter…Crafter…' Lord Warner muttered under his breath, wracking his brain.

The name of Crafter was vaguely familiar to Lord Warner. The minor noble Crafter family had a castle in The Southstones, he knew. He could not recall one of them being called Edmon, but he knew that the head of the family had many sons. Lord Warner had not concerned himself with learning the names of all members of this unimportant noble family.

'Have you come from Eagle Mount?' he demanded, shouting down.

'Yes, my lord,' Sir Edmon called back up to him. 'We are survivors from the battle.'

Lord Warner felt a tightening in his chest.

'Battle? Enter then, sir,' he shouted. 'You will tell me everything.'

He descended the steps that led down into the castle's modest courtyard, ordering the gates to be opened. He reached ground level just as Sir Edmon swung himself wearily from his saddle. Up close he looked awful. His face was surprisingly young, but he appeared exhausted and filthy. A splash of dried blood stained his surcoat, but he gave a reassuring shrug when he saw Lord Warner glance at it.

'It's Jacelyn blood, my lord, not mine.'

'What has happened?' Lord Warner demanded.

Sir Edmon gestured for the baron to walk with him. They stepped away from Lord Warner's soldiers, as though Sir Edmon did not want to speak openly in front of them.

'Eagle Mount is lost, my lord,' he said. 'It happened on the day of the wedding between Sir Rayden and Lord Roberd's daughter. The Jacelyn prisoners in the dungeons rebelled, under the leadership of the boy who had been Lord Roberd's ward. He had returned to the castle without anyone knowing, I think. And then the townsfolk joined in, and we did not stand a chance against such numbers.'

'And Sir Rayden?'

'Dead, my lord,' Sir Edmon said with a rueful shake of his head.

'Dead?' Lord Warner repeated.

'Slain by the boy's own hand. Many of our soldiers were killed too, and the rest were captured.'

'How did you get away?' Lord Warner asked, his eyes narrowed.

He had no time for cowards who would rather flee and save their skin rather than die with honour. He glanced at the three other men who had accompanied Sir Edmon to Hightop Castle. Their Monfort uniforms showed that they were some of Lord Aric's own soldiers, but like Sir Edmon they were filthy and showed signs of battle. Lord Warner's own men were helping them from their saddles and passing them water from the well in the corner of the courtyard, which they accepted gratefully.

'Some of us managed to escape Eagle Mount when we realised the battle was lost. It gives me no pleasure to admit that we left, rather than stay and fight, but I knew it was important for us to reach you here,' Sir Edmon said. 'We split up. Some planned to head back to The Southstones, to tell Lord Aric what has happened. I knew that you were the only remaining force of Monfort men left in The Head, so I came this way to inform you of this ill news. I only regret that it has taken so long for me to get here. For a week we have been hunted by Jacelyn search parties. We have been travelling only by night, and have had to take the longer route to get here to avoid their patrols. Even so, we lost several men along the way in skirmishes with their outriders.'

Lord Warner nodded and put his hand on Sir Edmon's shoulder.

'You have done well, Sir Edmon.'

'Thank you, my lord,' Sir Edmon said, smiling wearily, and he allowed himself to be steered inside the castle keep.

'Come to my study, I want to hear all the details. Leave nothing out. And I will have a chamber prepared for you. There are plenty spare.'

Sir Edmon glanced at the empty bedchambers as they passed them.

'What did you do with the previous owners of this castle, my lord?' he asked in an offhand way.

'The Leclarcs?' Lord Warner said. 'They are still here, down in the dungeons. I was going to put them to the sword, but you never know when hostages might come in useful.'

'Very wise, my lord,' Sir Edmon agreed.

They arrived at the study, and while Sir Edmon lowered himself, achingly, into a chair, Lord Warner went to the window that faced south. He gazed out, looking towards the distant shape that was the great castle of Eagle Mount. He clenched his hands behind his back.

He was unsurprised to find that he was not concerned about the death of Sir Rayden. He would certainly not mourn him, and he doubted Lord Aric would either. However, the fall of Eagle Mount was a terrible loss. Lord Warner was concerned about how his beloved duke would react to this news. Did he already know? Lord Warner knew he should send a messenger of his own, to make doubly sure that the news managed to reach The Southstones. But, with the Jacelyns back in control of The Head, the road would be dangerous.

And this boy who had slain Sir Rayden caused Lord Warner some uneasiness. He may have had no love for Lord Aric's son, but he could not deny that Sir Rayden was a fine swordsman. That he had been bested by an untrained boy unsettled him.

'Tell me about this boy,' he said, his back still turned to Sir Edmon.

'He names himself "Merric", I believe. His parents were the lord and lady of Ryding before their deaths, but he is half Jacelyn I hear.'

'And he styles himself as Duke of The Head now, I suppose?' Lord Warner said, scathingly.

'I understand that to be the case, my lord, yes,' Sir Edmon confirmed.

'Lord Aric will want this upstart boy's head,' Lord Warner muttered to himself.

'Sorry, what was that, my lord?'

'Nothing,' Lord Warner said, studying the distant castle of Eagle Mount where even now this Merric boy was likely revelling in his victory over the Monforts. The idea of it made Lord Warner feel sick to the stomach.

'Sir Rayden should be ashamed of himself,' he growled. 'He, a knight, being bested by little more than a child.'

'What do you plan on doing with the Leclarc family, my lord?' Sir Edmon inquired, looking at Lord Warner's back. 'Barter them in return for safe passage out of The Head?'

Lord Warner kept on looking out of the window, but after a moment he shook his head.

'I have no intention of fleeing back to The Southstones,' he said. 'Eagle Mount may have fallen, but I will not make the same mistakes as Sir Rayden. I will hold out here, and when Lord Aric returns at the head of his army, he will find me here still.'

Sir Edmon shifted in the chair slightly, as though he was desperate to leave The Head at the first opportunity.

'And if this Merric boy attacks you before Lord Aric returns?' Sir Edmon asked. 'From what I can gather he's become a bit of a beacon of hope for folk here in The Head. They have been inspired by his victory, and they will not allow us to remain here.'

'If the boy is foolish enough to try and take this castle by force then he will receive a true Camoren welcome,' Lord Warner smirked, turning to face the young knight. 'We have taken in the crops from every field within a league of here. We have enough food stored to last us six months, so if they think they can lay a siege and try to starve us out then they will be sorely disappointed. If they choose to try and take the castle by force then we Camorens are experts in siege warfare and know how to defend a fortress. The Jacelyns will give up long before they breach these walls, and they will lose a hundred men to every one of mine killed.'

'And the Leclarcs?'

'If this upstart boy thinks to draw his sword against this castle then I will execute them atop the walls myself, for all The Head to see. Their blood will be on his hands.'

'But what if they do manage to capture the castle?' Sir Edmon inquired.

'I would gladly sacrifice myself for my duke.'

'All of The Southstones has heard of your honour, and your courage, my lord,' Sir Edmon said, sounding slightly disturbed by Lord Warner's willingness to fight to the death. 'But I do not think Lord Aric would want his closest friend to give up his life needlessly.'

'It would not be needless, young sir,' Lord Warner said, his hand forming a fist and his eyes glowing with hardly contained pride. 'If we are destined to die here then all The Southstones will be inspired by our sacrifice. Where Sir Rayden failed, Lord Warner Camoren, Baron of Pooltyn, will carve his name into history.'

The look of worry on Sir Edmon's face must have been obvious, as Lord Warner adopted a softer tone and even forced himself to smile. The young knight was barely out of boyhood himself, and he had yet to even begin to grow a beard on his face.

'Do not fear, young knight,' he said. 'You will share in the honour and glory. Our deaths will be remembered in the annals of history.'

The words did little to remove the nervousness from Sir Edmon.

'If you choose to stay here, and they attack us, then my men and I will stand beside you, of course,' he vowed, 'but this castle holds little strategic value to Lord Aric now. Surely it would be better to abandon it and make our way back to The Southstones? Then we could fight for Lord Aric again, if he makes another attempt to take The Head. We would be no good to him dead.'

'You have been through an ordeal, I know,' Lord Warner said, almost fatherly, putting his hand on the knight's shoulder. 'But have courage, son. When Lord Aric returns he will either find us here, standing victorious on a pile of Jacelyn corpses, or instead he will discover us as the valiant dead ourselves, with us having honoured our duke to our final breath.'

Sir Edmon knew that Lord Warner could not be discouraged from his determination to remain in Hightop Castle, no matter what fate that may bring.

'You are certain that Lord Aric will return and try to retake The Head, my lord?' he said, as though wanting that reassurance that they would not be holding out on their own for long.

'I am,' Lord Warner guaranteed. 'I do not know when, and I do not know how, but mark my words. I know Lord Aric, and he will not give up this easily. When the king learns of Sir Rayden's death then he is sure to lend his aid to our cause. As far as the king is concerned, this Merric boy murdered the Jacelyns, and we will do nothing to discourage that view. And now the boy has killed Rayden too; the king's own nephew! With the combined strength of The Southstones and The Kingsland, these Jacelyns will not stand a chance. Especially if the boy, who you say has become a beacon to rally around, can be brought down from his perch. We here will resist as long as we can. We will fight to the last man if needed, and we will show these easterners how men from The Southstones fight and, if necessary, die.'

* * *

Later that night, once the rest of the castle was asleep, Sir Edmon left his bedchamber and crept quietly down the deserted hallways of the castle. If Lord Warner could not be encouraged to leave Hightop Castle and return to The Southstones, then only one course of action was left. Despite the Baron of Pooltyn's desire for a glorious death, such bloodiness was unnecessary and would achieve nothing. Sir Edmon was determined not to see any more pointless death.

As he sneaked through the chilly hallways of the castle, his heart was in his mouth. Lord Warner's soldiers had been more disturbed by the news from Eagle Mount than their baron, and had been on high alert ever since. If any of them were to discover him on his night-time mission then his head would likely be mounted on a spike by daybreak.

Reaching the moonlit castle courtyard, Sir Edmon crouched in the shadows cast by the moon, awaiting the signal. He only needed to wait a few moments before he heard the muffled sound of a struggle as the men who had accompanied him from Eagle Mount crept up to the soldiers standing sentry atop the walls, and seized them round the necks until they fell unconscious. They gently laid down the lifeless bodies, keeping as quiet as possible, before looking down at Sir Edmon and giving him a nod.

With the coast clear, he dashed across the courtyard towards the castle gates. Reaching them, he glanced over his shoulder to make sure there were no eyes watching him in the darkness. Satisfied that no one was going to raise an alarm, he turned his attention back to the gates. They had been barred with a heavy locking pin. He heaved, but could not lift it on his own. He looked back up to the walls and waved urgently. Moments later, his three men had joined him at the gate, having discarded in disgust their jerkins bearing the Monfort family symbol. Between the four of them they lifted the heavy wooden bar from its brackets, dropping it silently to one side.

While his men heaved the gates open with barely audible grunts, Sir Edmon took hold of a burning torch and waved it back and forth into the night, looking into the dark trees that lay a hundred paces away down the hill.

At once, shadowy figures poured out of the wood, hurrying noiselessly towards the castle and the now opened gates. They were led by two huge knights, identical in matching green surcoats bearing the oak tree symbol of the Oakheart family. They wore no armour to allow them to move silently, and their swords were in their hands, blackened with soot so they would not shine in the moonlight. Behind the two knights came a flood of soldiers, their faces shining with silent excitement.

Sir Edmon stood to one side, letting the men into the castle. He reached out and touched the arm of one of the Oakheart knights as they passed.

'They're in the dungeons,' he muttered.

The Oakheart knight nodded and was gone, disappearing with his men through the door that led into the castle keep.

Moments later came the sound Sir Edmon had been anticipating. A cry of alarm echoed from somewhere deep inside the keep as Lord Warner's men discovered that the castle had been overrun by enemies. There came loud shouts from the attackers, demanding that the Camoren soldiers yield and throw down their weapons.

Sir Edmon ran back into the keep, his sword drawn. In the hallway he passed the Leclarc family who were being escorted up from the dungeons. They looked hungry and tired and confused by their sudden rescue. Sir Jay and his son, Sir Ralph, glanced at Sir Edmon in curiosity as he hurried past, a determined look on his face.

He dashed upstairs, glad that he did not encounter any of Lord Warner's men on the way. He paused outside the door into Lord Warner's study. He took a deep breath to compose himself, before hurrying through the door.

'My lord!' he exclaimed.

'Sir Edmon!' the Baron of Pooltyn said. 'We have been betrayed!'

He was hurrying to belt his sword around his waist. Sir Edmon stiffened, but Lord Warner did not seem to suspect him.

'It seems that the time to die for The Southstones is upon us already,' Lord Warner said. 'Will you stand with me?'

'It is not too late,' Sir Edmon said, looking anxiously at the door behind him. 'We do not need to die. They will allow us to surrender, I am certain of it.'

All around them there was the sound of Lord Warner's men yielding and giving themselves up to the attackers. But Lord Warner himself looked furiously at Sir Edmon, as though disgusted by his lack of courage, and pushed past him.

'Tell me,' he said, as Sir Edmon followed him downstairs, 'do you flee from every battle you face? It is time you actually showed some courage for once!'

They rounded a corner and came face to face with the hulking shapes of Sir Oskar and Sir Orsten Oakheart who were blocking the passageway. Beyond them, Lord Warner's soldiers were being led into the courtyard, their hands raised.

Lord Warner gave his men one revolted look, before turning his eyes to the two Oakheart knights before him.

'For The Southstones!' he bellowed fearlessly, raising his sword.

The two Oakheart knights lifted their own swords, ready to defend themselves, but Lord Warner had noticed Sir Edmon standing still behind him. He turned and saw that the young knight had his sword aimed directly at him.

'What are you doing?' Lord Warner demanded, looking from Sir Edmon to the sword tip hovering near his chest.

'Put down your sword, my lord,' Sir Edmon urged. 'It's all over.'

'It was you! You let them in!' Lord Warner gasped, realisation setting in. 'You yellow-bellied coward!'

With a roar of fury, he thrust his sword at the traitor, who hurriedly parried it away. Lord Warner continued to strike at Sir Edmon again and again, who repeatedly blocked the attacks, stepping backwards.

'Stop, my lord!' Sir Edmon pleaded. 'The castle is lost.'

'I am Lord Aric's most loyal baron,' Lord Warner snarled. 'I told you: I will win, or I will die for my duke, with honour!'

The sound of steel on steel rang out again, as Lord Warner launched yet another attack. Sir Edmon gave way before the baron's fury but did not attempt to strike at his opponent. The two Oakheart knights hurried after them, ready to intervene.

'No!' Sir Edmon said to them. 'Do not kill him!'

'Fight back!' Lord Warner spat.

'Your men have yielded,' Sir Edmon said. 'You do not need to die. They have chosen to become prisoners rather than corpses. I urge you to do the same! The castle has been taken, with not a drop of blood spilled.'

'I will yet spill yours!' Lord Warner vowed.

Sir Edmon parried away one final strike, before sheathing his sword and raising his hands.

'I am unarmed,' he said.

'I care not. I will strike you down regardless, you traitor,' Lord Warner seethed, raising his sword to deliver the killing blow.

'There is no honour in killing an unarmed opponent,' Sir Edmon reminded him. 'Especially when you would shortly follow me to the grave yourself. Is that how you would want to be remembered?'

Lord Warner glanced over his shoulder at Sir Oskar and Sir Orsten, who were stood with their weapons drawn, aimed directly at his back. He looked furiously at Sir Edmon.

'Men who kill unarmed opponents rarely live on in history,' Sir Edmon reminded him, praying that his gamble would pay off. 'I should know; I've read more books than most.'

'Then draw your sword. I will die with honour, you rogue.'

'No, my lord.'

When Sir Edmon made no move to lower his hands, Lord Warner let out a bellow of frustration and anger. His sword tip lowered slightly. A heartbeat later he let go of it entirely.

'Have it your way then.'

The sword fell to the flagstone floor, and the clang echoed off the walls. Sir Oskar reached down and retrieved the sword, while Sir Orsten firmly took hold of Sir Warner's shoulder.

Sir Edmon breathed out slowly, relief flooding through him.

'Lord Aric will hear of your treachery,' Lord Warner promised him. 'He will not rest until you, Sir Edmon Crafter, have been punished for betraying The Southstones.'

'Then I fear he will be chasing a phantom,' Sir Edmon said simply. 'Sir Edmon does not exist.'

Lord Warner frowned at him, not understanding the meaning of his words.

'Congratulations, my lord,' Sir Oskar said to Sir Edmon. 'Your plan worked perfectly.'

'You sound like you doubted it, brother,' Sir Orsten said, grinning. 'I always knew it would work.'

Lord Warner turned his head to frown at Sir Oskar, confused. But then, a look of realisation passed over his face. With gritted teeth he understood that he had been fooled from the very beginning.

'I assume,' Lord Warner said with begrudging admiration, turning back to the young man who had defeated him, 'that I address Merric Jacelyn?'

- CHAPTER TWO -

The spriggan

The men sweated as they heaved on the ropes, grunting from the effort. The heavy stone was lifted slowly, inch by painful inch, off the ground.

'Put your backs into it, boys!' the foreman shouted. 'You're nearly there!'

Sir Paravell Porcourt watched the men work, hands clasped behind his back. The work on the new priory was almost complete, and most of the folk of the village of Porby had turned out to watch the final stones being placed. Sir Paravell felt their admiring eyes watching him, but he modestly tried his best to ignore them.

Porby was not a rich village, but the folk who lived there were happy enough. Sir Paravell himself had seen to that. He had provided the coin for the construction of the new priory out of his own pocket, stripping away a large portion of his inherited wealth in the process. But to him it had been an easy decision to make. The tired wooden building that had been the village's old priory had been in desperate need of repair. The stained glass windows had faded, and the holes in the roof had let in the rain, leaving a smell of damp. Prior Simms had wept in thanks when Sir Paravell had announced his plans for the construction of the brand new stone priory, and the village folk had been equally grateful.

'Heave!' the foreman bellowed.

The workmen gritted their teeth and pulled hard on the ropes. Most were stripped to the waist and their bare torsos were glistening with sweat from the effort. Slowly but surely the block of sandstone edged higher into the air. The foreman stood below it and peered upwards, with his hand shielding his eyes from the sun.

'That's it, that's high enough boys! Now, swing it across,' he ordered. 'A bit more…a bit more.'

A sudden loud crack cut through the air and the wooden scaffold that supported the weight of the stone splintered. The crowd of village folk who had assembled to see the completion of their new priory gasped in alarm. The workmen shouted out in pain as the rope began racing through their hands as the stone fell.

Seeing the sudden danger, Sir Paravell dove forward, grabbing hold of the end of the rope. He dug his boots into the ground and leant back. His heels left deep gouges in the grass as he was pulled forwards by the weight. With his strength behind the rope, the falling block of sandstone came to a rest just a few feet above the foreman's head.

The foreman wiped a bead of sweat off his brow and staggered away in shock, taking a swig of a drink from a flask he had pulled from his pocket. Sir Paravell directed a pair of men to secure the rope, while the rest went about repairing the scaffold. He let go of the rope now that the danger was over, and tugged a cloth from his belt which he used to clean the dirt from his hands.

'It looks like you should have become an engineer, sir,' Prior Simms said, when Sir Paravell had left the men to their work.

The young prior was stood nearby and looked impressed at Sir Paravell's timely intervention.

'It seems much too perilous,' Sir Paravell smiled back. 'I shall stick with being a knight.'

Sir Paravell was a tall man, broad of chest, and he kept his long hair tied behind his head. His father had died three winters previously, but Sir Proudlock Porcourt had not been a good man. He had ruled his lands with an iron fist, feared and hated by his folk in equal measure. No one had been sad when Sir Proudlock had died, and Sir Paravell had sworn that day to be everything that his father had not.

He was popular among the folk who lived in the land around the village of Porby. When he had taken his vows and become a knight he had sworn to look out for the weak and defenceless, and whether that meant riding to war to keep them from harm or building a new priory for them to pray in, he had promised himself that he would not disappoint them. He may only rule over a small village, but he would act just the same as if he had been a baron, or even a duke. It was the duty, and the privilege, of the highborn noble families of High Realm to do so.

'Sir Paravell!'

The call came from behind him. Sir Paravell tore his eyes from the construction work and turned to see his castle's steward striding through the village square towards him.

'Milas,' Sir Paravell greeted him. 'Have you completed your check of the winter stores?'

It was the beginning of autumn, and it would be just a matter of weeks now before the winter would set in. Castles across High Realm were busy preparing for the cold months and making sure they had enough food and firewood not just for themselves, but for the common folk that would need it too.

'Forgive me, sir, but I was drawn away from the task,' Milas said. 'This could not wait.'

He indicated another man, who Sir Paravell had not noticed at first. He was a farmer from the looks of him. His dirty grey hair poked out from beneath a grubby hat, and his threadbare clothes were just as scruffy. He was old and stooped, and his lined face was drooped in sadness.

'I regret to say that there's been another attack, sir,' Milas said.

'Tell me,' Sir Paravell said, suddenly serious, looking from his steward to the elderly farmer.

Milas glanced uneasily at the nearby village folk.

'It's not a matter to be discussed here, I fear,' he said.

A few minutes later, Sir Paravell was seated in the hall of Porby Castle. It was a modest castle, but it offered all the comforts that he and his small family could need. The hall could seat a few dozen, which Sir Paravell liked to do sometimes by inviting the village folk to dine with him. Most knights and lords would never allow common folk to dine in their halls, except for on special occasions, but Sir Paravell was not like most. Neighbouring knights would laugh behind their cups at him and call him things like the Peasant Knight. Sir Paravell knew they said this, but he did not mind in the slightest. In fact, he took the name as a compliment. He had more than enough gold and food for himself, so considered it an honour to be able to share it with the folk who lived in his land. It gave him comfort to know that he could make up for some of his father's heartlessness.

But now the hall was empty apart for himself, Milas, the elderly farmer and the single Porcourt soldier stood by the door. Sir Paravell sat uneasily as he listened to the farmer's story. The old man was stood before him, his filthy hat in his hand and his head drooped in misery.

'He's dead, milord,' he wept.

'I am merely a knight, not a lord, so you do not need to address me as one,' Sir Paravell said kindly and patiently. 'Tell me, my good man, *who* has been killed?'

'Me son, sir,' the old man replied, wiping his bulbous nose with his free hand. 'He'd just got back from the market in the next village, you see. He was stowing the wagon in the barn. I should have done it meself, the Mother forgive me. I found him, I did. Him lying there, with his head hewn clean off his body.'

'You poor fellow,' Sir Paravell said, full of sympathy for the man.

It had been the third such death in just a week, and it was starting to not look like a coincidence.

'Brigands, perhaps? Outlaws?' he wondered aloud, looking to Milas, who nodded wisely.

'If you'll pardon me, sir,' the farmer said, taking a step forward. His hands clutching his hat were trembling. 'It weren't no brigands that killed my son.'

'You know who killed him?' Sir Paravell asked keenly, sitting up straighter in his chair.

'Not *who*, sir, but *what*. It was a spriggan that killed him, you mark my words!'

'Spriggan?' Milas repeated, confused.

Milas had been born and raised in the nearby town of Eaglestone, and so had not grown up learning village folktales like this.

'They say the spriggan is a spirit, a spectre,' Sir Paravell explained to him.

'It's the ghost of a bloodthirsty giant, some reckon,' the farmer said, fearfully. 'Monstrously ugly, and fearsome to boot. And angry too, looking for vengeance.'

Sir Paravell did not believe in such tales himself, of course, but they were popular stories among the common folk in this part of The Head, especially when parents wanted to scare naughty children into behaving.

'Did you see it?' Sir Paravell asked the old man.

'No, sir,' the farmer replied with a sniff. 'But, I heard my son screaming. It was a scream of terror. I've never heard anything like it before.'

Sir Paravell had no doubt that the poor victim had been in terror in the moments before his death, but that did not mean the culprit was an evil spirit from children's stories.

'Had anything been taken?' Sir Paravell asked. 'Besides the life of your son?'

'A couple of sacks of grain from the barn were missing,' the farmer shrugged, looking confused by the question. 'Does it matter, sir? They can be replaced, but my son can't. The Mother curse the spriggan!'

Sir Paravell tried to give the old man a kindly smile.

'I assure you that the spriggan is not real, my friend. And nor would it kill to steal food. The last I checked, vengeful spirits do not eat grain. The murderer of your poor son is made of flesh and blood like the rest of us, and we will bring this villain to justice. This I vow to you.'

The old man bowed and was led out of the hall by the Porcourt soldier who had been listening to the conversation with increasing unease on his own face. Clearly he was not so quick to discard the old farmer's theory that a monster had been responsible. When they were alone, Milas approached Sir Paravell with a doubtful expression on his face. Sir Paravell looked deep in thought, his fingers steepled beneath his chin.

'Do you believe him?' Milas asked.

'That his son has been murdered? Certainly,' Sir Paravell answered. 'The fact that the spriggan is a creation of the imagination of the common folk does not matter. The poor man was terrified by the very thought of it, and others will be too.'

'Three murders,' Milas agreed with a concerned shake of his head. 'Likely all committed by the same villain. Should we take this matter to Lord Merric?'

Sir Paravell took a few moments to answer, a frown on his brow.

'No,' he said at last, coming to a decision. 'Lord Merric is Duke of The Head and has enough on his plate without him worrying about a few murders that I should be able to handle myself. Afterall, my family was given this land hundreds of years ago, and it is my responsibility to see to it that things run smoothly here. I cannot ask for help from Eagle Mount whenever I am faced with a challenge. No, we must deal with this murderer ourselves.'

'After everything The Head has been through recently,' Milas said sadly, shaking his head. 'After Lord Roberd Jacelyn's death and all this business with the Monforts, I thought crimes like this would stop. What brings someone to murder his own kind at a time like this?'

'Desperate men do desperate things,' Sir Paravell suggested. 'Who can say what his motive is? But we will see him pay. It is my responsibility, and my honour, to defend the folk in these lands. And by the Mother I will see justice done.'

He rose from his chair and asked Milas to order six soldiers to prepare to ride with him.

'Shall I come with you as well, sir?' Milas asked.

'No, you stay here,' Sir Paravell said. 'I need a good man to oversee the castle while I'm gone. And see to it that the inventory of the winter stores is completed.'

He left the hall and went to his bedchamber, where his servant met him with his armour. The servant helped Sir Paravell dress, pulling the chain mail coat over his head, followed by his surcoat. He passed the knight his helmet, before rechecking and tightening all the belts and straps.

'Thank you,' Sir Paravell said. 'Kindly prepare my horse, if you will.'

'Yes, sir,' the boy said, and hurried off.

Sir Paravell knelt, his armoured knee loud on the stone floor. He offered a quick prayer to the Mother, before rising again and heading off in his servant's footsteps. He paused outside another chamber and knocked before entering. His wife lay lying in a bed, attended by her handmaids. There was sweat on her brow, and one of the handmaids was dabbing at it with a cloth. The air was filled with the scent of candles. Sir Paravell sat on the edge of the bed and put his hand on his wife's belly.

'He is a fighter, I can tell already,' he smiled. 'He will be a great knight himself one day.'

His wife was in some discomfort, but she managed to smile fondly at her husband.

'What makes you so certain it is a boy?'

'I can just tell,' Sir Paravell said with a grin, before turning to one of the handmaids. 'How is she?'

'She is doing well, sir,' the girl assured him. 'The baby too. You'll have a child by this time tomorrow, I'm certain.'

Sir Paravell beamed at his wife.

'You are doing wonderfully,' he said, and took her hand. 'I must go, but I will return before the birth, I promise.'

In the small courtyard of the castle he met the six soldiers who would be accompanying him. All had purple shields strapped across their backs, emblazoned with the white crescent moon symbol of the Porcourt family. Each man had armed himself either with a crossbow or a spear and looked nervous at the thought of going on the hunt for the killer. No doubt some of them believed the stories of the spriggan, just as the old farmer did, and did not relish the prospect of hunting an evil spirit.

Sir Paravell's servant appeared from the stables, leading his warhorse. The knight thanked him and took the reins, swinging himself into the saddle. He drew his sword and tested the edge of the blade, hoping that this casual action would help calm his nervous men. He looked up at them.

'You know what we are off to do,' he told them. 'Folk under our protection are dying, and it is up to us to put a stop to it. We will bring the culprit back here, alive or dead, to face justice.'

He paused to let his words sink in. He was determined for the soldiers to see that he had no fear at the prospect of the task ahead of them.

'Let us be off!'

With a shout he kicked back with his spurs and led the soldiers through the castle gates at a trot. The procession of horsemen passed through the village square where the finishing touches were being put to the new priory. The village folk watched him go, and Prior Simms raised his hand in farewell. Sir Paravell felt slightly guilty for thinking it, but part of him was secretly glad to be leaving the construction behind. He knew he would be expected to give some sort of speech to announce the completion of the new priory, and was happy to delay that awkward event for as long as he could.

Within minutes, Sir Paravell and his men had left the village of Porby behind them. Fields spread out to either side of the road, which provided the village folk and the castle with their food. The fields were almost empty now, with the last harvest almost finished being brought in. Sir Paravell just hoped there was enough to last until the next spring. They passed a small wood where the young

Paravell Porcourt had gone hunting with his father in years gone by. He found himself short of time for such leisure activities these days, and hoped that when his own son was old enough he made the time to do things together.

The serjeant who commanded the detachment of soldiers rode alongside Sir Paravell.

'Do we know where we're heading, sir?' he asked.

'The latest killing was at a farm north-east of here,' Sir Paravell said. 'We will go there and see if we can pick up the murderer's trail.'

The serjeant looked hesitant.

'And if there is no trail to follow?'

'The killer is a person, serjeant,' Sir Paravell assured him, 'and all folk leave tracks.'

They rode for an hour, arriving at a small farmhouse just as the sun was beginning to set. An old woman came out of the cottage at their approach, wiping her hands on her apron, and squinting against the setting sun to see who the visitors were. She started in surprise when she saw the white crescent moon symbol of the Porcourt family on Sir Paravell's surcoat.

'Milord!' she gasped and struggled to lower herself into a bow.

'There is no need to name me so,' Sir Paravell said, long since used to the common folk making the mistake.

'Are you here about the death of Fromm?' the woman asked, breathless. 'Our son?'

'I am, my lady. Your husband spoke to me at Porby Castle this afternoon and explained what has happened. I am truly sorry for your loss.'

'Thank you, sir,' she gasped, the grief evident on her face. 'It's good of you to come.'

Sir Paravell gestured with his hand to show that no gratitude was necessary.

'Where was your son found?' he asked.

'Over there, sir, in the barn.'

She pointed through the twilight to where a barn lay beside some fields, almost lost in the shadows.

'Thank you,' Sir Paravel said, turning his horse in that direction. 'And fear not, we will bring this man to justice.'

'Man?' the old woman called after the soldiers as they rode off towards the barn. 'It was no man, it was the spriggan!'

But they were out of earshot and her words were lost to the settling night, so the old woman just fingered the leaf-shaped amulet around her neck.

'May the Mother protect you,' she muttered.

Sir Paravell came to a halt beside the simple barn and dismounted, passing the reins of his horse to the serjeant. It was a sorry excuse for a barn. The roof was half missing and there were gaps between the planks of wood that made up the walls. Ivy was creeping all over it, and Sir Paravell had to admit that the tumbledown old barn was more than a little spooky to look at, especially in the failing light.

Their horses whinnied and shifted uneasily, as though they knew that something terrible had happened there.

Sir Paravell strode into the barn, his sword in his hand. His chain mail and spurs rang with every step. In the low light he could see a dark stain on the hay-strewn floor that could only be blood. The blood had splattered all over the barn, and Sir Paravell could only imagine the ferociousness of the strike that had killed the unfortunate victim. There were drag marks leading out of the barn, to where a pile of freshly dug earth nearby showed where the man had been buried by his mourning parents.

There were shelves on one side of the barn, and moving over to them Sir Paravell founds sacks of hoarded food, common among farmers who were organised enough to prepare for the winter. A gap in the shelves showed where some of the sacks had been recently removed.

Sir Paravell lifted one of the sacks and tested its weight. It was not too heavy, so the missing ones could have easily been carried by one man. It looked like they were probably hunting a single murderer who acted alone. Sir Paravell and his six men should be more than capable of capturing him, if they could find him.

He left the barn and remounted his horse.

'Did you find anything, sir?'

'Unless we have come across a particularly hungry ghost, the culprit is a living man, as I thought. He will be no match for the seven of us.'

'Yes, sir,'

The serjeant was not so quick to disregard the old couple's belief that the spriggan was responsible. He had been raised believing the bed-time stories, and being this close to the murder scene was making the superstitious old soldier uncomfortable. The serjeant had fought fearlessly in battles before, but there was something about their quarry that night that filled him with dread.

Sir Paravell peered at the ground around them and saw a set of footprints heading north, away from the barn. Looking in that direction, he saw a hill a mile away that rose up beyond the farm, a dark silhouette against the inky sky.

'All three murders have happened within a couple of miles of Old Tor Wood,' Sir Paravell said, looking at the great tree-covered hill. 'I would wager that is where we will find our killer.'

He ordered a couple of the soldiers to light some torches as night fell, which they then distributed to the other men. They headed off towards the wood, each soldier holding a burning torch to light their way. Sir Paravell noticed that the faces of several of the men were pale with fear in the torchlight.

'When we find the murderer, we will try to take him alive,' Sir Paravell said confidently, in an attempt to encourage them. 'He is likely a fugitive, escaped from someone's dungeons.'

Sir Paravell recalled the amount of blood that had stained the inside of the barn, and wondered what kind of man could swing a blade with such force. He decided not to share that particular thought with his soldiers.

The ground started to rise as they neared the wood. There was no path they could follow, so they simply cut across fields. The land got rockier as they reached the first of the trees, and Sir Paravell ordered them to dismount.

'It would not do to have one of our horses trip and break a leg in the dark,' he explained.

So they hitched the reins of the horses to a nearby tree, where the beasts huddled close together. Sir Paravell and the others set off on foot. The men fingered their spears and crossbows warily as they stalked through the wood, their eyes darting about. Their breathing started to become more laboured as the ground steadily rose, and their progress slowed as they tried to negotiate the rocky, uneven ground.

The dark trees closed in around them, and the soldiers peered about, torches in hand. They seemed tense, but saw no sign of the murderer they hunted. The sun had fully set now, and it was the darkest night Sir Paravell could recall. It was made all the darker by the thick press of trees around them. The moon had risen, but it only formed a thin crescent in the inky black sky above, and this did little to lighten the night. The shape of the moon vaguely resembled the symbol of the Porcourt family, and Sir Paravell told himself that it was an omen from the Mother, and he pointed this out to his soldiers.

A sudden rustling sound came from their right, and all of them turned their heads to look in the direction it had come from. A shape darted out of the gloom, and in a panic one of the soldiers shot his crossbow at it. The crossbow bolt missed by some distance, and the deer grunted in alarm as it fled past them.

The men sighed in relief.

'Courage, boys,' Sir Paravell urged, looking around at their torch-lit faces. 'Let us make Porby proud of us this night.'

This seemed to steel their resolve somewhat, and they gritted their teeth and continued onwards. The only sounds they could hear were their own footsteps crunching on the twigs and fallen leaves that littered the ground, the crackle of their torches and the occasional distant hoot of an owl. They stalked forward for another few minutes, until one of their number tripped on an exposed tree root.

The serjeant turned to look at Sir Paravell.

'It's no use, sir,' he said. 'We don't stand no chance of finding anything in this darkness. Maybe we should wait until morning.'

Sir Paravell knew that the man was right. They were making so much noise as they blundered blindly through the forest that their quarry would hear them coming and could easily avoid them. He gave a quick nod, disappointed that they would leave the woods empty-handed.

Looking thoroughly relieved, the serjeant turned to his men.

'Alright boys, back down the hill. Carefully now.'

'We will be back for the villain in the morning,' Sir Paravell promised them.

'Hold up, where's Coops?' one of the soldiers asked.

Sir Paravell did a quick head count. They numbered only six, himself included.

'Coops?' the sergeant called, and then shouted his name a second time, even louder.

'He's not here,' one of the other soldiers said, his voice shaking.

'He likely just got turned around in the dark,' Sir Paravell said. 'Let us head back down the hill. We will most likely find him waiting for us by the horses.'

A sudden scream, a horrible scream, sounded from further up the hill.

'Help!' it called desperately, sounding almost inhuman in its terror.

The men whipped around and looked into the darkness in the direction it had come from.

'Coops!' one of them shouted. 'Is that you?'

The scream came a second time and, as one, the soldiers sprinted up the hill towards it. Sir Paravell ran with them, trying to keep control of his panicked men.

'Where are you, Coops?' one of them called breathlessly as he ran.

'Keep shouting, lad, we'll find you!' roared the loud voice of the serjeant.

They started spreading out as they ran blindly through the trees. The woods grew darker as each man went in his own direction, taking their torch with them.

'No! Stay together, men!' Sir Paravell called.

But it did no good. In their panic and fear, his order was ignored. Sir Paravell was soon all alone. An unexpected sensation began to creep over him. The hairs on the back of his neck began to prickle, and his palms were becoming clammy with sweat. He was beginning to feel fear.

He had faced many dangers in his twenty years, but he had never felt fear before. His unwavering belief and trust in the Mother had always kept him safe, and his determination to do the right thing by his duke had always seen him to victory. But this foe was something different. He had brutally killed three innocent farmfolk in cold blood, and now he had seized one of Sir Paravell's own soldiers from under their very noses.

Suddenly, Sir Paravell tripped over something solid as he hurried blindly through the dark, trying to rally his men together. He threw his arms out and managed to grab hold of a tree and stay on his feet. He turned back and lowered his burning torch, illuminating the ground. Among the moss and the first fallen leaves of autumn he saw the legs of a figure lying prone in the undergrowth. He moved the torch closer and saw the wound across the dead soldier's throat. Blood was still flowing from the ghastly injury, staining his jerkin. But that did not stop Sir Paravell from seeing the symbol of the crescent moon stitched onto the dead man's chest.

It was Coops.

'Over here!' Sir Paravell shouted to the night. 'I have found him!'

A few moments of silence passed, before...

'Sir?' a voice called from nearby.

'Here,' Sir Paravell said.

The serjeant crashed through the undergrowth and appeared at Sir Paravell's side. He had lost his torch and looked relieved to be no longer alone, but his eyes widened at the sight of one of his men lying dead on the ground.

'Where are the others?' Sir Paravell asked him.

The serjeant did not reply. His eyes were glued to the grim spectacle on the ground before him.

'Serjeant!' Sir Paravell said, more roughly than he intended, his own nerves beginning to show.

'I don't know, sir.'

The serjeant was an older man, a veteran of dozens of fights. The men looked up to him normally, but right now he looked as frightened as a fresh recruit.

Sir Paravell looked around them. He could only see the whereabouts of a couple of the other soldiers, their positions given away by the burning torches they held. They were far away through the trees, and the torchlight was growing more and more faint with every passing moment.

'They are going the wrong way,' Sir Paravell muttered, before raising his voice. 'Over here! This way!'

Either the men could not hear him, or else they were too panicked to pay any attention. Either way, they did not follow his calls. Sir Paravell looked after them, feeling frustrated and helpless. But he was determined not to show his fear in front of one of his soldiers.

'Come on, serjeant, this way.'

He sheathed his sword and picked up the crossbow lying at Coops' feet. The dead soldier would no longer be needing it, after all. He checked that it was loaded, before gesturing for the serjeant to follow him.

He led the way through the dense trees, leaving Coops' body behind. They would have to come back for it later, once they had found the rest of their men. Sir Paravell kept the crossbow up as he edged through the darkness, ready to shoot if he saw anyone that he did not recognise.

'Let's get out of here, sir,' the serjeant said, not even attempting to hide his fear.

Sir Paravell nodded but knew that in the darkness the motion would go unseen.

'We will, serjeant, once we have found the others.'

'They could be anywhere!'

'I saw a couple of lights this way,' Sir Paravell said.

He stopped short suddenly. The woods up ahead were pitch black, with not a light in sight.

'Where?' the serjeant asked. 'I don't see them.'

Sir Paravell did not answer him, and peered around. They had been there, not a moment ago, but now he could not see anything at all.

Another scream sounded in the trees, only to be silenced almost immediately.

The serjeant fell to his knees, whimpering, and Sir Paravell rounded on him.

'Pull yourself together, man. I need you here with me. Stand with me against this. You are a soldier of Porby, a soldier of The Head!'

The serjeant looked as though he would rather be anywhere in the world than here in these dark woods, but he nodded and got back to his feet. He gripped his sword tightly in both hands and breathed out slowly.

'Very good, serjeant. Now, this way,' Sir Paravell said.

Rather than following the sound of the latest scream, they headed further up the hill and into the heart of the woods. There was something about finding higher ground that brought a sense of comfort to Sir Paravell. He also felt better to have a plan of action. He did not know what he would find when he reached the top of the hill, but he would worry about that when he got there. For now, he just focused on putting one foot in front of the other and keeping his ears pricked and his eyes peeled for sight of the one they were hunting.

Suddenly there came a rustling from behind him, and Sir Paravell span around, the crossbow raised.

'Get behind me,' he ordered the serjeant.

He continued to edge up the hill, walking slowly backwards with the crossbow aimed back the way they had come. He peered into the blackness, trying to catch a glimpse of what had caused the noise. But he saw nothing.

The serjeant led the way up the rough slope, and Sir Paravell continued to stare unblinkingly into the dark trees behind them. No figure materialised out of the blackness, and Sir Paravell assumed that the rustling was nothing but the wind or some nocturnal animal that had been disturbed by their passing.

'I do not think he is following us,' Sir Paravell said after a few minutes.

There was no answer.

'Serjeant?'

He tore his eyes from the trees and risked a glance over his shoulder.

He was alone. The serjeant was no longer behind him.

Sir Paravell was more curious than anything else. The serjeant had been there mere seconds ago. He had heard his laboured breathing as they had struggled up the hill. Yet now, he was gone. There was no sign of him at all. It was as though the man had simply disappeared into thin air.

'Serjeant?' he said again, quietly.

He did not expect a response, and he did not receive one.

He realised that he had never known the soldier's name, and felt a surge of guilt at the thought. He knew it was an absurd thing to think at this time. He knew the names of nearly every villager in Porby, but not those of his own soldiers. He hoped they had not judged him for that.

Somehow, Sir Paravell knew that he was going to die that night. He no longer cared whether the one he was hunting was a man or a monster. It almost seemed like it did not matter anymore.

He threw down the crossbow. It was not a knight's weapon after all, and he drew his sword instead. He was sad that he would never be able to pass the blade down to his son when he himself became a knight, and he wondered whether someone would one day discover his body and the rusted remains of the blade. He knew he could turn tail now and flee back down the hill, but how could he survive when his men had died? He had led them here, to their deaths. It was only right that he died with them.

He strode up the hill, strangely calm. The trees ended, and he emerged into a clearing. The sliver of silver moonlight brightened the night just enough for him to make out a cliff face up ahead. The shadow of a cave entrance was just about visible at the base of the cliff. Somehow, he knew that was where he had to go, and he moved towards it.

'I am the sword of the helpless,' he murmured. 'I am the champion of my lord.'

He recited the vows and oaths he had sworn when he had first become a knight.

'I am the paragon of virtue. I am the paladin of the Mother.'

He reached the mouth of the cave and saw that it delved deep into the ground. A strong smell of damp air assaulted his nose. The light from his torch could not penetrate the darkness. He turned and looked behind him, but nothing moved among the trees on the edge of the clearing. He took a deep breath and stepped into the cave.

'I am the guardian of the realm. I am the servant of the king.'

His words seemed to echo all around him, speaking back like they were old friends. Water dripped from the ceiling, and the walls of the cave looked wet and slimy. The ground was slippery underfoot and he had to walk carefully. Something caught his eye in the torchlight, and he headed towards it.

He came across some stored sacks of food, and a blanket that was laying on the ground beside it. Sir Paravell sheathed his sword and picked up the blanket. A man had been sleeping here from the looks of it, and was using the cave as a hideout.

'Oh dear, you really should not have come here,' said an unfriendly voice.

Sir Paravell spun around, dropping the blanket. There was a flutter overhead as some bats, disturbed from their slumber, awoke and flew out into the night air.

A man stood in the entrance to the cave, his sword drawn.

Sir Paravell approached him slowly, redrawing his own blade.

'In the name of Lord Merric Jacelyn I am taking you to Porby Castle for the murder of three innocent people,' he said, his voice filled with determination. 'You will give up your sword and accompany me.'

He knew the man would never do as Sir Paravell had commanded. He just laughed.

'Three people? I have murdered nine by my count,' the man corrected him, casually, flicking fresh blood from his sword onto the rocky floor of the cave. 'Soon to be ten.'

'You will accompany me back to Porby Castle,' Sir Paravell repeated. 'I am a knight, and in the name of Lord Merric I'm taking you so that justice may be carried out.'

'I think not,' the man said, a hint of amusement on his face which was illuminated by the flickering flames of the torch.

Sir Paravell had barely raised his own sword in defence when the murderer's cruel blade had come swinging out of the gloom.

The burning torch dropped from his lifeless hand as he fell, dead, to the ground.

- CHAPTER THREE -

A small measure of peace

Ana whooped and laughed as she galloped her horse across the field, with Merric close behind her. A hedgerow appeared up ahead of them, but she did not slow. With a mischievous grin over her shoulder at Merric she spurred forward and her horse leapt neatly over the hedge. Merric hesitated for a moment, long enough for Ana to let out a hoot of laughter.

'Come on, Merric!' she teased. 'I'm tired of waiting for you to catch up!'

Merric kicked back his heels and his horse, who he had named Nosy, darted forwards and jumped high into the air. Merric felt his heart in his mouth, but the horse landed safely on the far side of the hedge. He almost slipped from the saddle, but a desperate fumble of the reins kept him from losing his seat.

Chuckling, Ana turned her horse and set off down the lane, leaving Merric barely a moment to catch his breath. Wiping a bead of sweat from his brow, Merric felt himself grin and set off after his friend. The sky was clear and blue, and while summer was over there was enough heat in the sun blazing overhead to give a pleasant warmth to the day. In this moment, there was nowhere Merric would rather be.

He rode through the dust that was being kicked up from the dry road by the hooves of Ana's horse, feeling the fine orange powder cling to his clothes and face. He urged Nosy onwards, desperate to overtake her and let her taste a mouthful of his dust instead for once.

Birds tweeted as they flew overhead, either singing to each other as birds did or else watching the race happening on the ground below them. Either way, they seemed just as happy and at peace as the two youths on their horses were.

Merric and Ana galloped through a tiny hamlet, which was little more than a cluster of cottages gathered around a central green. A group of small children, who had been gathered outside one of the cottages playing with a kitten, leapt to their feet as the two horses ran past. The children chased after them, giggling and cheering gleefully, but they soon got left behind when the hamlet faded into the distance.

The country lane along which Merric and Ana rode was lined with thick hedgerows that were teeming with life. Bees were buzzing around the bright flowers and birds fluttered to and from their nests in the thickets. Ripe blackberries grew in swathes, and Ana reached out and grabbed some of them as they rode past. She smirked at Merric as she ate some of them, before throwing a couple back to him. Merric fumbled the catch, but was able to lick the deep red juice from his hand with a grin.

They tore around a bend in the lane and suddenly came face to face with a rotund prior who was sitting on the front bench of a wagon heading towards them.

'Whoa!' the fat prior exclaimed in alarm at their sudden appearance, tugging on his reins to stop the two oxen that were pulling the wagon. The barrels of mead that were stacked behind him wobbled dangerously, and the prior shook his fist at the two youths as they galloped past.

'You ragamuffins!' he shouted in irritation, completely unaware that one of the offenders was his own duke.

'Sorry!' Merric called back over his shoulder, while Ana just laughed.

The angry prior and his shouts faded away as they rode further along the lane. Ana led the way, looking natural on the horse and her dirty blonde hair was trailing out behind her. Trees grew out of the hedgerows now, creating a shaded gloom along the lane. Here and there, where there was a gap in the branches overhead, shafts of sunlight cut through the air like swords, casting a dappled pattern on the heavily rutted lane. A large pond appeared to their left, and the shade of the trees had left its surface clear of algae. Ducks drifted across its surface, quacking and turning their beaked heads to look curiously at the two riders as they tore past.

Ana and Merric reached a fork in the lane, and without a moment's pause Ana turned to the left. Neither of them knew where the lane headed, nor did they really care. Merric was simply loving the moment.

It had been nearly a month since he had been named the new Duke of The Head, following the recapture of the castle of Eagle Mount from the Monforts. Since then, Merric's life had been vastly different to how it had been before Lord Roberd and his wife and son had been murdered. Even something as simple as spending a day in the company of his best friend away from the castle had done much to remind Merric that he was still really just a boy of fifteen years.

Ana swerved off the road and darted through an open gateway in the hedgerow. Merric followed her and they were plunged once more into blazing sunshine as they rode into the open meadow, leaving the shaded lane behind. Flocks of sheep scattered at their approach, bleating in surprise. A young couple, their arms linked while they took a stroll across the rolling grasslands, raised their hands to shield their eyes against the sun and look at the two youths galloping along. They grinned at the happy expressions on the two riders' faces. Daisies grew in patches where the sheep had not eaten them, and Ana, who harboured a love of all living things, took care to avoid trampling the wildflowers beneath her horse's hooves.

They slowed to a canter when they reached the crest of a hill, giving their horses a moment to catch their breath. They discovered a spectacular view ahead of them. The meadow gave way to a patchwork of fields and woods and streams that stretched into the distance for miles and miles. Not for the first time, Merric thought about how lucky he was to live in such a beautiful part of the world. It was a peaceful, picturesque scene, and he never wanted it to end.

Nestled between the gently rolling hills that lay ahead, they could see a small market town. Smoke was rising from chimneys, and the towers of a priory were just visible through some trees. Farmers were working in the fields surrounding the village, most likely preparing to bring in the final harvest before winter. Merric did not want to return to Eagle Mount just yet, and neither did Ana.

She angled her horse towards the town and led the way towards it. They rode up and down the sides of the low, sunlit hills, and leapt over the wooden fences that divided up the meadows and fields. She shouted cheerful greetings at the farmers who were tending their fields, who could only half raise their hands in puzzled acknowledgement in reply as she and Merric rode past. They splashed through a shallow stream and darted between the trees of a small wood, startling a rabbit who hopped hurriedly away. The twilight of the trees ended and they found themselves on another narrow lane. Glancing to their right they could spy the buildings of the town.

Ana at last slowed her horse to a walk, and Merric gratefully did the same, finally able to ride alongside her rather than trailing behind. The lane was surprisingly busy, with folk heading towards, or coming from, the town. Some were on horses, and they touched their hats politely at Merric and Ana as they passed. Others walked on foot in happy groups, and Merric felt a pang of envy that these folk were able to live like this every single day.

The market town was busy, but it was nothing like the hustle and bustle of Eaglestone on market day. The shouts of the vendors selling their wares were more sing-song and pleasant, and the folk wandering from stall to stall did so at a leisurely pace. Most seemed to know each other as well, and were calling out friendly greetings to each other as they shopped. Some faces turned to look up at Merric and Ana as they rode into the town square, but not recognising them the townsfolk simply gave them a polite smile before turning back to the stalls.

Ana dismounted, looking around happily at the pleasant town. Merric climbed down from Nosy as well, and he and Ana walked around the town square leading their horses by the reins. Ana was the same age as Merric, but she was taller than him. Or, as she liked to tease him, he was shorter than her. He was both short and skinny for his age, and this had done little to boost his confidence growing up. He felt that his short, wavy brown hair added to his boyish look, and he touched his smooth jaw almost every morning, waiting for the first signs of a beard to begin growing. But while Merric was not happy with his outwards appearance, Ana clearly saw none of the negative things that he did. While one hand was gripping onto the reins of her horse, with the other she took hold of Merric's hand and they walked through the market together.

There was a delicious smell of freshly baked bread coming from a nearby baker's stall, and Ana led Merric over to it.

'You're not from around here are you, my dear?' asked a smiling woman standing behind the stall.

Ana shook her head.

'From Eaglestone,' she said.

'Lovely! I don't go there too often myself,' the friendly-faced woman admitted. 'A little too busy there for my liking. What an honour it must be, living so close to our dear young duke!'

Ana turned and winked at Merric, who reddened slightly.

'What a sweetie he is,' the lady continued, taking one of her fresh loaves of bread and wrapping it in brown paper. 'Imagine doing what he has done, and at his age too. My sister Jil lives in Eaglestone, and she tells me he's doing a marvellous job.'

Fortunately, she did not look up from the bread as she said this. If she did, she may have seen Merric's face flush an even deeper shade of red.

'Here you are,' the woman said, passing Ana the bread. 'No, no, I insist,' she added, brushing aside Ana's protests. 'A gift, baked by my husband and me. Our countryfolk ways must seem strange to you, but I wouldn't want you to get the wrong impression of us here in Domadge Bartyn. Doolot's my name. It's a pleasure to meet you, young lady. I do hope you'll come and visit our town again.'

Ana thanked Doolot and stowed the loaf safely in her horse's saddlebag. Once they had walked through the town for a few minutes, and were away from the market, Ana turned to Merric.

'Didn't fancy announcing yourself?' she grinned.

'I think she would have been disappointed if she knew I was the one she was talking about,' Merric replied.

'Don't be daft,' Ana said to him.

They spotted a tavern sitting on the opposite side of a wide pond to the manor house of the noble family that ruled the town. Merric wracked his mind for a moment, recalling his teachings. If this was the town of Domadge Bartyn, which was a few hours' ride north from Eagle Mount, then the manor house belonged to the Freemont family. Merric had not yet met Sir Albet Freemont since he had been made duke, though he had seen him plenty of times from afar when Sir Albet had travelled to Eagle Mount to visit Lord Roberd.

'Let's have a drink before riding back home,' Ana said, looking cheerfully at the tavern.

Merric hesitated for a moment, and Ana clicked her tongue.

'You saw Doolot,' she urged. 'No one here would recognise you. We common folk know the highborn only by their name and by the banners that fly over their castles. No one here knows your face, and I've seen the portrait that was painted of you the other week. I'd eat my anvil if anyone would recognise you from that,' she laughed.

Merric glanced over at the manor house that was by far the largest building in the town. He doubted that Sir Albet would recognise Merric either. It was not that Merric was wanting to hide himself, but the idea of being swamped by the townsfolk of Domadge Bartyn, all thinking he was some hero to be praised and adored, was something he did not desire.

It was true that he had been the one who had led the revolt that had challenged Rayden Monfort, who had unlawfully made himself Duke of The Head. And it had been he who had killed Rayden in single combat, freeing Eagle Mount and the rest of the dukedom from Monfort rule. But Merric knew that had been a fluke. Rayden had been one of the greatest swordsmen in High Realm, and Merric had just gotten lucky. And he could not have done it at all without help. He found it uncomfortable when folk treated him as though he was some hero, like from the stories Merric liked to read in his books.

Merric and Ana tied their horses to the hitching post beside the tavern and sat down at one of the tables clustered beside the road. The landlady bustled over.

'What can I get you, my loves?' she asked.

'Two ales, please,' Ana said.

The woman gave the two youths a quick look before wagging a finger at them.

'Fine, but I'll add extra water to them,' she said with a chortle.

She came back with the drinks a few moments later, and Ana passed her a few coppers.

'It reminds me of Little Harrow,' Ana said fondly, looking around the town. 'It's bigger, of course, but it feels the same.'

Little Harrow was the village in the west of The Head where they had lived for a short while that summer, when Merric had been forced to flee Eagle Mount.

'Me too,' Merric admitted. 'I'd love to live somewhere like this. It's so peaceful.'

Ana did not miss the meaning behind Merric's words.

'It would definitely be a simpler life, wouldn't it,' she said.

Merric smiled knowingly and took a drink of the ale. It was cool and refreshing, and he had not noticed how thirsty the sun and the dust from the road had made him.

Ana gazed at Merric as he watched the townsfolk going about their afternoon, a peaceful expression on his face. There were times when she could not help worrying about him. She had protected him and looked out for him all the years they had been friends, and she wondered if perhaps she was just struggling to come to terms with the idea that others were taking on that role now. After all, the Duke of The Head did not need a blacksmith's daughter to look out for him when he had all his barons and knights and servants to do that.

Merric had never expected this burden of responsibility that had landed on him, and he had certainly never asked for it. He never openly said that he did not want to be the duke, and Ana knew that he would not want to abandon the role that had been forced upon him, but she knew he did not find it easy. Quite the opposite in fact, and she did not blame him in the slightest. She understood that most barons and dukes in High Realm, and even the king himself, will have grown up knowing that they would one day inherit the title. They would learn the role from their fathers as they grew up, and would be ready to take over when their time came. But not Merric. He had not even known he was a Jacelyn, let alone knew that he was in line to inherit the title of Duke of The Head. Merric's own parents had died when he was very young, and he had been raised at Eagle Mount by Lord Roberd Jacelyn. Merric had been completely unaware that Lord Roberd was in fact his uncle. When he had been murdered, along with his son and heir, Tristan, Merric had unknowingly become next in line to be duke. Ana could not imagine how it must have felt to be told that, and Merric had never really spoken to her about it either. He was not one to talk openly about how he was feeling.

While he may not have felt ready to become the duke, no one in the entire dukedom was doubting him. No one, that is, except Merric himself. He had freed Eagle Mount from the tyranny of the Monforts, and he himself had then come up with the plan to recapture Hightop Castle without a single drop of blood being spilled. Anyone else would be encouraged by those achievements, but Merric could not help but compare himself to Lord Roberd, and wondered how better a job Tristan would have done had he lived long enough to become the duke himself. Ana knew that Merric would always feel like he was in their shadow, and she knew that must be a difficult place to be.

'He'd be proud of you, you know,' Ana said.

'Hmm?'

Merric had been distractedly looking at the Freemont soldier stood beside the gateway that led into the manor house.

'Lord Roberd,' Ana said. 'He'd be proud of you.'

A flicker of a forced smile played across Merric's face.

'I hope so,' he said.

He looked as though there was more that he wanted to say, but he closed his mouth again. With a jangle of reins and chain mail a knight trotted past, heading towards the manor house. By the proud way he held himself, Merric assumed he was one of Sir Albet's sons. He felt a pang of envy at the confident way that the knight rode along, one hand raised in greeting at the townsfolk who called out, welcoming him home. The sight of the capable young knight seemed to encourage Merric to say what was on his mind.

'I just feel like folk have the wrong idea about me,' he said. 'I don't know if I can meet their expectations. I'm not one of *them*.'

He nodded at the figure of the knight as he disappeared through the gate. Merric was highborn, with his father having been the baron of the now ruined village of Ryding, but he did not feel like he really fitted in with the nobility of The Head. He felt like an outsider, though he could not really say why.

'And I think you overestimate what us common folk want,' Ana retorted.

Merric stared at her, not understanding.

'What do you mean?' he said.

'Folk don't care what their lord's name is, or how well they ride a horse, or carry a sword, or how well they can give a speech,' she said. 'All we really want is to feel safe, and to have a duke who genuinely cares about us.'

'Of course I care about the folk,' Merric said, 'but-'

'Exactly,' Ana said, interrupting him and taking a casual swig of her ale. 'That's all that matters. And you've already proven that you can protect them. Look at what you did at Eagle Mount. Look at what you did at Hightop Castle! Sure, you might make some little mistakes here and there, but who doesn't? No one's perfect, Merric, especially when they're new at doing something. But when it really matters I know that you'll make the right decisions, and the folk of The Head can rest peacefully in their beds.'

'But Lord Roberd-' Merric countered, as though trying to find an argument to Ana's words.

'Lord Roberd was the duke for years and years,' Ana cut across him. 'I bet when he first started he was just as unsure as you are now.'

'But at least he was prepared. He knew he was going to be the duke.'

'True,' Ana admitted. 'But you shouldn't compare yourself to him. Everyone else is different, so why shouldn't dukes? You're not Lord Roberd, you're *you*. What does it matter if you end up doing things a little differently to how he did, or how Tristan would have done if he had taken over from his father? You heard what that lady at the bread stall was saying. The folk here love you for what you've done, and for what I know you'll keep on doing.'

Merric's hand was lying on the rough wooden table beside his tankard of ale, and Ana took hold of it. She was pleased when Merric did not flinch away. He gave her hand a squeeze and they sat in silence for a while, drinking their ale and watching the world go by. A group of men trooped past the tavern, longbows over their shoulders, laughing heartily with each other. Merric sniggered suddenly and looked back at Ana.

'Do you remember, back at Little Harrow, when I was trying to learn to shoot a bow?'

'You were awful,' Ana agreed.

They spent a while laughing and fondly reliving their short time in Little Harrow, and wondering what Kasper, the hunter who had led them to his village, was up to now. There was a part of Merric that would dearly have loved to have stayed and started a new, simpler life there. But then he would remember how Sophya, Lord Roberd's daughter and the last surviving member of his family, had been destined to spend her life living beneath Rayden Monfort's cruel hand, and how the folk of Eaglestone and the rest of The Head had been mistreated by the cruelty of their new Monfort rulers. Merric had chosen to do the right thing, rather than the easy thing. That thought gave him heart that he was perhaps made of more lordly stuff than he gave himself credit for. There was a part of him that would always be proud of what he had managed to do. And, if he was honest with himself, he knew that Lord Roberd, and Merric's own parents who he could not remember, would be proud of him too.

Ana gave a slight shiver, which drew Merric's attention. The sun was getting lower in the sky, and where they were sitting was now draped in a shadow cast by the tavern. Merric took off his cloak and put it around Ana's shoulders. He remembered a time when she would have clipped him around the ear for daring to do such a chivalrous act, but Merric was not the only one who had grown up more than normal recently. She smiled gratefully at him, accepting the gesture of kindness.

'We'd better be heading back, I suppose,' Merric said. 'Sir Oskar will be furious if I'm back after dark. You'd think that being the duke would mean I can do whatever I want, but no!'

They finished their drinks and went back to their horses.

'Ready for another ride, boy?' Merric asked Nosy, patting his neck affectionately.

The horse whinnied eagerly in reply. Clearly he enjoyed being away from the confines of the castle as much as Merric did.

He climbed back up into the saddle and Ana did the same beside him. They turned their horses towards the road that would lead them back south towards Eagle Mount, but before Merric could set off Ana had reached across and took hold of the collar of his shirt. Pulling him towards her, she kissed him deeply on the lips.

When at last she let go, she kicked back her heels.

'Yah!' she urged her horse, and it darted forwards.

Grinning, Merric spurred after her. She had beaten him here, but he was determined to win on the way back.

- CHAPTER FOUR -

An unfriendly welcome

The rider walked his horse towards the gates that led into the town of Eaglestone. He joined the throng of folk queuing to enter the town, keeping his head down and taking little notice of the others stood around him. He knew that it would be best for him to avoid attracting any attention. He waited, patiently and calmly, as the queue shortened. Within a few minutes he had reached the front of the queue and was stopped by two men wearing the uniforms of Jacelyn soldiers. They peered up at the rider atop his horse, trying to see beneath his hood.

'You're an ugly one,' the first soldier chuckled, catching sight of the stranger's face. 'No wonder you keep your face hidden.'

The stranger made no response, allowing the soldier his jest. It was nothing the stranger had not heard before, and he had long since stopped paying attention to the words of lesser men.

'What's your business in Eaglestone?' the second soldier, an older man, asked.

'I seek a meal, and a bed,' the stranger said simply.

'Aye? Well you'll find both inside the walls,' the older soldier said. 'Got any weapons?'

The stranger pulled back his cloak to reveal that he was unarmed. He knew that trying to bring his sword into the town would lead to questions that he would not be able to answer.

'Alright then, head on through,' the older soldier said, stepping aside and clearing the way for the visitor to ride his horse beneath the arched gateway. 'Keep out of trouble, mind.'

But the stranger had already gone through the gate and disappeared into the crowd beyond. The younger of the two soldiers turned to his companion.

'He was a strange one, wasn't he,' he said.

But the older soldier simply shrugged and turned to face a farmer waiting to enter the town with a wagon of vegetables.

Once he had entered Eaglestone, the stranger steered his horse off the main street that led towards the heart of the town and disappeared down a side road. It was much quieter down here, away from the hustle and bustle of the main street, but the stranger did not remove his hood. There were some in Eaglestone who may recognise him, and even those who did not know his face would not be able to help themselves from stopping and staring at him as he passed.

He knew the town well, but after several weeks spent by himself, living alone in the wild and far from prying eyes and the hubbub of folk going about their lives, he felt no pleasure in his return. But he was not there for his pleasure. He had a job to do.

He knew exactly where he was heading. The street twisted between buildings, past workshops and yards and shops. The stranger ignored the sights and smells of the bustling town, focusing on his mission. Eventually the eastern town walls of Eaglestone loomed overhead, and he reached the corner of the town dedicated to the stables that housed the horses of the richer occupants of the population. He dismounted, feeling the mud squelch beneath his boots as he led the horse into the gloomy interior of one of the larger stables. The groom in charge approached him, wiping his hands on a filthy cloth.

'You want a stall for your horse? And some fodder?' the groom asked.

The stranger shook his head.

'I'm looking to sell the beast.'

The groom raised his eyebrows and moved closer to the horse, examining it closely.

'A destrier,' he said, walking around the animal. 'A warhorse. A favourite among knights. Sixteen hands, I'd say. Maybe even seventeen. How old is he?'

'I don't know.'

The groom paused in his examination of the horse's teeth and looked at the stranger.

'Do you have the papers?' he asked.

'No,' the stranger said, as though daring the groom to ask him why not.

The groom was much too wily to ask such foolish questions. Not having the papers that proved ownership meant that the animal was likely stolen, and he had no desire to cross a horse thief.

'I can take him off you, but without the right papers I'll struggle to sell him. I can give you two silvers for the animal.'

'Ten,' the stranger replied, flatly.

'Ten?' the groom laughed heartily. 'No chance, my friend. Judging by the state of your clothes I'd say you're pretty desperate. I'll give you six silvers, and that's my final offer.'

He held out the coins in his hand.

The stranger snarled and took the offered coins. He disliked the groom's manner, but six silvers would be enough for what he needed. He pocketed the coins without another word, and turned and left the stable.

He headed further uphill, his eyes taking in the sight of the soaring castle of Eagle Mount that towered over the town ahead of him. The sky blue banners of the Jacelyn family were flapping in the wind, in an almost taunting manner. He pushed his way through the crowd of townsfolk completing their tasks before heading home for the evening. The sun was setting below the western walls of the town, and the narrow street along which he was walking was gloomy and blanketed in shadow. A pair of children ran giggling across the street in front of him, ignoring the shouts of their mother to return home. One of them, a little girl no taller than the stranger's boot, stopped when she noticed him looming over her. She looked up and gasped in fear when she saw his face in the shadowed folds of the hood.

The man ignored her, taking a moment of pleasure to imagine how he could end her life in a heartbeat if he chose to. But he pushed this thought from his mind, knowing he had a more important task to complete.

The street grew emptier as he climbed higher into the town. Soon he was surrounded by the clamour of hammering metal and the whooshing sound of bellows. He had reached the blacksmith district of Eaglestone, and he could feel the heat from the forges even through his heavy woollen cloak. There were dozens of blacksmiths' workshops lining the street, but the stranger had already chosen which he would approach. This particular blacksmith had something of a reputation that the stranger remembered from his time in the town. He approached the wooden door and knocked heavily. It opened after a few moments.

The blacksmith was stripped to the waist, revealing his considerable belly that was streaked with sweat and soot. Only his arms were free from fat, forged into muscles by his work.

'Yes?' the blacksmith asked impatiently, looking curiously at his visitor.

'I want to buy a sword,' the stranger said.

'Join the Jacelyn army then,' the blacksmith said dismissively. 'Only soldiers and knights are allowed to carry weapons in the town.'

He went to close the door, but the stranger stopped it with his foot.

'I say, look here!' the blacksmith protested.

'I want to buy a sword,' the stranger repeated, more forcefully this time.

'Look, like I told you,' the blacksmith said, wiping the sweat from his brow. 'I *can't* sell you a sword, on orders from Eagle Mount.'

'I'll give you six silvers.'

The blacksmith ceased his protests, and his walrus moustache quivered slightly. The stranger knew that this blacksmith could easily be swayed by the lure of coin. The man poked his head out of the door and glanced up and down the street, to make sure no one was overhearing them. Seeing the coast clear, he looked back at the hooded stranger and lowered his voice to barely above a whisper.

'For six silvers I'd only be able to give you one of my more basic items, like what the Jacelyn soldiers carry.'

'That will do me just fine.'

The stranger knew that he could easily overpower the blacksmith and take as many swords as he wanted by force, but there was a risk that the commotion would draw attention, and he could not risk anything interfering with his plans.

The blacksmith looked nervously up and down the street once more, before pulling the door wide open and letting the stranger inside. He followed him indoors before hurriedly closing the shutters on the windows. It was gloomy inside, with only the glow of the forge for illumination.

'The coins?' the blacksmith asked, rubbing his hands together.

The stranger tossed them onto a table, where they span and danced across the wood.

'Take one of these,' the blacksmith said, gesturing at a stack of plain but sturdy swords laying on a nearby workbench.

The stranger took one and tested the weight of it in his hand, and checked the sharpness of its edge. Apparently satisfied, he turned to leave. But as he did so, the glow from the forge lit up his face. The blacksmith did a double take.

'Wait, don't I recognise you from somewhere?'

The stranger paused, one hand reaching for the door handle. He sighed, before turning back and looking the blacksmith in the eyes. The blacksmith took a step back in horror when he remembered where he recognised the face from.

'What a pity,' the stranger smirked, locking the door behind him and trapping them both inside. 'You should have just taken your coins and not said another word.'

It only took a moment. The stranger unlocked the door and stepped outside, re-emerging into the settling gloom of the evening's twilight. He hid the blood-stained sword beneath his cloak, and disappeared into the shadows. He began making his way back down towards the main street that led from the town gates to the castle at the top of the hill. He knew that the boy would be passing through any moment now.

* * *

Merric led the way through the gates and into Eaglestone, waving shyly in response to the cheers and calls of the folk he passed. He felt like he would never get used to their reactions, but with a smile he decided that cheers were much better than being pelted with rotten tomatoes, as some less popular dukes had been in the past.

He returned the salute of the two Jacelyn soldiers standing beside the gate. While he would be sad to say goodbye to Ana, he was already looking forward to getting back to the castle. If he had timed it right, then once he had washed and changed his grubby clothes, his squire, Tomas, would be knocking on his chamber door and announcing that it was time for dinner. A small part of him felt guilty that he had left the day's duties to be carried out without him, but Sir Oskar and Sir Orsten Oakheart were more than up to the task. And, he reasoned, it had been his cousin, Sophya, who had encouraged him to spend some time away from Eagle Mount with Ana.

'It'll do you some good!' she had said to him. 'You deserve a break.'

A fanfare by the trumpeters high on the walls had heralded his return, and despite his dirty appearance the townsfolk easily recognised their beloved young duke, and called out friendly greetings.

'Good evening, my lord!'

'Welcome back, Lord Merric!'

'The Mother praise you, my duke!'

A little girl even approached him atop his horse and handed up a small bunch of flowers to him. Merric thanked her, and she hurried back to her beaming mother and buried her blushing face in her skirt. Merric glanced across at Ana, who just laughed.

'Don't worry, I don't get jealous that easily,' she said.

Merric unsuccessfully tried to brush the worst of the dust from himself, in an attempt to at least slightly appear more lordly. The townsfolk did not seem to care how he looked, and Merric realised that there must have been some truth to Ana's earlier words at the tavern in Domadge Bartyn.

He and Ana rode up the Lord's Way, the main street that led up through the heart of the town all the way to the castle of Eagle Mount. More folk waved to them, but the street was growing quieter as many returned home for their suppers. As they passed through the Fountain Court, a square halfway up to the castle which was a popular meeting place for the townsfolk, they saw a knight who was asking a richly dressed merchant for directions.

'A Ouestorian,' Ana muttered with dislike, hearing the knight's flowery accent.

Merric clicked his tongue, amused by his friend's prejudice. It was true that High Realm and Ouestoria, the kingdom that lay to the west beyond the Border Peaks, had been at war many times throughout history, but there had been years of peace since the two had last crossed swords. The two kingdoms got on well enough now. Some were less happy to forget the past than others.

Another pair of knights were trotting down the street towards them from the direction of the castle. They were dressed in the pristine armour of the elite Eagle Guard, and no doubt they had been dispatched to greet Merric and return him promptly to Eagle Mount.

'This is where I say goodbye then,' Ana said with a disappointed sigh.

Merric handed her the flowers that the little girl had given him, and she accepted them with an amused smile. He would have loved to have kissed her before they each returned to their own lives for a while, but here, under the watchful gaze of the two Eagle Guard, Merric would never have dared.

'I'll see you soon,' he said to her, hoping that the look in his eyes would tell her how much he had enjoyed their day together.

'You'd better,' Ana grinned, before turning and disappearing down a side road that led towards her father's workshop.

Merric went with the Eagle Guard, who rode silently on either side of him. Even though they were there for his own protection, he felt somehow trapped by them. He wished more than ever that his day with Ana out in the countryside had never needed to end.

Lights were twinkling up ahead as candles were lit in the castle as the darkness settled all around, and Merric admitted that he would at least be glad to be out of the saddle and into a comfortable chair. Ana often laughed about his 'lordly backside', and how he was too soft and needed hardening up.

A grin crossed Merric's face as he remembered her saying this, and the visored helmet of one of the Eagle Guard glanced across at him. Always professional when on duty, the knight did not ask his duke what had amused him. Merric was privately very grateful for this.

'My duke,' one of the Eagle Guard said, breaking the silence as they rode up towards the castle. 'Sir Oskar has requested your presence when we have returned, if you are agreeable. He wishes to advise you of the day's happenings.'

Merric nodded, feeling his spirits sink a little. Dinner, it seemed, would have to wait a bit longer.

A hooded figure stepped out into the road ahead of them, and stood immovable in the path of their horses. Merric and the two Eagle Guard came to a halt. Assuming the figure was perhaps a blind beggar, the Eagle Guard to Merric's left spoke loudly but patiently.

'You there! Careful now. Step aside for your duke.'

The hooded figure did not move, and so the knight spoke again, a little more forcefully this time.

'Make way for Lord Merric!' he ordered.

Still the figure stood as though a statue, giving no indication that he had even heard the command. The Eagle Guard walked his horse slowly towards the figure, while the other stayed close beside his duke. Merric felt a rising sense of unease as he saw the Eagle Guard beside him loosen his sword in its scabbard. It was their job to be ever watchful and vigilant, as the life of their duke was of the utmost importance. But surely this lone figure was no threat to them.

The first Eagle Guard walked his horse right up to the figure standing in their way, and came to a halt right in front of him. Sat on his horse, he towered over the hooded figure.

'Do not make me ask you again,' the Eagle Guard said, slowly and firmly.

The figure reached up suddenly and grasped hold of the bridle of the Eagle Guard's horse. Before Merric could even register what he was seeing, the figure had drawn a sword from within the folds of his cloak and had thrust it up into the knight. It struck him right through the gap between the chest plate and helmet.

The second Eagle Guard let out a shout of fury as his comrade fell, dead, from his horse. The armoured body toppled onto the ground with a metallic crash as the steel struck the cobblestones. The second Eagle Guard drew his sword and the hooded figure spun to face him, the sword held confidently in his strong hands.

'My duke, back to the castle!' the knight ordered Merric, and before waiting to see if the order had been commanded he bore down on the hooded assailant.

But Merric had not moved. He could only watch, frozen with shock. He stared at the body of the dead Eagle Guard, and then his eyes were drawn to the second knight who was duelling desperately with their attacker. Their swords rose and fell, but despite being on horseback and his opponent being unarmoured, the Eagle Guard was unable to find an opening. The Eagle Guard were among the greatest warriors in all The Head, hand-picked to serve as the Jacelyn family's loyal protectors, but this hooded figure almost seemed to be toying with him.

'Please, my duke!' the Eagle Knight shouted. 'You must get back to the castle! Go! Save yourself! I will hold him off!'

But Merric could not flee. He did not know whether it was the shock that stopped him from moving, or a desire not to abandon the knight. One of the Eagle Guard had already fallen to the assailant's ruthless sword, and Merric could not let the other follow him to the same fate. As Merric watched, transfixed, the hooded figure slashed his sword at the knight's horse. The animal cried out in alarm and fell sideways onto the ground, trapping the Eagle Guard's leg beneath it. The assailant advanced on the helpless knight, raising his sword.

'No!' Merric shouted, leaping from the saddle and tugging his own sword from its scabbard, glad that Sir Oskar had insisted that Merric take it with him.

'Run!' the Eagle Guard pleaded at him, but he was silenced by a ruthless death stroke delivered by the hooded figure.

The assailant turned quickly and met Merric's charge. He blocked *Hopebearer* as Merric swung his father's old sword at the murderer of the two gallant knights. The counter strike was more powerful than Merric could have imagined, and he staggered backwards. The hooded figure chopped down at him again and again, and it was all Merric could do to block the attacks as best he could. He had been taught to defend himself against sword attacks, but this assailant was fighting in a style Merric had never seen before. Ruthless and ferocious, almost animal-like. Merric could only back away, fighting for his life, fearing that each blow would be the one that killed him.

As he backed away from the savage attacks, Merric's foot struck the fallen shield of one of the Eagle Guard. Before he could even think about trying to keep his balance, he had stumbled and fallen backwards onto the cobbles. The hooded figure raised his sword with both hands, ready to swing it down and finish Merric as he lay prone on the ground, completely defenceless.

Another sword appeared from nowhere and blocked the descending blade in a shower of sparks. Merric glanced to the side in surprise and saw that his rescuer was the Ouestorian knight he had seen earlier. He had not donned his helmet in his rush to come to Merric's aid, and his long brown hair flew free in the light evening breeze. The assailant let out a noise of frustration and turned to face the new challenger, furious that his murder of Merric had been interrupted.

The Ouestorian knight raised his grey shield, which bore the symbol of a candle. The shield was dented and scratched in places, as though it had seen a great deal of use. The hooded figure roared in frustration again and swung his sword viciously at the Ouestorian, who blocked it with the shield, adding another gouge to its surface and sending chips of grey paint flying. The heavy blow had knocked the shield to one side, and the Ouestorian knight was forced to strike forward with his own sword to parry away the assailant's next attack.

'Stop this!' the Ouestorian shouted at the hooded figure, who ignored him and continued raining blows down upon him.

The Ouestorian knight spun gracefully away from the sword one more time, his teeth gritted. He then began his own attack, trying to get through the hooded figure's defences. At last, he spotted an opening. Feigning with his blade, he switched at the last moment. The weighted bronze pommel at the bottom of his sword connected loudly with the side of the assailant's head. There was a sickening crunch. The hooded figure let out a grunt and fell to the ground, knocked out cold.

Shouts came from the direction of the castle, as soldiers hurried down the street towards them. They held torches in their hands and wore anxious expressions on their faces. Clearly they had been alerted by the sound of fighting in the street.

'My duke!' they shouted.

'I'm here,' Merric called back, from where he laid on the ground.

Wiping the sweat from his brow, the Ouestorian knight turned to Merric. He sheathed his sword and reached out a hand to help pull Merric back to his feet.

'Are you okay, *mon duc*?' he asked in his throaty accent.

'Yes, I'm fine,' Merric said, shakily. 'Thank you, sir. Thank you.'

He edged cautiously towards the prone figure lying on the cobblestones, but the knight held out a hand.

'Careful!' he warned. 'Let me.'

He knelt down and pulled back the hood of the assailant lying unconscious on the ground. As he did so, Merric recoiled in horror. The Ouestorian looked up at him.

'Do you know this man?' he asked.

'Yes,' Merric managed to say, looking at the familiar bald head and the scar that pierced the man's cruel, horrifying face.

The face that had haunted his nightmares.

CHAPTER FIVE

The Ouestorian

It was fair to say that Sir Oskar and Sir Orsten Oakheart were furious. The twins had arrived on the scene shortly after the Jacelyn soldiers had tightly bound the hands and feet of the unconscious figure of the scarred knight who had attacked Merric. They had quickly arranged for an escort to take their duke back to the castle. Merric had been led to his study where he had slumped, still in a state of shock, into the chair behind the great desk. A short while later, after they had overseen the bodies of the two fallen Eagle Guard being returned for burial, and the captive being taken down to the dungeons, the Oakheart twins had joined Merric in the study.

'What have I said, time and again?' Sir Orsten said in frustration, speaking as much as to the room itself as to his brother and Merric. 'It is not safe! Our duke cannot go wandering around without protection.'

'I agree with you, brother,' Sir Oskar said, his anger mixed with the same shock that Merric felt. 'Though I never thought that someone here in Eaglestone would try and cause him harm.'

'He's not from here,' Merric said.

The Oakheart twins both stared at him.

'Do you know who the attacker was, my duke?' Sir Oskar asked, surprised.

'Yes,' Merric nodded, 'and so do you. You've met him before.'

Sir Orsten looked puzzled, but understanding passed over Sir Oskar's face.

'He was a knight who served Lord Aric,' he said, remembering. 'He was the one who came to Oaktyn that day, to get father to bend the knee to the Monforts.'

'I forgot about him,' Sir Orsten admitted.

Merric had witnessed the confrontation between the scarred knight and elderly Lord Horin Oakheart. The proud old Baron of Oaktyn had been reluctant to pledge his loyalty to the Monforts, and so the scarred knight had taken his two sons as hostages. It had only been when Merric had returned to Eagle Mount and freed them from the dungeons that they had been able to get revenge on their captors. But once the dust had settled after the Battle of Eagle Mount, the scarred knight had not been among the dead or captured.

The Oakheart twins were both of great height and strength, equally matched in battle. But there the similarities ended. While Sir Oskar had a sharp mind, his brother preferred to let his sword do the thinking for him.

'I had always assumed that he'd gone back to The Southstones with Aric,' Merric said.

'By the state of his clothes I would say he has been living rough these past weeks,' Sir Oskar said thoughtfully. 'Perhaps he thought that he could get revenge for the death of Rayden Monfort by killing you tonight.'

Merric gave a shudder, knowing just how close the scarred knight had come to succeeding in his plan.

'It was he that killed my parents, too,' he said, feeling like he may as well be completely honest with the Oakhearts.

Sir Oskar opened his mouth in surprise, and Sir Orsten frowned. Merric had not often spoken to anyone about the deaths of his parents. He himself had never really known what were true memories, and what were just nightmares created by his over-active mind. But when he had seen the scarred knight with Rayden Monfort, standing over the body of Tristan, Merric had known at once that he was the same man that he had seen as a young boy in the ruins of his home village.

'I'd always thought it had been common bandits that had raided Ryding,' he said. 'But if that scarred knight had been working for the Monforts even all those years ago then it looks like Aric has had his eyes on The Head for a long time. Tonight wasn't the first time that I've been at that man's mercy.'

'You do not need to worry, my duke,' Sir Oskar assured him. 'He is in chains down in the dungeons, and there will be guards outside his cell day and night. He will not be leaving.'

Merric nodded, not entirely reassured. The scarred knight had killed his parents, and had played a part in the murder of Tristan, and likely the murders of Lord Roberd and Lady Cathreen too. And tonight, he had nearly succeeded in ending Merric's own life. He had been responsible for almost all of the horror that Merric had experienced in his life. But, he reminded himself, the villain was only acting on the orders of Aric. And what would Aric do once he learned that his assassin had failed to kill Merric? Would he send someone else?

He had tried to allow himself to believe that Aric had given up on whatever his plans for The Head were, and would leave them in peace. Especially now that Lord Warner Camoren had been removed from Hightop Castle and was also down in the dungeons below Merric's feet. But it looked like Aric would not so easily be discouraged, and losing his son and his most loyal baron were not going to stop him.

Merric felt like he wanted a moment to himself. Rising to his feet he could feel that his legs were shaking. He hoped that the Oakheart twins would not notice, as he did not want them to think he was weak. He was slightly intimidated by the men, but was grateful for all the support they had given him over the past month. Less than a week after he had become Duke of The Head, he had named them joint Lord's Counsel, whose responsibility it was to advise and aid their duke. They had been proud to be offered the position, and had proven themselves more than capable of the role. And they had certainly made Merric's life a lot easier. They were good, honourable knights from an old, stoic family, and Merric did not want them to think less of him now, seeing him so shaken after the evening's events.

'My duke, before you leave,' Sir Oskar said, stepping forward. 'I do not think it wise for you to leave the castle without an escort going forward, at least not until we have discovered whether any further threats to your life are out there. We will question the captive, and I hope we are able to gain information from him. Though I do not know how willing he will be to talk.'

'We know the girl saw you safe from harm during your wanderings in the summer,' Sir Orsten said, 'but an assassination attempt is something else entirely.'

Merric nodded. He just wanted to return to his bedchamber. He was even able to ignore the way Sir Orsten had referred to Ana simply as "the girl".

'What my brother means to say,' Sir Oskar said, slightly more tactfully, 'is that you are far too important to The Head. If Lord Aric still seeks to take this dukedom for himself, then your death would go a long way to achieving that ambition.'

'I understand,' Merric said, saying whatever needed to be said in order to be able to leave.

He excused himself and left the study. He hurried upstairs towards his bedchamber, grateful that he did not see anyone in the corridors on the way. Word of the attack must surely have spread across the castle, and he did not much like the idea of having folk stare at him.

As Duke of The Head he was entitled to use the vast bedchamber that offered spectacular views of the surrounding land, but to Merric that would always be Lord Roberd's. And so he was happy to continue using the simple bedchamber that he had slept in since he was very young.

He pushed open the door and leant against the basin in the corner of the chamber. He breathed in and out slowly with his eyes screwed shut. It was a very strange feeling, knowing that he had been so close to his own death. Only an hour ago he had been feeling so happy after a perfect day spent with Ana. He felt shaken, but also strangely alive. He supposed that was something that happened when you suffered such a close call. His heart was pounding and his legs continued to shake. He kept on taking deep breaths, feeling himself begin to calm. He realised, with some surprise, that he still held *Hopebearer* in his hand. He had been holding it, without realising, during his whole conversation with Sir Oskar and Sir Orsten downstairs. He put the sword down at last, propping it against the wardrobe next to him. His hand was sweaty, and he noticed that he had been gripping the sword so tightly that the pattern from the leather on the hilt was imprinted into his palm. He used his hands to splash some cold water from the basin onto his face, leaving his hair plastered all over his forehead. He glanced again at the sword he had inherited from his father. When he had faced Rayden in battle it had been *Hopebearer* that had won the day, he was sure of it. But this time, it had been a knight from Ouestoria.

There was a knock at the door and, before Merric had even had a chance to answer it, Sophya Jacelyn hurried in, looking anxious.

'Oh, Merric!' she cried, rushing over and wrapping her arms around him.

'I'm all wet!' Merric warned her, his face still dripping from when he had splashed water on it. He was worried about ruining the dress she was wearing.

'Don't worry about that,' Sophya said with a relieved laugh, still hugging him tightly. 'I was so worried when I heard what happened. I thought it was all my fault!'

'Your fault?' Merric said, puzzled.

Sophya finally let him go.

'Yes, it's my fault,' she said, dabbing at her eyes. 'I encouraged you to leave the castle today. But how was I to know that monster would be waiting for you?'

'Don't be silly,' Merric said, forcing himself to smile. 'How could you possibly have known? It's no one's fault.'

'Yes,' she agreed, also smiling slightly, 'you're right. I'm just being silly. But I was so worried that I'd lost you too.'

She and Merric had never been close growing up, and Sophya had in fact found the younger boy to be incredibly annoying when they were children. But now they were the only family that the other had left, and that had brought them closer together. Merric had noticed a remarkable change in Sophya in the past few weeks. She had grown from a girl that was prone to fits of petulant sulks and who had allowed herself to become infatuated with Rayden Monfort, into a young woman who had matured quickly beyond her years. As though determined to make up for her behaviour when she had believed Rayden's lies, and had been convinced that Merric was the real enemy, she had taken it upon herself to support her cousin in any way that she could. Perhaps inspired by her own mother, who had been more than just the wife of the duke, Sophya had decided to shoulder some of Merric's burdens. She had done a remarkable job at keeping the castle of Eagle Mount running while Merric had been weighed down with the responsibilities of ruling the whole dukedom. Before, she had enjoyed nothing more than relaxing with her friends and trying to catch the eye of every handsome knight that visited the castle, but now she carried out her duties with a determined passion. And it turned out that she was good at it

Merric was not confident when it came to entertaining guests to the castle, nor penning letters to local merchants to secure the provision of grain to fill the food stores ahead of the coming winter, but this is where Sophya excelled. Her natural charm made her a delight for folk to deal with, and she seemed to be enjoying herself and took pride in her work. Merric was reminded of Lady Cathreen every time he looked at Sophya now, and wondered what it must have been like living under the influence of cruel Rayden Monfort for her to have matured so quickly.

'So,' she said, taking Merric's hand and leading him over to the bench beneath the window, where they both sat, 'how was it?'

'Scary, I suppose,' Merric said, feeling awkward by the question.

'No,' she said, smacking him gently on the arm. 'I mean, how was your day with Ana?'

'Oh,' Merric said, grinning despite himself and feeling even more awkward. 'It was…nice.'

Sophya rolled her eyes.

'*Nice?*' she said. 'Honestly, what are you boys like!'

While he was much too shy to speak openly about his feelings for Ana, and even hearing Sophya mention her name made his face flush, he liked the fact that she was asking. It made him feel like a normal boy of his age. Aside from Ana, Merric did not really have any friends his age, and certainly none who would take him aside and treat him like a normal fifteen-year-old boy.

And, since becoming duke, most of his time had been spent with Sir Oskar and Sir Orsten, rebuilding The Head in the wake of the brief Monfort rule. Then there had been the visit of the various barons of The Head, who had come to vow allegiance to their new duke. None of them had questioned Merric's right to rule, nor expressed any concern at his young age, but Merric had been very aware of the fact that they were all men far older than he was, and far more experienced than him too. Elderly Lord Horin Oakheart, Baron of Oaktyn and father of Sir Oskar and Sir Orsten, had been ruling his lands since even Lord Roberd had been a child. They had not sought to make Merric feel like the odd-one-out, but that had been the result none-the-less.

Not many fifteen-year-old boys were expected to rule a whole dukedom, and so Merric appreciated times like this where he was able to act like the young person he really was. While he felt so comfortable around Ana, she could never truly understand how Merric was feeling. Sophya seemed to understand only too well. Merric supposed this was what having a brother or sister would be like. He had annoyed her growing up, naturally, but he knew that she would always be there for him.

There was another knock on the door, and when it opened this time Merric saw another friendly face. Tomas, his old servant, entered the bedchamber with a tray of food. The round-faced boy had accompanied Merric and Ana when they had fled Eagle Mount that summer, and he had shown incredible loyalty and bravery. Every time anyone called Merric the hero of the Battle of Eagle Mount he would counter this by saying that Tomas was the true hero. It had been he who had put aside his own fears and roused the folk of Eaglestone to come to Merric's aid when the battle looked lost. And Merric would never forget it. He had promoted Tomas to be his squire now, and this put the boy one step closer to his ambition of one day becoming a knight.

'I thought you might be hungry,' Tomas said, gesturing at the tray.

Merric felt calmer now, helped by the companionship of Sophya. His shock had given way to hunger. He smiled appreciatively at Tomas.

'You read my mind!' he said. 'But you're not my servant anymore, Tomas. You don't need to do this.'

'I know, my lord,' the boy said, 'but I wanted to.'

Merric could think of no one more deserving of becoming his squire than Tomas. Sir Orsten had approved of the promotion. He, too, had noticed the bravery that Tomas had shown, and recognised its potential. The Oakheart knight had even taken it upon himself, when he had a spare moment or two, to school Tomas in the art of being a knight. He had a long way to go before he would be ready, but Merric could tell that the timid, shy boy positively swelled with pride whenever he imagined himself one day being a knight. It was not something that happened very often to normal boys from the town of Eaglestone.

'Come and sit with us,' Sophya said kindly to Tomas.

The three of them sat there for a couple of hours, picking at the food while Sophya and Tomas tried to coax Merric into telling them more about his day with Ana, but he kept tight lipped. Sophya instead told them about the funny things she had overheard that day, and it was not long until the attack in the street that evening was pushed to the back of Merric's mind. They talked long into the evening, and it was only when Tomas fell asleep in his chair that Sophya decided it was time to leave Merric to go to sleep.

'Thank you, for this,' Merric said to her as she turned to leave.

She smiled knowingly at her cousin, before giving him a curtsy.

'Goodnight, my lord,' she said.

* * *

The next few days passed without anything out of the ordinary happening, and Merric tried to forget about the attack as he refocussed his attentions on running the dukedom. As though attempting to keep him from dwelling on the fact that he had almost been killed, Sir

Oskar and Sir Orsten were keeping Merric so busy with his work that he had barely a free moment to think of anything else. There were piles and piles of documents to be signed, inspections of soldiers to carry out, meetings to be had with local noblemen, and punishments to deal out to wrongdoers.

Both the Oakheart twins and the castle jailer had questioned the scarred knight who had carried out the attack on Merric, but they had been able to gain little information from him. He had kept a stubborn silence, no matter what they tried. Despite his unwillingness to talk, they could make some guesses about their grim-faced prisoner. Judging by his filthy appearance and the fact that no one had seen him since the Battle of Eagle Mount, they could assume that he had been living out in the wilds. It seems that he had been biding his time, waiting for the right moment to strike against Merric.

'Are you aware of the Porcourt family, of Porby?' Sir Oskar asked Merric.

'I think so,' Merric replied, looking back at the huge map that covered the rear wall of his study. Porby was a village just north of Eagle Mount, and Merric knew that the Porcourts were a minor noble family that had held lands there for generations.

'We have received unfortunate tidings from the widow of Sir Paravell Porcourt, who it appears was killed by a brigand living in their lands,' Sir Oskar said. 'It seems that there had been several murders there before Sir Paravell had attempted to apprehend him.'

'And you think that our prisoner here is the murderer?' Merric asked.

'It certainly seems so,' Sir Orsten growled. 'The murders did not begin until after Eagle Mount was retaken, and that was the last time the rogue was seen here. The timings fit.'

'Attempting to murder me is one thing, but killing innocent folk? And he calls himself a knight,' Merric said, shuddering.

'From what you have told us about the man he is far from an honourable knight,' Sir Orsten said. 'Leading the attack that destroyed your village and stabbing Sir Tristan in the back are hardly the actions of a man of honour. From the way he speaks I would guess he is a man from the mountains, not of noble birth.'

'Lord Aric has been known to bestow a knighthood on wild brigands as a reward for carrying out his dirty work,' Sir Oskar explained. 'I would not be surprised to find out that this is the case here, too.'

'I always thought that he didn't seem like he was a real knight,' Merric agreed.

While the prisoner had not given any more information, the Oakheart twins were convinced that his attempt on Merric's life showed that Lord Aric had not given up on his plans. They believed it likely that Lord Aric had given his scarred henchman instructions to cause as much chaos in The Head as he could. And that was exactly what the scarred knight had been doing these past weeks. Perhaps it was all part of a plan by Lord Aric to cause unease in The Head, ahead of him making another attempt to seize control of the land for himself. There had been no further signs of Monfort activity since the scarred knight's capture, but Sir Oskar had explained that they could not be too careful.

'With your permission, my duke, I think we should write to Lord Tymon Conway,' he said. 'As the Baron of Bridge Ford we should ask him to double the guards there.'

Merric thought this was a sensible move, and signed the letter that was written. There was only one way of crossing over the Rush, the roaring river that separated The Head from the rest of High Realm. If Lord Aric chose to take control of The Head again, this time by using brute force, then this bridge that was guarded by Lord Tymon Conway would be the first line of defence against the Monfort armies.

Merric had been able to see Ana again a couple more times, but it had not felt the same as it had been before. Because of the extra security precautions, Ana had been required to come to the castle, rather than Merric go to her in the town. It had not been as enjoyable spending time together when everywhere they went there was a member of the Eagle Guard stood watchfully nearby. Ana's eyes had been filled with concern the first time she had seen Merric since the attack, and she had looked unhappy as well. Merric felt like he knew why.

That summer, when they had fled Eagle Mount with Tomas to escape the Monfort swords that were hunting them, Ana had been able to protect Merric. With her trusty crossbow she had helped keep him safe from harm, and it was that which had propelled their friendship forward into something more. Merric's feelings towards Ana had not turned to love simply because he had been grateful for her support and protection, but rather that the shared danger had made them both realise how they felt for each other. Now that he was duke, the role of protecting Merric had fallen to the Eagle Guard and the Jacelyn soldiers. Ana knew that they could protect Merric far better than she ever could, and they were trained to do that very role, but there was something about passing that duty on to others that Ana struggled with.

'I wonder what it's like to have a normal life?' she had half joked, and Merric had imagined what things would be like in ten years' time. How would things be between the two of them? Would they be married, as he privately hoped they would be, or would the natural gulf between a duke and a blacksmith's daughter have driven them apart?

Whenever there was a gap in his duties and he was not daydreaming about Ana, Merric felt his mind wander to the knight who had come to his rescue that evening. He had asked Sir Orsten about him one day, and the knight had just shrugged.

'We get a lot of knights coming and going,' he said. 'I am afraid that I do not know his name, nor recognise his family's symbol.'

Sir Orsten did not seem interested in the identity of the knight, but was merely glad that he had done what he did. He had explained to Merric that it was a knight's duty to do what is right, always, and so him coming to Merric's aid was not as unusual a thing as Merric was making it out to be. Nevertheless, Merric wished to thank the knight for saving his life. Eventually, he asked Tomas if he would go into Eaglestone and see if he could find the Ouestorian knight.

'He had the symbol of a candle on his shield,' Merric told him. 'Perhaps he's still in the town. Maybe check the inns?'

'If he's still here, I'll find him,' Tomas said enthusiastically.

It did not take Tomas long. Merric had been walking the walls of Eagle Mount, gazing out to the west and wondering what Lord Aric was doing at that moment, when he heard his name being called. He turned, and saw Tomas climbing the stone steps that led up onto the wall, with the Ouestorian knight behind him.

The knight bowed when he reached Merric.

'Thank you, Tomas,' Merric said.

The boy smiled and turned and walked back down the steps to the castle courtyard below.

The knight was not as old as Merric had first thought, perhaps only two or three years older than himself. His long brown hair framed his handsome face, and there was a wisp of a beard growing on his chin. His eyes were friendly and there were lines framing his mouth, as though he was regularly quick to laughter. Up close, Merric could see that the knight's chain mail and surcoat was looking a little worn in places, as though it had been a long time since a castle blacksmith had given it any attention.

The knight gazed at him with his grey eyes, waiting politely for Merric to speak. Now that he was stood in front of him, Merric suddenly felt a bit awkward and nervous about speaking to the knight one on one.

'I wanted to thank you,' he said lamely, 'for what you did.'

'I did what any knight would do, *mon duc*,' came the modest reply in the flowery accent of Ouestoria.

'That's what Sir Orsten, my Lord's Counsel, said,' Merric smiled.

'A wise man,' the knight conceded. 'You have a magnifique view from up here, no?'

He began walking around the walls, looking admiringly at the spectacular view of the lands surrounding the hill on which Eagle Mount was built.

'Yes, I'm very lucky to call it home,' Merric admitted, walking beside him.

'I heard a rumour that this has not always been home to you? But I was not sure if such rumours were false.'

'No, that's true,' Merric admitted. 'I was born in a village called Ryding, but I was brought here by Lord Roberd Jacelyn when my parents were killed.'

The knight nodded, looking sympathetically at Merric, but he said no more.

'You're from Ouestoria?' Merric asked, hoping the question did not sound rude.

'Yes,' the knight replied, looking embarrassed at having forgotten his manners. 'My apologies, *mon duc*. Allow me to introduce myself. My name is Sir Sebastien, of Montré.'

'It's a pleasure to meet you,' Merric replied. 'I'm afraid I don't know too much about Ouestoria. Tell me about Montré. Is that your castle where you were brought up?'

'It is a beautiful place. Our chateau is high up in the mountains. Pine trees grow up to the snowline, and there are more flowers in the meadows than you could even imagine.'

'What brought you to High Realm?' Merric asked, curiously interested.

'Sadly, my mother passed away many years ago,' Sir Sebastien said, 'and my father and I grew apart. We have chosen to follow different lives, you see, and would hardly recognise each other now.'

'I'm sorry to hear that,' Merric said, knowing how pathetic his words sounded. He needed Sophya with him, as she would find much better things to say.

'You and I are more alike than you first thought, no?' Sir Sebastien continued. 'We have both learned to live without our parents. I expect my father has now passed away. He was an old man. Had I stayed at home I expect I would be the Count of Montré by now, but my younger brother will hold that title. Is it not funny how things work out?'

Merric knew exactly what he meant.

'My father was the Baron of Ryding, and while I was growing up here in Eagle Mount there was always a part of me that wondered how different things would have been if my parents had never died. I'd have become the baron myself one day.'

'And now look at you, *mon duc*,' Sir Sebastien said, grinning across at Merric and gesturing at the whole of Eagle Mount.

Merric could not help but smile as well.

'Yes, and I can't say that I've really got used to it yet.'

The grin faded from Sir Sebastien's face, and he put a hand on Merric's shoulder.

'These people here say they understand what you're going through, I am sure,' the Ouestorian said, quietly, 'but no one but you can truly understand it. I hope you will not take offence when I say it, but for one as young as you, it is a great burden.'

'It's hard,' Merric agreed, feeling surprisingly grateful that someone was saying it. He was tired of hearing folk tell him how good a job he was doing, and how Lord Roberd would be proud of him. 'You know, it's nice to hear someone else say that too.'

'We rise to our greatest accomplishments when we are being most tested,' Sir Sebastien said. 'My mother used to tell me that when we were young, but the saying sounds better in our Ouestorian language. The common tongue you speak here in High Realm is a far less poetic language.'

Merric laughed, and they walked in silence for a few minutes, continuing their circuit of the castle walls. Up here the autumn wind tugged at Merric's cloak, and the Jacelyn banners flapped noisily.

'So, what happened after you left home?' Merric asked, switching the conversation back. He was curious about the Ouestorian knight, who seemed to be living a fascinating life.

'I decided to carry on with my life alone. I spent a year or two wandering through Ouestoria, but there was too much there that reminded me of my dear mother.'

'I'm surprised you would want to come to High Realm,' Merric said, with a knowing smile.

'We Ouestorians hold no grudges against High Realm,' Sir Sebastien said. 'It has been many years since our homelands fought one another. I am much too young to have fought in the last war, and you were yet to even be born I would guess. There are some who do not let old rivalries die, I know this. But I hope to be judged by my own actions, not those of our fathers.'

Merric nodded with a smile. He liked Sir Sebastien.

'Have you been long in The Head?' he asked.

'Only since the Monforts left. The border was shut before then. I have been travelling from town to town, but you would be surprised how many distrust me because of my Ouestorian accent.'

Merric grimaced, recalling Ana's own reaction to hearing Sir Sebastien's voice when they passed him in the street. Her grandfather had fought and died in the last war with Ouestoria, and Merric suspected that she was not quick to forget.

'Are you a sellsword?' Merric asked Sir Sebastien. 'A mercenary?'

'My goodness, no!' Sir Sebastien said, with a laugh of mock outrage. 'I am a knight, not a sword for hire, *mon duc*. I take my vows seriously. I have no need for gold, as my father was very rich you see. No, I travel from place to place seeing if I can offer my sword to those in need. Perhaps I have read too many stories of gallant knights killing dragons and saving maidens. But it looks like I arrived at Eaglestone at the right time!'

He laughed, and again brushed aside Merric's gratitude as he once more tried to thank the knight for coming to his aid.

'I am just glad to have been able to help,' Sir Sebastien said.

'I know you enjoy the life of a wandering knight, sir,' Merric said, 'but if you wanted to settle somewhere and make a home then I know that The Head would welcome you. I would be glad to offer you a place on the Eagle Guard, if you'd like to join them.'

Sir Sebastien laughed again.

'A Ouestorian serve in the Eagle Guard? Even in Montré, beyond the Border Peaks, we have heard of the great protectors of the Jacelyn family. I do not think your folk would welcome me joining their noble ranks.'

Merric knew that Sir Sebastien was probably right. Members of the Eagle Guard were men born and raised within the noble families of The Head, and it was the greatest honour to become one of them.

'Do not worry, *mon duc*,' the knight said, sensing the awkwardness that had settled over Merric. 'I do not seek a reward for what I did. Your friendship is prize enough for me.'

- CHAPTER SIX -

A difference of opinion

Sir Sebastien laughed as Merric threw the spear, which went sailing high and wide of its target, disappearing harmlessly into the bushes. Sir Orsten shook his head in despair at Merric's pitiful attempt, but his twin brother frowned, unimpressed, at Sir Sebastien's behaviour. One should not laugh and mock a duke.

Sir Oskar handed Merric another spear, offering him some words of advice for his next attempt.

'A valiant attempt, *mon duc*,' Sir Sebastien chuckled, speaking over Sir Oskar. 'Perhaps next time, eh?'

Merric scowled good-naturedly at the Ouestorian and took the offered spear from Sir Oskar. Sir Orsten spurred forwards and rode ahead with the rest of the knights and squires that had accompanied them on the hunt, crashing through the undergrowth of the forest in pursuit of the boar that had so easily dodged Merric's poor throw. Merric was content to let them ride off ahead, and he followed at a slower pace. Sir Sebastien fell in beside him and the two picked their way between the trees, avoiding the gnarled roots and rabbit holes that littered the ground. Sir Oskar and a clutch of knights of the Eagle Guard followed along behind, keeping a watchful eye out for any sign of approaching danger.

Sir Sebastien hefted his own spear and held it overarm, the tip pointing straight ahead of them.

'Hold it like this,' he taught Merric, 'and when you throw, make sure you follow through, like this.'

'I think I'll leave the spear-throwing to you, Seb,' Merric laughed. 'I'll stick with the sword.'

Sir Sebastien tutted.

'You cannot hunt with a sword.' He turned and looked over his shoulder at Sir Oskar. 'Do you not teach young noblemen how to hunt over here in High Realm?'

'Our duke has had little time for such leisure activities,' Sir Oskar said, putting emphasis on Merric's title, as though wanting to remind the Ouestorian who he was referring to.

'Then we must fix that,' Sir Sebastien said, grinning across at Merric. 'Back in Ouestoria the ladies love a man who can hunt. Come, let us catch up and give you another throw.'

Merric had never before shown an interest in hunting, and had always stayed behind whenever Lord Roberd and Tristan had gone riding into the Greenwood. It was not that he had anything against it, and he certainly enjoyed eating what they had managed to catch, but it was just one of many things that Merric had chosen to avoid when growing up. He had shown no interest in any of the activities that associated him with being from a noble family. It had been a kind of protest in his younger years to avoid learning to competently ride a horse, wield a sword and act like a young nobleman. He felt like such skills were unnecessary to a boy with no future. Now, Merric could only smile at the thought of his ten-year-old self seeing him now, and realising what a mistake that had been.

It had been Sir Sebastien who had suggested that they go on the hunt, and he had a way of getting Merric to try new things where no one else could. The Ouestorian had spent more and more time in Eagle Mount, and while the two of them had become good friends, he had complained often of the lack of excitement in the castle. When he had heard some of the other knights in Eagle Mount planning on going for a hunt, he had encouraged Merric to accompany them.

'There is nothing quite like it for the soul,' Sir Sebastien had said, visiting Merric at Eagle Mount one afternoon after the new duke had completed a long and tiresome day. 'Blow those cobwebs away, eh?'

There were a lot about Sir Sebastien and Merric that were different. The Ouestorian was handsome and confident, outgoing and charismatic, all traits that Merric secretly wished that he possessed himself. But there were a great many things about them that were the same as well. Both had lived without their parents for a long time, and both had spent the most important years of their lives struggling to identify their place in the world. There were some things about Merric that Sir Sebastien simply understood better than anyone else did, and sometimes they were things that the Ouestorian had noticed that Merric had not even identified in himself. He had quickly grown to value the companionship of the knight, and he was grateful that Sir Sebastien seemed to enjoy his company just as much as Merric enjoyed his.

Up ahead in the Greenwood, Merric could hear the whoops and cheers from Sir Orsten and the other knights as they continued the hunt. If Sir Sebastien was wishing he was up there with them then he had the grace not to show it. He chose instead to keep Merric company, riding alongside him and simply enjoying the fresh air.

'Have you ever been married?' Merric asked him as they rode through the dappled green light beneath the leaves.

'Me? No! I would not be tied down with one woman,' the Ouestorian laughed. 'I would not deprive the ladies of High Realm of my charm. I was betrothed once, it is true, back in my homeland. My mother had matched me with the daughter of a neighbouring count. I was only a boy at the time, and when my mother died the count sought an alternate husband for his daughter.'

He went quiet for a moment, though whether he was thinking about what could have been had the planned marriage gone ahead, or if he was thinking about his mother, Merric did not know. He then looked back at Merric, with a knowing twinkle in his eye.

'Why do you ask, eh? Is there a young maiden that you have your eyes upon perhaps?' he asked with a devilish laugh.

Merric did not answer, but turned a little red. This only spurred Sir Sebastien on. The Ouestorian hooted with glee.

'But of course! I have heard you talking,' he said. 'I have heard you talk about a girl to your cousin, the Lady Sophya. What was the name of this girl again? Ana, I think it was.'

'Been eavesdropping, have you?' Merric asked, his eyebrow raised.

'It is not my fault if we Ouestorians are born with exceptional hearing,' Sir Sebastien said, unabashed. 'Who is she? Do not tell me she is a Monfort or something!'

Merric could not help but laugh at this.

'No, she certainly isn't! She's not from a noble family,' he said. 'She's my best friend. Her father is a blacksmith.'

'She is not a lady?' Sir Sebastien asked, sounding disappointed.

Merric did not know whether to be offended on Ana's behalf or not, but he knew that she would wrinkle her nose in disgust if anyone tried to call her a lady to her face.

'No, she's not a lady,' Merric confessed

'And you like this girl?' Sir Sebastien probed, playfully.

'Yes,' Merric said, smiling, with his eyes fixed on the trees in front of him and not looking at his friend.

Sir Sebastien did not speak and just stared at Merric, his eyebrows raised as though waiting for him to go on.

'I think I love her,' Merric conceded.

'Aha!' Sir Sebastian whooped. 'I knew it!'

'We went through a lot together this summer,' Merric said, as though he needed to explain himself.

'Ahh Merric,' Sir Sebastien said, sounding almost sympathetic. 'I have been there, my friend. I know how you are feeling. Maybe you love her, maybe you do not. It does not matter.'

'It doesn't matter?' Merric said, not understanding. 'What do you mean?'

'You are Duc of The Head,' Sir Sebastien said, as though his meaning was obvious. 'You cannot be marrying some fishmonger's daughter.'

'Blacksmith's daughter,' Merric corrected.

'Quite so,' said Sir Sebastien dismissively. 'You will be expected to marry a noble lady, of good stock. It seems unfair, I know.'

Merric bit his lip. It was something that had bothered him ever since he had first realised the feelings he had for Ana back in Little Harrow, and that had been before he had become burdened with being the duke. Such worries were twice as bad now. He would always tell himself that it did not matter, and that he could fall in love with whoever he wanted and marry them if he chose. But Lord Roberd had been married to the daughter of the Duke of The Dale, and even Lord Aric's wife was daughter of the king.

He did not care what others thought, and it would not matter to him in the slightest if folk would talk about him behind their hands if he married Ana. But there could come a time where he would need to marry someone not of his choosing in order to help secure an alliance or bring two families together. Many dukes in the history of High Realm had not been able to enjoy the simple luxury of marrying the one they love, and it caused Merric genuine worry when he thought that he could be one of those unfortunate dukes. He did not know how to broach the subject with Ana, and so chose to push such worries aside when he was with her.

Sir Sebastien seemed to know that he had said something to trouble Merric, and so he changed the subject. They talked about happier things, and the Ouestorian was soon teasing Merric again about his awful attempt at throwing a spear.

An hour later the small party of knights and squires left the Greenwood and headed back towards the castle. Merric had given up trying to be a good hunter, but he caught sight of Tomas and the other squires all talking excitedly. Tomas had a hunting falcon perched on his arm and was stroking the bird fondly. He was thoroughly enjoying his time with the other squires, and Merric knew that his old servant was fitting into his new role perfectly. The other squires were all sons of other knights and lords, each training to one day become a knight themselves. They had welcomed Tomas into their midst warmly, not caring at all that the boy was not from a noble family. They recognised the heroism Tomas had shown during the Battle of Eagle Mount, and that was enough for them.

Sir Orsten was riding at the head of the group and was loudly retelling the story of exactly how he had taken down the boar, to anyone who would listen. Sir Oskar rode up beside Merric, shaking the young duke out of his thoughts of the feast they would be having that evening.

'I never thought I would see you enjoying a hunt, my duke,' Sir Oskar said with a smile.

'There's a first time for everything, I suppose,' Merric said.

'I always thought you were like me,' Sir Oskar said kindly. 'My brother always preferred the more raucous of activities, and so I left the hunts and the jousts to him. Some of us have to be a little more respectable.'

'Is everything okay?' Merric asked, looking across at the knight.

Sir Oskar towered over him. He was enormous for such a gentle man, and his great warhorse only added to his size. It was said that the boys of Oaktyn wrestled bears on their tenth birthday, in order to prove themselves a man. Merric doubted that such folktales were true, but he imagined that even as a child Sir Oskar and his brother would have been more than a match for a fully grown bear. Whether it was Sir Oskar's mind or Sir Orsten's fearlessness, Merric was thankful every day that the Oakheart twins were on his side. He would not like to be their enemy.

'Of course, my duke,' Sir Oskar said, but Merric could see straight through the forced smile that was spread across the knight's face.

'One of the reasons I chose you to be my Lord's Counsel was because I knew you would always be honest with me,' Merric said.

'And I hope I always will be,' Sir Oskar said, with a slight bow of his head.

Merric continued to look inquiringly at him. Sir Oskar hesitated before continuing.

'Will you permit me to speak openly, my duke?'

'Of course,' Merric said, frowning up at him.

'I confess that I am a little troubled by your friendship with Sir Sebastien,' Sir Oskar said, as though the words had been on his mind for some time.

Whatever Merric had been expecting, it was not this.

'What do you mean?' he asked, taken aback.

'We do not truly know the man, and so we cannot be certain of his intentions.'

Merric felt a slight jolt of anger.

'He is my friend!' he said, hotly.

'With respect, my duke, you do not know him'

Merric knew he could not argue with this, as it had only been a week since he had met Sir Sebastien.

'He saved my life!' he said instead, reaching for his next argument.

'As any good and honourable person would do,' Sir Oskar said, not put off. 'Especially a knight.'

'I don't care if a knight is *expected* to do something like that, the fact is that he *did* do it. If it weren't for Seb I'd be dead right now.'

'A fact that fills me with cold dread whenever I think of it,' Sir Oskar admitted. 'And for that I will always be grateful to the man. But I am not sure that it is the right time for a stranger to be spending so much time at Eagle Mount these days. We are living in uncertain times.'

'He is not a stranger,' Merric insisted, looking ahead to where Sir Sebastien rode, deep in merry conversation with another knight. 'You can't order me not to spend time with him. I'm the duke, and can choose my own friends.'

'Of course you can, my du-'

'Is it because he's Ouestorian?' Merric shot across at him.

'You know it is not,' Sir Oskar said. 'But given the situation we are in, and what has happened since this summer, we must be extra vigilant. Any new faces are ones we should treat with caution, until we know for certain what their intention is.'

'His intention is to be my friend,' Merric said, spurring forward away from Sir Oskar. 'Something that no one else seems to understand.'

* * *

Sir Oskar did not raise the subject of Merric's friendship with Sir Sebastien again, and the next few days blurred together as Merric was kept too busy to think of much else. He was gradually becoming used to the day to day activities of being duke, and what had previously made him nervous had now begun to become boring instead. His least favourite thing to do was to hold court, which happened twice a week in the Grand Hall of Eagle Mount. A long line of petitioners would stretch from the doors all the way out into the courtyard, and sometimes it would carry on through the castle gates and into the main square of Eaglestone beyond. Folk would travel from across The Head to come to their duke with their troubles which needed resolving, and Merric would spend hours sat in the hard chair that sat on the raised dais beneath the great stained glass window in the Grand Hall, forcing himself to smile patiently down at them and listen to them all.

Farmers would come to him with a dispute regarding the boundaries between their fields, and priors would appeal for additional funding to make much-needed repairs to their priory roofs. A knight from a minor noble family a day's ride from Eagle Mount had come to apologetically inform Merric that they would be unable to raise the additional soldiers as requested, as his lands only included one small village and all the able-bodied folk had already been recruited. A couple of weeks previously, at the Oakheart twin's advice, Merric had requested that all lords and knights increase the number of soldiers in their employment, in case war with the Monforts was forced upon them, but he excused the knight and promised that he did not expect him to arm small children in order to reach his quota. A minstrel named Poe Tadge had asked permission to host a performance in the Grand Hall of Eagle Mount.

'Here?' Merric asked, surprised, looking about at the high vaulted stone ceiling.

'For the acoustics, my lord,' Poe said, strumming his lute as he spoke, letting the notes ring off the stone walls.

The first court session since Merric's afternoon spent hunting in the forest ended in a murmur of excitement when a young nobleman stepped forward, smartly dressed in his finest doublet and emerald green cloak.

'Sir Marc!' Sir Oskar said in surprise when he looked up from the parchment on which he was taking notes.

Merric did a double take. Sir Marc was one of the knights of his Eagle Guard, but he rarely saw him without his helmet on, let alone without his armour. He had not recognised him straight away. A timid-looking young woman with auburn hair was holding onto Sir Marc's arm, and the knight looked slightly nervous as he looked up at Merric. In his armour and atop his warhorse, Sir Marc was as fearsome a warrior as the rest of the Eagle Guard, and Merric was slightly amused to find himself surprised to see that these valiant guardians of the Jacelyn family were normal folk really, at the end of the day.

'My duke, this is Lady Jeyna of Allertyn,' Sir Marc said, introducing the lady on his arm. 'With your permission, we wish to marry.'

It was not forbidden for members of the Eagle Guard to marry and have families, but most chose not to.

'I know it is not normal practice,' Sir Marc pressed on, 'but…'

He hesitated, and looked at Lady Jeyna,

'But with war looming, we may not have another opportunity.'

Merric, of course, gave his permission. He watched as the two young lovers walked from the Grand Hall with broad smiles on their faces, while some of the others gathered cheered them on and offered their congratulations.

But rather than feel joy at the thought of one of his Eagle Guard finding love and getting married, Merric felt a familiar weight of dread in his insides. Was war indeed coming? Was he going to have to lead The Head through it? Many of the folk seemed to think so, and he wished he shared their confidence that they would win against their Monfort enemies.

When he was not carrying out his lordly duties, Merric found opportunities to spend time with Sir Sebastien, who had now been given a chamber within the castle walls. The two could often be found in the courtyard, where the Ouestorian was helping Merric improve his horse riding and swordsmanship.

'I will teach you the Ouestorian way,' Sir Sebastien said cheerfully, raising his own sword. 'We are fluid, like water or wheat in the wind. We are always moving, and that makes the sword feel lighter, do you see?'

'If you say so, Seb!' Merric said, sweat on his brow and an ache in his arms.

He did not like to say it, but he found this Ouestorian way to be even harder than the High Realm technique that he had been taught by Sir Gerard of the Eagle Guard that summer, and which Sir Orsten had sought to improve in recent weeks. But the more time he spent with his sword in his hand the more Merric felt used to its weight, and he could feel his strength growing. He knew he would never be a great swordsman, but he listened to every word Sir Sebastien said during the lessons, hoping that one day it would come in useful.

'It may seem like the High Realm way is more powerful,' Sir Sebastien said, 'but it is all about technique, you see? If you strike just right, a Ouestorian blow could cut a bull clean in two.'

Merric saw Ana as often as he could, and when the two of them spent time together Merric tried to ignore what Sir Sebastien had said to him in the Greenwood, when he had told Merric that there was no future for him with her. He knew that Sir Sebastien had meant well when he had said that, and that the Ouestorian would be mortified if he had known the effect of his words. Merric tried to convince himself that if Sir Sebastien knew Ana then he would not so easily dismiss her, but he had not dared let the two mix. He was worried that Sir Sebastien would say something to Ana that would tell her that they had been talking about her, and the thought of that filled Merric with dread.

But with the threat of war hanging over them all, Merric knew that neither Ana nor Sir Sebastien could be his number one priority at that moment. The Head had to come first.. A week after the Ouestorian had become a resident of Eagle Mount, the Oakheart twins came to Merric's study. They closed the door behind them, and their serious expressions told Merric that they were there to discuss something important.

'What's wrong?' Merric asked them.

Sir Oskar and Sir Orsten were looking tired. It was no easy task being Lord's Counsel, even with the role being split between the two of them. Whenever Merric got to bed late after a long day's work he always reminded himself that the twins had worked even longer, and even harder, than he had.

'We still have not been able to get any more information from the prisoner with the scarred face, nor from Lord Warner Camoren,' Sir Orsten said, a hint of frustrated disappointment on his face.

The captured Baron of Pooltyn was in the cell next to the scarred knight. He was so loyal to Lord Aric that Merric had never truthfully expected the man to talk. He had been so willing to die for Lord Aric in Hightop Castle that the discomforts of the dungeons would hardly be likely to loosen his tongue and make him spill all of his duke's secrets.

'While we cannot know exactly what Lord Aric is planning, we have to allow for the worst, my duke,' Sir Oskar said. 'We still do not know why Lord Aric sought to take The Head, but there is nothing to indicate that he will give up now.'

'I'd have thought that losing your son and your most trusted baron would be enough to put you off,' Merric said.

'I fear Lord Aric is not like most men, my duke.'

'You think that there will be war then?' Merric asked, nervously.

'We have no choice but to prepare for it,' Sir Oskar said wisely. 'He has tried to take over The Head through stealth and intrigue, and that has failed. Brute force is his only option now, and The Head does not possess the strength to hold back the might that The Southstones can throw at us. The Monforts can muster armies far greater than we can, and I feel like Lord Aric will not hesitate to arm every man and boy from his dukedom, if that is what it takes to win.'

'The crossing at Bridge Ford-' Merric began, but Sir Orsten cut him off.

'It would buy us time, but that is all,' he put in. 'Lord Aric certainly has the numbers he needs to assault the bridge, and he would not hesitate to lose hundreds if not thousands of his men in the attempt to capture the bridge. If he does not care about the life of his own son then he certainly does not care about the lives of the common folk that he rules with an iron fist.'

'Well, we've asked the barons and knights to recruit more soldiers,' Merric said, hopefully.

'I fear it will not be enough, my duke,' Sir Oskar said with a rueful shake of his head. 'I have been doing the calculations. Not even if we arm every man, woman and child would we have enough to equal the Monforts' numbers. And do not forget, the king himself is Lord Aric's father-in-law. If he has managed to convince the king that his version of events are true, and that you are the true culprit in the murders of Lord Roberd and his family, then he will have the full support of The Kingsland as well. We would be outnumbered five to one, at the very least.'

Merric gave a shake of his head.

'How could anyone believe Aric? How could anyone believe that it was *me* who murdered Lord Roberd, and that Aric and Rayden were trying to help the folk of The Head?'

'King Cristoph is not the wisest king we have ever had,' Sir Orsten said, laughing humourlessly. 'Some say that he loves Lord Aric, and others say that he fears him. Either way, the king will believe anything that he tells him.'

'You know, I've been thinking about the king,' Merric said, shifting in his seat slightly. 'We've not heard a word from him since Lord Roberd died. I would have thought we'd have heard *something* from him. If he believes Aric then why hasn't he sent a message, demanding I hand myself over or something? Demanding that The Head gives in?'

'I know what you are thinking, my duke,' Sir Oskar said. 'But do not take the king's silence as evidence for him staying out of this dispute between The Head and The Southstones. There is a chance that his realm will be cloven in half, and even a king as passive as King Cristoph will not be able to sit idle and allow it to happen. If he has not openly pledged his support to us, then we have to assume that he is against us.'

Merric found this to be a troubling thought. He had, of course, never met King Cristoph. He lived far away, on the far side of High Realm, but Merric had heard all the stories about him. He may not be an inspiring leader like kings of years past, but he was still the rightful ruler of High Realm. The folk of The Head loved the Jacelyn family, and as such they had grown to love Merric too, but how would they feel if their dukedom was at war with their very king? Would their loyalty to the Jacelyns hold firm, or would their duty to their king beat this? No, he convinced himself; Aric murdered Lord Roberd, and if the king sided with him then surely the folk of The Head would consider him to be no king of theirs.

'I expect that Lord Aric is keeping the king up his sleeve,' Sir Orsten said. 'He is not the kind of man to willingly be indebted to others. If he can get what he wants by himself then he will not call on the king's support. But he knows he has got him there in his pocket, in case he needs him.'

'Regardless of the king's silence on the matter, we cannot hide from the fact that the situation facing us is dire,' Sir Oskar said. 'Like my brother wisely says, the king may not be issuing a royal decree, insisting that The Head kneels before Lord Aric, but we would be fools to imagine that he has not already gifted him with his army and the other things that he will need to wage war against us.'

Merric looked between the two of them. They had always been able to offer a solution before, and he was trusting that they had the solution now as well. They were painting a very grim picture of a fight that was hopeless and destined to fail before it had even begun.

'So what can we do?' he asked, hoping they had an idea.

'There is one place we can turn to for aid, my duke,' Sir Oskar said. 'Somewhere which so far has remained neutral.'

In an instant Merric knew where Sir Oskar was referring to. He spun around in his seat and looked up at the enormous map behind him.

The Dale.

The dukedom of the Florin family lay to the north-west of The Head, nestled behind the Silver Peaks. A land of rolling grassland, The Dale was the fourth dukedom of High Realm. Merric knew little of The Dale, but had always heard Lord Roberd speak very highly of the Florin family. From Merric's reading in the library of Eagle Mount, he knew that the folk of The Dale were proud and honest, often choosing to stay out of the squabbles between the other dukes. But when High Realm itself was threatened the Florins had always risen to the moment and come to the king's aid.

'Do you think they would side with us?' Merric asked.

'Lady Cathreen was the sister of Lord Godfrei Florin, the current Duke of The Dale,' Sir Oskar said. 'He would want justice for the death of his sister.'

'Assuming he does not believe Aric's lies too,' Merric pointed out. 'The last thing we need is for them to join with Aric.'

'I do not think they would believe Lord Aric's story,' Sir Oskar said thoughtfully. 'If he did then he would likely have already declared his loyalty to the Monforts. We must take his silence as indication that he has not yet chosen a side.'

'He has never been one for war,' Sir Orsten countered. 'Lord Godfrei is not his father. Now *there* was a man with a strong sense of duty.'

'I agree, and yet Lord Godfrei is the duke nowadays. And so it is he that we must appeal to.'

'I do not like the idea of outside help,' Sir Orsten muttered grudgingly, 'but I admit we cannot fight alone.'

'We must reach out to him,' Sir Oskar said firmly, turning to Merric. 'We must seek an alliance with The Dale if we are to have any chance of survival should war break out. Without their support I fear we will be helpless against the combined strength of both The Southstones and The Kingsland, and will be forced to accept Lord Aric's rule once more. And this time it will be for good.'

Merric had never met Lord Godfrei, nor anyone from Lady Cathreen's side of the family. He had no idea whether they would agree to march to war. But, like Sir Oskar said, surely the Florins would be angry at the death of Lady Cathreen, just as folk from The Head were. Sir Oskar was right, they had to try. If the Monforts recaptured The Head then the folk here would suffer beneath their rule once more, and Merric knew that Lord Aric would not allow him to remain living. While the folk of The Head would be destined to life beneath Monfort tyranny, he himself would be executed for the murder of the Jacelyns. The thought of such injustice pained him more than the thought of death itself.

Merric nodded.

'You're right,' he said. 'We have to try.'

'I beg the honour of being your envoy,' Sir Oskar said, rising to his feet and bowing his head. 'Allow me to travel to The Dale on your behalf, and speak with Lord Godfrei. I will not return until I have been able to secure an alliance with him.'

Merric thought about this for a moment. He knew what he wanted to say, but the Oakheart twins would be unlikely to approve of his suggestion.

'Thank you, Sir Oskar,' he said, glancing up at him uneasily. 'But I was thinking that perhaps Seb, I mean Sir Sebastien, should go.'

As expected, a dark expression passed over Sir Oskar's face. Merric felt like he ought to explain himself.

'It's not that I think you wouldn't do a good job. But Aric will know that we need the support of the Florins, and that we'll be sending an envoy to The Dale, and so he'll likely be keeping a lookout. You and Sir Orsten are too easily recognisable, and they'd stop you before you even managed to take one step into The Dale. Even if Aric knows who Sir Sebastien is, he would have no reason to think that he is working for us. So he's more likely to make it all the way to Lord Godfrei without being stopped. And he knows his way around High Realm better than anyone.'

Merric could see that Sir Oskar saw the sense in what he was saying, even if he did not like it. Encouraged, Merric pressed on.

'And I need you here,' he admitted to Sir Oskar. 'I made you and Sir Orsten be my Lord's Counsel because I can't do this on my own. I need you to help me lead The Head.'

The Oakheart twins did not know Sir Sebastien like he did. If they had gotten to know him they would have every faith in him, as Merric did. He knew that the Ouestorian would not let them down. He would succeed in his quest to gain Lord Godfrei's support, or, Merric thought with a nervous gulp, he would die in the attempt.

The twins were loyal and obedient, and while they did not like the idea of the fate of The Head being in the hands of Sir Sebastien, they could not readily refuse Merric's wish.

'You are our duke,' Sir Oskar said with a reluctant bow of his head. 'If you trust Sir Sebastien to see it done, then I will prepare the letter for him to carry.'

- CHAPTER SEVEN -

The messenger

Sir Sebastien set off that very evening. He choose to leave under the cover of darkness, just in case anyone was watching and sent the Monforts word of what he was doing. It was vital that his quest remained a secret if it stood a chance of succeeding. Only Merric, Sir Oskar and Sir Orsten were there to see him off, and Merric felt a pang of guilt that his friend was attempting to save The Head and yet no one knew. He deserved a hero's send off, not this secretive farewell.

Rain was falling heavily, and Sir Sebastien wore a heavy cloak over his grey surcoat. He had the hood pulled up over his head, but the rain did not seem to be dampening his spirits. He grinned down at Merric, who was stood with his shoulders hunched and a grimace on his face as the rain dripped down the back of his neck.

'Do not worry, *mon duc*,' Sir Sebastien said good-naturedly. 'I am well used to being on the road. The rain and I are old friends.'

The letter to Lord Godfrei Florin, written by Sir Oskar and signed by Merric, was stowed safely in a waxed canvas bag on Sir Sebastien's saddle, to protect it from the rain. It had been with some reluctance that Sir Oskar had handed the vital letter to the Ouestorian, but he knew that it would be too late now to change Merric's mind and send someone else to The Dale instead. With the letter now safely in Sir Sebastien's possession, Sir Oskar and his twin brother stood a few paces away, giving Merric and the Ouestorian a chance to say their goodbyes.

'I have something for you,' Merric said.

From beneath his cloak he produced a sword, and he held it up for the Ouestorian to take.

'For me?' Sir Sebastien said.

The scabbard was made from sleek black leather, and when he drew the sword a few inches the raindrops danced off the polished steel blade.

'It's beautiful, *mon duc*,' Sir Sebastien said. 'But I cannot take this.'

'It's a gift,' Merric insisted. 'I had it made for you, as my way of saying thank you.'

'I do not need your thanks,' Sir Sebastien said, smiling down at his friend. 'It was my duty, and my honour, to protect you.'

'I'm not only thanking you for saving me that day,' Merric corrected him. 'You're a real friend.'

Sir Sebastien waved this away, but he politely accepted the sword, and buckled it onto his belt, beside his tired old blade that had seen better days.

Sir Sebastien leaned down from his horse and shook Merric's hand.

'If Lord Godfrei says no in response to your letter, shall I threaten him?' he grinned.

'Better not,' Merric smiled back. 'I don't fancy ending up at war with The Dale too.'

'Give me two weeks and I will be back with his reply.'

'Be safe, Seb,' Merric said, the smile fading from his face.

Sir Sebastien could see the concern in his friend's eyes, and became serious himself.

'Do not worry about me, Merric,' he assured. 'I know my way around this kingdom better than most who have lived in High Realm all their lives. I can keep off the road, and avoid being seen by unfriendly eyes.'

'Don't try anything heroic,' Merric pleaded with his friend. 'Not like when you came to my aid. The road to The Dale passes close to The Southstones. If you see any Monfort patrols you turn in the opposite direction and run. Just…be careful.'

Merric wished that he could send some soldiers to accompany Sir Sebastien, but that would raise too much suspicion once he had left The Head and was in the dangerous lands that lay beyond. And besides, Merric knew that Sir Sebastien would argue that he would travel faster alone. A detachment of soldiers would only slow him down.

'You know me,' he said, flashing his cheeky grin again. 'I am always careful.'

He clicked his tongue and his horse set off at a trot. Merric watched him as he went through the gates and into the streets beyond, until the darkness and the hammering rain swallowed him up.

'May the Mother grant him speed,' Sir Oskar muttered somewhere behind Merric.

Feeling strangely sad at the idea of Sir Sebastien being gone from the castle, Merric turned and walked back towards the keep, splashing through the puddles that were forming in the courtyard.

To Merric, the castle somehow felt emptier over the next few days with his friend gone. Sir Sebastien may have only been one person out of hundreds who lived and worked in Eagle Mount, but his presence was missed, and not just by Merric. The Ouestorian had always been the one to laugh the loudest during mealtimes in the Grand Hall, and had quickly befriended the Jacelyn soldiers. His easy-going and down-to-earth nature, which was missing from many of the other knights who spent their days in the castle, made him easy to like. To many, Eagle Mount simply seemed like a much drearier place without Sir Sebastien brightening its halls.

Merric's lessons with him, where he had been slowly but surely improving his swordsmanship and horse riding, had made the days go by faster. Now, there was less to distract Merric from his duties of ruling The Head. This was something that Sir Oskar had commented on too, but while Merric had been saddened by the lack of the distractions, Sir Oskar had seen it as a good thing. Merric knew full well that while Sir Sebastien was hugely likeable and had made many friends in the castle, there were some, Sir Oskar and Sir Orsten among them, who had not warmed to the Ouestorian knight. Merric understood their reservations. With the threat of war ever growing they were hesitant to befriend strangers. But if they put aside their caution and their natural distrust of those from High Realm's oldest enemy, they would have seen how important Sir Sebastien had been in making Merric feel happier and more confident in his role as duke.

Most unfortunately, Ana had shared the same view as the Oakheart twins. She had never met the Ouestorian, but Merric had talked about him often during the times that he and Ana had been able to spend time together. Like Sir Oskar, she felt that Merric's close friendship with Sir Sebastien was a cause for concern, rather than comfort. The morning after Sir Sebastien had departed for the Dale, Merric had gone down into Eaglestone with an escort of a pair of Eagle Guard and knocked on the back door of her father's workshop. She had been pleased to see him, but if she had hoped that Sir Sebastien's departure would mean that Merric would talk less about the Ouestorian then she had been quickly disappointed. She had been dismayed when Merric had spent almost the entire visit talking about him.

'I can't believe that of all those you could have chosen to act as your envoy you chose *him*,' she said, not troubling to keep the tone from her voice.

Merric knew that she would have been glad to make the journey to The Dale herself.

'It's a dangerous journey,' he tried to explain. 'I couldn't ask you to go. And besides, Seb knows High Realm like the back of his hand. He was the most sensible choice.'

'Danger is hardly new to me, Merric. Or perhaps you have forgotten that,' she snapped back, before her voice turned softer and she took hold of Merric's hand.

'Sorry,' she apologised. 'It's not that I'm saying that I wanted to be the one to go. To be honest, I wouldn't want to go. I want to be here, where you are.'

'Then what is it?' Merric asked, still annoyed by Ana's continued lack of warmth towards Sir Sebastien. No matter what he had said about his new friend, it had seemed to make Ana dislike him more.

'Look,' she said, speaking carefully, not wanting to make him upset, 'I'm glad that you have a new friend. And I'm not stupid, I know there are things you can talk about with him that you couldn't talk about with me, or anyone else for that matter. But I'm worried that you're pushing others aside in favour of him. When did you last spend time with Sophya? Or Tomas?'

'I had breakfast with them this morning!' Merric said defensively. 'And I have meetings with Sophya almost every day. It takes both of us to keep the castle running, you know.'

'Oh Merric,' Ana said, half smiling and half scowling in exasperation at his ignorance. 'Work doesn't count. When did you last spend time with her just as cousins? You've just built a good relationship with Sophya, and I know how much it means to her to have you as family. Please don't push it all aside.'

'Who says I'm pushing anyone aside?' he said. Then he noticed the piece of parchment lying on a table strewn with tools of Ana's blacksmithing trade. He recognised the handwriting. 'Has Sir Oskar been writing to you?' he demanded.

Ana had the good nature to turn a little red.

'Yes,' she admitted. 'But only because he has your wellbeing at heart. He knows that you and I are close.'

'Since when has everyone been so interested in who I'm friends with?' Merric said crossly, standing and pacing angrily over to the window. The two members of the Eagle Guard stood outside were waiting patiently, their helmeted heads looking up and down the alley.

145

'And since when have you been so quick to ignore those who are looking out for you?' Ana replied, just as hotly.

'You're just jealous of me being friends with Seb,' Merric said, not caring if his words hurt her. 'All of you are.'

He thought Ana was going to argue back, but she just shook her head in a dejected, defeated way.

'That hardly sounds like something the Duke of The Head would say,' she said.

'Yeah? Well, what's new?' Merric said, feeling the fight burn out of him.

His shoulders slumped and he bit back whatever he had been wanting to say. He just stood there, looking blankly out of the window. After a few minutes of awkward silence, Ana rose and went and stood beside him.

'I'm sorry,' she said, putting her arm around him. 'I don't want to fight.'

'Me neither,' said Merric, giving her a hug.

He returned to the castle soon after, pondering Ana's words. He was feeling frustrated. Before he had met Sir Sebastien, he had felt like there was a hole in his life. He had Ana, and he had Sophya, and Tomas, and Sir Oskar and Sir Orsten too, but he had not had someone who he felt he could really open up to and be completely honest with. Someone like an equal, or a brother. Sir Sebastien simply understood Merric far better than anyone else did. Sometimes he wondered if this was how it would have been had Tristan still been alive. Sure, he and Tristan had grown apart in recent years, but in the final days of the older boy's life they had begun to make up for lost time. Tristan had been ripped away from him, but now that Merric had found someone that filled that missing part of his life, everyone seemed to want him to go back to how he was before.

Merric kicked angrily at a pebble and sent it skidding across the cobblestones. He did feel bad that he had been neglecting his other friends, and he vowed that he would fix that. There was no reason why his friendship with Sir Sebastien meant that his relationships with Sophya and Tomas had to be affected. With war threatening to fall across the realm, Merric knew it was more important than ever for them to stick together. Perhaps Sir Sebastien being away for a couple of weeks would help Merric to mend his fraying friendships, and then when the Ouestorian returned to Eagle Mount maybe everyone would be much warmer towards him.

With that thought comforting him, Merric began trying to make amends with his friends the very next day. At breakfast, he learned in conversation with Sophya that she was good friends with Lady Jeyna of Allertyn, who was due to marry Sir Marc of the Eagle Guard that very afternoon in the Grand Priory of Eaglestone. Given that Sir Marc was one of his loyal protectors, Merric felt like he ought to make an appearance at the wedding. Such things were expected of a duke. Not wanting to go alone he offered to accompany Sophya. She had eagerly accepted, and had talked excitedly non-stop during the rest of breakfast of what Lady Jeyna and her betrothed had been planning. Merric, who knew little of weddings, could do no more than listen and act as though her infectious excitement was rubbing off onto him.

Sophya seemed to be in her element as her handmaids got her ready in her bedchamber, dressing her in one the gowns that she had not worn since before her family had died. Merric could barely remember a time in the past few weeks when he had not seen her hurrying across the castle carrying out her tasks, inspecting orders and checking the food stores in the basement. But when she emerged from her bedchamber in her dazzling gown and perfectly styled hair there was not a single scroll of parchment or a quill in her hands.

Merric, dressed in his finest sky blue doublet, offered her a clumsy compliment.

'You look lovely,' he said.

'Thank you,' she beamed, looking at her reflection in one of the windows. 'It's nice to act like a lady again, now and then. To think I used to dress like this every day! I had far too much time on my hands.'

Laughing, she took Merric's arm. They walked out of the castle together, with a trail of Eagle Guard behind them. As they headed across the town square towards the Grand Priory, Sophya beamed at the admiring glances and comments she received. Merric walked along with her, feeling a little self-conscious.

The wedding service was a simpler affair than the only other one Merric had witnessed. When Sophya had been married to Rayden Monfort no expense had been spared. There had been so many guests there, no doubt at Rayden's order, that they were packed shoulder to shoulder into the Grand Hall of Eagle Mount. While Sir Marc and Lady Jeyna's wedding was a more modest ceremony, Merric could not help but notice the love they had for each other. He thought back to what Sir Sebastien had said, and wondered what his own wedding would one day be like. Would he be standing beside Ana, feeling the same love that Sir Marc and Lady Jeyna did? Or would he be marrying a faceless lady from some noble family, who he was marrying purely for political reasons? He forced himself to push such thoughts from his mind, and he applauded along with everyone else when Sir Marc and Lady Jeyna kissed. Why concern himself with something that he would not need to worry about for many years yet?

As much as he enjoyed his day with Sophya, helping to celebrate the marriage of Sir Marc and Lady Jeyna, his responsibilities as duke were never far away. He envied those previous dukes who had enjoyed years of peace and calm during their times where they ruled, with nothing more complicated to think about than preparing for the next winter. The shadow of approaching war seemed to cover everything, and the prospect of potentially leading

The Head into war in his first few months as duke terrified Merric more than he would ever admit. While no one openly talked about it, everyone in Eagle Mount seemed nervous of what the future would bring.

Merric asked Sir Oskar if he would do him the honour of leading the army of The Head, should war indeed become unavoidable. Merric could think of no one he would rather have in command of the army. Sir Oskar had shone with visible pride at the request, and while he prayed to the Mother that it would not come to war, he swore to Merric that he would lead the army with honour should the need arise. Sir Orsten did not share his brother's view, and even seemed eager for the opportunity to draw his sword against the Monforts once more. He had never forgiven them for imprisoning he and his brother in the very dungeons that now housed the scarred knight and Sir Warner Camoren.

With Sir Sebastien gone, Merric asked Sir Orsten if he would continue training him, and help turn their boy duke into a warrior. While Sir Oskar would lead the army in battle, and oversee things from a strategic point of view, Merric would be expected to ride at the head of the army as it marched to war. The army would need him as a figurehead to follow. He would likely be in the thick of the action, and a duke who could not suitably defend himself would not last long in battle. Sir Orsten had made his typical jokes, good-naturedly mocking Merric's mediocre sword skills, and tutting in disapproval at the Ouestorian-style of fighting that Merric had adopted under Sir Sebastien's tuition. But the Oakheart knight had committed himself fully to continuing where Sir Sebastien had left off, as though wanting to prove that anything the Ouestorian could teach he could teach better.

Tomas had joined them for the lessons too. He sweated and frowned in concentration as he applied himself every lesson. He was determined to hang onto every word that Sir Orsten said. There were a few times when Merric had discovered Tomas by himself, in some quiet part of the castle, sword in hand and practicing the moves Sir Orsten had taught them. Merric could only be inspired to work harder himself when he saw the effort that his squire was putting in. He was proud of the knight that Tomas would one day grow to be.

After one such lesson, Merric and Tomas were leaning beside the well in the courtyard quenching their thirst after the effort of practicing. Sir Orsten was a harsh drillmaster, and he had kept them at it for hours.

'Have you heard anything from Kasper?' Tomas asked.

Merric lowered his cup in surprise. He had not heard Kasper's name since he and Ana had mentioned him during their visit to the tavern in the town of Domadge Bartyn. He had not heard a thing from the hunter since Merric had told him to go back home to his village, but he had not really expected to either. Kasper was hardly the type to send a letter. In the aftermath of the Battle of Eagle

151

Mount, Kasper had pledged his longbow to Merric's service. His protection and guidance had been welcome that summer, when they were beset with danger on all sides, but with Eagle Mount reclaimed Merric knew it was time for Kasper to be with his family.

'No,' Merric said to Tomas, 'but I'm sure he's absolutely fine. He's where he needs to be, with his wife and daughter.'

'It would be nice to see him again,' Tomas said, thoughtfully.

Merric nodded. They had all been a little afraid of the grizzled archer when they had first met, and they had not known where his loyalties had laid. But they had all warmed up to Kasper, who had revealed himself to have a kind heart behind his stony-faced exterior.

'I thought maybe you would have asked him to be the one to go to The Dale and deliver your message,' Tomas said. 'If anyone can stay hidden from the Monforts then it's him.'

Merric felt a pang of irritation, but bit his tongue. He knew that Tomas did not mean to antagonise him about Sir Sebastien, and he did not want to fall out with him as well. But why was everyone trying to make him feel like he had sent the wrong person?

'I'm sure he would have gladly done it, if I'd asked,' Merric agreed. 'But his place is with his family now.'

Autumn was setting in, and the woods around Eagle Mount were turning from green to orange. After the pleasant warmth of the summer, folk began wearing cloaks as standard whenever they went outdoors, to protect themselves from the slight chill in the air and the frequent downpours of rain. Whenever the heavens opened and rain hammered down, Merric thought of Sir Sebastien and wondered whether it was raining wherever he was. He hoped that the rain, which could quickly turn roads into quagmires, did not slow him down too much.

Despite his insistence that the Ouestorian had been the best choice for the job, Merric had begun to grow concerned about Sir Sebastien. It had been nearly three weeks since he had set off on his journey to The Dale, and the Ouestorian had boasted that he would return within two weeks. While Merric had known that this had merely been bravado, even if Lord Godfrei had proven difficult to convince then Sir Sebastien should really have been back by now.

When Merric confided in Sir Oskar and Sir Orsten, they told him not to worry. But he could tell that unspoken words of unease filled their own minds. He often caught glimpses of them glancing at each other when they thought Merric was not looking, and he knew they were wondering whether they had been right all along in their argument not to have Sir Sebastien carry the message. A couple of times he had heard them in whispered conversation, debating whether a second envoy should be sent in Sir Sebastien's footsteps, just in case he had been distracted from his task and the letter had still not reached Lord Godfrei in The Dale.

'A second letter doubles the chance of Lord Aric finding out what we are doing,' Sir Orsten had warned.

But a few days later, Sir Sebastien's absence was explained, and it confirmed Merric's worst fears.

With his duties for the day completed, he was sat high up on the roof of the castle keep with Ana. She had come to visit him, and Merric was grateful for the distraction. Neither of them had mentioned Sir Sebastien since their argument in her father's workshop, and it was as though they had some unspoken agreement to put it behind them. At that moment Merric was not worrying himself about what future he may or may not have with Ana. He was just enjoying her solitary company, with no one overlooking them. Up here, at the highest point of the castle, where the birds nested amongst the turrets of the towers, they were in no danger of being disturbed. While the dizzying heights of their perch had made Merric's stomach lurch when they had first emerged onto the roof, it was soon something else entirely that was making his insides do somersaults.

Ana only broke off the kiss when she spied a commotion in the streets far below where they sat.

'What's that?' she asked.

Merric looked round, dismayed that she had ended their kiss. Ignoring the sick feeling he got whenever he looked at the ground from this height, he glanced over the battlements to peer down at the town far below. At this height, Eaglestone was little more than a maze of tiled roofs and narrow streets. Even the huge building that was the Grand Priory looked like little more than a model that Merric would have played with when he was a small boy. Peering down to see what Ana had spotted, Merric saw that there was a crowd making its way up the main road that led to the castle, and while they were much too far away to hear their voices, the ant-like folk that made up the crowd seemed to be surging around a lone horseman who heading towards Eagle Mount. Whoever the horseman was, they seemed to be causing a great deal of excitement or unrest among those running alongside him.

'It's Sir Sebastien!' Merric exclaimed.

'You can't possibly tell from here,' Ana said, staring just as intently down at the tiny specs in the streets.

But Merric had already jumped to his feet and was hurrying along the walkway behind the battlements towards the door that led down into one of the towers. Ana came after him, a little frustrated at Merric's sudden distraction. Together they ran down the spiral stairs, taking the steps two at a time. They were not the only ones drawn to the excitement of the approaching horseman. Servants, handmaids, Jacelyn soldiers and the knights who liked to loiter around the castle to be at the beck and call of their duke, all emerged into the staircase which wound around and around all the way to the ground floor of the castle.

They emerged into the entrance hall, and Merric dashed out through the oaken doors, with Ana hot on his heels. Sir Oskar and Sir Orsten and half a dozen others had beaten them to the courtyard, and Merric skidded to a stop when he reached the spot where they were huddled, awaiting the return of Sir Sebastien. Moments later, the horseman rode through the gates.

With a sinking feeling in his stomach, Merric knew at once that it was not Sir Sebastien.

The horseman was not anyone that Merric recognised. He was a middle-aged man, who was a nobleman by birth judging by the strong jaw and prominent cheekbones that defined his proud face. He wore rich-looking but plain clothes that carried no family symbol. He was completely unarmed but for the banner he carried boldly aloft. While Merric did not know the man, he felt a jolt inside himself when a small gust of wind plucked at the cloth of the banner the horseman was carrying, and he saw what was on it.

It was a Monfort banner, with the symbol of the black knight marching across a white background.

'Who are you?' Merric demanded, his shock and disappointment causing him to forget his manners.

The man was clearly unimpressed by the less than polite greeting, though his arrogant expression betrayed that he had been expecting little more than this from the boy stood before him.

'My name is unimportant. I speak with my master's voice, and that is all you need to know. You are him, then?' he asked, looking down at Merric. 'The boy they now call Duke of The Head?'

Sir Orsten let out a snarl of anger and reached for his sword. His brother laid a calming hand on him.

'He comes unarmed, Orsten.' Sir Oskar muttered, warningly. 'We cannot touch him.'

'Listen to him,' the horseman advised Sir Orsten in a patronising tone. 'I am here to break words with you, and then I will be leaving your dukedom. Fear not, I will not stay a moment longer than is required.'

Merric, who had been so convinced that the approaching rider was Sir Sebastien returning, could feel himself deflating. He had been so excited to see his friend again, and hear Lord Godfrei's reply. He had not even taken a moment to wonder why a messenger from Lord Aric had arrived at Eagle Mount. Seeing Merric struggling, Sir Oskar took a step towards the horseman.

'My name is Sir Oskar Oakheart, Lord's Council to Lord Merric Jacelyn, Duke of The Head. You bring word from Lord Aric?'

'I do.'

'Then come, let us move away to Lord Merric's study,' Sir Oskar said, gesturing politely towards the castle keep behind him. 'There we can discuss whatever message it is that he has sent us.'

The man did not move to dismount from his horse.

'I see no need,' he drawled. 'The message I bring does not require discussion. It is not a request, but a demand.'

All those gathered bridled at the man's words. While an unarmed messenger could not be harmed, he was expected to at least treat his hosts with respect. It was clear that this messenger from Lord Aric had no intention in pleasantries. This seemed to bring Merric out of his silence.

'Aric doesn't have any authority here. He can't demand anything of us,' he said, using every strength he had to resist balling his hands into fists.

He did not want the messenger to see that his words were angering him, as that would only prove to Lord Aric that Merric was every bit the child he thought him to be. The messenger looked a little amused by the sight of Merric. He raised his voice so that all who had gathered around the courtyard would be able to hear him.

'Listen carefully, all of you. We have captured Sir Sebastien of Montré attempting to sneak his way into The Dale. We have reason to believe that he was doing so on your behalf. Though what a Ouestorian was doing with you I could not begin to imagine.'

Merric felt a thrill of fear pass through him at the mention of Sir Sebastien, but after a warning look from Sir Oskar he stayed silent.

'But Lord Aric is merciful,' the messenger continued. 'He proposes a trade.'

Merric felt a rush of hope. There was a chance yet to save his friend. Behind him, Sir Oskar and Sir Orsten glanced uneasily at each other.

'The trade that Lord Aric proposes is thus: your Ouestorian friend in exchange for noble Lord Warner Camoren, Baron of Pooltyn, who we are led to believe was captured recently at Hightop Castle. You have three days to bring Lord Warner to a neutral location one league west of Bridge Ford.'

The messenger looked around all the assembled faces, before settling his eyes on Merric's.

'You must bring him yourself, Lord Merric,' he said, using the title half-mockingly. 'Though you may be accompanied by ten others if you are too fearful to travel beyond your border alone. Lord Aric will meet you there, with the same number of men. If these demands are not met, or the three-day deadline expires, then your Ouestorian friend will find himself shorter by a head.'

Merric stepped forwards, unable to restrain himself, but the Monfort messenger had already turned his horse and trotted away towards the castle gates. Merric could only watch him go, helplessly. A Jacelyn soldier followed the messenger as far as the gate, before turning back and confirming that he had gone. Merric slowly turned around, looking at everyone who had gathered to hear the messenger's words. Dozens of eyes looked back at him. Sir Oskar looked sympathetic, and Sir Orsten angry. Ana, meanwhile, looked worried.

'If we set off today,' Merric said, 'we can make it to the meeting place in time.'

His words were immediately received by a clamour of voices as many of the gathered folk talked at once.

'My duke,' Sir Oskar said, stepping forwards to make sure his voice was heard. 'We must stop and think.'

'We cannot negotiate with Monfort filth,' Sir Orsten said, punching a fist into his palm.

'Surely you can't trust them to keep their word?' Ana said, disbelieving. 'Did the events this summer not teach you anything?'

'I know you are fond of Sir Sebastien,' Sir Oskar continued, speaking over the others, 'but Lord Warner is a dangerous man. Think of how far we had to go in order to capture him in the first place. We cannot let him go free.'

'I hate to say it,' Sir Orsten said, 'but my brother is right. It is simply not a logical trade.'

Merric could not believe what he was hearing.

'So you would let them kill Seb?'

'My duke,' Sir Oskar said, raising his hands to calm him, 'of course we do not wish it. But it is the only course of action we can take. We cannot free Lord Warner. He is Lord Aric's most trusted and valued baron.'

'And Seb is a trusted and valued friend. I will not let you sacrifice him. He is a good man.'

'But, my duke, how many good men of The Head will die if Lord Aric has his most capable baron at his side once more?' pointed out a knight whose name Merric did not know.

There was a ripple of agreement from many of the other knights and soldiers who were gathered around.

'Seb left the safety of The Head to try and help us,' Merric said, looking angrily around at them all. 'And this is how you would thank him? He risked his neck for us.'

'Merric, listen' Ana put in nervously, looking uneasy at speaking in front of all the gathered knights, many of whom had not noticed the girl standing in their midst. 'He knew the risks when he agreed to help. He knew the danger.'

Merric's worry about his friend caused him to become furious at them all.

'No, *you* listen. All of you!' he snarled. 'I am the duke, not any of you. You can't stop me. None of you liked Seb from the beginning,' he accused, looking at Ana and the Oakheart twins with his jaw clenched.

'It's not like that,' Ana said, her own temper rising. 'Think about what you're saying! You're willing to risk the lives of everyone here in The Head just for one man.'

'Yes I am,' Merric agreed, daring them to continue trying and stop him. 'You just don't like him because he's from Ouestoria, or because you're jealous of him or something. Well, I'm sorry that you're all jealous that Seb understands me better than any of you ever could.'

He looked at Ana.

'And I'm sorry that Seb has opened my eyes to the fact that you and me would never work. It was a dream, what we had, and that's all. It's time to wake up.'

He could never recall being so angry or worried, nor ever speaking with such coldness in his voice. Ana looked at him as though he had hit her. Her mouth opened slightly, but no response came.

It was silent in the courtyard, but for the flapping of the banners in the breeze. Sir Orsten and Sir Oskar looked as though they wanted to continue their appeal to stop Merric from agreeing to the trade.

'Prepare the prisoner,' Merric ordered before they could speak, and a pair of the Eagle Guard reluctantly turned and headed towards the keep.

'Wait,' Sir Oskar said, holding out a hand to stop them. 'My duke, even if the trade was one that we could agree to, the demands are far too dangerous. They are asking you yourself to leave The Head. You were nearly killed by a Monfort attacker in the very streets of Eaglestone, not half a mile from this very spot. We could never vouch for your safety beyond the border of The Head, especially with only ten men by your side.'

'You're right,' Merric said with a tone of finality in his voice, 'you can't guarantee my safety. And when I was attacked it was Seb who came to my rescue. It wasn't you, or Sir Orsten, or you Ana. It was Seb, and I'm not going to abandon him now. What kind of friend would I be if I wasn't willing to face the same dangers that he faced for me?'

He pushed past them all, making his way back into the castle keep. While the Eagle Guard went down to the dungeons to unshackle Sir Warner and prepare him for the journey, Merric headed up to his bedchamber. He walked past Sophya in the corridor. She had clearly not heard what had happened in the courtyard outside. She had her eyes glued to a letter, but looked up when she saw his thunderous expression.

'Merric?' she said uncertainly.

He ignored her and continued upstairs. He pushed his bedchamber door open and went over to the rack that held his armour, eying the steel plates and trying to remember how to put it all on. The door opened behind him and Tomas hurried in.

'What's happening?' the young squire asked. 'I heard shouting down in the courtyard.'

Merric felt a slight twinge of regret for the way he had spoken to them all, but he pushed that out of his mind. They had deserved it, and right now he could only think of Sir Sebastien. He did not have time to worry about them.

'Seb has been captured,' Merric said. 'Will you help me with my armour?'

Tomas, who had no knowledge that Merric was being firmly advised against going to rescue Sir Sebastien, hurried to help Merric put on the armour. Merric had worn it on a couple of occasions, but only for ceremonial reasons. He had not yet gotten used to the weight of the heavy steel and chain mail. When Tomas pulled the surcoat over his head and Merric caught a glimpse of the Jacelyn eagle emblazoned across his chest he felt encouraged that his course of action was the right one. He knew that Lord Roberd would never have allowed a friend to suffer at the hands of the Monforts either.

Tomas handed him *Hopebearer*, and Merric buckled the leather scabbard onto his belt. He left the chamber without bidding farewell to Tomas, and found the Oakheart twins waiting for him in the corridor outside.

'We are going with you, my duke,' Sir Oskar said.

'You heard him, I am allowed to take only ten with me,' Merric said, striding straight past them.

'Then take us and eight of the Eagle Guard, my duke, I beg of you,' Sir Oskar said, hurrying to walk beside him.

'If you cannot be talked out of this then we will at least watch out for you,' Sir Orsten added.

'No,' Merric said, and hurried down the staircase towards the entrance hall.

Right now he was not ready to forgive them for disagreeing with him in front of everyone else. He was the duke, and they ought to remember that.

'I'll just take the Eagle Guard with me,' he said to the Oakheart twins. 'They're all the protection I need.'

'My duke!' Sir Oskar objected, hurrying to keep up with him. 'Please, my duke. You are not thinking clearly.'

Merric ignored him, reaching the courtyard and climbing up onto Nosy's back. A groom had saddled him and brought him from the castle stables. Ten members of the Eagle Guard were waiting for him, along with Lord Warner who was looking a little worse for wear but otherwise unharmed from his spell in the dungeons. His clothes were dirty and his beard unkempt, but he sat with an arrogant pride atop the horse. There was no sign of Ana, and Merric assumed she had gone back to her home in the town.

Merric could not worry about her right now, not when Sir Sebastien was in mortal danger, and only he could save him.

- CHAPTER EIGHT -

The ride to glory

For two days they rode hard. The further west they went the more Merric was convinced that his decision to agree to the trade of prisoners was the right one. He knew they made a gallant sight as they galloped along the Great East Road, and it was the first time Merric truly felt like a duke.

In every town and village they passed through great crowds were gathered, cheering as their duke and the Eagle Guard thundered past on their horses. They did not know where Merric was heading, but he made such a glorious sight in his shining armour and pristine surcoat that they had no doubt that he was carrying out some heroic deed.

While he felt a sense of concern for Sir Sebastien, he could not wait to see his friend's face when Merric arrived at the meeting place. Then they would be even, with each of them having come to the rescue of the other. Merric could not believe how he had ever thought himself unready and unworthy of being Duke of The Head. All he had needed, it turned out, was for something like this to happen. Something that would really test him, and give him the opportunity to show that he was capable of being a leader. Something to spur him on.

He did not blame Sir Oskar or Sir Orsten for wanting him to stay at Eagle Mount. Their priority was keeping him safe, and that had blinded them to what really needed to be done. Merric had made the right choice, and the cheering, adoring crowds calling his name and waving from the roadside proved that.

Lord Warner Camoren looked almost as satisfied as Merric did. While he looked far from lordly with his grubby clothes and unkempt beard, he was smug with pleasure at the idea that Lord Aric had arranged for his return to The Southstones. Merric did not like the idea of having to maybe face Lord Warner in battle one day, especially after he had tricked the Baron of Pooltyn into losing Hightop Castle, but he knew that was a problem for another day.

Merric insisted that they keep up a fast pace, not wanting Sir Sebastien to suffer as a Monfort prisoner for a moment longer than he needed to. They rode all day, stopping at night only when it became too dark to continue on their way. Merric had barely slept, being both excited and nervous in equal measure. He had risen well before the sun in the morning, eager to be on his way again.

They rode through the Greenwood where that summer Sir Gerard Velion, the captain of the Eagle Guard, had been killed fighting off the Monfort yeomen who had been hunting them. And they road past The Yielding where Merric had journeyed on his flight to Little Harrow. They did not pause as they galloped through Oaktyn, and Merric felt a slight pang of guilt when he saw elderly Lord Horin Oakheart, father to Sir Oskar and Sir Orsten, who had come out to greet his duke. Merric could not afford to lose any time, so merely waved at the elderly Baron of Oaktyn as he rode through the town.

A few miles beyond Oaktyn they rode past the junction in the road which led towards the distant village of Little Harrow, which had almost become Merric's new home until he had learned that Sophya still lived. With a jolt, Merric realised that this was now the furthest he had ever travelled from Eagle Mount. And every step his horse now took along the road was taking him further and further west than he had ever been before.

After two days of hard riding Merric, Lord Warner and the ten Eagle Guard arrived on a ridge that overlooked the Rush; the vast, raging river that marked the western border of The Head. Merric had never seen the great river before, but he had grown up hearing stories about it. At this point the river was half a mile wide and impossible to cross, apart from over the bridge that lay before them.

The castle of Bridge Ford lay at the bottom of a low valley directly ahead of Merric, sitting across the Great East

Road on the eastern bank of the river. Anyone wanting to go in or out of The Head would have to pass between the great towers of Bridge Ford, and it was this fortress that the Monforts would have to attack if they wanted to invade The Head. The stone bridge beyond the castle spanned the great river with countless impressive arches that had been built many centuries ago, and which stoically withstood the heavy pounding of the rushing water as it thundered past. Merric's imagination had never been able to accurately imagine what the river was like, and even at this distance the thundering of the water as it churned past on its way to the distant sea assaulted his eardrums.

Merric led the way down the road as it headed towards Bridge Ford. The land was barren here, with the soil not suited to the growing of crops. Some goats grazed on the swathes of patchy grass, but aside from that there was little sign of life. It was a hard existence for the Conway family who ruled Bridge Ford and the surrounding lands, living in a fruitless part of The Head and relying on the more fertile areas of their barony to provide them with the food they needed. Living with the thunderous crashing of the river, and the knowledge that they were on the very edge of The Head, had made the Conways into ill-tempered and private folk, always preferring to keep to themselves rather than attend the banquets and other highborn occasions hosted by the dukes of Eagle Mount.

Normally, the road down to Bridge Ford would be dotted with folk travelling to and from The Head. But evening was beginning to fall, and so most travellers will have already sought an inn to spend the night further to the east towards Oaktyn. There were no inns, or even farms, in the valley where the Rush roared past, leaving the Conways to their solitary life.

As they approached Bridge Ford, Merric could see faces on the battlements looking down at them curiously. He knew that the gates would be shut at dusk, barring all crossings until morning, but Merric could not wait. While he knew that Lord Tymon Conway would be obliged to offer his duke rest and food, Merric knew he would not be able to sleep knowing that Sir Sebastien was so close.

'Sir Marc,' Merric said, turning to the Eagle Guard directly behind him. 'Would you go ahead and ask if Lord Tymon could keep the gates open a little longer for us to pass through?'

Sir Marc looked momentarily surprised, as though he had been expecting them to wait until morning before crossing the river and leaving The Head. But, being an obedient Eagle Guard, he merely nodded and spurred off ahead.

The castle was built from weather-beaten stone, but its walls were thick and its towers tall. It commanded an imposing position, offering dominating views of the lands in all directions. Two banners fluttered from the tallest towers. The blue chained bear of the Conway family flew from one, while the eagle of the Jacelyns flew from the other. The stirring sight of his family's banner filled Merric with a thrill, and he hoped that Lord Roberd was looking down on him, watching proudly as Merric brought honour to the Jacelyns.

When Merric passed beneath the eastern gate of Bridge Ford he was greeted by a thin, nervous-looking man who was hurrying towards him, adjusting his sword belt as though he had been suddenly roused from his chambers. He had a narrow face and a small beard which did not entirely hide his weak chin. He was beginning to bald, which did nothing to improve his generally frail appearance. Merric had never met Lord Tymon Conway before, but he had no doubt that this was the man standing before him.

'My duke,' Lord Tymon said, stooping to a hurried bow. 'I was not aware of your visit. I would have made arrangements for your arrival, had I known.'

He gestured for a groom to come and take Merric's horse, but Merric waved him away.

'Thank you, but your hospitality is unnecessary,' Merric said. 'I'm journeying across the river straight away.'

Lord Tymon blinked and looked over his shoulder at the western gate, which was still standing open. Through the yawning gateway the sky was orange as the sun was setting, and in an hour it would be dark.

'With so few men?' Lord Tymon asked uneasily, scratching his bald patch.

He spotted Lord Warner amongst the Eagle Guard, and the look of confusion on his face only increased.

'I'm afraid I don't have time to explain,' Merric said, though his apologetic tone was tinged with impatience.

Lord Tymon chewed on one of his fingernails absent-mindedly.

'I do not mean to contradict my duke,' he said, looking agitated, 'but I am not sure that it is a good idea for you to leave The Head at this time. Normally I would not say anything, but you know better than I that we are in uncertain times. I cannot vouch for your safety once you have crossed the river.'

The horses of the Eagle Guard shuffled around restlessly, and Merric bit his tongue. He did not have time to listen to Lord Tymon.

'I appreciate your concerns he said.'

'I have heard reports that there are Monfort patrols across the river,' Lord Tymon warned. 'And only a couple of days ago we could see movements of Lord Aric's soldiers from the tops of our towers.'

Merric clicked his tongue impatiently.

'You don't need to worry. I know of the movements you're talking about,' he said.

Merric would have thought it strange if the Conways had *not* seen Monforts across the river. That was where the meeting place was after all, so Lord Aric and his men would be heading this way, with the captive Sir Sebastien with them..

'Oh, okay, my apologies. I just thought you ought to know, my duke,' Lord Tymon said, bowing his balding head once more.

Lord Tymon was not what Merric had been expecting. He had known that the Baron of Bridge Ford was a man who had earned little respect or admiration from the folk who lived in his barony. Merric had always assumed it was because Lord Tymon was uncaring towards his folk, but he sensed now that it was because the baron was simply a man who few could be inspired by. Merric could see that Lord Tymon was not the cold and authoritative figure that he had imagined, but rather an insecure man whose failings towards the folk who depended on him were down to his own shortcomings. Merric had to admit that he would be concerned if the fate of The Head rested on Lord Tymon alone, should the Monforts choose to declare war. But fortunately the soldiers who served the Conways seemed to be good, dependable men. They were gathered around, curious to catch a glimpse of their new duke. They were all strong-looking men with chiselled jaws, made so by the harsh life of living here on the edge of The Head.

'Will you allow me to send some of my men to accompany you, at least' Lord Tymon suggested.

'Thank you, but they will not be needed,' Merric said, an eye watching the sun as it sank lower and lower in the sky to the west.

He brushed aside Lord Tymon's final, feeble attempts to appear a gracious host and offer Merric and the others beds for the night, and then led Lord Warner and the Eagle Guard across the courtyard of Bridge Ford and towards the western gate. Lord Tymon walked beside him, accompanying his duke as far as the gate. Merric knew that the moment he had left the castle then Lord Tymon would be hurrying to his study to write a letter to Eagle Mount, making his concerns known. But Merric's path was clear to him, and when he returned with Sir Sebastien safely retrieved from his Monfort captors then Lord Tymon would see what could be accomplished with the courage to do the right thing. It was the time for bold action, and Merric and his ten Eagle Guard would be the ones to carry it out.

As soon as they passed beneath the archway of the western gate Merric felt the spray from the churning river on his face, and he gave an involuntary shiver. The bridge stretched out in front of him seemingly forever. As he urged Nosy forward, and took the first few steps out onto the stone bridge, he imagined that he could feel it shifting below, but he put that down to his mind playing tricks on him. The bridge was wide enough for two wagons to pass each other, and was flanked by stone walls to stop any careless travellers from tumbling to their watery deaths below. But even so, out of the corners of his eyes, Merric could see the water rushing past and he had to fight to keep a sudden heave of nausea from rising up from his stomach.

He forced his eyes to focus on the far bank of the river instead.

He did not know what he had been expecting, but the western bank of the Rush ahead of him looked much the same as the eastern bank. Rocky hills rose up to the south and he could make out the treetops of a dense forest to the north, but apart from that it very much resembled The Head that he was leaving behind him. He could not tell whether he was disappointed or reassured by this. Part of him had expected the land beyond the border of The Head to look like another world, but he supposed that had been stupid of him to think.

He realised that he had been setting a quick pace as he rode along the bridge and so, not wanting the Eagle Guard or Lord Warner to think that he was afraid of the river surging beneath them, he slowed Nosy down. The Eagle Guard looked as steady as always, and Merric knew that crossing the bridge would not cause them any unease, despite the raging torrent that flowed beneath them. Lord Warner looked positively cheerful, plainly excited by the prospect of being reunited with his beloved duke and returned to his own homeland. Merric could not be bitter towards him; he would gladly trade ten Lord Warners for his own friend.

The bridge ended and Merric walked his horse onto the western bank, pausing to dignify the moment. It was his first time ever leaving The Head, and he knew he would want to remember it for the rest of his life. He was on a quest, leading these fine, valiant knights on a noble errand to rescue Sir Sebastien. Perhaps even minstrels would sing of this day in years to come.

But no quest was ever easy, and Merric had to admit that he was feeling nerves in the pit of his stomach. Even though it was a simple exchange of prisoners, being outside of The Head and on the other side of the great river began to make Merric feel uneasy. He was no longer in his own dukedom, and potential danger was now everywhere. He felt oddly vulnerable, and was silently grateful for the presence of Sir Marc and the other Eagle Guard.

They set off, continuing along the Great East Road as it headed through The Hinterland. This was the neutral land between the four dukedoms, and not a soul lived there. The absence of any farms or other signs of folk living nearby made even the lands around Bridge Ford feel well-populated by comparison. The road wound between wild hills topped with rocky outcrops, and within half an hour even the great towers of Bridge Ford were hidden from view behind them. The forest to the north that Merric had spied from the bridge spread for miles, rising all the way to the foothills of a huge range of mountains. That way, somewhere, lay The Dale. Merric wondered how far Sir Sebastien had gotten in his journey to carry the message to Lord Godfrei Florin before he had been caught.

For the first time since leaving Eagle Mount, Merric's mind turned to Lord Aric. This would be the first time Merric had been face to face with him since he had become the duke, and he had no idea how he would feel seeing the man who had arranged for the murder of Lord Roberd and his family. He knew that he would have to remain polite, for fear of Lord Aric changing his mind and refusing to release Sir Sebastien. Merric only hoped that he would be able to keep his hatred in check.

The rocky hills on the south side of the road grew taller, and the ground to the north was becoming hilly too, leading up towards the trees of the gnarled forest. It was an unwelcoming place, and Merric was not surprised that no one had chosen to make this land their home. The Eagle Guard looked around themselves vigilantly, watchful for any dangers to their duke.

'I do not like this,' Sir Marc said, riding up beside Merric. 'These hills are too steep for our horses. We could get trapped here in this valley.'

'We'll make the prisoner exchange and then return to Bridge Ford as quickly as we can,' Merric promised him.

By Merric's reckoning they were close to the location for the exchange, a league from the river. Sure enough, as the road rounded another outcrop of rock, a group of horsemen appeared in the distance, just visible in the dusk, awaiting them. Merric let out a breath of relief, admitting to himself that a part of him had been concerned that the Monforts would not keep their word. But fortunately, Lord Aric appeared to be honouring the agreement.

Merric could count eleven horsemen, but as he got closer he could see that the figure leading them did not appear to be Lord Aric. Merric put his hand up to his eyes to shield them from the sunset, in order to get a better look. No, it was definitely not Lord Aric. And when he looked closer at the cluster of horsemen he realised that he could not see the figure of Sir Sebastien among them either.

Merric frowned and looked across at Lord Warner who was likewise peering ahead at the distant horsemen.

'Where is he?' Lord Warner wondered aloud, but Merric could not tell whether he was referring to Lord Aric or Sir Sebastien.

Merric pushed aside his concerns, deciding that they were probably keeping Sir Sebastien out of sight and under guard somewhere, until they had confirmed that Merric had brought Lord Warner as agreed.

When they had ridden within shouting distance, the knight leading the distant horsemen that were waiting for them cupped a hand to his mouth and called out a greeting to Merric.

'Merric Jacelyn?' he shouted.

Merric noticed that the man had not addressed him with his correct title, but now was not the time to worry about such trivial things.

'Yes, that's me!' Merric called back. 'I have brought Lord Warner Camoren, as agreed.'

The distant knight spoke to his companions before turning back to Merric.

'You are to come with us!' he shouted.

Merric's brows furrowed in confusion, and the Eagle Guard around him stirred uneasily.

'Where is Sir Sebastien?' he demanded.

'You will come with us, Merric Jacelyn,' the knight repeated, ignoring Merric's question. 'Or we will shoot.'

Merric noticed movement out of the corner of his eye, and turning his head he saw figures rising up from the crests of the hills on both sides of the road. There must have been a hundred of them. Merric gritted his teeth in anger and sudden fear. The figures had their crossbow bolts aimed at him and the cluster of Eagle Guard.

'That was not the deal,' Merric shouted across to the knight. 'Lord Warner in return for Sir Sebastien, that is what Aric offered.'

In response the knights up ahead just laughed, and Merric's blood boiled. He gripped his reins tightly, and Sir Marc laid a calming hand onto Merric's.

'This is a trap. We should turn back,' he advised, but Merric did not move.

'No,' Merric insisted. 'They've got him here somewhere. We can't go back without Seb.'

The men on the hills peered down the sights of their crossbows, ready to unleash death should Merric try anything foolhardy.

'If anything has happened to Sir Sebastien then Aric will never get his beloved baron back,' Merric warned.

Lord Warner looked doubtfully at Merric, knowing that the words carried little threat. Merric was not a murderer, and would not kill him in cold blood.

Again, laughter sounded from the distant knights.

'Save us your empty threats,' their spokesman said. 'All Lord Aric desires is you, boy. So come with us now and the rest of your men can leave in peace.'

'We are not leaving you, my duke,' Sir Marc said grimly.

The distant knight was tapping his saddle impatiently with his steel-gauntleted hand.

'If you will not come willing then we will need to use force,' he threatened.

'What about Lord Warner?' Merric shouted across to the Monfort horsemen. 'If you do anything to me then he dies.'

At his words, one of the Eagle Guard drew his sword and held it towards the captive Lord Warner, to demonstrate the seriousness of Merric's words.

'His sacrifice is one that Lord Aric is willing to make,' came the simple reply.

The Monfort horsemen started walking their horses forwards, drawing their swords from their scabbards. A look of shock and sudden terror passed over Lord Warner's face, and a moment later a crossbow bolt whistled out of nowhere and struck him cleanly in the neck. He slipped from the Eagle Guard's grasp and was dead before he hit the ground.

Merric looked in horror at the body of Lord Aric's most trusted and loyal baron.

'Do not harm the boy!' the knight shouted, as he spurred his horse forward to a gallop. 'We must take him alive. Kill the rest!'

A storm of crossbow bolts came shooting from the hilltops, and the Eagle Guard raised their shields. Most of the shots missed or hammered harmlessly into their wooden shields, but two bolts found their mark and one of the Eagle Guard toppled from his saddle, impaled by them both.

'My duke!' Sir Marc cried. 'We must fall back!'

'No!' Merric insisted, horrified by what was happening. 'We must find Seb. We must find him!'

He kicked back his heels and Nosy lurched forwards. The Eagle Guard raced after him, with no choice but to protect their duke. The Monfort knights ahead of them showed surprise on their faces to see the sudden charge, but this quickly gave way to smirks as they looked eagerly at their prey. The Eagle Guard closed in around Merric as they charged, swords pointed towards their foes. Merric held *Hopebearer* in his clenched fist, all sense of fear giving way to his determination to find Sir Sebastien and bring him safely back to The Head.

The Monfort knights were fifty feet away from them, and the crossbow bolts continued to rain down on Merric and his protectors. Another of the Eagle Guard was struck down by a bolt that found a gap in his armour, and he fell heavily from his horse. His body bouncing along the road in the wake of his fellows. The enemy knights were now just twenty feet away, and the Monfort crossbowmen in the hills ceased shooting for fear of hitting their own side. They were ten feet away, and the Eagle Guard clanged down the visors of their helmets, ready to fight to the death to protect their duke. They were five feet away, and Merric was suddenly filled with absolute terror as the true nature of their circumstances struck him. He could not rescue Sir Sebastien if he himself was dead, and charging headfirst into the midst of their ambushers could only end one way. He felt *Hopebearer* begin to slip from his grasp.

The two sides came together with a deafening crash of metal, shouts of men and neighing of horses. A sword came from nowhere and aimed to knock Merric from his horse. He instinctively tightened his grip on *Hopebearer* and brought it up to block the strike. More blows came his way and all his training from Sir Sebastien and Sir Orsten disappeared out of his head as he clumsily defended himself as best he could. He held his sword like an infant, in the heat of battle forgetting even the most basic things he had learned. He felt himself slipping from his saddle as he tried to avoid the swords of his enemy, and only his desperate scrabbling at the reins kept him from toppling to the ground and being trampled by the hooves of the closely pressed horses.

To either side of him the Eagle Guard were faring better, and Sir Marc roared in defiance as a Monfort knight fell dead beneath his blade. There were few who could match the Eagle Guard in battle, but they were outnumbered and the greater numbers of Monfort men were taking their toll. Another Eagle Guard was lying dead on the ground, and with the blaring of a horn Merric saw more Monfort horsemen were appearing from around the corner of the road ahead of them. The Eagle Guard were going to be even more outnumbered than they already were.

The Monfort reinforcements crashed into the sides of the Eagle Guard, who fought back valiantly. But it was ultimately fruitless. More of their noble number fell, and despite their desperate defences there were soon only three of the Eagle Guard remaining, pressed in close on either side of Merric, determined to fight to their last breath to protect their duke. They were surrounded, with each Monfort knight wanting to be the one to capture Merric. The swords of the Eagle Guard rose and fell with disciplined strokes, and a gap appeared in the press of Monfort men who were encircling them, giving them a path to retreat back towards the bridge.

'Go!' one of the Eagle Guard shouted.

Terror filling all of his senses, Merric urged Nosy through the gap. Two of the Eagle Guard went with him, slashing at the enemies with their swords as they went. The third Eagle Guard remained behind in an attempt to hold the Monfort horsemen off. He kept them at bay for a few crucial moments before he fell to their cruel swords, just as his brothers had done before him.

Merric and the other two knights galloped as hard as they could back down the road. Crossbow bolts once more screamed down onto them, and one of the two remaining Eagle Guard fell from his horse, wounded. He rose quickly to hit feet, pulling out the crossbow bolt and throwing it to the ground. He turned to face the pursuing Monfort horsemen, his sword raised fearlessly as he prepared to sacrifice himself to give Merric a fighting chance of escaping back to The Head.

'Keep going, my duke!' the last Eagle Guard said.

Merric recognised the voice of Sir Marc, and he could not help but think of the knight's young bride back in Eaglestone. Sir Marc's armour was covered in blood. His brand new surcoat was torn, and he had lost his helmet in the desperate fight. His teeth were gritted, his expression hard.

The two of them rode as fast as they could, heading back eastwards along the road. Merric sheathed *Hopebearer* and bent low over his saddle, trying to urge every bit of speed out of his horse. They had ridden out of range of the crossbows, but from the thundering of hooves behind them Merric knew that the Monfort horsemen were in hot pursuit. Their horses were fresh and well rested, whereas Nosy and Sir Marc's own horse had been riding hard for two days ever since they left Eagle Mount. Already, Nosy's breathing was sounding laboured.

'On boy, on!' Merric pleaded, his insides cold with fear.

In the final orange glow of the sunset Merric could see the towers of Bridge Ford as they rounded a corner in the road. The roar of the river could be heard, but the sound of their pursuers was even louder. The Head was so close. Just a few more minutes and they would safely be back at Bridge Ford.

'Do not let him get away!' one of the pursuers behind him called.

Merric could make out the bridge itself now, and he could see figures moving along it. They were Conway soldiers. The sentries high in the castle's towers must have spotted Merric's plight, and Lord Tymon had dispatched soldiers to come to his aid. Nosy gave a final push and Merric dared to believe that they would manage to escape.

There was a bright flash and flames erupted at the western edge of the bridge. A cluster of Monfort soldiers had been hiding in wait, in case Merric escaped the ambush and tried to do exactly what he was doing, and had piled bundles of firewood and set it alight. The way to the bridge was blocked. There was no way their horses could jump over the flaming barrier, and by the time the Conway soldiers had cleared the obstacle the Monfort riders would have caught up with Merric.

Sir Marc, seeing their escape route blocked, steered his horse off the road, and Nosy followed. They rode south across country, desperately trying to keep ahead of their pursuers who were still hot on their tail. Merric held on for dear life as Nosy ran across the uneven ground and leapt over ditches and wild bushes. They rode with the roaring river on their left and the rocky hills to their right, and with no other option than to keep going forwards.

'My duke,' Sir Marc said calmly, looking over his shoulder and seeing the Monforts close behind. 'Keep riding. Do not stop. Do not let them catch you!'

'What are you doing?'

Sir Marc had pulled his horse around and turned to face the Monfort knights who chased after them. His sword was held firmly in his hand as he challenged their pursuers.

'No!' Merric screamed.

He could not watch. He looked forward and heard the sounds of Sir Marc desperately fighting off the Monforts. He heard shouts, cries, and a scream of pain. He did not look back, and moments later the sounds of the enemy's pounding hooves were close behind him once more. Merric closed his eyes, despair flowing through him.

It was his fault. It was all his fault.

Nosy whinnied in panic and Merric's eyes flew open. He had been riding directly towards an outcrop of rocks that blocked his path, and the horse skinned to a halt in fear. Merric was thrown forward out of his saddle and he was sent tumbling to the ground. His head hit the rock and he felt a splitting pain sear behind his eyes. He staggered to his feet, one hand clasped on the cut over his eyes and the other grappling blindly as he tried to draw his sword.

He was vaguely aware of the Monfort knights reining in around him, their jeering voices filling his ears. Nosy reared in panic at the sight of their swords and lances and took off, galloping away and out of sight. The Monforts let the horse go. It was Merric they wanted. One of their number leapt neatly from his saddle and approached Merric, his sword pointing directly at him. Merric stumbled backwards away from the blade, looking over his shoulder. He was stood right beside the river. The water of the Rush flowed past a few feet below him, littered with branches and logs and other debris being carried downstream in its powerful rapids from the mountains to the north. The Monfort knights continued to close in around Merric, as though daring him to try and resist them further.

But he would not let them take him. He only had one option. With a tear in his eye at the thought of all the good men who had died that evening because of him, he let himself fall backwards. He toppled for several feet before hitting the pounding torrent of the river.

The last thing he remembered was just how cold the water was.

- CHAPTER NINE -

A quiet life

Kasper walked through the trees, stepping high over a tangle of brambles, and adjusted the boar that was draped over his shoulder. He carried his longbow in his other hand, and the feeling of the smooth yew wood was so familiar that it felt like an extension of his own arm. He hummed quietly as he walked, enjoying the feeling of peace and isolation that his hunts alone in the woods offered him. A thin drizzle of rain had fallen that afternoon. It had not been enough to soak him, but just the right amount to bring the clean, fresh smell that often accompanied rain. His long, dirty blond hair was tied back behind his head, to keep the wet strands from falling into his eyes, but little else had changed in his appearance over the past weeks. Despite his wife's attempts to keep him well-groomed, his jaw was still thick with the course stubble that had grown during his adventures that summer. He had to admit that he quite liked the look.

He smiled fondly to himself as the trees began to thin as he neared his village and his nose caught the familiar smell of woodsmoke. He reached the edge of the woods and emerged into a field thick with the bristles of recently-cut wheat. He walked across the well-trodden trail that led through the middle of the field. Out of habit he nodded a greeting at the scarecrow that stood sentinel in the middle of the field, and made his way towards the far fence and the cluster of cottages beyond. Smoke drifted lazily from the chimneys, completing the welcoming image of the village. His smile broadened.

Friendly voices called out in greeting as Kasper climbed over the fence at the far end of the field and emerged onto the dirt road that led through the village. He waved his bow arm in response to the greetings. He loved this village and the folk who called it home. When he had first arrived back in Little Harrow, after his adventures with Merric, he had been surprised by how quickly he had returned to his old life of hunting and providing for his family and the other villagers. A part of him felt a sense of anti-climax to be returning to his old life, after the dangers and adventure he had experienced. Though of course he never said as much to his wife. In the times when he was alone, stalking through the woods with his longbow in hand, he could not help imagining that every twig snap and rustle of leaves was coming from some Monfort soldiers hidden among the trees.

After returning home from Eagle Mount that summer he had taken his wife's hands in his own, and felt ashamed to see how relieved she had been to find him safely returned to her. He had told her that his days of adventure were in the past. He had not told her that he had in fact offered his services to Merric, and had been a little disappointed when the new duke had politely declined and urged him to return home to his family.

Before that summer, Kasper had possessed a very low opinion of the highborn families of High Realm, helped in no part by his own baron, Lord Tymon Conway, who had shown little interest in insignificant villages like Little Harrow. But his time with Merric that summer had helped Kasper to see that perhaps he had been too quick to judge, just as many noble folk were too quick to judge the commoners who lived their simple village lives.

He was proud that he had helped Merric, and was delighted that the boy was now the duke. He knew that Merric could be great at the role. He may be young but he was clever too, and he had wise advisors surrounding him who would keep him on the right track. If he was honest with himself, part of Kasper's desire to return to Eagle Mount that summer had been in order to fulfil a personal vendetta. While he had been eager to help Merric, especially when he had discovered the boy locked up in the castle dungeons, the opportunity to settle the score with Orderix, the cruel Lord's Counsel who had helped betray the Jacelyns, was one he did not want to miss. Now,

Orderix was dead, slain by Kasper's own arrow, and things had returned to normality at Eagle Mount.

Kasper had to admit that there was nothing more that someone like him, a simple hunter, could do to be of service to the Duke of The Head. He had dozens of archers to command now, and one extra longbow would make little difference. He knew that Merric was right; it was time for Kasper to serve his family now. The journey back to Little Harrow, while disappointing, had given him time to look forward to returning to his old life.

Although, Kasper had to admit that things in the village were not exactly how they had been before. The aftermath of the events that summer, with the Jacelyns and Monforts going at each other's throats, was beginning to be felt even in this tiny village on the edge of the dukedom. Not long after Kasper had returned to Little Harrow then Sir Hestor Peggleswade, the portly knight who ruled the village, had nailed a notice to the wooden post at the centre of the village. The Peggleswade family had ruled these lands for generations, and Sir Hestor had received a letter from Lord Tymon Conway, on behalf of Merric himself, ordering that he strengthen his force of soldiers, in case their duke required them to march to war. Considering that Sir Hestor kept only three soldiers to guard his simple walled house, he needed nearly every man from the village to join his tiny army in order to meet the quota that had been requested.

'I require the services of a dozen spearmen and a dozen archers,' the notice said, 'to report to Harrow Manor two days hence.'

Few of the villagers of Little Harrow could read very well, so most turned up at the manor house the very next morning, rather than in two days as requested. Sir Hestor usually liked to sleep in late most mornings, most likely as a result of the heavy eating and drinking he partook in most evenings. He was roused from his morning lay in by a confused looking soldier. Sir Hestor came out of his house, still in his nightclothes, to inspect his new recruits. He made an uninspiring sight in his stained nightgown, but his recruits looked little better. They had varying degrees of skill and experience, but few looked like real soldier-material. Most were too old or too young, or else had stooped backs or eyesight so bad that no one would trust them with a longbow.

Feeling a rush of eager anticipation, Kasper had put his name forward immediately. He had promised his wife that he was doing so just to look out for the others in the village, but he privately felt excited by the prospect of breaking the routine of village life. He stood there in Sir Hestor's yard with his longbow, along with a handful of other bowmen whose weekly practices had made them half-decent shots. All the other recruits were either leaning on pitchforks or had their blacksmithing hammers over their shoulders. They certainly looked nothing like soldiers.

The prospect of becoming a part-time soldier was exciting to the villagers, who had never held a spear or seen a battle before. But it turned out that, aside from having to stitch the Peggleswade family symbol onto the breast of their jerkins, signing up to join Sir Hestor's small band of soldiers had actually meant very little. When the new recruits had begun to realise that they were not going to be marching straight off to war with their duke their enthusiasm had started to wear off, and they mostly went back to their old lives and gave soldiering little more thought.

In the aftermath of helping Merric get rid of the Monfort rulers who had taken over Eagle Mount, Kasper had been anticipating something happening. He gave little thought to the games being played by the dukes of High Realm, but he had thought that surely the Monforts would try and retake The Head, or else The Head would march to war against The Southstones. But as far as he could tell, nothing had happened at all. A couple of weeks ago one of the village farmers had returned from market in Oaktyn to report excitedly that he had seen Merric and a band of knights galloping westward along the main road. This had caused a surge of anticipation among Sir Hestor's new recruits, who expected that their wait was over and that they were sure to be summoned soon.

'If Lord Merric is riding to war, surely he'll be needing us!'

'The boys of Little Harrow will march at the front of the army of The Head,' another agreed, getting carried away in his enthusiasm and forgetting about the fact that nearly all of them could barely tell one end of a spear from the other.

But no rider came to their small village, and Kasper assumed that either Merric was just travelling to visit Lord Tymon, or else the army of The Head had marched off to war already and the small knot of recruits in Little Harrow had simply been forgotten. Life in the peaceful village slept on peacefully.

Kasper pushed open the door of his cottage and immediately felt something crash into his legs.

'Hullo Daysee,' he laughed, dropping the boar heavily onto the table and hanging his bow from the hooks hanging from the ceiling beams. He reached down and picked up his daughter and gave her hug, before turning and giving Maryl a kiss.

Kasper listened rather than talked while they ate their dinner that evening. He smiled as Daysee told him about her day, while Maryl shook her head in amused resignation. From what Kasper could gather, his daughter's day had consisted of chasing the chickens, chasing the village cats, chasing the village dogs, and otherwise generally getting under her mother's feet.

'Perhaps your pa could take you hunting with him tomorrow instead?' Maryl said, winking at Kasper.

'Oh please!' Daysee pleaded. 'Can I?'

'Maybe when you're a little older,' Kasper laughed.

Daysee spent the rest of the meal sat with her little arms folded and a cross pout on her face.

That evening, after Daysee had been reluctantly put to bed, Kasper went to the inn at the centre of the village. There he was met by the familiar warmth and sound as he went through the door. As always, the inn was packed with smiling, relaxed villagers, and they cheered when Kasper entered. One unexpected benefit of his adventures with Merric that summer was that Kasper had not had to buy himself a single drink since his return. All of the villagers were eager to hear about the Battle of Eagle Mount, and hear about how many Monforts Kasper had personally killed. Kasper had felt no pleasure in taking lives that summer, except for Orderix of course, and he had only done so to protect his friends. This did little to dissuade the village folk from their image of Kasper striding heroically through the battle, dispatching enemies left right and centre.

As he walked up to the bar, Kasper nodded a greeting at Ketch the miller. Ketch was almost unrecognisable now from the selfish man he had been before, when he had used his power as the only miller in the village to bully and take advantage of those who depended on him for a supply of flour. It had been Merric who had solved that particular problem. Ketch was frowning in concentration at the playing pieces of a game of Kings of Castles that he was playing with Patt, a farmer with a bulbous nose. Both

Ketch and Patt had been among those to volunteer to serve their village in Sir Hestor Peggleswade's tiny army. Howel, the village fool, was dancing like a lunatic in front of a fiddler who was playing a jaunty tune.

Kasper reached the bar and ordered a tankard of ale from Lora, the charming landlady who was easily the most popular person in the whole village. But before he could pass over the coppers a hand clapped him on his shoulder, and Kasper turned to see the toothless grin of Hamm.

'Not this time, Hamm,' Kasper said to the elderly farmer. 'Let me pay for a drink for once.'

'Nope,' Hamm said, passing the coins to Lora. 'That Podmore was a good lad, and you kept him safe. That's worth a drink at least!'

Kasper smiled, remembering the false name Merric had adopted when in Little Harrow to avoid any attention being drawn to him. He raised the tankard in thanks to the farmer, who shook his head in bewilderment.

'To think that boy is a duke now! Well I never…'

There was a call from behind Kasper, and he turned and saw a couple of men waving at him from a table by the fire. Aulden, the village blacksmith, and his son Jule both had rough faces and broad chests. They were the strongest men in the village, and they, too, had been among those who had volunteered to be soldiers.

Kasper joined them at their table and clinked his tankard of ale against theirs.

'Cheers, boys,' he said.

'Our glorious leader is here, did you see?' Aulden said, chuckling and nodding to the far corner.

Sir Hestor, looking as dishevelled as ever, was drinking a cup of wine with the portly prior who presided over the services held in the small village priory. They seemed to be singing some song that was wildly inappropriate for a noble and a prior to be singing, and their antics were drawing laughs from those nearby.

'If we go to war, we could always just leave him behind,' Kasper laughed, taking a swig of ale.

'Do you reckon it will come to war?' Jule asked, looking at Kasper. His face seemed more serious than his father's.

He tried to sound confident, but Kasper could hear the hint of nervousness in his voice. Like everyone else, Jule considered Kasper to be an expert on the subject of warfare. He was the only person from Little Harrow who had been in battle, and he had become friends with the new duke as well, so many thought this meant that Kasper knew exactly what Lord Merric would be planning.

'My advice is to not try and understand politics,' Kasper said, kindly. 'Leave that to the nobles.'

Aulden made a noise of dislike, and Kasper turned to him.

'They're not all bad,' Kasper assured him.

'You've changed your tune.'

'Yes, well,' Kasper smiled. 'I got to know one of them. And I liked him. And so did you, coming to think of it!'

'Well, I didn't know he was a noble at the time. I thought he was just a simple boy from Eaglestone,' Aulden laughed, 'so that doesn't count.'

'Just know this,' Kasper said, confidently. 'Merric is not like the other lords. He will always put the folk first. Whatever ends up happening, it'll be for the best. He's got a clever head on his shoulders. Not like you two simpletons.'

'What are you saying?' Aulden asked in mock outrage.

'You're hardly the sharpest tool in the shed, father,' Jule pointed out.

'You're not wrong there, son,' the blacksmith laughed. 'Don't need no brains to beat hot metal, that's what I always say.'

'Well I don't think Sir Hestor would let you bring your hammer to a battle,' Jule said.

'True. Better get practicing with that spear, boy,' Aulden said, winking at his son.

Kasper reached out and put a hand on each of their shoulders.

'If it comes to war then just keep an eye out for each other. Try and keep yourselves out of trouble, and you'll make it home safe and sound.'

'I'll drink to that,' Aulden said, chinking his tankard against theirs.

The fiddler started playing a new tune, and it was a song they all knew. Within seconds the whole inn was singing along, and Kasper, Aulden and Jule joined in with the rest, all worries of war pushed from their minds.

The next day Kasper was awoken to the sounds of a tired old wagon trundling past with wheels that squeaked loudly. Kasper groaned, rubbing his sore head. The blacksmith and his son had kept him at the inn for half of the night, and he had come staggering home cursing himself for having drunk so much ale. The sound of the wagon rolling past his cottage felt as loud as if Aulden and Jule were smashing his head with their hammers, and he reluctantly clambered from his bed and hobbled out of the cottage. Maryl watched him struggling, an amused look on her face.

Once Kasper had dunked his head into the barrel of water at the side of their cottage he felt slightly more awake. He looked towards the centre of the village and saw that the wagon had pulled up outside the priory. It belonged to Old Vigga, the slightly eccentric elderly lady who lived on a farm a couple of miles outside the village. Most of the villagers steered well clear of her, which is exactly how she preferred things. Some of the children in Little Harrow would sneak onto her farm for a dare, but she would chase them off with her walking stick or else set her cats on them. But her cows were their main source of milk, and now and then she made a rare journey into the village to make a delivery. As well as carrying out his religious duties, the village prior did a roaring trade turning the milk into butter and cheese.

His head was pounding, but Kasper could not stand by and watch Old Vigga struggling to unload the milk pails from the wagon by herself. Wincing at the pain of the headache, Kasper walked over and offered to give her a hand.

'Ooh, thanks dearie!' she chuckled, pinching his cheek as though he was a child.

'Erm, no problem,' Kasper said awkwardly, and he climbed up onto the wagon and took over the unloading.

'I'm getting a bit old for this,' Old Vigga said, chuckling once again.

'A bit?' Kasper repeated under his breath.

Old Vigga, as her nickname suggested, was older than anyone else in the village. No one knew quite how old she was, and they doubted whether even she knew. But she had seemed ancient even when Kasper was a small boy. She had not always been so eccentric, but Kasper assumed this was a result of her living on her own with no one but her cats and cows for company.

'Maybe you should hire some help, Vigga,' Kasper called down to her, raising his voice as her hearing was failing. He had half unloaded the wagon by now, and the sun blazing overhead made Kasper begin to regret his offer to assist her. He needed some shade, and a nap.

'Why, are you volunteering, young man?' she crooned, beaming up at him.

'I'm not a dairy farmer, I'm afraid,' Kasper apologised, thinking quickly. 'I bet there's someone in the village who would be eager for the job though.'

He doubted that was true, as everyone thought Old Vigga was odd and best avoided, but it did not seem right to see such a frail old lady having to carry out such back breaking work.

'Oh don't worry about Vigga,' she said. 'I've got my son back at the farm. He looks after me.'

Kasper clicked his tongue sympathetically. Old Vigga's son had died many years ago, and even her grandchildren had long since moved away to seek something more than the simple lives of a dairy farmer and their dotty grandmother. No doubt she was getting confused in her old age. As strange as she was, the thought of Old Vigga returning to her lonely farm and unhitching the oxen from the wagon by herself made Kasper feel a pang of sadness and guilt.

'I'll tell you what,' he said, once the unloading of the milk was completed and he had hopped down off the wagon, 'I don't really need to go hunting today. I'll come back with you, and give you a hand, if you like?'

'My son would be delighted to meet you,' Old Vigga said, clapping her hands together.

Kasper went back home to grab his jerkin, while the prior emerged from the priory to inspect the milk delivery, looking as though his head hurt just as much as Kasper's did. When Kasper told Maryl where he was going, she hurriedly packed a basket with food items for Kasper to take with him to give to Old Vigga. She packed some apples and loaves of bread, and a cheese made from Old Vigga's own milk wrapped up in a cloth.

'The poor old dear,' Maryl said. 'She really ought to move out of that farm and into a cottage here in the village. That place must get so cold in the winter! At least I can make sure she has a good meal tonight.'

The road to Old Vigga's farm was little more than a track. It was in desperate need of repair, but no one used it apart from her. It was wildly overgrown and the uneven wheels of the wagon bounced in and out of the ruts in an alarming way. It did little to help Kasper's headache. He drove, leaving Old Vigga to point and remark in excitement at completely normal things, such as bumblebees and daffodils. It was tiresome to listen to, but Kasper supposed if these little things kept the old lady happy then who was he to question it?

The track wound between fields where some of the villagers worked, harvesting the last of the wheat. But before long the fields ended and they passed through wild grasslands thick with wildflowers and dotted with occasional copses of trees. To the east the Pink Hills rose, creating a dramatic backdrop to the peaceful scene. Soon, there was not another soul in sight.

'It's very beautiful, but do you not get lonely out here, by yourself?' Kasper asked.

'Oh no,' Old Vigga said in her quiet, high pitched voice. 'Vigga likes the peace and quiet, and I have my cats and cows. Besides, my son is home now too.'

'Mmm,' Kasper said, not wanting to encourage her confusion.

Her farm came into view. It was a simple place, with a small yard and a field where half a dozen cows could graze. Her home was in desperate need of repair, but Kasper was surprised to see that it was actually looking a little tidier than it had done the last time he had seen it a few years ago. The yard had been recently swept and the windows had been thrown open to let some air into the musty old cottage. Still, there were tiles missing from the roof and the wood of the lean-to where Old Vigga stored her dairy farming equipment was rotting away. Kasper thought that perhaps he would round up some of the folk from the village and bring them down here and fix her home up as best they could. If the previous summer had taught Kasper anything it was that the villagers would always look out for each other.

He brought the wagon to a halt in the yard and climbed down.

'Shall I unhitch the oxen for you?' he asked, patting the tired beasts who looked as old and frail as Old Vigga did.

'No, no!' she chuckled, 'I can manage.'

203

She untied the oxen with well-practiced hands and steered them towards a small paddock with a strength that was surprising for such a small, old lady.

Kasper took the basket of food from the wagon and put in on the simple wooden bench that sat beside her front door.

'I'll just leave this here,' he said. 'It's just some bits from Maryl.'

'Oooh!' Old Vigga said, her eyes lighting up as she shuffled over to take a look. 'All my favourite things. I'll share these with my son. Where is he I wonder? Oh, here he comes!'

Kasper turned in surprise when he did indeed hear footsteps approaching behind him. A young man walked around the side of the house from the direction of the cow field. He had a shovel in one hand and a bucket filled with manure in the other. He stopped short when he saw Kasper, a look of surprise appearing on his face.

Kasper's mouth dropped when he recognised him. It was certainly not Old Vigga's son.

'*Merric?*'

Merric put down the shovel and bucket and turned around, hurrying back around the cottage and out of view.

'Oh, he's very shy,' Old Vigga said, apologetically.

But Kasper did not hear her. He had hurried after Merric, going around the side of the cottage and pushing his way through a gate which was already beginning to swing shut. He dashed into the field, looking left and right.

He spotted Merric running across the field and vaulting over an old tumbled down stone wall at the opposite end. Kasper ran after him.

'Merric, wait!' he called.

The immediate shock of suddenly seeing Merric again quickly wore off, but instead confusion was setting in. What on earth was the Duke of The Head doing here, shovelling cow dung at Old Vigga's farm?

Merric did not stop, and so Kasper kept running after him. Up ahead, Merric skidded to a halt when he reached a wild hedgerow, and after a moment's indecision he turned left and sprinted that way. Kasper hared after him, and became vaguely aware of the sound of the river over the hammering of his own feet sprinting across the ground. Merric ducked past a tree and disappeared from sight again, but Kasper followed, determined not to lose him.

The wide expanse of the Rush spread out before him, flowing calmly but swiftly southwards towards the sea. Even as a small child his parents had scared him silly by telling him stories about the great river, and as such he had never dared to even dip a toe into the water, despite living only an hour's walk away from it. Down here the river may not have been the churning, raging torrent that it was further to the north, but the current was still strong and would likely drag someone to their deaths if they were to foolishly decide to take a swim.

Merric was standing on the shingle that led down to the water's edge. He was standing still at last, with nowhere left to run. His shoulders were slumped and his head was bowed. Kasper slowed down to a stop ten feet away from him, not wanting Merric to run off again.

'Merric,' Kasper said. 'Merric? What in the name of the Mother are you doing here?'

Merric seemed reluctant to turn around, but he did so, slowly. Kasper peered at him, not recognising the hollow look in Merric's eyes. There was evidence of a recently healed injury on his forehead, and his clothes were simple and rough spun from wool, as though they were pieced together from the odd garments that Old Vigga had in her cupboards.

Merric kept his head down and looked as though he did not know how to answer Kasper's question.

'What happened to you?' Kasper urged him, taking a couple of steps towards him, the shingle crunching beneath his feet.

Have you not heard?' Merric said at last.

'Heard?' Kasper asked, confused. 'Heard what?'

'I thought all The Head would know by now.'

Kasper could hear the shame in Merric's voice.

'Well, you know our village is in the middle of nowhere,' Kasper said, trying to bring a smile to Merric's face. 'News travels slowly around here.'

Merric looked as though he wished that Kasper *had* already heard whatever it was that he had to tell him. As though he would rather not be the one to have to say it.

He made to speak, but his voice broke before he could get any words out. He steeled himself and tried again.

'Kasper, I've really messed things up.'

Merric spoke, and Kasper listened. He told him about Sir Sebastien, and how they had become friends. And how the Ouestorian had attempted to deliver a message to The Dale on Merric's behalf, but had been captured by the Monforts on the way. He spoke about how everyone had attempted to discourage him from his determination to attempt to free his friend, but he had ignored them all. And he told Kasper what had happened when they had reached the meeting place and were ambushed.

'It's my fault,' he finished. 'It's all my fault. They were good knights, all of them. And Sir Marc! He…he had just been married, and he died. All to protect me. Because of my stupid decisions.'

'What happened to you?' Kasper asked, not knowing how to process all this information. 'How did you end up here?'

'I don't remember much of it,' Merric said with a shrug. 'I hit my head when I fell from Nosy.'

Merric stopped speaking, swallowing hard. Kasper knew that he had grown close to that horse, and it was causing Merric yet more pain to know that Nosy was lost somewhere on the other side of the river.

'I remember falling into the river,' Merric said, his eyes unfocussed as though recalling it. 'It was so cold, and I thought I was going to drown. And I think I wanted to. They wanted to capture me, and all I was doing was trying to stop them from doing that. But I remember feeling a log floating in the river, and I somehow held onto that. My armour was heavy but I managed to stay afloat on the log. I think I must have passed out. The next thing I knew I was washed up on the shore here. And the old woman was standing over me. She dragged me all the way to her house. I have no idea how. She made some sort of paste and used that to help my head heal. She seems confused, and keeps calling me Ren. I don't know who he is, but she seems to like me being around.'

Kasper did not know what to think, but that did not matter. He put a hand on Merric's shoulder, and he felt it start to shake as tears filled Merric's eyes. Kasper pulled him in close and held him tightly as Merric cried. He did not try to stop him, or try to tell him that everything was going to be okay. He just let Merric cry.

'It's all my fault,' Merric sobbed into Kasper's shoulder.

Kasper did not reply, and just put his hand on the back of Merric's head and continued to hug him in exactly the same way that he held Daysee when she was upset. Maryl would try and sooth her and try to help fix whatever had made her cry, but Kasper knew that sometimes it was better to say nothing and just be there for her. Sometimes no words could help. Sometimes it was better to just let the tears come.

CHAPTER TEN

The boy duke

Kasper insisted on taking Merric back to Eagle Mount. He could not remain here, working on Old Vigga's farm, no matter what he had done. Merric was reluctant to go back, too ashamed and feeling too guilty to ever want to see anyone again. He had thought that he had known better than everyone else, and that had cost good men their lives. He had acted like the stupid boy that he was, not like a duke.

'Yet you are still our duke,' Kasper told him, when Merric confessed this. 'Would you prefer to hide out here and pretend that you had died as well? Would you want Ana to live with that grief? That's not fair on her, or fair on any of them.'

Mention of Ana's name made Merric feel even worse, and did nothing to discourage him from wanting to hide out here. He would never forget the look on her face when he had spoken to her for the last time, when he had told her that they were stupid to think they could ever have a future together.

'We all make mistakes,' Kasper said, trying a different approach when he felt a fresh wave of despair pass over Merric's face. 'And you've got to live with those mistakes, Merric, and learn from them. You can make it up to everyone, if you come to Eagle Mount with me.'

'I can't face them,' Merric said, looking broken. 'I can't bear the idea of it.'

Kasper could not bring himself to judge Merric for what he had done. He had no idea what it was like to rule something, let alone the whole dukedom. On the other hand he could not say how everyone back at Eagle Mount would be feeling about Merric, but even if they did judge him for his mistakes then it was something that Merric would have to face up to. He could not spend his life hiding away. The guilt would eat at him more and more until it became unbearable. It was always better to accept a fault, and move on from it.

'Well if you don't go to them then they'll come to you,' Kasper said, with a sense of finality.

'What do you mean?' Merric asked him, suspiciously.

'Merric, come on,' Kasper said, shaking his head wearily. 'I can't just forget that I've seen you. If you don't go back to Eagle Mount then I'll have to ride there myself and tell them where they can find you. They must be worried sick about you. Think about the folk of

Eaglestone! We might not have heard about what happened here in Little Harrow, but surely they have in the streets of Eaglestone. They must be wondering whether their duke even lives or not.'

'I wish I had died,' Merric said, his voice quavering a little as he thought of the Eagle Guard who had lost their lives protecting him. 'Or I wish they had just let the Monforts take me.'

'Don't be stupid,' Kasper said, his voice suddenly impatient. 'And don't be so quick to throw away your life, after all we did this summer to help keep you alive. Now, would you prefer to come with me, or would you rather it if all the highborn of The Head found you here at Old Vigga's farm, shovelling dung all day long?'

Merric had finally run out of energy and excuses and so, after one last look at the great river that had nearly taken his life, he gave a weary nod and accepted Kasper's offer to take him back. Together, they walked back to the farm, where Kasper explained to old Vigga that her "son" needed to travel to Eagle Mount on business for the duke.

'He's an important man, my son,' she said proudly, giving Merric a pat on the head. 'I know you will do me proud. Don't forget your things!'

His few belongings were stowed in a sack beside the mattress he had been sleeping on in the corner of her cottage. Inside were the remains of his armour that had not come off and become lost in the river, but Merric told her that he did not want it. For all he cared, Old Vigga could sell it and take the money as thanks for taking him in and healing his injuries. But when Merric had gone outside, Kasper peered inside the sack and saw the hilt of a sword amongst the armour. He pulled it out and hid it beneath his cloak.

Together they walked along the track that led away from the Old Vigga's farm and headed towards Little Harrow. Merric glanced back and saw the elderly lady watching them leave, her arm waving in farewell and a pair of black cats rubbing themselves up against her legs.

Merric and Kasper walked in silence. Kasper's mind was filled with the thought of leaving Maryl and Daysee again, and wondering what his wife would say. But, he assured himself, this time would be different. He was only taking Merric home, not heading towards danger like he had that previous summer. He glanced across at Merric, who was walking beside him, staring at his own feet. Kasper knew he could not abandon Merric. Even if he did not harbour a concern that Merric would turn around and walk in the opposite direction if he was given the choice, Kasper knew that the boy needed to be close to at least one person who was not going to be holding his actions against him. He knew that Merric needed a friend.

After an hour, the chimneys of the village came into view and Kasper held out an arm to stop Merric.

'Wait here,' he said, 'and please don't go anywhere. I'll need to say goodbye to Maryl and Daysee. I had promised them that I was done going on journeys away from the village, but they'll understand.'

He was back before long, with a pack of provisions on his back and his longbow over his shoulder. He was glad to find Merric sat on the verge where he had left him, playing absent-mindedly with a length of grass between his fingers and waiting for Kasper to return. Part of him had expected Merric to run away while he was gone, but it seemed that the boy had accepted that he needed to return to Eagle Mount and was willing to go without a fuss.

With his farewells to his wife and daughter done, Kasper led Merric on a path that skirted the edge of the village. He knew that Merric would not want to be bombarded with questions by the village folk, and so did not take him directly through the centre of Little Harrow. Merric appreciated that more than Kasper could ever imagine.

Merric remembered little of the journey back to Eagle Mount. They walked most of the time, and when they were lucky they came across farmers with wagons who were happy for them to hitch a ride on, giving their feet a rest. Whether they were walking or bouncing around in the back of a wagon, Merric kept his hood up. Even though there was a seemingly constant drizzle of rain falling, Kasper was not fooled; he knew that the hood was not to keep the rain off, but rather Merric was hiding his face, not wanting any of the other travellers on the road to recognise him. Merric mostly stayed silent as they travelled, held prisoner by the thoughts that assaulted him. He had no idea what he would say to Sir Oskar and Sir Orsten when he saw them, or Tomas, or Sophya, or especially Ana. But he knew he had to face them. He was ashamed with himself for how he had acted, and doing another shameful act would likely only make him feel worse.

They slept under the stars, as they had done that summer. They found what shelter they could beneath trees or behind hedgerows. But the weather was colder now than it had been in their last journey through the great outdoors, and Merric shivered under the blanket that Kasper had brought for him. He could not complain though, and in a way he liked the feeling of discomfort. It made him feel like he was being punished, which he knew he deserved. He felt guilty that Kasper was suffering the same cold and damp nights as he was, but if it was bothering the hunter then he did not say so.

They arrived back at Eagle Mount several days later. Merric kept his hood up and the Jacelyn soldiers at the gate did not recognise him. When they walked through to the streets beyond Merric could sense a different mood in the town. People seemed a bit more downcast and less cheerful than they had been before, though that could just have been because of the weather. The light rain was still falling, reminding everyone that autumn had arrived. But Merric was not so naïve as to think that it was only the weather that was dampening the spirits of the town. The Eagle

Guard were famous in The Head, with children growing up learning each knight's name and what heroic deeds they had accomplished. The death of so many of their number was no doubt contributing towards the sad feeling within Eaglestone.

They headed up the Lord's Way, walking up through the rain-washed street towards the hazy image of Eagle Mount ahead, their feet soaked by the flow of water cascading down the hill in the gutters. The castle was swathed in low clouds, looking almost ghost-like. Merric kept his eyes downwards all the way to the castle, following behind Kasper as he made his way through the sombre crowds going about their business. They stopped when they reached the castle gates, finding their way barred by a cluster of Jacelyn soldiers.

'What do you want?' one of the soldiers asked.

He must have been a new recruit, as all those Jacelyn soldiers who had fought at the Battle of Eagle Mount knew Kasper by face. The soldier peered at the soaked archer, noticing the smaller figure behind him, hunched beneath his cloak and hood.

'Send for one of the Oakhearts,' Kasper said to the soldier.

A minute later Merric recognised the voice of Sir Orsten, and forced himself to look up.

'Kasper?' said Sir Orsten in amazement, seeing the hunter waiting at the gates. 'What are you doing here?'

Then he spotted Merric, and he swore loudly and in a fashion unbecoming of a knight.

There was a sudden burst of activity. Hands took hold of Merric and guided him through the arched gateway and into the castle courtyard. Voices clamoured and yet more soldiers crowded around, wanting to get a good look at him.

'Back away, back away there!' Sir Orsten barked, putting a hand on Merric's back and steering him away from the ogling onlookers. Merric turned his head and glanced back at Kasper, who looked back at him with an encouraging smile on his face. And then Kasper disappeared from view as Sir Orsten led Merric up the steps and into the castle keep.

'Merric!'

Sophya cried out when she caught sight of him. She had just left the Grand Hall and froze when she saw Merric there in the entrance hall with Sir Orsten. Clutching the side of her face in disbelief she ran up to him and gave him a hug.

'Thank the Mother you're safe!' she cried. 'We thought you were gone!'

Merric smiled weakly at her, but he could not bear to see the pleasure on her face at seeing him returned, alive. He did not deserve her love.

Sir Orsten took him straight upstairs and to Merric's study, leaving a shell-shocked Sophya in the entrance hall. Merric could not help feeling like a condemned man being led to the gallows. He felt powerless to resist, and just allowed the Oakheart knight to guide him. Even Sir Orsten's face, usually so emotionless, was pale with the shock of seeing Merric again. When they reached the study he ushered Merric inside. and ordered the soldier stationed outside the door to go and find his brother. Like everyone else they had passed on their journey through the castle, the soldier's jaw dropped in disbelief at the sight of his duke. Sir Orsten had to repeat the order, more loudly this time, before the soldier hurried off in search of Sir Oskar.

'Sit down, my duke,' Sir Orsten said to Merric once they were alone inside the study.

The fire in the grate was not lit and the room was cold. Merric sat down in his chair behind the desk, but could not look at Sir Orsten. He could feel the knight's eyes boring into him, and Merric wished he would stop. They remained in silence for a few minutes. Sir Orsten, stood by the cold fireplace, did not know what to say, and Merric did not want to say anything at all. The silence was painful, but it was preferable to talking about what had happened.

The door crashed open and Sir Oskar burst in.

'Brother, is it true?' he blurted out.

He paused when he saw Merric.

'My duke!' he exclaimed. 'I can scarce believe it!'

He collapsed onto one of the chairs facing Merric, but his brother stayed standing, his arms folded.

'We thought you were dead, my duke,' Sir Oskar said, when it became clear to him that Merric was not a figment of his imagination

'We heard from Lord Tymon at Bridge Ford,' Sir Orsten added. 'He told us what had happened, and we had no choice but to assume that you had fallen too.'

Merric still did not speak. He did not know what to say. Nor did he know what they wanted him to say. Did they want him to say that he wished he had died with his men?

'You need some rest, I'm sure,' Sir Oskar said, glancing at his brother. They shared a troubled look, disturbed by Merric's silence. 'We will make an announcement , telling The Head that you are alive. I know it will give them…heart.'

Merric noticed Sir Oskar pause, and when he glanced up the two brothers were looking a little uneasy. He knew what they were thinking. If The Head had been told that he had died, then they had likely also been told the circumstances in which he had fallen. The folk would know that their duke had acted rashly and stupidly, and not in the way that a duke should act. Merric was not sure that they would be pleased to know that he still lived. They had been so quick to love Merric when he had retaken Eagle Mount, and captured Lord Warner at Hightop Castle, and he had always known that they should not have thought so highly of him. Now they will have seen him for the stupid boy that he really was. The bubble had been burst, and they would be ready to move on to a new leader. A better leader.

'What happened with Sir Sebastien?' Sir Orsten asked.

Merric shrugged, and finally broke his silence.

'I don't know. I don't think they even meant to trade him. They killed Lord Warner themselves, and then came after us.'

'They killed Lord Warner?' Sir Orsten said, his eyebrows raised.

'Yes. They said that Aric did not even care about him. They only wanted to capture me.'

'They were trying to capture you?' Sir Oskar asked, taken aback.

'Yes,' Merric said.

He was a little frustrated by the way they were just repeating everything he was saying.

'I don't know why they wanted me,' he admitted. 'If they wanted to kill me with the others then I'd be dead, but they wanted me alive for some reason.'

'I knew they would try something like this,' Sir Orsten said, pacing angrily up and down the study. 'I knew it! That is why we tried to stop you!'

'I'm sorry,' Merric said, his voice breaking. 'I should have listened to you.'

'The important thing is that you are safe,' Sir Oskar said, giving his brother a calming look as if to say that this was not the time.

He turned to face Merric once more.

'My duke,' he said, in his gentlest voice. 'We need you to tell us exactly what happened, and don't miss anything out. It is important, so we can decide what to do next.'

Merric left the study half an hour later. He felt drained after reliving the events of what had occurred when he had crossed the river, and the whole time he spoke he could see the faces of the Oakheart twins darken, grimacing as they heard what had happened. He went back to his bedchamber, glad that he did not pass anyone in the hallways. He could not face more people rushing over to him, exclaiming over his return and wanting to hear about what had happened. His isolation ended abruptly, though, when he reached his bedchamber door. Before he could reach out for the door handle it opened in front over him.

He came face to face with Tomas, who was leaving the bedchamber.

'I'd heard you'd come back, but I couldn't find a servant,' Tomas said, not looking Merric in the eye, 'so I've lit a fire in the hearth.'

'Thank you,' Merric muttered, awkwardly.

Tomas forced a smile, but still kept his eyes down.

'I'm glad you're safe, my lord,' he said.

He disappeared down the hallway and out of sight. Merric watched him go, not surprised that Tomas felt so uncomfortable around him. He wondered how many others would feel that same way.

* * *

Merric had not imagined that life would quickly go back to how it had been before, and a part of him knew that it would never truly be the same again. He felt that he deserved every single stare that he received, and he knew that folk were muttering to each other behind his back. He could not blame them, and he even felt a kind of savage pleasure at the knowledge that he was being punished.

Once the initial shock of seeing their duke back at the castle had worn off, the looks Merric received from the folk around Eagle Mount were far from welcoming. Servants and soldiers who had previously admired Merric, and even adored him, now looked at him with disappointment and judgement. Old Myk, the strict castle steward, had always been friendly enough to Merric in the first few weeks after he had been made the duke, but now he acted as though Merric was a mere boy, not worthy of his time or energy. Everyone knew that Merric had thought himself above everyone else, ignoring their advice and opinions. He had thought that he knew better, and had allowed his personal feelings to lead to the deaths of the valiant Eagle Guard.

Sir Oskar and Sir Orsten were not angry with Merric for not listening to them, but rather their reaction to Merric's return to the castle was far worse. Merric would have preferred it if they had shouted at him, or openly

222

showed that they no longer trusted their duke's judgement. But instead they treated him almost like a child. They spoke in calm, quiet voices around him, as though worried he was going to explode with rage as he had done that day he had set off to try and rescue Sir Sebastien. They explained everything to him like he was too simple or too immature to understand. They knew he had ruined his chance to be a good duke. It was almost as if they felt like they needed to hold his hand every step of the way, to stop him from making any more stupid choices. Though whether they did that for Merric's own benefit, or for the benefit of The Head, he could not tell.

He found that the Oakheart twins took an ever more active role in the running of The Head, with Merric being pushed to the back. It was as though no one trusted him anymore. He would occasionally be passed things to sign as a formality, but apart from that Sir Oskar and Sir Orsten, along with Sophya, looked after everything themselves. When they had carried out discussions about what they should do about The Dale, Sir Oskar had asked Merric for his thoughts, but he knew that they would not take his views into account when making a decision.

Despite what had happened, nothing had changed in regard to the fact that they needed to secure an alliance with The Dale. But it was looking more and more likely that further attempts to reach the Florins would fail, just as Sir Sebastien's attempt had. Without safely crossing the river, and getting past the Monfort patrols that were guarding the route to The Dale, there was no way for them to reach Lord Godfrei at his home of Bluewall Castle. They could not ask anyone else to attempt the journey in Sir Sebastien's footsteps, as to do so would be sending someone to be killed or captured for certain. They spent long hours in the study, trying to decide on the best course of action. Merric had spoken little, knowing that his words added little value. Sophya made up for this, as though wanting to show the Oakheart twins that there was some strength left in the Jacelyn family. Their conversations only seemed to go around in circles, with them agreeing that they needed the support of the Florins, but not knowing how they could hope to communicate with them without sending more messengers to share the same fate as Sir Sebastien. And that, Sophya insisted, was something they would not do.

Merric's sense of uselessness only increased when Sir Oskar and Sir Orsten had even taken over the running of the court sessions. While they themselves listened to the petitioners and responded to them, all Merric could do was sit quietly and alone on the raised dais, feeling all eyes watching and judging him. When a teary-eyed Lady Jeyna had come forward, dressed all in black and asking whether the body of her beloved husband had been recovered, Merric had been unable to stand the accusing stares and had to leave the Grand Hall.

Sophya had tried her best to make Merric feel better. She alone seemed to be holding onto a hope that his mistake would not be repeated, and that he was still capable of being a good duke. She had spent time with him when her duties allowed, but she could never quite work out what to say to him. She did not know whether Merric wanted to be reassured, or cheered up, or simply to have his mind taken off his current misery. If anything, Sophya's attempts to help only made Merric feel even worse. Not only was she taking after her mother and doing a splendid job at keeping things at the castle running smoothly, but every day she was resembling her father more and more as well. Merric knew that it was his own pitiful attempt at being the duke that was forcing her to rise up and fill the void he was leaving, but this did not help lift his spirits. He could even see Lord Roberd's kind features in her own face when she had tried to comfort him. He could not help but compare himself to her, and he pitied The Head's poor fortune when he had inherited Eagle Mount rather than her.

He had not seen Tomas since the day he had returned to the castle. He was not sure whether his squire was deliberately avoiding him, or whether he was genuinely being kept busy. Merric suspected, when he was at his lowest, that the Oakhearts were keeping Tomas away from him, in case Merric's poor judgement rubbed off on the young squire who had such promise as a knight. Merric had watched Tomas one day from his bedchamber window, sparring with Sir Orsten in the courtyard below. He had continued his lessons without Merric, and he seemed to be coming along quickly. If anything, Merric's absence from the training was spurring him on. Tomas had once admired Merric, and that feeling had only grown during their flight from Eagle Mount that summer, when Merric had been tested time and again. But now Tomas, along with everyone else, must surely know that Merric was not the person everyone believed him to be. One day Tomas would be a knight, and memories of the quiet, shy boy would be all but forgotten. As would the memories of how highly he had once thought of Merric.

But nothing made Merric feel worse than he did when he came face to face with Ana again for the first time. A week had passed since he had returned to Eagle Mount, and he had not caught a single glimpse of her, not even from afar. He knew that she would likely never want to see him again after what he had said to her. She would certainly not go out of her way to visit him in the castle, that was for sure, and Merric was much too ashamed to go into the town to find her at her father's workshop.

Merric had been walking aimlessly around the courtyard, avoiding everyone's company, when he heard the trundle of wheels and saw Ana and her father, Danell the blacksmith, steering their wagon through the castle gates and towards the stables. Merric had ducked into the shadows and loitered by the well. When the wagon came to a halt, she hopped down from the seat, her blonde hair tied up in the way that Merric liked. He had watched her as she began unloading their delivery of horseshoes. But she seemed to sense someone's eyes on her. She turned and saw Merric watching her, half hidden in the shadow at the far side of the courtyard. He nervously smiled at her. She just turned back to her work as though she had not even seen him. Danell, stood on the back of the wagon and passing the crates down to his daughter, saw who Ana had been looking at. He gave Merric a small nod of recognition with an expression that might have been sympathy or might have been disappointment.

Merric wanted to go over to Ana, to tell her that he was sorry. But the damage was done. He could not take back what he had said, and he would not expect her to accept his apology. He had hurt her, deeply, and he was supposed to be the one person who would never do that to her.

It was the final straw to Merric. He was not the duke that the folk of The Head deserved, and he had even ruined his friendships. Sophya was being kind to him, but he could see the disappointment in her eyes whenever she looked at him. Tomas seemed to be avoiding him like the plague, as though Merric's foolishness was contagious. He knew he had lost the respect of the Oakheart twins, who had been so full of praise for the way Merric had acted that summer. He knew that all the barons would feel the same, and every other noble, knight and commoner across The Head would know what he had done. Part of him feared that with their respect for him gone, the folk of The Head would lose their enthusiasm to stand up against the

Monforts. Perhaps they would prefer to just look the other way and let Lord Aric do whatever it was that he was planning. Their willingness to stand against their rightful king might not be so strong without a leader they would be happy to follow.

And, perhaps worst of all, Merric had even ruined things with Ana. Just as their relationship had begun to grow he had thrown it all away. All to try and save a friend, and he had failed at that too. Sir Sebastien was likely dead by now, or else locked so deeply in the dungeons of Lord Aric's fortress of The Citadel that he would never again see the sun.

By the time Merric had returned to his bedchamber that night he had made up his mind. He could not fix everything, but he could make sure that the folk of The Head did have a leader they could look up to. The Jacelyns had ruled these lands for hundreds of years, and Merric was determined to make sure that a Jacelyn would continue to do so.

The sky was pitch black outside by the time he had finished, and Merric was surrounded by crumpled up pieces of parchment covered in crossed out attempts. But, at last, he was satisfied with what he had written.

Dearest Sophya,

It pains me to write this, but I know that I must. I'm not thinking about what I want, but about what The Head needs.

I'm not the duke that The Head deserves, nor the duke that the folk need right now. It's best that I step down, and allow someone more deserving to take over. I had a chance to prove myself worthy to continue Lord Roberd's legacy, but I see now that only his daughter can do that. I hope you will not hate me for leaving you with this burden, and I'm sorry, but I'm confident that you will make him proud where I've failed.

I know that you would ask me to stay in Eagle Mount, but it's a place that now only fills me with shame and sorrow, and is a reminder of the mistakes I've made. I will not darken the castle with my presence for one more night, and by the time you read this I will be long gone. I do not mean to leave without saying a proper goodbye to you in person, but I know that you would try to convince me to remain here, and that is something I just can't do.

I hope that we'll one day meet again, when I have made up for what I've done.

Look after Tomas. I'm certain that he'll become a fine knight one day, and serve you with pride.

Your friend and cousin
Merric

Merric finished rereading the letter, and felt a great sadness at the words. He knew it was the right decision, but he could still feel tears stinging behind his eyes. Before he could change his mind, he laid the letter on the desk where he knew it would be found in the morning. He rose from the chair and crossed to his wardrobe and pulled out his plainest clothes, dressing quickly. He pulled out a warm cloak of dark green wool and put that on over the top, knowing that the weather was only going to get colder. He packed a few basic items and a small purse of coins into a pack, which he hoisted onto his back. Walking over to the door he opened it a crack and peeked out, making sure the coast was clear. Seeing and hearing no one, he slipped out of the door and hurried down the hallway beyond.

Just like he had done many times in his life, he snuck down into the courtyard and across to the stables. Fortunately it was a moonless night, and the dark clouds were cloaking everything in darkness. The driving rain that had started falling that evening meant that the soldiers on guard duty that night were huddled in what little shelter they could find, and would never notice the figure of their former duke hurrying across the courtyard. Merric pulled open the trapdoor in the stables that revealed the secret passage that led all the way into the town beyond the castle walls. For the second time in his life, Merric disappeared down through the passage, expecting this to be the final time he would ever be in Eagle Mount.

The streets of Eaglestone were almost deserted. Those townsfolk who were not already at home and tucked into their beds were hurrying through the rain, heading to or from the town's vibrant taverns. They paid no notice to Merric. He pulled his hood close over his head but even that did little to shelter him from the downpour, and his fringe was quickly plastered to his forehead by the rain. He gave a shudder, and made his way down towards the town gates. He found them closed, as he had expected them to be. Two soldiers were milling around them, yawning widely and leaning on their spears, shivering against the cold rain. Merric could tell they were newer recruits, just as he had hoped they would be.

Glancing around, to make sure there was no one else nearby, Merric cleared his throat and hurried towards the two soldiers, trying his best to look panicked and alarmed.

'Thank goodness!' he gasped, reaching them and clutching at the elbow of the nearest man. 'I've been robbed! He went that way!'

The soldiers looked at him in alarm, shaken awake from their daydreams. They stared in the direction Merric was pointing, the rain plinking noisily on their helmets.

'If you hurry, you'll catch him!' Merric added pointedly, by way of encouragement.

The two soldiers dashed away towards the side alley Merric indicated, clutching onto their helmets as they ran to keep them from falling off. Merric turned to the gates, and with a great heave he managed to swing one of the big oak doors open far enough to squeeze through. Pulling it back into place behind him, so that the returning soldiers would not notice anything amiss, Merric turned and disappeared into the night.

- CHAPTER ELEVEN -

The vagabond

Merric travelled all through the night, shoulders hunched and head bowed against the beating rain. Still, the cold rain was finding its way down the back of his neck, soaking him within minutes and sending him into uncontrollable shivers. He made slow progress, walking on foot in the pitch dark, but he knew he had to put as much distance between himself and Eagle Mount as he could. Come morning, his letter would be discovered and they would know that he had left the castle. He had no doubt that they would come after him and drag him back to Eagle Mount, and he had no desire to make that easy for them.

He did not really know where he was heading, but his subconscious mind had chosen north, and so it was northwards that he walked. He trudged across fields and clambered over fences, feeling the long wet grass of the rain-sodden meadows soaking his breeches. His feet inside his boots were sodden, and the rain seemed to be getting through to his very bones. Owls hooted overhead, but apart from that he neither saw nor heard any other signs of life. He found the isolation strangely comforting, with no accusing eyes watching him for the first time in days.

He came across a lane, and it seemed to head in the rough direction that he was travelling in. He knew that travelling on roads and paths would make it more likely that he would be discovered by other travellers, but he welcomed the break from walking across country. The cloying mud that sucked at his boots from the waterlogged fields had been slow and difficult going. Besides, he reasoned that in the middle of the night he would be unlikely to come across other folk, and even less chance that any would recognise him.

He kept going for a couple more hours, walking through the darkness and yawning widely, before finally stumbling as his heavy eyelids began to droop. He decided it was time to stop and get some rest, before he fell asleep on his feet. It was so dark that he could not even make out his immediate surroundings, let alone see the shape of Eagle Mount on its high hill behind him, but Merric hoped that he had travelled far enough to mean that anyone looking for him in the morning would have their work cut out to find him.

He stepped out of the lane, pushing his way through the hedgerow, cringing as the cold, wet leaves brushed against his face like icy fingers. He saw the outline of a tree a handful of paces away and he curled up in its roots, trying to get as much shelter from the rain as he could. He wrapped his soaked cloak tightly around himself, his teeth chattering, and was so tired that he fell asleep quickly. But his dreams were anything but peaceful.

When he awoke the sun had fully risen behind the blanket of grey clouds in the sky, and he knew that he had slept for longer than he ought to. The rain was still falling just as hard as it had been during the night, and the sky above gave no sign of letting up. To make matters worse, Merric was dismayed to see that he had not travelled as far as he had thought. The hill of Eagle Mount stood only a few miles away to the south-east, and the castle itself was still clearly visible, silhouetted against the grey clouds. Even at this distance the castle was high in the sky, and Merric had to look upwards to see its tall towers. He could still make out the proud Jacelyn banners, hanging limply in the rain-filled air.

Getting no satisfaction from the imagery of the sad-looking banners, which mirrored his own mood, Merric decided to lay low for a few more hours. He was still tired, and with being this close to Eagle Mount still he stood a good chance of being spotted if he travelled by day. He looked about at his surroundings and reasoned that it was not a bad place to rest a little longer. He was in a shallow hollow to the side of the narrow lane. Trees grew all around him which kept the worst of the rain from falling on him, apart from the occasional dripping from the leaves above him.

He lay there, in the nook between the roots of the tree, listening to the pattering sound of the rain on the trees above. He stared ahead, watching as the rain lashed down onto the meadows and fields that lay before him. A few times he saw farmers dashing about, but none of them looked his way. They were much too concerned with completing their chores quickly and getting out of the rain to notice the boy huddled in his cloak in the shelter of the distant copse of trees. Merric tried to go back to sleep, but he was cold and miserable and his damp clothes were uncomfortable. He cursed his bad fortune that, on top of everything else, it was raining.

His eyes were just beginning to close, as he sat there listening to the rhythmic pattering of rain on the leaves, when suddenly his ears picked up another sound. He sat bolt upright, straining with all his might to listen. He was sure it had been a voice, and not the distant sound of the farmers' calls to their sheepdogs. It had been a more authoritative voice, closer at hand.

'Merric?' came the shout, and others echoed the call from further away.

Merric leaped to his feet, pulling his pack back onto his shoulders. He stooped low, hiding behind the tree and watching the nearby lane. He was wide awake now, and crouched there for several minutes, listening. Had it just been the sound of the wind playing tricks on his ears? He thought that he could now hear hoofbeats over the sound of the rain as someone walked their horse in his direction.

He peered around the tree, his eyes scanning up and down the lane along which he had travelled the previous night.

A sudden movement caught his eye, and he instinctively ducked out of sight. It had been a head, too difficult to identify through the veil of pouring rain, bobbing up and down beyond the hedgerow as someone rode a horse along the lane. If it were someone looking for Merric then they would ride close by his hiding place. From their high vantage point atop their horse it was too much to hope for that they would not spot him. The tree behind which Merric crouched was too small to hide him completely.

He glanced around urgently, looking for a better hiding place. The ground sloped away down from the lane and towards the fields where Merric had spied the farmers at work. If he descended a little further then he would be hidden completely from the lane. He glanced back towards the rider, whose head was turned the other way, and seeing his chance Merric scrabbled down the damp slope, slipping and sliding, using his hands to keep himself from falling. He froze when he heard the voice again, much closer this time.

'Merric?' it called.

He skidded behind another tree, holding his breath. He was afraid for a moment that the rider had spotted him, but the shout came again, distorted a little as though the rider had cupped his hands to his mouth to help the sound travel further.

Merric could make out the voice now. It was Sir Orsten, he was sure of it. It was as Merric had expected; they had found his letter, and were now trying to find him. No duke had ever given up his responsibilities before, and to do so would bring the greatest shame upon him. But Merric did not care about that. He could not imagine feeling any more shame than he already did. What would they do with him when they found him? Would they drag him back to Eagle Mount to make an example of him? It would be better if they would just let him lose himself in the wilderness and be forgotten, as he wanted.

'No sign of him over that way, sir,' another voice said.

'Curse this rain,' Sir Orsten said. 'We will never find him in this.'

'We can't give up, sir,' the other voice said.

'I know we can't,' Sir Orsten said, sounding dispirited. 'We have half the dukedom out looking for him. He cannot have gone far. He is not one for outdoor living.'

Merric felt a surge of bitterness. He had survived well enough in the outdoors that summer. But then again, he had not been alone. He had Kasper and Ana and Tomas looking out for him. But he would show them; he would do just fine on his own.

He hurried along, leaving his pursuers behind as he continued heading north. He wanted to keep on putting as much distance between himself and Eagle Mount as he could. The further away he got from his hunters, the more likely it was that they would accept that he was truly gone, and abandon their search. Based on this idea, Merric kept well clear of the lane and once more travelled across country. The going was slower and harder, but he had no desire to stumble across Sir Orsten or the other search parties. He stuck to the cover of trees as often as he could, using them to help hide himself from any eyes that were on the lookout for him, trusting that the shelter of the trees and the driving rain that fell in sheets would keep him obscured. When there were no trees to hide amongst he hurried along quickly, dashing across rain-soaked meadows and fields, looking around cautiously and ever watchful for signs of his hunters.

At one point he saw two horsemen riding along ahead of him, and he threw himself flat onto the ground to hide from view. He cringed as he felt the mud soak into the elbows and knees of his clothes. The two riders were looking around beneath their hoods, clearly searching intently. Merric kept himself flat, resisting the urge to run in the opposite direction. When they had passed out of sight, he rose back to his feet and hurried onwards again. The riders had been travelling along a sunken road that passed between two fields, heading towards a village that Merric could just make out to the west. Steering clear, he crossed over the road and continued along the next field, trying not to think longingly of the inn in the village, with a roaring fire and hot food on offer.

He carried on like this for the rest of the day, hiding whenever he spied anyone approaching. Sometimes it was horsemen from Eagle Mount looking for him, shouting his name and appealing for him to come to them if he could hear their calls, and other times it was simply farmers and village folk going about their normal lives. As the afternoon wore on Merric could not pretend that his stomach was not gnawing with hunger. He could not hunt as Kasper and Ana had been able to, and even if he had the skills he had nothing to hunt with. He had brought a small dagger with him from his bedchamber in the castle, but nothing that would be even remotely useful in hunting for something to eat. He had a handful of coins, but the search parties out looking for him were sure to converge on any villages or roadside taverns, and so he did not risk trying to buy something to eat. He found some berries in a hedgerow and he had greedily eaten as many as he could pick, but they had done little to fight off the gnawing pains of hunger in his stomach. The one benefit of the rain was that all the streams he came across were swollen from the downpour, and so he did not struggle to find water to drink. At least he would not die of thirst.

A sudden barking, just as the light was beginning to fade, gave Merric something to worry about other that his hunger. He froze, looking around behind him. It sounded like his hunters had brought some hounds with them, to try and sniff out his scent. They really did seem desperate to locate him, and Merric again wished that they would just leave him alone. He hurried onwards, finding a stream barring his way. It was too wide to jump, and there were no steppingstones with which he could use to cross, so there was nothing for it but to splash across the stream. Gritting his teeth he stepped in, and his already wet feet were immediately completely waterlogged, and were beginning to go numb from the cold.

The braying of the hounds behind him was growing louder, and he had sudden nightmarish visions of the dogs catching him and wrapping their teeth around his ankles and wrists. He paused for a moment, his feet and shins submerged in the water, thinking hard. Quickly reaching a decision, he turned and hurried along stream, lifting his knees high with every step to keep himself from stumbling in the cold water. The stream led uphill, weaving between trees and rocks. The barking grew louder still and, hearing the voices of the men tending the dogs, Merric ducked down behind a rock.

Glancing out from behind his hiding place he could see a cluster of dogs, their tails wagging happily and excitedly, sniffing and scurrying around the spot where Merric had entered the stream. He could not hear the words that were spoken, but the dogkeepers seemed to be looking around in indecision. As Merric had hoped, the stream had washed away his scent, and the dogs had lost his trail. Some of the men were looking up the stream in Merric's direction, while the rest were staring ahead across the fields to the north.

'Go on,' Merric muttered, urging the dogkeepers and their hounds to fall for his trick and head north, away from him.

They dogkeepers were cheerful men and had always been kind to Merric during his life in Eagle Mount, and the dogs were a friendly, playful pack really, but that was before. In this moment, Merric knew that everyone from the castle were now his enemies, seeking to drag him back to whatever miserable fate awaited him.

He exhaled in relief when the dogs, barking eagerly, dashed across the stream and into the fields on the opposite side, their handlers close behind. Not wanting to be too close to them, Merric continued wading along the stream. With the dogs so close he could not risk them picking up his scent again.

As night fell the rain finally stopped, but the sky continued to be thick with overcast clouds. Without the moonlight to help illuminate his way, Merric did not fancy another night of staggering blindly through the darkness. He found a cluster of boulders beside the stream and huddled between them, savouring the shelter from the breeze which chilled him in his still damp clothes. He felt like he would never be dry again. He took his boots off, hoping that he could at least drain out the stream water, making the journey the following day a little more bearable. He was getting blisters from the wet leather, and his exposed feet were icy cold. He wrapped himself up in his cloak, tucking his numb feet beneath him. He wished that his pursuers would just give up and call off their hunt, but until they did so he knew it would be far too risky to even attempt to light a fire.

He awoke the next morning feeling thoroughly depressed. He ached, he was cold and he was painfully hungry. The only good thing was that the rain had continued to hold off during the night, and the sky was even starting to look a little brighter. But his clothes were still so damp that it hardly seemed to make a difference. He set off once more, and as he walked he did not see or hear any sign of those who were searching for him, either human or canine. He dared to believe that the hunters had moved onto a new area to search, and it gave him a grim satisfaction to think that he had been able to avoid their attempts to find him.

With that worry gone for the time being, Merric instead found himself fixating on his hunger. He had to accept that a few berries found now and again in hedgerows was not going to keep the hunger at bay, and without the means to hunt for food it left him with only one option. His journey took him within sight of another village that afternoon, and so he made the decision to go and have a look and see if he could find anyone willing to sell him something to eat. He had no idea how far he had travelled since he had left Eagle Mount, and so did not know what village it could be. Would the folk living there know that their duke was missing, and so be on the lookout for him? It was a risk he would have to take.

As he neared the village he could see it was larger than he had first thought. There was even a small castle sat on the far side, surrounded by a simple wall and a water-filled moat. A priory stood at the centre of the village, its stones gleaming as though it had only recently been built. The air was filled with chimney smoke and the sounds of village life. Dogs barked, chickens clucked and somewhere nearby a blacksmith was hammering away at his anvil. Merric crouched behind a fence, looking carefully for signs of anyone who would be looking for him. He could not see anyone who looked like they had come from Eagle Mount.

Deciding that he had to just go for it and hope for the best, Merric hopped over the fence and onto the road that led into the village. Doing his best to look like a normal traveller, he walked casually into the village. There were not too many folk wandering about, but those he saw gave Merric uneasy glances. Whether they realised who he was, or else this village was simply wary of strangers, he could not tell. He decided that he would not linger here, just to be safe. He would get in and out of the village as quickly as he could, as soon as he had found something to eat. A couple of soldiers were stood in the small square at the centre of the village, and they narrowed their eyes at Merric as he passed them. Their shields were purple, and the symbol of a crescent moon was painted onto them. Merric tried to recall the name of the family who had that as their symbol, but at that moment all he could think about was searching out some food.

He smelt the delicious aroma of pies baking, and his mouth began to water. He looked around to find the source of the enticing smell, and he moaned in longing when he spied a bakery just around the corner from the newly built priory. He reached for his coin purse and was about to head over to the bakery when he felt a hand clap him on the shoulder.

Merric span around, coming face to face with a small man with wiry grey hair and a threatening expression plastered across his face. He was flanked on either side by another two soldiers with same moon symbol on their shields. The small man took a moment to examine Merric. He looked into his eyes, before peering at his filthy and travel stained clothes.

'You're not from around here,' he said at last.

It was not a question.

'No,' Merric agreed, looking uneasily at the soldiers who were studying him with the same suspicion as the small man was. Had they spotted that his clothes, while simple in design, were clearly richly made? Surely only someone from a noble family would have clothes such as this, and Merric was sure that he must be the only boy from a noble family who was wandering around in this area of The Head.

'I'm just travelling through,' he added, hopefully, cursing himself for coming into the village. If they worked out who he was, he would be back in Eagle Mount before he knew it.

'Just travelling through, are you?' the man repeated, doubtfully. 'What's your name?'

Merric reached out for the first name he could think of.

'Podmore,' he said, giving the same false name he had used when he had lived in Little Harrow that summer.

But he had taken a second too long to answer. His moment of hesitation had been noticed by the man, whose lips curled in satisfaction.

'I think you're lying to me aren't you?'

'No!' Merric said, trying to sound convincing. 'My name is Podmore, from Eaglestone. I'm just travelling through, on the way to visit my uncle.'

'Okay then,' the man said, humouring Merric's lie for a moment. 'Where does your uncle live?'

Merric's mind searched around hurriedly, trying to think of somewhere.

'Bartyn?' he attempted.

'You mean *Domadge* Bartyn?' the man challenged.

'Yes, that's what I meant.'

'Well you must be hopeless at following a map,' the man said, looking at Merric with a growing dislike. 'Porby isn't on the way to Domadge Bartyn from Eaglestone.'

'Wait, I didn't mean…'

'Enough!' the man barked. 'Stop lying, filth. I know why you're here in my village, and you're not going to do any more killing. Seize him!'

Before Merric could react, the two soldiers had grabbed hold of him. He struggled against them, but their grips were too strong and they were looking at him with absolute loathing. Merric was confused by their sudden aggression. He knew he must now be widely disliked by all that knew of what had happened, but he had never imagined that he would be so roughly handled. Was this on Sir Oskar and Sir Orsten's orders? He could not believe that they would have wanted to treat him in this way.

The man grabbed hold of a tuft of Merric's hair and gave it a painful yank down, so that they were looking into each other's eyes.

'We have you now, scum,' he said.

* * *

Merric did not know how long he had been down in the dungeons of the small castle. It could have been hours or it could have been days for all he knew. With no window to see outside he had no concept of the passing of time. After two nights of broken, uncomfortable sleep in the cold rain he was exhausted, and he felt himself passing in and out of sleep in the dark cell. Sometime after he had been thrown roughly into the dungeon, and the jailer had bound his wrists to manacles attached to the wall, the door had opened and a bowl of something resembling porridge had been pushed towards him. It looked disgusting, but Merric had been so hungry that he had wolfed it down, his chained hands tipping the bowl up so that he could gulp down the dregs.

Several times the man from the village square with the wiry hair came to question him. It quickly became clear to Merric that they did not know who he was, and had no idea that the person they had chained up was their ex-duke. However, this brought Merric little relief. The reality of his situation was, in fact, far worse. From what Merric could gather from the questioning, this village had been plagued recently by a murderer who had killed several of their number. A few weeks ago the knight who ruled the village had himself been killed, after leading some of his men in a manhunt to try and catch the murderer. For reasons that Merric could not grasp, the man believed that he was the murderer. The man, who turned out to be the steward of the castle, seemed to believe that eventually he would be able to force a confession out of him. Again and again Merric pleaded his innocence, but each time it fell on deaf ears.

Despite his predicament, after a couple of these interrogations Merric had actually begun to feel a little sorry for the steward. From what little information Merric had been able to get from him, the knight who had died had been a beloved leader of the village, and he had left behind a wife and a new-born baby. The folk of this village must be scared, and so the steward would be under a lot of pressure to find the culprit. Merric was not convinced that the steward truly believed that he had caught the real murderer, but he was so determined to find someone to blame that he did not care. He had to be seen to have achieved something, to ease the villagers' fears. If this was the same village that Sir Orsten and Sir Oskar had been talking about before, then they believed that the scarred knight in the dungeons of Eagle Mount was the one who had been committing the murders. If that was true then the village was already safe, and the steward was worrying unnecessarily.

But no matter how much Merric sympathised with the steward's position, he knew that his own situation had worsened considerably. He toyed with the idea of telling the steward who he really was, and that the murderer was already caught, but the idea of being taken back to Eagle Mount was almost as bad as spending the rest of his life in this dungeon. And besides, he doubted the steward would believe him anyway. It would seem like a very farfetched story. And so Merric instead continued to plead his innocence, trying to convince the steward that he was not the murderer and hoping for him to see reason. Merric explained to him that if he *was* guilty why would he have returned to the village, several weeks after the last murder had occurred?

'Don't ask me to understand how the mind of a murderer works,' the steward had said. 'You're a vagabond and an outlaw. I'd wager you're an exile too, not welcome anywhere.'

Merric did not say so, but the steward had got that last bit correct at the very least.

He knew that if he could not convince his captors of his innocence, and that he was not guilty of the crimes he was being accused of, then it was likely that he would meet his end here. He supposed that the only reason why he had not already been executed was because they were first wanting to draw a confession from him. Well, he reasoned, they would be waiting a long time for that.

The door rattled and it opened once more. Merric anticipated another interrogation, but it was not the steward this time. A young soldier came in. He glanced nervously at Merric, before depositing a cracked water jug onto the floor. Without saying a word he made to back out of the room again.

'Wait!' Merric croaked, his throat dry.

The young soldier hesitated.

'How long have I been down here?' Merric asked.

'Two days,' the soldier said, his eyes downcast to avoid the prisoner's gaze.

The more Merric looked at him the younger the soldier seemed. He was perhaps only the same age as himself. He had grown the faintest hint of a wispy moustache on his top lip, as though he was trying to look older in front of his fellow soldiers.

'What are they going to do with me?'

The soldier looked up and into Merric's eyes, trying, and failing, to look intimidating.

'You're going to pay for what you did to those folk you killed,' he said.

He looked alarmed at his own daring.

'Do you really believe it was me?' Merric asked him, sure that this boy must see that the steward was wrong about him.

The soldier continued to look at the prisoner's face, and there was hesitation etched into his expression. At last, he shook his head and looked back down at his own feet once more.

'I'm just travelling through, I promise,' Merric pleaded to him.

'It doesn't matter,' the soldier said, glancing at the door to the cell, worried that he would be in trouble if anyone overheard him talking to the prisoner. 'Milas is a good steward, but my father always used to say that once he got an idea in his head then nothing would make him change his mind.'

'Your father, is he a soldier too?'

'He was,' the soldier corrected. 'He's dead now.'

'Was he one of the soldiers who went with your knight to try and catch the murderer?'

The young soldier nodded. Merric sighed and let himself slide down the wall and into a sitting position.

'My father is dead too. And my mother,' he said truthfully. 'I never knew them.'

'I still live with my mother,' the soldier piped up eagerly, as though glad to have something that his prisoner did not.

'I'm sure she's very proud of you,' Merric said, 'being a soldier and everything.'

'I've only been a soldier a short while. Since Milas said he needed replacements. Sir Paravell took most of his soldiers with him, and none of them came back.'

'What's your name?' Merric asked him.

The young soldier hesitated for a moment, but then seemed to decide that it would do no harm to say.

'Warbric,' he said.

Despite his precarious predicament, Merric felt himself grin for the first time in days.

'That's a good name for a soldier,' he said.

Warbric smiled as well, before biting his lip hesitantly.

'They say that war might be coming. If the duke calls us up, then we'll have to march with him to war. I've never even seen a battle,' he said, as though it was a shameful thing to admit.

'I have,' Merric said.

'You have?'

'Just keep your head down, and listen to your leaders. Don't try and do anything heroic.'

Warbric nodded, thoughtfully. A shout came from outside the cell and he jumped. As he turned to leave, Merric tried his luck.

'Wait, Warbric. Do you think you could loosen these manacles? I can't really drink with both hands bound.'

Warbric dithered for a moment, weighing up Merric's request. Reasoning that even with one hand free the other would still be chained to the wall, he decided that it could do no harm to grant the prisoner's request. He moved forward and, giving Merric an uneasy glance, took a key from his belt. A few seconds later one of the manacles dropped away and Merric rubbed his freed wrist in relief.

'That's better,' Merric said, smiling at Warbric.

He reached forward and picked up the water jug and drank deeply from it. Warbric left the cell, locking it securely behind him. Merric closed his eyes and leant his head back against the rough stone wall of the cell. He knew that he could not stay there. If he was having to choose between being executed for a crime he did not commit, or being sent back to Eagle Mount, then he did not like the sound of either option. By asking the young soldier to free one of his wrists he had chosen a third option instead: Escape.

He had no idea whether it was day or night, but if he waited any longer then the choice between trying to escape and staying put might be taken away from him. He had no desire to meet his end at the hands of an executioner here in this village. So, the next time the door was unlocked and a soldier entered, Merric made his attempt. It was not Warbric who entered, but an older soldier with a thick red beard covering his jaw. Merric was glad; he would have found his escape attempt much harder had it been sweet, innocent Warbric. When the bearded soldier stooped down to collect the waste bucket, Merric swung the water jug with his freed hand, bringing it crashing down onto the soldier's head. He fell flat on his face, knocked out cold.

The crash had been loud and Merric froze for a few seconds, listening intently with bated breath, hoping that no one had heard. There was no shout of alarm. He stooped down and plucked the key from the soldier's belt, using it to free his second wrist. Free at last, he crept across the straw-strewn floor to the cell door and peered out. There was nothing there except for a stool and a table, where the soldier would sit when on guard duty. If there had been a second guard then Merric's escape attempt would have been that much more difficult. A single candle stood on the table, along with Merric's own pack that had been taken off him when he had been seized. He quickly checked through it, making sure that all his belongings were there, before hoisting it onto his shoulder. Moving quickly, in case anyone else was about arrive, he snuck up the stairs that led out of the dungeons.

Up ahead he could see a black sky, and he thanked his luck that he had timed his escape to be during the night. He emerged into the courtyard of the castle and crouched in the shadows, looking around. The simple castle keep stood to his left, and the gate to his right. A soldier was sat next to the gate, dozing lightly, and Merric knew he would never be able to get out that way without waking him and causing an alarm to be raised. He could silence the guard while he slept, using the dagger in his pack, but these soldiers were men of The Head. They had not done anything wrong, and certainly did not deserve to have Merric turn a blade on them.

Merric instead turned his attention to the walls. A single soldier was walking around the battlements, but his gaze was facing outside the walls at the surrounding land, not inwards into the courtyard, and so he did not see Merric. The walls were not tall, maybe only slightly taller than Merric himself. He knew that if he could get up there then he could climb over the battlements and drop silently down the other side.

He waited for the soldier up on the wall to reach the far side of the castle, before hurrying over to a ladder and quickly climbing up onto the walls. Reaching the top he crouched down again, glancing back, but the shape of the soldier on the far side of the walls did not seem to have heard him. Merric hopped up so that he was sat on the battlements, before swinging his legs over. The drop looked deceptively long in the darkness, but he knew that he would be fine. He took a breath and threw himself forward. His heart caught in his mouth for a moment, but a second later his feet hit the ground. He stumbled on landing, but managed to stop himself from falling flat on his face. Looking out at the darkened fields around him,

Merric could not help but smile at his successful escape. There was just one obstacle left.

The water-filled moat surrounded the castle, and while Merric doubted it was deep and he was sure he could easily wade across, he knew that the splashing was sure to draw the attention of the soldier on the wall. He therefore turned left and hurried around the base of the wall towards the gate, where a wooden bridge spanned the moat. He was halfway there when he saw shadowy shapes appear out of the darkness in front of him.

There were three of them, and they were heading right for him. Hurriedly, Merric pulled off his pack and reached in to grab his dagger. He heard the click of a crossbow being raised, and the scrape of a sword being drawn. In desperation, he reached forward and grabbed the closest of the shadows, putting his dagger to the figure's neck.

'Stop, Merric!' the shadow said in an urgent, hushed tone, and he recognised the voice of Kasper.

Stunned, Merric let him go. Kasper massaged his neck, before turning and speaking to his two companions.

'Ana? Tomas? It looks like we've found him.'

CHAPTER TWELVE

Four is company

Merric stared at the three of them in stunned surprise. They were the last people he had expected to come face to face with in the dead of night, here outside the walls of Porby Castle.

'What are you doing here?' he hissed in disbelief, whispering so as not to alert the soldier patrolling the battlements somewhere above them.

'Isn't it obvious?' Kasper muttered back. 'We've come to bust you out!'

Ana made an angry hushing sound, peering cautiously into the surrounding darkness, her crossbow in her hands.

'We need to get out of here, and quickly,' Tomas said, lowering his voice to an almost imperceptible whisper, looking just as anxious to be away from there as Ana did.

Without offering any more explanation, Ana hurried off through the darkness, with Tomas and Kasper following close behind her. With countless more questions spinning wildly around his head, Merric went after the others. They dashed around the curving base of the wall with the moat to their right. There was only a narrow strip of grass between the wall and the water, and Merric brushed one hand along the stones beside him to keep himself from toppling into the moat as he hurried along through the darkness.

A patch of orange light came into view ahead of them, silhouetting the familiar shapes of Kasper, Tomas and Ana as they led Merric to safety. Kasper was tall, with his long hair, broad shoulders and his longbow slung across his body. Tomas was short and had to pump his legs quickly to keep up with the others. Ana, at the front of the group, had her hair tied up in her usual style, the shape of her body hidden beneath the leather jerkin that she chose to wear.

The orange glow turned out to be coming from a brazier that was burning beside the closed gates, drenching the wooden bridge in light. As they drew closer Merric could see that the fire that crackled in the iron cage cast long shadows across the ground, and Merric knew that if the soldier on the walls looked down while they were crossing the bridge then he could not fail to see them. Ana crouched down, just outside of the patch of illuminated ground, and she put a finger to her lips. Kasper seemed to be listening intently as well, trying to hear the sound of the footsteps of the guard patrolling the battlements above. He and Ana seemed satisfied that the guard was on the other side of the castle and that the coast was clear. Kasper waved the others forward. They crept out onto the bridge, and Merric felt suddenly vulnerable and exposed in the bright light of the brazier.

They had almost reached the other side of the bridge when they heard the shout.

It was accompanied by the heavy tread of running feet, as someone hurried from the direction of the dungeons.

'Raise the alarm!' the voice shouted from within the courtyard. 'He's escaped!'

Kasper cursed, and throwing caution to the wind, they sped up into a run, not bothering to try and keep quiet. Another voice called out from above the gate, as the patrolling soldier finally spotted them.

'I can see him, he's on the bridge! You there! Halt!'

They did not stop, and the familiar voice of the castle steward shouted out.

'Shoot him!' he cried.

The soldier on the wall hesitated, having never shot at a person before. By the time he released the arrow, Merric and the others had reached the far side of the bridge and had disappeared into the darkness once more. The arrow sailed wide, clattering onto the road some way away. The castle gate crashed open at that moment, and half a

259

dozen figures came riding out on horseback, torches in their hands.

Ana lead the way as they sprinted through the village. The sound of hoofbeats was not far behind. They ran through the small square where Merric had been caught, and the newly built priory loomed out of the darkness. The door opened and the prior poked his head out, curious about the shouting that had broken the night. The horsemen behind them were gaining quickly, and it would only be seconds before they were caught. Thinking quickly, Ana made for the priory.

The prior instinctively stepped aside, letting the four figures run through the door and into his priory. It was in his nature to grant access to any who sought to commune with the Mother, but he quickly realised that the man and three youths who had just entered his priory were being pursued by the soldiers from the castle.

'I say!' the prior exclaimed. 'This is a holy place!'

'Sorry!' Ana called, genuinely, over her shoulder as they dashed between the rows of benches.

A few candles were lit, giving them enough light to see by. They ran all the way to the front of the priory, swerving towards a side door. At that moment their pursuers reached the front door, where the bewildered prior still stood in his nightgown.

'I am sorry, Milas,' the prior said, holding out a hand to stop the steward and the soldiers who had leaped down from their horses and tried to barge their way in. 'I cannot allow you to enter with your weapons.'

'Prior Simms!' the steward protested. 'They are getting away!'

'This is a house of the Mother,' Prior Simms insisted.

'Go around!' the steward said, turning back to his men. 'We'll cut them off!'

Ana, Merric, Kasper and Tomas ran through the side door, emerging into a small yard surrounded by a wooden fence where the prior seemed to keep his beehives.

'Split up!' came a shout. 'Don't let them get away!'

They vaulted the fence, Tomas with some difficulty, and hurried along the alleyway behind. Up ahead, where the alleyway spilled out onto a cottage-lined road, a pair of horsemen galloped past, their torches like bright yellow streaks in the blackness. Merric and the others hid in the darkness of the alley for a moment, checking the coast was clear, before darting out and running along the road. They were nearing the edge of the village, and Merric dared to believe that his escape from the castle would succeed. If they could just make it to the fields beyond the village then surely they would be able to disappear into the night, and be gone from here.

'This way!' Ana hissed, darting to the left when more torches appeared ahead of them.

They ducked between two cottages, listening to the shouts as the search party called out to each other. They hurried from garden to garden, leaping over fences and pushing their way through hedgerows, ignoring the faces of the villagers that were appearing at their windows, wondering at the commotion. A lane appeared in front of them, which appeared to lead out of the village. They turned onto it, making to disappear into the darkness, when the sudden snorting sound of a horse appeared behind them.

Spinning around, Merric saw one of the mounted soldiers galloping down their lane. The horse skidded to a halt at the sudden appearance of the four figures who were in its path. The soldier was just feet away from them, but he held the reins of his horse in one hand, and the burning torch in the other, leaving no hand free to draw his sword. All he could do was shout over his shoulder.

'Here! They're over here!'

Kasper swung his longbow like a club, knocking the torch from the startled soldier's hands. His horse reared in panic at the falling flames and the soldier could do nothing more than desperately try to stay in his saddle. With all of the soldier's attention focused on not falling from his horse, Ana led the others up the lane at a run, feeling the night close in around them as they left the village behind. The sound of hoofbeats was close behind them though, as the steward and the others responding to the soldier's shout raced after them. Looking around urgently, Kasper saw a narrow gap in the hedgerow.

'Through here!' he said. 'Quickly.'

They all struggled through the gap, Merric feeling his cloak catching on the brambles. Safely through to the field beyond, they crouched behind the hedge and watched as the soldiers galloped past their hiding place, Milas in their midst. Merric could see the steward's face in the light of their burning torches, his expression equal parts anger and disappointment at the thought of his prisoner's escape.

'They're gone,' Tomas said, peering through the gap in the hedge and looking up the lane towards the fading light of their torches.

There was the sound of a snapping twig and the four of them spun around. A soldier stepped out of the darkness with a loaded crossbow raised in his trembling hands. Merric recognised the young, scared face at once.

'Warbric,' he said calmly, raising his hands and indicating that the others should do the same. 'Don't shoot us.'

Ana narrowed her eyes, not wanting to take her hands off her own crossbow. She looked warily from Merric to the young soldier.

'I should call Milas back,' Warbric said, his eyes flickering in the direction that his fellow soldiers had gone in their hunt.

'You know I'm innocent,' Merric said to the young soldier, in what he hoped was a reassuring tone.

'Then why did you run?' Warbric demanded, brandishing the crossbow.

'We can't linger here,' Kasper muttered to Merric, leaning in close.

He had one eye on the lane behind them. The soldiers would realise their mistake soon enough, and when they rode back this way the game would be up.

'What are you whispering?' Warbric demanded, aiming the crossbow at Kasper instead.

'I know you're just wanting to serve your village,' Merric said to Warbric, 'and I can see that you're a good lad. But killing me and my friends won't bring back your father and the others.'

There was a sound of hoofbeats further up the lane as the steward and the others began heading back this way, and Merric looked pleadingly at the young soldier. Finally, Warbric lowered his crossbow

'Go,' he said, simply.

Kasper and the others did not need telling twice. They dashed into the field, away from the sound of the returning search party. Merric lingered just long enough to give Warbric a small smile and a nod, before hurrying off after them. Soon, the shape of Warbric and the village behind him were swallowed up in darkness. Somewhere, back in the direction of the village, Merric could hear the roar of frustration as the castle steward realised that his prisoner was gone for good. He hoped that Warbric had the sense to not say that he had seen them, and that the young soldier would not suffer any kind of punishment for letting them get away.

Merric, Kasper, Ana and Tomas kept going for another hour. The going was much easier than it had been the last few times that Merric had trekked through the pitch black of night. Kasper seemed to be able to see just as well in the dark as he could during the day. He had never before been to this part of The Head, but his natural comfort in the outdoors meant that he appeared to find the easiest paths to take with little effort. All Merric had to do was follow in his footsteps. They walked in silence, Kasper and Ana leading the way, followed by Merric with Tomas bringing up the rear. Merric's old squire was pacing along with his sword drawn in case any pursuers appeared, and there was a determined look on his young face.

They stopped for the night once they were confident they had put enough distance between themselves and the village to mean that they were in no danger of any pursuit stumbling into them. They took shelter in a dell nestled within a copse of trees, and Kasper even dared to light a fire. Merric savoured the heat of the flames and he held his hands out towards them. He had been shivering almost non-stop since he had left Eagle Mount days ago, and the cold, damp dungeon had done little to help. Now he felt warm for the first time in days.

Ana offered to take the first watch. She walked away from their simple camp, leaving Merric, Kasper and Tomas to enjoy the fire down in the bowl of the dell, while she climbed up into a tree. She sat there, in the crook between a branch and the trunk, and looked out into the night. She had not spoken a word to Merric as they had travelled, and had avoided even looking at him. Though, if he was being honest with himself, he would not have expected her to act any differently. He was just surprised to have been reunited with her at all, even more surprised than he was to see Kasper and Tomas.

'Just give her time,' Tomas said quietly, sitting himself down next to Merric.

Merric shook his head sadly.

'Time won't help,' he said. 'I really hurt her, Tomas.'

The young squire did not answer, and Merric knew this meant that Tomas agreed with him. There was a shower of embers as Kasper threw a few more branches onto the fire. The hunter yawned widely and laid himself down beside the fire, opposite where Merric and Tomas sat.

'How did you know I was there?' Merric asked, looking at him through the flames.

'I tracked you as far as the village,' Kasper said, his arms behind his head as he looked up at the night sky. The clouds were thinning at last, and even a few stars were visible in the sky above, mixing with the sparks floating up from the fire. 'While we were looking around the village we heard the folk talking about how the killer of someone called Sir Paravell had been caught.'

'We thought it would be too much of a coincidence that you had passed through the village at the exact same time that some criminal they had been hunting for was caught,' Tomas continued, looking at Merric. 'We figured that it was you they had locked up in their dungeons.'

'But why did you even come after me in the first place?' Merric asked, quietly. 'I'm not going back to Eagle Mount, so if that's why you came then it was a wasted journey.'

He did not want to sound ungrateful, but if that was their plan then Merric may as well have told the castle steward his real identity and saved them all a lot of bother. He swore to himself that not even these three could convince him to return to Eagle Mount.

'That's why everyone else is looking for you,' Kasper admitted.

'Did you see them?' Tomas asked Merric. 'Sir Orsten and Sir Oskar, and all the soldiers from the castle? Pretty much everyone has been out looking for you.'

'Yeah, I saw Sir Orsten,' Merric admitted.

'Then why didn't you go to him?' Tomas said.

'I didn't want them to find me,' Merric said, but he knew they would not understand. 'If you're going to try and talk me into going back then I'm leaving right now.'

He even stood up and reached for his pack.

'Sit down, Merric,' Kasper said, not moving from his laying position beside the fire. 'We're not going to try and talk you into anything.'

Merric looked at Tomas, who nodded reassuringly at him. Merric slowly sat back down again, glad that he would not have to leave the warmth of the fire at least.

'So if you're not going to drag me back, why did you come?'

'We just want to make sure you're alright,' Kasper said, with a kindness that Merric had never heard before.

He looked across at Kasper, feeling a surge of gratitude towards him. The hunter seemed to be the only one not judging Merric for the mistakes he had made. Tomas was being friendly towards him, but Merric could see that there was a different look in his eyes now. There was a look of disappointment behind his friendly smile.

'You shouldn't have come,' Merric said.

'The castle was in uproar when they found your letter,' Tomas explained. 'Everyone was really worried about you. Sir Oskar and Sir Orsten immediately led search parties to try and find you, and I went looking for Kasper. I knew we had to help find you, and Kasper can track better than anyone.'

'You had stayed in Eaglestone?' Merric asked Kasper.

A week had passed between Kasper hand-delivering Merric back to Eagle Mount, and Merric choosing to leave in the dead of night. He had assumed that Kasper had long since returned to Little Harrow.

'I stayed, just in case. I thought you might do something stupid,' Kasper said, chuckling. 'It turns out I was right.'

'I've been doing a lot of stupid things lately, it seems,' Merric said. 'If you could track me so easily, why didn't you help the Oakhearts to find me rather than come out here by yourselves?'

'We felt like you might not want to face them quite yet,' Kasper reasoned. 'Folk don't just run away for no reason, and I figured you wouldn't want to go back just yet.'

Merric nodded, and glanced up at the dark shape of Ana perched up in the tree with her back to them.

'And what about Ana?' he asked, keeping his voice low in case she overheard. 'How did you convince her to come along? I thought coming to try and find me would be the last thing she'd want to do'

'What do you mean?' Tomas said, confused. 'It was Ana's idea to come and help you in the first place.'

* * *

The following morning dawned a little brighter, but while the rainclouds seemed to have moved on it was clear that autumn had well and truly arrived. The sun no longer carried as much warmth in its rays, and Merric gave a shiver when he awoke. The fire had died out during the night, and Kasper stirred it back into life with some kindling. Ana slept on, wrapped tightly in her blanket. Kasper had taken over the watch from her halfway through the night, and he told Merric that he had not seen or heard a soul.

It had taken Merric a while to fall asleep, and it had been a long time after Kasper and Tomas' snores had echoed around the dell before sleep had finally taken him. His mind had raced around in circles while he had tried to decide what to do next. Going back to Eagle Mount was out of the question, but nor could he remain here. In his final moments before he had fallen asleep he had realised that there was only one real path he could take, and it was a path that he needed to take too.

With Ana now awake as well, Merric knew he had to speak to them all. He went over to where they were sitting together beside the fire that was slowly coming back to life.

'Thank you for coming to find me,' he said to them, 'and for looking out for me.'

'I sense a "but" coming,' Kasper smirked at Tomas. Merric ignored him.

'I can't tell you how much it means to me, to have friends at this time,' he continued.

'Of course we're still your friends,' Tomas said, as though he could not believe that Merric would ever doubt it. Ana, though, continued to avoid Merric's eye.

'But,' he said, confirming Kasper's suspicions, 'I need to try to make things up to The Head.'

'Then come back to Eagle Mount,' Tomas insisted. 'You've got to come back. It's your home. You're the duke! I know you made a mistake, but no one is blaming you as much as you're blaming yourself.'

Merric just shook his head.

'I *was* the duke,' he corrected Tomas, 'but I'm not anymore. I had a chance and I messed things up. No one would trust me to rule anymore, and The Head deserves a better leader.'

Tomas did not reply. Merric knew that he agreed with what he was saying, even if he was too kind to say such a thing out loud.

'So what will you do then?' Kasper asked, and Merric was glad that he at least had seemed to accept that Merric was not going back.

'Even in exile I can still serve The Head, and that's what I want to do. Maybe I can try to make up for the mistakes I've made. If I can do something that will make me forgive myself, then maybe The Head will be able to forgive me too.'

They looked at him expectantly. Kasper did not seem to like what he was getting at, but made a gesture to suggest that Merric should just spit it out. Ana was looking into the embers of the fire, remaining silent.

Merric sat down heavily beside them, hugging his knees to his chest.

'When Sir Sebastien was captured he was carrying a message to The Dale, to try and get Lord Godfrei Florin to agree to an alliance between The Head and The Dale,' he said. 'If I can get there, to Bluewall Castle, then maybe I'll be able to convince him to join the fight against the Monforts. Without them, we'll lose The Head to Aric.'

Kasper raised his eyebrows and rubbed the back of his head, letting out a whistle. Tomas looked at Merric in no small measure of alarm. Ana got to her feet and walked away, shaking her head.

'I mean, that's quite a journey,' Kasper said at last, breaking the silence that had greeted Merric's words.

'I know,' Merric said. 'But if there's a chance that I'm able to do some good for the dukedom then I have to try.'

'What makes you think you'll be able to make it to The Dale?' Tomas asked. 'Sir Sebastien wasn't able to. What if they capture you too?'

'It doesn't matter,' Merric shrugged. 'Without the support of the Florins, The Head will stand no chance. If I'm able to do this thing then I will gladly try, no matter what it might cost. I owe it to everyone.'

Kasper and Tomas looked at each other.

'Well, what do you think?' Tomas asked Kasper.

'I don't think we have a choice really.'

Merric knew what they were thinking.

'No way,' he said. 'I've had enough of others getting hurt because of me. I'm going on my own.'

'This sounds familiar,' Tomas said, surprising even himself by smirking slightly. He recalled a very similar conversation that had happened that summer in the Greenwood.

'But you have a good life,' Merric said to Tomas. 'You're going to be a knight! You can't throw all that away for me.'

'Who said I'm doing it for you?' Tomas retorted, still smiling slightly. 'We need to get The Dale on our side. Nothing is more important to The Head than that. What kind of knight would I be if I turned my back on that?'

'Okay then,' Merric tried again, turning to face Kasper instead. 'What about your family? I thought you'd had enough of adventure, and wanted a quiet life now? It's not like last time. Before, we were getting away from danger, but this time we'll be walking straight into it.'

'If the last summer has shown me anything,' Kasper said, getting to his feet and stretching as though the matter had already been settled, 'it's that you highborn folk could barely tie your bootlaces without my help. You won't get halfway to The Dale without me.'

Merric looked furiously at the two of them. He would be lying if he said that he was not grateful to them, but the last thing he wanted was to put them into unnecessary danger. He was doing this because he had gotten good folk killed, and leading Kasper and Tomas out of The Head hardly seemed like a good way to try and make up for that mistake. But he knew he would never be able to change their minds.

'What about Ana?' he asked them quietly, not wanting her to overhear.

She was several paces away, doing her best to ignore their conversation and was busying herself with rolling her blanket and slinging it over her shoulder with her crossbow.

'Oh, she's definitely with us,' Tomas said, grinning.

'Don't count on it,' Ana called without turning to face them.

Tomas' grin just widened, and Merric smiled nervously back at him. It was the first time she had spoken a word to him. He would take all the progress he could get. He hoisted his pack onto his shoulders, pulling out the small dagger that was his only weapon and sliding it into his belt.

'You're going to need more than that toothpick,' Ana said in a mocking tone.

'Yeah,' Merric admitted, looking down at the rather pathetic weapon.

Compared to Ana with her crossbow, Tomas with his sword and Kasper with his longbow, he may as well have been armed with a dandelion.

'I'll be on the lookout for something better,' Merric suggested.

Tomas cleared his throat.

He went over to his pack and untied a long, thin item that had been strapped to the side. He unwrapped the cloth that was tightly bound around it, revealing a sword.

It was *Hopebearer*.

'Perhaps, this?' Tomas said.

- CHAPTER THIRTEEN -

The bannerless

They travelled west, taking the most direct route towards the border of The Head, and The Dale which lay beyond. They walked through lands that none of them knew, but they knew that if they kept heading west then they would eventually reach the river, and then it would be a simple case of following it downstream to Bridge Ford where they would hopefully be able to cross. Merric did not know how easy it would be for them to pass through the castle of Lord Tymon Conway without being recognised. And he did not even know whether they would even still be allowing travellers to pass over the river, with the threat of war looming. But that was a problem they would not need to worry about for a few days yet.

The land grew steadily wilder in this northern part of The Head. The rolling landscape of sprawling meadows, patchworks of fields and pleasant little woods gave way to steep valleys and windswept hilltops, crisscrossed with dry stone walls. The soaring peaks of the Storm Mountains rose up to their right as they walked. Their summits were shrouded in clouds and the first of the year's snow, and their flanks were covered with dense forests of pine trees. The land along which they travelled was dotted with great rocks that jutted out of the mossy undergrowth like mountains straining to break through the ground and join their giant brothers to the north. It was tiring hiking across this hilly, uneven land.

'You didn't think to bring horses with you?' Merric said, half-jokingly.

'We would if we could,' Tomas admitted.

He explained that when Merric's disappearance had been discovered, Eagle Mount had been a hive of activity. Everyone had wanted to help with the search.

'There wasn't a horse to be found in the castle or in Eaglestone,' Tomas admitted.

And so they travelled on foot. Occasional flocks of sheep bleated and scurried away when Merric, Kasper, Ana and Tomas walked past, but apart from them and the occasional shepherd they saw little sign of life. The farms they passed were small and simple, and even from the tops of the craggy hills Merric could not see any villages or towns for miles.

They sheltered the next night in the ruined remains of an old castle, long abandoned, sitting on a lonely hilltop. The stones were bare and weather-beaten, and not even moss or ivy grew on the ancient walls. It had collapsed in some places, and yawning holes gaped in the walls, but it at least offered a small amount of shelter. Still, the wind that howled between the ancient stones chilled them, and Kasper's attempts to light a fire were fruitless. There was no roof above them, and so they were at least thankful that it was not raining. Tomas and Merric huddled close together beneath their cloaks for warmth, while Ana preferred to sit by herself, her arms hugging her knees to her chest.

They set off again the next morning, aching from their restless and largely sleepless night. If anything, the wind had gotten even stronger since the previous evening. Merric's legs were sore from the constantly rising and falling ground, and every time they reached the crest of the next hill he would hope that it would be the last. But, every time, when they reached the top they would be greeted by the monotonous sight of yet another valley and another wild hill beyond it.

On occasion they would find their way forwards blocked by cliffs of rock that were much too tall and steep for them to attempt to climb. When they came across such obstacles they had no choice but to walk north or south, parallel to the cliff, looking for a point where it was low enough for them to scale without fear of falling.

As harsh and inhospitable as the land was, Merric had to admit that there was a beauty to it. This part of the dukedom had been largely untouched by the hands of people, and there was something oddly peaceful about the wild hills and the jutting outcrops of rock and the pine forests, and the tumbling streams that wound between them. If he were not in such a hurry to reach The Dale, and if the wind that blew across the exposed hills was not so cold, then he could have enjoyed his time there. But, as it was, the difficult terrain was exhausting him, and the cold was making him dispirited.

Signs of wildlife were scarce on the barren hilltops. But, in the valleys, they sometimes came across small pine woods, growing defiantly in the shelter where the wind could not batter them. When they discovered these small woods Kasper and Ana would hurry ahead, their longbow and crossbow at the ready. Most times they came out of the trees moments later, shaking their heads in disappointment, but one time Kasper emerged with a catch over his shoulder, smiling triumphantly. They quickly made a fire there and then, and ate hungrily before continuing on their way, their spirits momentarily lifted by the meal. But, after a couple of hours, the memory of the food had faded and they were once more thinking only about the challenges of the journey.

They talked little as they walked. They were so out of breath from the difficult hiking that all they could do was try and save their energy. Even when they did try to speak they had to shout in order to be heard over the howling wind that tugged on their cloaks. As fate would have it, the wind was blowing from the west, directly into their faces. At times, when the gale was at its strongest, it felt as though they took one step back for every step forward. If the others were regretting their decision to so willingly accompany Merric on his journey then they were gracious enough not to say so. Each of them just walked with their head bowed to the wind, focusing on putting one foot in front of the other.

They did not follow a particular path, but it was simple forward enough for them to keep heading in the direction they needed to go. Even with the overcast sky hiding the position of the sun it was not hard for them to keep going straight. The great Storm Mountains were to the north and the Greenwood lay miles to the south, visible as a great green blanket from their vantage point, so all they had to keep doing was walk straight between them.

It was such difficult going that on several occasions Merric wondered whether they would have done better to have travelled south to the Great East Road, and then journeyed along that through the Greenwood and onwards towards Bridge Ford. But every time he thought this he reminded himself that route would take them close to Eagle Mount and Oaktyn, where he was sure that the everyone would still be on the lookout for him. And travelling along the Great East Road, while certainly easier, carried a much higher risk of being recognised. But the fact that he was taking this more difficult route through the highlands out of choice gave him little comfort as he trudged wearily across the wild land.

When they stopped by a stream to drink from the cold water, Tomas saw Merric stood on a hillock, staring to the north. He approached him, asking Merric what he was looking at.

'There's Storm Hall,' Merric said, pointing.

Tomas looked in the direction indicated. There was a castle nestled in the mountains in the far distance. Its walls rose in levels as the castle clung to the steep side of a mountain face.

'The home of Lord Temothy Bloom?' Tomas asked.

He had been studying the noble families of The Head as part of his training to one day become a knight.

Merric nodded.

'An impressive sight,' Kasper said, a little impatiently. Clearly he did not think it was the time for sightseeing.

Merric turned away from the distant castle and hopped down from the hillock. He did not know this land, but he had assumed that they had crossed into the barony of the Bloom family. The Blooms were a dour folk, due to their harsh lives in the storm-ravaged mountains in the north of The Head. Merric had once seen Lord Temothy Bloom, Baron of Storm Hall, when he had visited Eagle Mount to discuss matters with Lord Roberd. He had looked fearsome with his wild beard and leathery and weather-beaten face, and he and his men had resembled brigands in their leather and wool clothes. But that evening Lord Roberd had explained to Merric that there were none more loyal to The Head than the Blooms; whenever battle was called, it would always be the Blooms who answered first. Merric's mind drifted up to the mountains to the draughty chambers of Storm Hall, where Lord Temothy likely was right now. He wondered what the grim baron must think about him. He was a proud man, dedicated to his duty as Baron of Storm Hall, and would surely have little respect for someone who was too ashamed of their actions to continue with their own duty as the duke. He knew that his decision to leave The Head to Sophya had been the right one, and he knew she would do a better job than he had done.

As the sun began to set that evening they kept their eyes open for somewhere they could shelter. None of them much fancied another uncomfortable night exposed to the wind. There were certainly no inns around this wild part of The Head, and they had not even seen a farmhouse in hours. The hills stretched onwards as far as their eyes could see in the failing light, and the ruined old castle they had slept in the night before was starting to sound luxurious. Just when they were thinking that they would probably have to settle for curling up between a jumble of rocks, their luck at last turned. As they descended into another steep valley they spied a tumbledown old barn at its bottom. The roof looked patchy and its walls old, but it was better than they could have hoped for. If nothing else, it would keep the wind off them and keep them mostly dry if it started to rain.

Emboldened by their discovery, they walked a bit faster as they picked their way down the side of the hill towards the barn. Merric thought excitedly about the good night's sleep he would get, and he knew the others felt the same. None of them had been able to sleep more than an hour or two the night before, and their journey across the highlands had been exhausting and their legs ached terribly. The barn looked like it was used to house sheep during the winter months when snow settled in these exposed highlands, but Merric had no shame in pretending he was a sheep for one night if it would give him shelter. Even Kasper, who normally never gave any signs of discomfort, looked eager to be indoors and out of the wind. He led the way towards the barn, but he drew up short when they were just twenty paces away. He threw out an arm to stop the others.

'What's wrong?' Merric asked him, keen to be inside.

'I can see someone moving around in there,' he warned.

Surprised, Merric peered through the twilight. He could just make out something moving inside the barn, visible through the small window. There was a small flicker of light.

'Shepherds?' Merric guessed.

'Could be,' Kasper said.

'Maybe they would let us stay there with them?' Tomas said hopefully.

'Hold it right there!'

All four of them spun around at the voice and saw a young man, stubble growing on his jaw, pointing a longbow at them. He had the arrow aimed directly at Kasper, the most threatening-looking of their group, and when he spoke he directed his words at him.

'Don't try anything, now,' the young man said.

Ana reached for her crossbow, but Kasper stopped her with a wave of his hand.

'Don't!' he hissed at her.

Ana reluctantly removed her hands from her crossbow, but looked dangerously at the young man who was threatening them. Merric had been on the receiving end of that stare before, and was not surprised to the see the archer gulp nervously.

'We didn't know this barn was taken,' Kasper said. 'Our apologies. We'll move on.'

Figures emerged from the barn, no doubt drawn by the sound of voices. There were three of them, each armed to the teeth with spears and swords. They were dressed like soldiers, but the symbol that had been stitched onto their jerkins had been roughly torn off, leaving threads hanging there. Merric thought they looked like deserters.

'Well, well, well,' said one of the soldiers, a strong-looking man with a rust coloured beard. 'What do we have here?'

'Caught them skulking around the barn, serjeant,' the archer said, his longbow still aimed at the four of them.

'We weren't skulking,' Merric objected, feeling slightly insulted despite the danger.

'We're just passing through,' Kasper said to the serjeant with the beard who seemed to be their leader. 'We didn't know you were here. All we sought was shelter for the night.'

'A likely story,' the serjeant said, waving his sword menacingly at them. 'Hunting us, more like.'

'Hunting you?' Merric said, nonplussed.

'Who are you?' Tomas asked, trying his hardest to not look concerned by the weapons pointing at them. He was not sure that he felt ready to put his newly learned sword skills to the test quite yet.

The soldiers ignored him.

'Get in there and grab a torch. I want to get a good look at them,' the serjeant said to one of the soldiers stood behind him, a hulking man holding a spear in his strong hands.

As the huge soldier turned and went to go into the barn, Merric caught a glimpse of the shield he had slung over his back. While it looked like he had tried to scrape away the symbol painted on its surface, Merric could clearly make out the black marching knight on the peeling and flaking paint.

'They're Monforts!' he said, his hand automatically reaching for the hilt of *Hopebearer*.

'Ah, ah, ah!' the serjeant said warningly with a smirk, and the young man with the longbow switched his aim to Merric instead.

'Keep your hands where I can see them!' the archer demanded.

Gritting his teeth, Merric released his hand from his sword.

'You're just passing through, eh?' the serjeant said when he was satisfied that Merric was not going to do anything foolish.

Kasper nodded, with his arms outstretched to assure the Monfort men that he was no threat to them.

'We don't know who you are,' he promised the soldiers, 'and we're certainly not hunting you.'

'No one travels around this forsaken place,' the fourth soldier said, standing behind the serjeant and sniffing at them disapprovingly with an upturned nose.

'Only those who don't want to be discovered,' agreed the serjeant.

'Like you?' Merric said, filled with hatred at the sight of the Monfort men.

'Shut up,' Ana hissed angrily at him, quiet enough that no one else would hear.

Merric ignored her. He hated everyone who served Lord Aric, and he certainly did not want a conversation with them. He fought the urge to reach for his sword again.

'If they're thieves or outlaws then maybe they have something valuable on them,' the soldier with the upturned nose said with a sneer.

'I assure you, we have nothing of value,' Kasper said. 'It's true, we've been avoiding the Great East Road it is true, but not for the reasons you think. We're not thieves nor outlaws.'

The hulking soldier emerged from the barn with a burning torch in his hand, and the serjeant snatched it from him. He came closer, the torch held high above him to cast a light over Merric and the others. They winced and shied away from the harsh light that was blinding them.

The soldier with the sneering face got a closer look at the hilt of *Hopebearer* at Merric's waist, and his eyebrows rose in interest.

'That's a mighty fine sword you've got there,' he said, his eyes moving up to Merric's face.

He paused, a frown appearing on his brow. Merric could tell that the soldier recognised him, and was trying to place where he knew his face from.

'Are you…*him*?' the soldier asked, disbelief passing over his features.

'Who?' Merric asked, playing for time. If these Monfort soldiers discovered that they had Merric at their mercy then he would not fancy his chances.

'It *is* him!' the soldier said excitedly to the serjeant. 'I recognise him!'

The bearded serjeant stepped closer and his own face turned into a frown as he studied Merric.

'This boy? You think it's him who killed Sir Rayden?' he said, doubtfully.

Unable to contain his anger any longer, Merric wrenched *Hopebearer* free of his scabbard and held it out in front of him. Ana whipped up her crossbow, Kasper notched an arrow to his bowstring and Tomas' own sword appeared in his hands. The time for words were over.

'Calm yourselves,' the serjeant said, chuckling. He sheathed his own sword. 'You know what, I think you're right, Bryn. It's him. I recognise that sword.'

'Yes,' Merric said, seeing nothing to be gained by lying. 'It was me that killed Rayden. And I'll kill you too, for what the Monforts have done to The Head.'

But to Merric's complete surprise, at a gesture from the serjeant, the other soldiers also lowered their weapons. Even the archer behind them lowered his longbow and let the string go slack.

'What's going on?' Ana asked, eyeing them warily.

She kept her crossbow raised, and Kasper and Tomas showed equal signs of distrust and did not lower their own weapons either.

The serjeant gave a bark of a laugh and, ignoring *Hopebearer*, put his strong arm around Merric's shoulders.

'Come on, come inside,' the serjeant said cheerfully.

The man's grip was so tight that Merric could not have broken away even if he had tried, and had no choice but to allow himself to be steered into the interior of the barn. Kasper, Ana and Tomas followed close behind, their weapons only half lowered as they looked around suspiciously. Inside the barn, and out of the chilly wind, it was warm and comfortable. A small fire crackled in the centre of the floor, and the soldiers had found stored sacks of wool that they had used to make comfortable chairs to sit on. The serjeant sat himself down with a weary groan and took a long swig from a skin of wine and offered it up to Merric, who did not accept. The other soldiers edged past Merric and collapsed onto other sacks.

Merric looked around at the other three, dumbfounded. A minute ago they had been aiming at each other with weapons, and now their once-captors were lounging around casually.

'Who *are* you?' Tomas asked them.

'They're Monfort soldiers,' Merric said venomously.

'We *were* Monfort soldiers,' the serjeant corrected him. 'Come and sit down, all of you. You're making me uncomfortable, all stood there.

Merric ignored them, and remained standing.

'What do you mean you *were* Monfort soldiers,' he asked.

The serjeant took another gulp of wine and sat back, looking thoughtful.

'What you all need to realise,' he said, 'is that the first victims of Aric Monfort were the people of The Southstones themselves.'

288

'I don't understand,' Merric said.

'I know what the rest of High Realm thinks about us,' the serjeant said, 'but not everyone in The Southstones are like the Monfort family.'

'And yet you fought for Aric?' Merric said, accusingly.

'You think we had a choice?' the serjeant counted.

'Everyone has to serve in the army of The Southstones,' the soldier with the upturned nose said. 'It isn't optional.'

'Why do you think the Monforts are able to have such a big army?' the young archer added.

'Wait,' Merric said, not believing it for one second. 'You're telling me that the soldiers who fight for the Monforts are doing so unwillingly? I'm not stupid enough to believe that. I've seen first-hand what they're capable of.'

'No, we're not saying that,' the serjeant agreed. 'Don't get me wrong, the four of us are in the minority for sure. There are more like us, but most think the sun shines out of the Monforts' asses. That family has ruled The Southstones from day one. Imagine how much you lot here love the Jacelyns? Well that's what it's like in The Southstones with the Monfort family, except the Monforts come down hard on anyone who don't worship the ground they walk on.'

'It's been going on for hundreds of years,' the archer added. 'Now, folk don't even realise that their loyalty is down to fear more than anything else.'

'So how did you end up here?' Kasper asked.

'I bet they came with the lot who captured Eagle Mount,' Merric said with dislike. 'I bet they helped with the murders of the Jacelyns, too.'

'We never agreed with what happened,' the serjeant argued, raising a finger. 'But what could we do? Soldiers are trained to follow orders, and the Monforts have a way of dealing with those who disobey them. You're afraid of the Monforts? Imagine living beneath their rule.'

'So you ran away?' Tomas asked them.

'We were at Eagle Mount when you led the uprising,' the serjeant said, looking at Merric. 'As soon as we saw that Rayden was dead, we scarpered. We saw it as our chance to get away from the Monforts once and for all.'

Merric glanced at Kasper, who seemed to be believing them. The Monfort symbol that had been scratched off their shields and unstitched from their jerkins seemed to back up their story that they had abandoned their loyalty to Lord Aric.

'So what are you doing now?' Tomas asked the soldiers.

'We're not really sure, the truth be told,' the serjeant said, turning to the younger boy and scratching his beard beneath his chin. 'We're bannerless right now. Not really got a home, nor someone to follow or call our leader. Once the heat has worn off a bit we'll try and start a new life here, I guess.'

290

Now that it seemed the four soldiers were not a danger, Kasper and Tomas sat themselves down, and only reluctantly did Merric join them. He was glad to get his weight off his feet, but Ana remained standing near the door. The soldiers did not give her a second glance. As far as they were concerned, it meant more wine for them.

'So what in the Mother's name are you doing all the way out here?' the serjeant said to Merric. 'I thought you'd be over in Eagle Mount, preparing to fight this war with Aric.'

Merric did not want to admit to these strangers that he had given up his role as duke, so he skirted around the question.

'You know, there's still a hope in The Head that it won't come to war,' he said.

The soldiers all looked at each other and then burst out laughing.

'What's so funny?' Ana said, eyeing them suspiciously. She seemed unready to befriend the men who had served the Monforts up until recently. To her, it seemed that uniforms and loyalties could not so easily be discarded

'I like your positive outlook,' the serjeant said to Merric, tears of laugher in his eyes, 'but if the Monforts are wanting war then that's what'll happen. Aric always gets what he wants.'

'Well, we don't know for certain what exactly it is that he wants,' Merric said hotly, not enjoying being

291

laughed at. 'He tried to have me captured, but he hasn't shown any sign of wanting to march his whole army into The Head.'

'Sorry, where have you been?' the soldier with the upturned nose said, disbelieving.

Merric and the others just stared at him, not understanding what he was getting at.

The serjeant looked back at them, equally confused.

'A whole damned army is camped right across the river. It sure looks like he's planning an invasion to me. The Mother help those poor souls at Bridge Ford who gotta to stop them.'

'Aric's army is just outside The Head?!' Merric exclaimed.

'How have you not heard that, back in Eagle Mount?' the serjeant said, just as surprised by the news that Merric did not already know.

'I've been gone a few days,' Merric said, pushing this aside. 'Are you certain of this?'

'That's what I hear,' the serjeant said, returning to his skin of wine. 'Ten thousand men have assembled there, that's what they're saying. Apparently they're led by one of Aric's nephews, Sir Axyl maybe. And that'll only be a tiny portion of the soldiers Aric has available to him, especially with the king supporting him too.'

Merric jumped to his feet, looking at his companions.

'We've got to get going,' he said to them urgently. 'If he's gathering his army, it won't be too long until he's ready to invade.'

'But,' Tomas protested, 'if they're waiting on the other side of the bridge then we would never be able to get across!'

'You're trying to cross the river?' the serjeant said, looking from Merric to Tomas. 'No chance. You'd walk straight into them. Do yourself a favour and get back to Eagle Mount instead.'

Merric sat back down again slowly, realisation sinking in. Of course, Lord Aric was not just preparing the army to assault Bridge Ford, but also to stop anyone from The Head from leaving. He had laid siege to the whole dukedom. And then, once Lord Aric had finished mustering his entire army of men from The Southstones and The Kingsland, he would march them to join these men at the river, and together they would launch their assault on The Head.

'I can't go back to Eagle Mount,' Merric said, dejectedly. 'If the invasion is really coming then I have to cross the river.'

'Well you can't,' the serjeant said simply, swigging some wine. 'Not unless you fancy seeing yourself as a corpse or a prisoner.'

'Although…' the young archer said, hesitantly.

'Although?' the serjeant prompted, impatiently.

The archer turned to Merric.

'Look, I've been thinking about this. When we came to Eagle Mount with Aric and Rayden we crossed over the river at Bridge Ford and came that way. But, a second force came after us, commanded by Lord Warner Camoren of Pooltyn. He waited in the Greenwood until…'

'Until Rayden and Aric had murdered the Jacelyns, and he swooped in with all his soldiers,' Merric finished with a scowl.

'Erm, yes,' the soldier said, looking uncomfortable. 'Anyway, that second force was much larger, right? Enough to overpower all your Jacelyn soldiers. You must have wondered where all those extra men came from that night, surely? Now, your baron at Bridge Ford would never have allowed them to enter The Head. So I was thinking that there must be another way of crossing the Rush.'

'There's only one way of crossing the Rush,' the soldier with the upturned nose said, rolling his eyes with his arms crossed. 'Everyone knows that.'

'Only one crossing that we know of,' the young soldier corrected, not discouraged. He sounded excited to be sharing this theory that he must have been thinking about for a long time. 'If there's another crossing, then it could be a way of getting over the river without running into the army waiting across from Bridge Ford.'

'You're just talking rubbish,' the soldier with the upturned nose retorted.

'Such things can wait until the morning,' the serjeant said, breaking up the argument. 'I'm tired, and need some shuteye. You lot should stay here tonight. No point in blundering around in the pitch black.'

But sleep did not come easily to Merric, despite the surroundings being much more comfortable than they had been in days. Was there really a second crossing over the river somewhere? He knew that what the soldier was saying made sense. Surely Lord Tymon Conway would never have let Lord Warner Camoren and the small Monfort army into The Head that summer? He would have known that Lord Aric and his knights and a handful of soldiers were visiting Lord Roberd, and would have given them permission to pass. But would he have allowed a whole column of soldiers, not expected by Lord Roberd, to march unobstructed into The Head? Surely not. That could only leave the option that there must indeed be some other way of crossing the river and entering The Head. Some way that was not common knowledge. And if you could enter The Head by this secret route then you could leave The Head by it too.

Merric knew that if the crossing really did exist then he had to find it. He had to get to The Dale. If the Monfort army was preparing for war then he had to secure the alliance with the Florins, or else The Head was doomed.

CHAPTER FOURTEEN

Rosewood

When they made to leave the next morning, after the soldiers had fed them a breakfast of bread and cheese, the serjeant had tried to discourage Kasper from going with Merric.

'You look like you're handy with that bow,' he said. 'Fancy joining my little band?'

Kasper politely declined the offer, and they set off while the sun was still low in the eastern sky behind them. Merric had eventually fallen asleep the previous night, his thoughts and worries finally pushed from his mind in favour of much needed rest. But even the relative comforts of the barn and a half decent breakfast did little to raise his spirits after the shattering news that the crossing at Bridge Ford was barred to them.

None of the others had attempted to discourage Merric when he told them that despite this set back he could not give up, and had to find a way to cross the river.

They knew that Merric would not be put off on his quest to reach The Dale, and they had promised to go with him.

'Do you think it's true?' Merric asked Kasper, walking along beside him as they left the soldiers and the barn behind them. 'That there's another way to cross the Rush?'

Ana and Tomas seemed to be listening in too, as though eager to hear whether their continued journey westward was pointless or if there was still a hope of reaching The Dale.

'I did hear rumours,' Kasper admitted, though he looked unsure.

'Rumours are the best thing we've got right now,' Merric said, looking sullen. 'What have you heard?'

Kasper looked reluctant.

'There are stories of a man who lives around here somewhere, in the mountains,' Kasper said as he strode along. 'According to the rumours he knows a way of crossing the Rush whenever he chooses to.'

'You think it's the same crossing that the soldier was talking about last night?' Merric asked him. 'The one that Lord Warner would have used with the rest of the Monfort soldiers?'

'I don't even know if the stories about this man are true,' Kasper said, not wanting Merric to get carried away. 'Some folk talk of there being a ford or something that can be safely crossed if you know where it is, and that's what this man uses. Other folk say that he can sprout wings and fly over the river.'

'That's not true, surely,' Merric said.

'Of course it's not,' Kasper said. 'It's complete rubbish. But that's what happens when rumours are started. The truth gets twisted and no one knows what is real and what is made up. This man definitely can't fly, of course, and he might not even know a way of crossing the river at all. Who knows, maybe the man himself doesn't even exist.'

'He exists,' Merric said, firmly, wanting to believe it. 'The crossing exists. And finding this man is our best chance of finding it and making it across the river.'

He was not sure why he was so convinced that the hidden crossing over the river was real. He had not heard about it before the previous night when the archer had spoken about it, and for his whole life he had grown up knowing that the Rush was impassable apart from at Bridge Ford. True, he had managed to cross the river when he had fallen in and washed up on the eastern bank, but that had been more luck than anything else. Many had tried to swim across the river, but none had made it.

But Merric just knew that there had to be another crossing, and he had never been so certain about anything before in his whole life. It was not just because of what the young soldier had said, about how surely Lord Tymon Conway had not allowed an uninvited Monfort force to march across the bridge, but because if there was not another crossing then Merric's quest to reach The Dale would have failed before it had even begun. And he knew that he could not fail. The fate of The Head depended on him not failing.

'Even if we do find the crossing, do we think it would be safe?' Tomas asked, sounding a little concerned. 'I don't fancy wading into the river and being swept away.'

'We've got to try,' Merric said to him. 'We need to find it. Not just so we can get to The Dale, but so that we can make sure that the Monforts don't use it again. If they already know about the crossing then surely they will use it again when they are ready to invade The Head, to outflank Bridge Ford.'

'That's true,' Tomas admitted. 'If we find the crossing then we'll have to send word to Sophya and the others.'

They had reached the top of the valley and the barn behind them disappeared from sight. Merric wondered what the deserters from the Monfort army would do next, but he could not think about them now. They still had a long journey ahead of them before they would reach the river. The one positive was that the clouds were beginning to clear, and they could see a hint of blue sky beyond. The morning was chilly and they wrapped their cloaks tightly around themselves, but they were all looking forward to feeling the sun on their faces.

'What do you both think?' Merric asked, looking at Kasper and Ana.

Ana's face was passive, as though she neither had an opinion nor cared. Her presence there with them, though, betrayed that she did care, even if she chose not to admit it. Merric wondered how long he would be punished by her for what he had said, and whether they would ever be friends again.

'Your logic makes sense,' Kasper said. 'We need to get to The Dale, and we need to make sure the Monforts aren't planning to use a back way into The Head.'

'You're all forgetting one thing,' Ana interjected.

'What?' Merric asked, trying to think of what he had missed.

'We have no idea where the crossing is. It could be anywhere.'

'I don't think so,' Kasper countered. 'It can't be south of Bridge Ford. The river there is far too wide.'

'Okay then,' Ana allowed. 'But even if it's somewhere north of Bridge Ford then surely that's still miles and miles for us to search. And I assume it would be really hard to find, otherwise everyone would know where it is.'

'Don't forget who you have with you,' Kasper pointed out. If I put my mind to it, I bet you I'll be able to find this crossing.'

'But you said there's a man somewhere in the mountains who knows where it is,' Merric put in.

'No, I said there are *rumours* of a man who knows where it is. A hermit living alone up in a cave, apparently. He's probably mad, if he even exists.'

'But there's no sense in looking blindly for the crossing when this man can tell us exactly where it is.'

'So we go and find him,' Tomas said, agreeing with Merric and looking to his right at the sheer wall of mountains that ran from east to west, like an enormous grey wave topped with storm clouds. 'If he knows where it is then it'll save us searching the river ourselves.'

'We'd never find him,' Kasper said, with a shake of his head. 'I only told you about him because the story about him tallied up with what that soldier said. He would be even harder to find than the crossing itself would be, and we don't even know for sure that either exists.'

'Someone must know where we can find him,' Merric insisted.

'What else do the stories about him say?' Tomas asked.

Kasper sighed, as though they would do better thinking about a plan for how they will find the crossing themselves, rather than waste time thinking about the stories of a man who may or may not even be real.

They splashed across a shallow river which barely reached the tops of their boots, and continued on when they reached the other side.

'The stories say that he is from Rosewood,' he said at last. 'Apparently he was a prior, before he decided to go

301

off on his own. The cloister in Rosewood is where he was taught.'

Merric thought back to the great map in his study in Eagle Mount. The village of Rosewood lay in the north-west of The Head, and could not be much further than a day ahead of them. He had heard of the cloister there, where young priors and prioresses lived and were taught, ready to be dispatched around the dukedom to serve in priories.

'He's a prior?' Merric asked, surprised.

'Apparently. Well, at least he *was*,' Kasper corrected. 'The stories say that he left, for some reason.'

'Then those who live at the cloister might know where he is,' Merric said, feeling encouraged. 'It's the best shot we have, anyway.'

He picked up the pace, glad to have a solid plan of action. Tomas went with him, while Kasper and Ana followed behind. Neither of them seemed as eager as Merric was to follow up on the lead. They walked hard all day. The land grew a little less wild as they headed further west. The hills began to flatten and the barren and weather-beaten grasslands turned into fertile fields. The sheep here were plumper and their woollen coats were whiter and more healthy-looking. Merric began seeing farmers at work in the fields, and the occasional farmhouse and small castle could be spotted on distant hilltops. For the first time in a couple of days they even came across a road, and while it was narrow and overgrown they enjoyed the feeling of having a hard surface beneath their feet rather than having to pick their way over uneven, stony ground.

Merric had been growing nervous of the idea of returning to Bridge Ford and crossing the great bridge that spanned the Rush there. Not only did he doubt that he would be able to pass through without being recognised, but the idea of revisiting the place where he had suffered the terrible defeat and gotten so many good knights killed had filled him with a cold panic. Now that he had been able to spend some time thinking about it, learning that the bridge was now barred to them by the Monfort army that waited on the other side was actually a slight relief to him. Now all they had to do was find this other way of getting to the other side of the Rush.

As the afternoon sun began to dip in the sky ahead of them they got their first glimpse of Rosewood. The village lay in the base of a valley and the buildings were clustered around a stream that wended its way along the valley floor. It was a large village, certainly bigger than Little Harrow, and this was most likely because Rosewood was also home to the cloister. Many folk visited the school for priors and prioresses, spending their coins at the inns of Rosewood and making the village into a wealthy place. That attracted more folk to come and live there, and over the years Rosewood had grown. To the east of the village stood the cloister itself, and Merric and the others had a good view of it from their vantage point on the hill that overlooked the village. The cloister was a large stone building with a courtyard at its centre and red tiles on its roof. A wall surrounded it, enclosing both the cloister and the orchards and gardens that made up its grounds. But the gate was open, and folk were coming and going freely. It looked like a friendly, welcoming place.

Feeling encouraged, Merric led the way down into the valley. They followed the road that was flanked on both sides by dry stone walls that kept the sheep in their fields. They began to see more travellers on the road, who greeted them in friendly tones as they passed. As the ground levelled out and the cloister drew nearer, Tomas hurried forwards to walk beside Merric.

'Do you think they'll be able to help us?' he asked.

'I hope so,' Merric said. 'If anyone will know where we can find that man we're looking for, then it'll be them.'

They reached a fork in the road, and followed the one which led up to towards the open gates of the cloister. A brown-robed novice stood beside them, and he looked up when he saw Merric and the others approach.

'Greetings, travellers,' he said, bowing his head in welcome.

'Greetings,' Merric replied. He looked awkwardly round at the others. 'Erm, we're wondering if you'd be able to help us find someone. He used to live here, we think.'

'Of course,' the smiling novice said. 'If you head on up to the main building then someone will be glad to assist you.'

He gestured for them to head on through the gates, and Merric and the others went through.

'They seem friendly,' Merric said, once the novice was out of earshot..

They walked up the path that led between beehives and orchards, where more novices harvested fresh honey and gathered baskets of ripe apples. Clearly there was more to learning to be a prior than just reading books. Some of the novices called out words of welcome to Merric and his friends as they walked past, while others carried on with their work, sweating a little in the thick robes worn by all the novices. Merric, too, had noticed a little more warmth in the day since they had left the highlands behind.

An older man in prior's robes was stood near the main doors that led into the cloister, and he must have seen them coming as he approached the new arrivals, spreading his arms out warmly.

'Welcome, all,' he said. 'Do you seek shelter? Food? We can offer either here.'

Tomas opened his mouth, possibly eager to take up the offer of food, but Merric took a step forwards.

'We're looking for some information,' he said. 'I'm wondering if you could help?'

The prior looked a little surprised, but bowed his head.

'If I am able to help then I will of course endeavour to do so.' He gestured with an arm. 'Come with me to my study.'

They followed him through the doors and into the interior of the Cloister. He walked gracefully, in the manner that all priors seemed to, with his hands clasped together beneath his wide sleeves and his back straight. They walked down hallways with high, vaulted ceilings, and Merric peered with interest through the doorways that they passed. In the kitchens novices were toiling over hot stoves, while in another chamber rows of yet more novices were listening intently to a prior as he gave a sermon. They passed more chambers of novices reading from great tomes and chanting in unison. Merric noticed that not all of them were young. Indeed, some had greying hair and looked to be in their winter years.

'Our novices receive the calling at all different ages,' the prior said to Merric, seeing him look in surprise at three older novices who walked past them in the hallway. 'It is never too late to answer the Mother's summons and dedicate the rest of their lives to Her service.'

'Do all priors study here?' Tomas asked.

'There are other cloisters in High Realm, so we cannot take credit for all the great priors who have lived,' the prior said modestly. 'However we pride ourselves in the esteemed alumni of graduates that we have taught here at Rosewood Cloister over the centuries. Odo the Pius, before he became king, was a student of ours; Prior Gallad, who first discovered the potion that can cure headaches; Prior Elbard who was a key advisor to Lord Lowan Jacelyn, the Sword of the East; and of course Simeon, the current Arch

Prior at Eaglestone. Once they are trained our graduates spread far and wide across The Head, serving in the priories.'

Ana was looking around with a sceptical eye. While she was a firm believer in the Mother, she had no interest in places like this. She had never attended the sermons at the Grand Priory, considering it to be a waste of time. She always said that there was more to worshipping the Mother than listening to old men preach about Her in their draughty old priories.

They followed the prior all the way to his study, which was a simple chamber free of any comforts. He sat at a simple desk and chair, and gestured for them to sit as well.

'So, what can I help you with?' he asked them patiently, looking from one face to the next.

He was an old man who looked like he had spent most of his life there within the walls of the cloister. His skin was pale and his thinning hair was colourless, but Merric would wager that the man would not consider it a wasted life. Quite the opposite, in fact.

'We're looking for a man who I think used to be a novice here,' Merric said.

'We have had many hundreds of novices come through our doors,' the prior said apologetically. 'I am afraid you will need to be more specific.'

'I don't think this particular novice completed his training,' Merric said. 'I heard that he left, maybe twenty years ago? I'm afraid I don't know his name.'

Ana looked doubtful, as though she expected the prior to say he had no knowledge of what Merric was talking about. However, the prior's face turned sombre.

'Sadly there have been a number of novices who never completed their studies to become priors,' he admitted. 'Other callings have taken priority for them; war, duty to their lord, love.'

Merric knew that priors were forbidden to take up weapons and were not allowed to marry or have a family. When they became a prior they left behind all their worldly belongings and gave up all ties to their old life. For some, such a sacrifice turned out to be too much.

'But I think I know the man you speak of,' the prior continued. 'His name was Adkyn. He was a promising student, but he decided that the priory was no longer suitable for him.'

Ana and Kasper exchanged a look of surprise. They had expected the visit to the cloister to be a wasted journey. Perhaps there was at least some truth to the rumours.

'Do you know why he chose to leave?' Merric asked.

'Each have their own reasons,' the prior said. 'Our novices are here by their own choice. None are forced to join us, and they are able to leave whenever they choose.'

'And do you know where he is now?' Kasper asked, wondering how much of the story he had heard would turn out to be true.

'I am afraid I do not,' the prior apologised, looking at him.

'In the mountains, maybe?' Tomas added.

'It is a possibility,' the prior agreed. 'He never loved being confined within these walls. I fear he felt that the cloister restricted his love for the Mother, rather than enhanced it, and sought to be closer to Her. Even before he left he would often take himself outside of our walls, spending time in the countryside and surrounding himself with the Mother's own bounty. The trees, the animals; they're all Her children, you see. We priors connect with the Mother through song and prayer, but for Adkyn that was not enough. He wanted more of a hands on connection with Her. We can only assume this is what led him to ultimately leave us for good.'

Merric could see Ana nodding understandably.

'We priors at the cloister always knew that he would not complete his studies here, though of course we hoped we were mistaken in our predictions. But then something happened to him on one of his trips beyond our walls, and we could see a noticeable change in him. We knew then that that his time with us was over. He left for good, soon after that.'

'And no one has seen him since?' Merric asked.

'We have heard rumours,' the prior offered, 'though I try not to listen to such gossip. All sorts of tales have reached us here, though which are true I could not say. But as for where he now resides, I am afraid I do not know with any certainty. I am sorry that I could not be more helpful.'

Merric did his best to hide his disappointment, and stood to leave. The others did the same. The prior could see the that his words had not been what his visitors had been hoping for, and he sought to offer some other hope to them.

'If you are determined to find him, then I am given to believe that his sister lives in Rosewood still.'

Merric glanced around at Kasper, who raised his eyebrows. It was not much of a lead, but it was something at least. They left the chamber and the prior escorted them all the way back down to the gates.

'May the Mother go with you, my young friends,' the prior said to them.

Dusk had settled by the time they turned back onto the road that led into the village of Rosewood. The road led between orchards of cherry trees, whose pink petals were turning an autumnal red. The air had a fresh fragrance to it, and down here in the valley, out of the desolate highlands, it was a pleasant evening. Smoke drifted from the chimneys of the nearest cottages, and with it came the smell of folks preparing their suppers.

The road emerged onto the main street that led through the centre of the village. A few wagons were rolling up the road from the direction of Oaktyn, filled with vegetables from the Yielding in the south, but apart from that the streets were looking quiet. Most folk seemed to already be at home. Merric and the others stood there for a few moments, looking around at the surrounding cottages, wondering if one of them could be the home of the sister of this Adkyn man.

'What do you think?' Merric asked them. 'It would take us ages to knock on every door.'

'And what would we say, anyway?' Kasper scoffed. 'Hello, do you happen to have a brother called Adkyn who went off his rocker and now lives up in a cave somewhere?'

Even Merric had to laugh at the absurdity of this idea.

I don't know about all of you,' Kasper said, his face brightening suddenly, 'but I think we should start looking there.'

He was looking at an inn, and without waiting for the others he walked towards it. The inn was a welcoming-looking place. It sat beside the street, three stories tall with pleasant light blazing out from the windows. The image of a goose was on the sign that was swaying gently above the door. Merric had to admit that they could all do with some home comforts, and so followed Kasper who led the way inside. They were immediately blasted by warm air. The innkeeper came over, smiling warmly at them all.

'Welcome to the Gambolling Goose! What can I be doing for you fine folk?' he asked Kasper.

311

'Food and beds for the four of us,' Merric said, pulling out the purse of coins he had brought with him from his bedchamber in Eagle Mount.

'Of course, young master!' the innkeeper said brightly.

They were led over to a table by a roaring fire, and a few minutes later a shy-looking serving woman brought over plates of food which they tucked into. Tomas and Kasper ate hungrily, though Ana toyed with her food more than anything. Merric sat back in his chair, chewing slowly, and gazed around the inn at the other patrons. It was getting crowded, and Merric wondered whether Adkyn's sister was among them somewhere.

'Any ideas where to start?' he asked when Kasper and Tomas had eaten their fill.

'The man's sister?' Kasper asked.

He looked around the inn like Merric did and sighed. 'Short of the standing on a box in the middle of the village and shouting for her, I have no idea.'

'She could be anyone,' Tomas agreed.

'She's our best bet though,' Merric said. 'Without her we'll never find Adkyn, and without him we'll never find the crossing over the river.'

'Don't forget,' Kasper warned, 'the stories about him could still all be a load of rubbish. We could be wasting our time on him.'

'But we have to try,' Merric insisted. 'If there's even a slim chance that he knows a way across the Rush then we have to give him a go. We have to get to The Dale if we're to have a chance in this war.'

'And if there is a crossing, and if the Monforts already know about it, then we have to let Sophya know,' Tomas reminded him. 'They might use it again.'

'Rather than going off looking for someone who is quite possibly half mad, I think we should just go and look for the crossing ourselves,' Kasper said.

'If it were that easy, loads of people would know about it,' Merric said. 'It must be a ford or something, which you wouldn't really be able to see.'

'Don't forget who I am,' Kasper said, taking a draught of his tankard of ale. 'I'm a tracker. If the Monforts used this crossing to bring a couple hundred men over the river then there will be signs. Even if the ford is hidden then the passage of hundreds of feet will be visible.'

'Even after all this time?' Tomas asked. 'It's been weeks.'

'Of course,' Kasper said.

'But that could still take ages,' Merric protested.

'I think we should try to find Adkyn,' Ana said.

Merric looked across at her, surprised. She had still barely looked at him since they had bumped into each other outside Porby Castle, and he had half expected her to disagree with him about what they should do purely out of principle. She had looked distracted since their visit to the cloister, but she was now looking determined. Perhaps something about this Adkyn person had struck a chord with her. They certainly seemed to share a lot of the same beliefs.

'How about,' Tomas piped up, looking between them all, 'me and Kasper go to Bridge Ford and then head north, searching along the river to see if Kasper can find the crossing, while you and Ana go and find Adkyn?'

'I don't think it's a good idea for us to split up,' Kasper said, and he gave Merric a concerned look.

Merric likewise glanced nervously at Ana, wondering how she felt about the idea of spending time alone with him. She kept her eyes firmly on Kasper and Tomas, as though acting like Merric's chair was empty.

'We'll stand double the chance of finding the crossing if we do it this way,' Tomas pointed out.

Kasper nodded thoughtfully, considering this. He looked between Merric and Ana. Clearly he, too, was wondering how they would fare if they only had each other for company.

'What do you think?' Kasper asked Merric, as the serving woman came over to take their empty plates.

'Erm,' Merric said, giving Ana one more look. 'Well, I'm definitely going to go and find Adkyn. I suppose it wouldn't do any harm if you went ahead and tried to find this crossing yourself. You know, just in case we can't find Adkyn, or if he can't help us.'

'We're getting ahead of ourselves, anyway,' Kasper said, with a shake of his head. 'We're still no closer to finding out where he lives. How about this - we'll give it until midday tomorrow. If by that point we're still no closer to finding his sister then you're all coming with me to look for the crossing ourselves. You're not going wandering aimlessly into the foothills of the Storm Mountains looking for him unless you have a clear idea of where you're going. It could be dangerous.'

Merric agreed, hoping desperately that he would be able to find Adkyn's sister the following morning before Kasper's deadline was reached. He knew that finding the man up in the mountains was their best chance of finding a way to leave The Head, though he would be lying to himself if he pretended that he was not also hoping for some time alone with Ana to try and repair their relationship.

They left the bar of the inn and headed through to the dimly lit staircase that led up to the bedchambers above. Halfway up the stairs they saw the shy-faced woman who had brought them their food. She was stood there, as though waiting for them, half bathed in shadows.

'Good evening,' Merric said politely to her as went to pass her, but she put an arm out to stop him.

Tomas instinctively reached for the hilt of his sword, but Kasper put a calming hand on his shoulder.

'You're looking for Adkyn?' the woman asked Merric, not looking him in his eye.

'Yes!' Merric said, looking at her with more interest. 'Do you know him?'

The woman nodded.

'Wait, are you his sister?' Tomas asked.

She nodded again. Merric looked back at the others, hardly daring to believe their luck. The very woman they were looking for must have overheard them while serving their dinner.

'My name is Saxta,' she said timidly. 'What do you want with him?'

She was looking suspiciously at the swords at Merric and Tomas' waists, and at Kasper's grim face.

'We do not mean him any harm,' Merric assured her, excitement coursing through him. 'We just wanted to ask him some things.'

'You're not the first to seek him out,' she said, 'and not all of them were friendly.'

'I promise we go to him as friends,' Merric said.

Saxta looked at him doubtfully.

'Many have said that before, but most either mean him harm, or else just want to mock him. He's not normal, not like you and me.'

Merric took a breath. He glanced around, and could see that the stairwell was deserted but for them. No one would overhear him, and Saxta did not seem to be the sort who would spread gossip. He decided that it was a time where he should be honest.

'My name is Merric Jacelyn,' he said quietly. 'You can trust me.'

'The duke?' Saxta said, her eyes widening as she recognised his name.

Merric felt himself redden.

'Until recently, yes,' he said quickly. 'I think your brother has some information which is vital to The Head.'

'Really? Adkyn?' she said, looking doubtful. 'My brother lives alone up in the hills. He spends his days dedicating his life to the Mother. What information could he possibly have?'

Merric hesitated.

'I'm really sorry,' he said with a shake of his head. 'I can't tell you. It's really important that no one knows what I'm trying to do. But I promise you that war with the Monforts is coming, and I think your brother can help us to save The Head.'

Saxta looked at him for a long minute. Then she peered over his shoulder at the others.

'Okay,' she said with a nod, deciding that she would trust them. 'I thought you felt different to the others who have sought him out over the years. That's why I decided to speak to you. But you have to know, Adkyn is not his old self. He's very wary of strangers. Even if you tell him who you are, I can't promise that he'll speak to you. Living up there by himself has made him a little wild. You'll have to be really careful.'

CHAPTER FIFTEEN

Wild encounters

Merric wanted to set off immediately, but the others were able to talk some sense into him. If he was being truthful, Merric had to admit that the idea of a good night's sleep in a real bed was an appealing prospect. But at the same time, he was itching to get going. Saxta had given them clear directions on how to reach her brother. Follow the northern road out of Rosewood for half a day, until you reached the rocks that resembled a perched eagle, then cut through the steep-sided valley. Merric hoped that the journey would be as simple as it had sounded

They awoke early the next morning and left the inn at dawn. The air was chilly, and they wrapped their cloaks tightly around themselves.

'I definitely can't persuade you to come with us?' Kasper asked them hopefully, one last time.

'No,' said Merric and Ana said together.

Merric glanced at her. He had a feeling that her determination to find Adkyn was driven by their shared beliefs, rather than the idea that he could help them find their way across the river. But if it meant having some company on the journey then Merric did not mind what her motivation was.

'Okay then. Be careful,' Kasper said to them, still looking uneasy at the idea of them wandering north by themselves. 'If you find Adkyn and he's able to help, and you find the crossing, then you must wait there. Do not cross without me, do you understand?'

Merric nodded.

Kasper did not look reassured.

'We'll see each other again in a few days then,' he said. 'Come on Tomas.'

The two of them turned and took the southern road out of the town. This led down towards Oaktyn and the Great East Road, but Kasper had said over breakfast that morning they would not need to go as far as that. He believed that any crossing, if it existed, would be north of the point where the Willowbank river met the Rush. So that was where they would start their search. Then it would be the simple case of travelling northwards along the eastern bank of the great river until they found a sign of this crossing. With any luck, they would meet Merric and Ana coming from the opposite direction, and between them they would find this hidden way to cross.

Merric watched Kasper and Tomas disappear into the dawn's early light, before turning to Ana.

'Shall we get going?' he asked.

He could not help but act timidly around her, as though worried that any wrong word spoken would trigger her wrath. Her response, as he had expected, was fairly cold.

'Come on then,' she said, impatiently, hoisting her pack onto her back, checking her crossbow was secure, and pacing off down the street between the rows of buildings.

Merric hurried to keep up with her, but she made it clear that she was not interested in starting a conversation with him. Despite the early hour, the folk who lived in the village were already beginning their day. Banging could be heard coming from the blacksmith's workshop, and the fishmonger was shouting out what he had on offer that day. Villagers began going from shop to shop, paying little mind to Merric and Ana. Clearly strangers were not an unusual sight in Rosewood, with the cloister drawing travellers from all four corners of The Head. A dog chased a cat across the street, and a laughing child ran after it. A queue was forming by a well in the very centre of the village, but Ana led Merric past it and continued onwards along the road.

As they left the village, and the cottages on either side of the road gave way to fields and meadows, Merric could see a detachment of soldiers training in a field under the watchful supervision of the knight who ruled these lands. A castle rose up beyond the field and the training soldiers, the symbol of a rose flashing proudly on the banners fluttering from the castle's towers.

The road on which Merric and Ana walked was narrow, and did not look like it was frequently travelled upon. The only thing ahead of them in this direction were the mountains, so apart from a few shepherds whose flocks grazed in the fields north of the village there was little reason for folk to come this way. Merric was unsurprised to see that the road leading into the distance ahead of them, climbing as it rose up into the hills, seemed to be empty of other travellers.

Rosewood had been a pleasant village, but now that the cottages and neatly tended orchards were behind them, the land around them was beginning to look wild again as they re-entered the highlands. Merric had grown up in Eagle Mount, surrounded by the pleasant, welcoming sight of fields, small woods, trickling streams and gently rolling hills. Here, on the northern edge of The Head, life was tougher and the landscape was more dramatic. Pine trees grew out of the rocky ground and the streams crashed their way down from the high mountains.

Ana led the way as they walked onwards, with the road winding its way around the craggy hills. The road was heading constantly uphill, with little opportunity for them to catch their breath. Merric ignored the painful stitch in his side as he struggled to keep up with Ana's fast pace. They spoke very little, and Merric did not try and force her into conversation. He was reminded of the days they had spent together, just weeks ago, when they had gone riding in the countryside by themselves. He could not help but smile ruefully at how different things were between them now. At the time, Merric had thought that his life could not get any more complicated, what with him having the dukedom thrust upon him. Now, he would happily return to those days if it meant he could go back to the beginning and do things differently the second time around.

'Those must be the Fingers,' Ana said, shaking Merric from his thoughts.

She had stopped walking and was stood on the verge of the road. Merric stepped up beside her, breathing heavily from the effort of the hike and with his hands on his hips. The road veered off to the east, but directly in front of them, to the north, the ground sloped away sharply. Further ahead, the foothills of the Storm Mountains stretched out towards them, like great clawed hands reaching south. Saxta had told them to look out for these Fingers, as she had called them, as it was an indication that they were going the right way.

'There,' he said, pointing.

Directly ahead of them, on the crest of one of the rocky hills, sat a pile of rocks that looked like they had once crashed down from the mountains and rolled down to their final resting place on this lower hill. If Merric squinted his eyes and tilted his head to one side, the pile of rocks *could* almost resemble an eagle perched, ready to take flight. It was just as Saxta had described.

Ana nodded. They left the road behind and she led the way down the slope. It was covered in loose scree and gravel, and they had to pick their way down carefully to avoid creating an avalanche of stones. More than once, Merric slipped and skidded a few feet down the slope, but each time Ana grabbed a hold of his arm and pulled him upright again.

By the time they reached the bottom of the slope the sun was high in the sky. Guessing that it was around midday, Merric suggested they stop and eat some of the food they had brought with them from the inn. Ana agreed, but peered around watchfully around as they ate.

Merric watched her out of the corner of his eye, and wondered if he should say something to her. Ever since Porby he had felt weighed down by the words that were left unspoken between them. He knew that she would never forgive him, but the fact that it had been Ana who had suggested to Tomas that they go and look for Merric when he had left Eagle Mount showed that she at least did not hate him.

'Ana?' he said, testing the water.

She shot him a look, before lowering her eyes to her food.

'Yes?' she said cautiously, as though she knew what he wanted to say.

'I just wanted to say…you know…I'm sorry,' Merric said, uncertainly.

Ana's eyebrows shot upwards, but she did not look up from her food.

'I just wanted you to know that,' he finished, feebly.

She did not answer, and Merric wished that he had not said anything. His words had felt so inadequate, and did not come close to covering what he had meant to say.

'Let's go,' Ana said, putting the last of her food into her mouth and rising to her feet.

'Okay,' Merric said quickly, clambering awkward to his own feet on the uneven stony ground.

They set off towards the rocky hill topped with the eagle-like shape, keeping to the left of it where the gap between it and the next hill beside it formed a v-shaped valley that headed further uphill to the north. So far, Saxta's directions seemed to be accurate. The going was even tougher now that they had left the road behind, and their route now required them to climb over and jump between the bounders that littered the valley bottom.

'Do you know what you're apologising for?' Ana said after a while, revealing that despite her silence she had been thinking about Merric's words.

Partly relieved, partly nervous, Merric tried to choose his words carefully.

'I'm apologising for what I said, that evening when I left Eagle Mount to try and free Sir Sebastien,' he said.

He recalled the look of shocked hurt on Ana's face when he had said what he had said, and this brought a fresh wave of shame.

'You're sorry because you said it, or you're sorry because you didn't really mean it?' Ana challenged, not looking at him and concentrating on where she was putting her feet.

'I don't know. I wasn't thinking properly. I was frustrated, and worried about Seb,' Merric said lamely.

She leaped across a crack in the rocky ground and turned and waited for Merric to follow.

'You know what,' Ana said, 'it's not like I ever wanted a marriage proposal or anything from you. I know that we're from different worlds, and that things might not have worked out between us.'

Merric leapt across the gap, slipping slightly on the gravel beneath his feet when he landed. Ana turned and continued on up the valley.

'But I was enjoying seeing how things were going,' she continued. 'We're young. I don't see why we couldn't have just carried on and seen how things went. So what if you had to marry some noble lady one day? Why does that mean we can't enjoy ourselves now?'

'I know,' Merric said, hanging his head. 'It's just what Seb was saying –'

Ana came to a stop and Merric almost bumped into her. She turned to face him, her finger jabbing into his chest.

'It had nothing to do with him,' she said. 'I know he's your friend, but this is about us, Merric, not him. Do you remember that day when you found out you were a Jacelyn? You kissed me then like you did not care about what the future might bring. That's who I fell in love with, not the Duke of The Head. Back then you would never have let someone else dictate how you felt.'

Merric opened his mouth, but he did not know what to say. Fortunately for him, Ana cut him off before he had even started to speak.

'Let's not do this now,' she said, sounding frustrated at having allowed herself to become emotional about it. 'We've got a job to do. This is about The Head now, not about us.'

They fell into silence again, and Merric did not know whether he felt better or worse for their talk. Ana looked like she was glad to get it off her chest though. She no longer looked so tense when she walked, and it was as though she felt that she no longer needed to give Merric the cold shoulder. She had said what she wanted to say, and that seemed to be enough for her for the moment.

They kept on climbing through the valley that led up the mountainside between the ridges of hills that flanked them. The sides of the Fingers had gotten steeper and steeper, and the valley now resembled more of a gorge. Merric did not like the feeling of being enclosed by the steep rock to either side of them, but they had no choice but to keep going onwards, higher and higher. The peaks of the Storm Mountains loomed overhead, impossibly tall with their tops hidden in clouds. It was growing colder. While the effort of their journey was causing sweat to bead on Merric's brow, his breath was misting in front of him as he climbed. When he stopped and looked back down the valley he could see that they had risen much higher than he had imagined. The land was stretched out in the distance, and if he used his hand to shield his eyes from the sun he could just make out the village of Rosewood where they had left that morning.

After what felt like a couple of hours of hard hiking Merric began to get the feeling that they were being watched. Every now and then he heard the sound of loose stones clattering down the side of the valley, but when they turned their heads towards the sound there was no sign of life. Merric supposed there were plenty of wild animals in these lands, although he was not sure that the thought comforted him. His fears were confirmed when he heard the sound of a wolf howling somewhere off to his right. It was answered, almost immediately, by another to his left.

Instinctively, Merric put his hand on the hilt of *Hopebearer*, and Ana unslung her crossbow and notched a bolt. They glanced uneasily at each other.

'Come on,' Merric said, leading the way now.

He tried to ignore the ominous sounds of the howling, but it did not take long for him to come to the conclusion that they were, indeed, being followed. More howls came, echoing around the valley. He caught glimpses of grey fur out of the corner of his eye as the shapes darted between the rocks that hid them from view. It became harder and harder to ignore the feeling that they were being hunted. There were howls behind them and in front of them, getting ever closer.

All of a sudden a wolf leapt onto a rock ahead of them. Merric and Ana stopped, looking up in fear at the snarling beast that was looking down at them with its yellow eyes. Merric instinctively used an arm to push Ana behind him, but more wolves were revealing themselves now. More of the slathering animals were behind them, growling menacingly. The wolves had encircled them, and were getting closer and closer. Their matted grey fur looked almost black in the long shadows that were being cast across the valley by the setting sun.

Merric looked from wolf to wolf, noticing their snarling yellow teeth and intelligent eyes. He pulled *Hopebearer* from its scabbard, but almost immediately Ana grabbed his hand and pulled it down.

'No! put it away,' she hissed, eyeing the wolves.

She had lowered her crossbow as well, though her face was white with fear.

'What?' Merric said, goggling at her. 'They're *wolves*, Ana.'

'We need to show them that we mean no harm,' she said. 'They're just guarding their territory.'

She slung the crossbow back over her shoulder and began walking slowly up the valley again, directly towards the nearest of the wolves. Merric noticed that she clutched the amulet around her neck that her father had made, to replace the one she had lost the previous summer.

Merric edged up the valley after her, looking fearfully around at the wolves.

'Your sword,' Ana urged him, glancing back.

Gulping, Merric slid *Hopebearer* back into its scabbard and raised his hands as though the wolves were enemy soldiers who could understand the gesture.

As one, the wolves leapt forward. Merric cried out and fell backwards, away from the snapping jaws. He raised an arm to fend them off, and just when he felt certain that he was about to feel their wicked teeth sink into him, he heard a harsh shout.

The wolves paused and looked around. The shout came again, and a figure came into sight waving a burning torch from side to side.

'Away! Away I said!' he bellowed, jabbing at the wolves with the torch.

They gave angry howls, but they turned and ran back down the valley, away from the fire. Merric felt a strong hand yank him to his feet.

'What in the Mother's name do you think you're doing?!'

Merric looked at their saviour as he pulled Ana back onto her feet as well. He was a big man, made all the larger by the thick furs he was wearing and the wild and bushy beard that half covered his face. He carried the burning torch in his meaty hand, and a wooden staff, roughly hewn from a tree branch, was slung across his back.

'You damned fools,' the man barked. 'Do you want to get yourselves eaten?'

'Are you Adkyn?' Merric asked him, still trembling from his close brush with death.

He knew the answer to his own question. How many other men could there be living up here in the wild?

The hulking figure of Adkyn glared down at him for a moment, before pushing him roughly away.

'Get out of here,' he ordered. 'Go on! Go back to Rosewood, or wherever you're from. I don't want you here gawping at me.'

'We need your help,' Merric tried to say, but Adkyn interrupted him.

'I've helped you enough already, unless you wanted to become the wolves' dinner. Go on, go!'

He actually brandished the flaming torch at them, as he had done to the wolves, and both Merric and Ana had to take a step backwards. Adkyn spotted the amulet around Ana's neck, which she was still fingering with one hand.

'What's that?' he asked, pausing in his outburst at them.

Before Ana could answer him there came the familiar sound of howling, getting closer once more.

'Curses,' Adkyn spat, peering into the dusk that was settling around them. 'It's too late. These wolves are getting bolder by the day. Come on then, follow me. And hurry!'

Adkyn turned and paced up the valley. Merric and Ana glanced at each other, before hurrying to keep up with the big man. It was easier said than done; Adkyn was limping from an old injury, but his strides were long and he knew this land well. He walked confidently across the uneven ground. The valley finally came to an end and opened out onto a wide plateau of rock, punctuated here and there by an occasional cluster of pine trees. Further ahead, the mountains continued to climb high into the sky. Adkyn led them further north, heading across the mercifully flat plateau towards the largest gathering of trees. Merric kept on glancing over his shoulder, but if the wolves were still out there then they seemed hesitant to attack while Adkyn was with them. It had seemed that the man had lived in these parts for long enough that even the wild animals knew to give him a measure of respect.

They walked through the trees for a few minutes, reaching a clearing which resembled a mossy bowl. At its depths Merric could make out a simple cottage, made from roughly cut logs. A homemade axe sat beside the front door, but aside from that there were little signs that anyone lived there at all. Adkyn led them down into the hollow and towards his cottage, pushing open the door that was also made from logs lashed together. Merric and Ana entered his home, and looked around.

While it looked like a cottage from the outside, really it was more of a cave. The floor, walls and ceiling were smooth rock which had been hollowed out of the mountainside in a time long before people walked the world. The front of his home had been built across the entrance to the cave, and here Adkyn kept a vast wooden chair which sat in front of an open fire. Back in the cave Merric could spy a pile of straw that must have been Adkyn's bed, along with piles of root vegetables that he had undoubtably been hoarding ahead of the coming winter. It appeared that he was preparing to hibernate, like one of the mountain bears that lived in these parts.

Adkyn closed the door behind him and Merric was grateful for the break from the cold mountain air. The man put the burning torch into the firepit, which soon roared into life. The flames leapt into the air, and the smoke coiled and drifted out of the small circular hole in the roof. Adkyn propped his staff against the wall of his simple home and lowered himself onto his chair.

'You can stay here tonight,' Adkyn said, reluctantly, 'but tonight only. At first light I'll take you down off the mountain myself, and get you out of my hair.'

'Thank you,' Merric said feebly, both for providing them with shelter and for saving them from the wolves.

'I might not want to see you get eaten by wolves, but you're very much mistaken if you think I'm happy having two children here disturbing my solitude.'

Ana was still fingering her amulet.

'I really thought they wouldn't attack us,' she muttered.

Adkyn let out a harsh laugh.

'Because of that thing around your neck? Ha! You may love the Mother, girl, and she may love you, but that won't protect you from a pack of hungry wolves. They need to eat, after all.'

'I guess I have a lot to learn still,' Ana said.

'Just don't bother with the priories,' Adkin said, using his toes to pull his boots off and stretching out in his chair, his bare feet by the fire. 'Nothing but a bunch of timewasters wanting a comfortable life. You think a book can teach you about Her? Or listening to some dusty old fool spout out his sermons?'

'I've never really enjoyed them,' Ana admitted. 'Da would always take me to the Grand Priory at Eaglestone, but I've always been more like my ma. I liked to see the Mother's world, and feel it, rather than just hear about it.'

Adkyn nodded, approving.

'Is that why you left the cloister?' Merric asked him.

This seemed to be the wrong thing to say, as a look of annoyance passed over the man's face.

'Is that why you're here, eh?' he demanded. 'Heard about me over in Eaglestone and thought you'd come and gawp at me?'

'No, no!' Merric said, not wanting to anger the man. 'Like I said, we really need your help, and your sister in Rosewood told us how to find you.'

'Saxta told you, eh? What story did you spin her to get her to tell you where I live? No, don't tell me,' he added, when Merric went to open his mouth to reply. 'I don't, in fact, care.'

'At the cloister they told us that something happened to you one day, and that's what led you to leave for good?' Ana asked him.

Adkyn looked at her for a moment, before sighing.

'Aye, that's true.'

Merric felt a flutter of annoyance. He had asked basically the same thing, and yet Adkyn had practically jumped down his throat.

'I'd like to hear about it,' Ana said, cautiously.

Adkyn looked like he was going to get angry at them again, but his face softened.

'I suppose we're stuck with each other until morning, so no harm in telling you. I was walking beside the Rush one day and a bear attacked me,' Adkyn said. 'I still carry the scars.'

Merric noticed the mountain man rubbing his leg as he said this, and he assumed that even after all these years this was the source of Adkyn's limp.

'We struggled, and I thought I was going to die. I managed to get away, but in doing so I fell into the river. I'll tell you what, I'll never forget how cold it was. When the water covered my head I felt certain that I was dead. But then I felt a hand reach down and pull me out. The Mother saved me that day, and I knew She had a need of

334

me. I wasn't going to spend another day holed up in the cloister with the rest of those mindless idiots.'

Merric gave a start. The same thing had happened to him that summer, when he and Ana had jumped into the Willowbank river to escape Monfort soldiers in Oaktyn. Merric, too, had been dragged below the water and smashed against the rocks by the current, before he had felt someone pull him out. At the time, Ana had assumed that Merric had pulled himself out but the shock had made him confused. But now, hearing Adkyn's similar account, she glanced curiously at Merric. Merric himself was biting his lip as he thought. Had it been the Mother who had saved him? Arch Prior Simeon had certainly seemed to think so, when he had told him about it later. But Merric could not help but wonder why She would bother saving him.

'And what do you do now?' Ana asked, turning back to Adkyn.

'Whatever the Mother requires of me,' Adkyn said simply. 'I could never hear Her in the cloister, but out here, in the wilds, She's everywhere.'

'I've heard you know of a way to cross the Rush,' Merric said, crossing his fingers for luck behind his back.

'Go to Bridge Ford if you're wanting to leave The Head,' Adkyn said dismissively, not even bothering to look at Merric.

'We've heard that you know of a way of crossing the river *other* than at Bridge Ford,' Ana added, to clarify.

Merric nodded eagerly.

'We need to get a message to Lord Godfrei Florin in The Dale,' he explained. 'But we can't cross the Rush at Bridge Ford as a Monfort army is waiting on the other side.'

Adkyn waved his hands impatiently.

'I am a simple man, trying to live a simple life. I have no interests in lords or wars. Jacelyns…Monforts…The Head…none of that means anything to me. My life is the Mother, that's all.'

'But you know of a way across?' Merric asked, biting back a retort. He knew it was not the time to get into the politics of what was happening in the realm and try to justify their cause.

Adkyn hesitated, scratching his beard.

'It's really important,' Ana said, pleadingly.

Adkyn studied them both for a minute, as though deciding whether he liked these two youths. He decided to buy himself a bit more time before deciding whether to answer their question.

'There's an ancient forest on the western bank of the Rush, just west of here,' he began. 'Probably the oldest forest in all of High Realm. Some folk say that it's the home of spirits, and I spent most of my childhood believing that nonsense myself. Folk talk of seeing ghosts and other such rubbish.'

'The Haunted Wood,' Merric said wisely to Ana, nodding. He could picture the forest in his mind's eye on the map in the study at Eagle Mount. He believed that it was the same forest he had seen to the north that day when he had ridden across the bridge and entered The Hinterland.

'Do not name it such,' Adkyn snapped at him. 'A foolish name given by the damned idiots who draw maps. Do not sully that place with such disrespect. That forest is the heart of the Mother's dominion in this world. It is an ancient place, full of power, and secrets, and truths. It is within that very forest that the Green Knight was blessed with a vision of the Lady of the Lake, the Mother herself in her earthly form.'

'The Lady is real?' Ana said, her face in awe.

'She does not reveal Herself to everyone,' Adkyn admitted. 'But I have seen Her.'

Merric could see the look of admiration and wonder on Ana's face.

'I've only ever dreamed of such a thing,' she said, her eyes misty.

'I make the pilgrimage to see Her once a season,' Adkyn went on

'And you use a secret crossing to reach the forest?' Merric asked excitedly, breaking the spell-like moment that had passed between Adkyn and Ana.

Adkyn looked at Merric in obvious irritation.

'And so the crossing must be close to here?' Merric asked, oblivious to the man's dislike. 'Can you tell us how to cross?'

Adkyn continued to eye him sceptically.

'That crossing is almost as sacred as the old forest itself. Had I not been saved from the river by the Mother that day I would never have discovered it.'

Ana sensed an opportunity.

'I know you want to protect it,' she said, 'but the Monforts know about it too. I don't know how they found it, but this summer they crossed it with an army and used it to try and take The Head for themselves. They're going to use it again.'

This did indeed seem to anger Adkyn. The wild man turned his attention back to Ana.

'I'll tell you how to get across the river, but this is not some toll bridge for anyone to use. I am not telling you so that this boy can reach The Dale. I'm telling you because to stand in the old forest is to stand in the Mother's very presence, and I will not deny you that opportunity.'

- CHAPTER SIXTEEN -

Leaving The Head

The next morning they took leave of Adkyn's mountain home. He went with them, just in case the wolves that had harassed them the previous day were still close by. The mountain man walked along with his usual limp, and with his heavy wooden staff held in both hands and his eyes watchful as they scanned the ridges around them.

'Surely the Mother wouldn't let the wolves attack when you're with us?' Merric pointed out.

He assumed that one so devoted to Her would be safe from harm.

'The Mother created the wolves, but she does not control them,' Adkyn replied, as though it were obvious.

'I don't understand,' Merric said.

'I've given up trying to explain it to him,' Ana said apologetically to Adkyn.

'The Mother created us all,' Adkyn growled. 'She created the animals, and the plants, and the folk who walk this world. But how we all act is down to us. Folk kill, and steal, and cheat, but that's not Her fault is it? It's the same with animals. They'll do what they have to do in order to survive, and so do we.'

'She can't take responsibility for what folk do,' Ana said to Merric in a voice of exasperation. 'The Mother created men like Aric Monfort, but it was through his own actions that he became the villain that he is.'

Merric nodded, but he knew that he would never truly understand. There were some, like Ana and Adkyn, who accepted the Mother without question, and nothing would sway them from their devotion towards her. Merric supposed this must be a source of comfort to them, and helped provide answers where none could be found through other means. But Merric had been brought up reading books, and this left little room for things that he could not see and touch for himself. The priory taught that folk should be selfless and care for others, and Merric could get on board with that. But when it came to believing in a goddess who created the world and all life then it became a stretch too much for him.

The journey out of the Fingers proved much easier than the climb the previous day. The sky was clear and blue, and while the air was chilly the sun beating down overhead soon warmed them. Either the wolves had moved on, or else the presence of Adkyn had acted as a deterrent, as they did not see or hear a sign of them as they hiked. Eagles circled high overhead, and Merric could not help but hypnotically watch the majestic creatures.

Adkyn glanced up at them too.

'Did you ever hear of Haerophon?' he asked Merric.

'Of course,' Merric said, surprised that anyone would think that he had not. How could anyone raised in Eagle Mount not know of Haerophon? But then, he remembered that he had not told Adkyn who he really was. The mountain man had no idea that he was speaking to a former Duke of The Head. 'He was the giant eagle that Jace rode when he first arrived in High Realm, wasn't he.'

'I'm impressed,' Adkyn said, raising an eyebrow. 'I thought that few common folk knew of Haerophon's name.'

He looked quizzically at Merric, who hurriedly wracked his brain for an explanation for his knowledge.

'There's a stained glass window in Eagle Mount that depicts him, and it has his name written on it too,' he said, hurriedly. 'I saw it once when I visited Lord Roberd's court.'

Apparently satisfied, Adkyn looked back up at the circling eagles.

'It's said that he was from these mountains,' he said. 'Once, many thousands of years ago, there were hundreds of giant eagles here. The Old Folk used to ride them, they say, but they gradually died away.'

'What happened to them?' Ana asked, stumbling slightly on the loose rocks beneath their feet. Merric reached out a hand to steady her, and she did not jerk it away.

'Some were hunted,' Adkyn said, 'and others just died. Sometimes that happens with animals. Some say that once there were all manner of animals that lived in this land, who died out long before folk arrived. Things that exist now only in myths and legends. But of the giant eagles, one remained when the rest were gone. And his name was Haerophon. He flew west, and he must have found himself in Ouestoria eventually. The next thing history tells us is that when Eldred, the first king of High Realm, crossed the Border Peaks and settled these lands, Jace came with him riding on Haerophon. He was the last of the eagle riders, because Haerophon was the last of the giant eagles.'

Merric knew that Jace was his distant ancestor, and that he had founded Eagle Mount and begun the Jacelyn family. When Jace had died, his eagle had flown away. The stories said that he had gone to be with his master in the afterlife.

'No one truly knows what happened to Haerophon,' Adkyn continued, 'but there are some that believe that he lives still, somewhere here in these mountains, far beyond the reach of us folk'.

Merric thought it was a nice story, but clearly a myth. There were no magical creatures like giant eagles in the world, and he was almost certain that they had never even existed at all. They made good stories, but that was all they were. He did not say as such to Adkyn though, as the rough mountain man seemed to be finally tolerating Merric's presence, even if he did not seem to like him.

Adkyn stayed with them all the way out of the Fingers, and did not leave them until the rocky hills were behind them and ahead lay swathes of fields and a distant forest.

'That is the East Wood,' he told them, looking at the distant forest. 'Head through there and you will reach the great river. Then follow the directions that I gave you earlier and you will find my crossing.'

Merric had been grateful for Adkyn's protection, but he was not sorry to bid farewell to him. He had spoken to Merric with little more than contempt and had often treated him like he was not even there. It was not something he was used to. On the other hand Adkyn and Ana had bonded easily, and they had talked for most of the journey out of the mountains, leaving Merric to follow them in silence.

Ana turned and waved to Adkyn, who was already walking back up towards the mountains, and Merric hoisted his pack more securely onto his shoulders.

'Well, that went better than expected,' Ana said. 'I half expected that we would not even find him.'

'He wouldn't have told us anything about the crossing if it hadn't been for you,' Merric said, truthfully.

343

Ana gave him a rare smile.

'I wonder how Kasper and Tomas are getting on?' Merric asked. 'If they haven't had any luck finding the crossing then at least our journey up there, and almost getting eaten by wolves, will have been worth it.'

They set off again, heading south west towards the forest that spread across the horizon. The Rush lay somewhere beyond the trees, and even further west loomed another mountain range, which Merric knew marked the border of The Dale. It was still a long way off though, and they could not think about reaching The Dale until they had at least crossed the great river. Adkyn's directions had seemed clear, but Merric would not be completely confident until they had found the crossing for themselves and reached the far bank of the river safely.

It felt strange to be seeing other folk again after the solitary isolation of the mountains. Shepherds were herding their flocks of sheep in the fields with the help of trained dogs, and Merric even spied a small castle with a lone tower as they neared the forest. Clearly they did not get many travellers in this part of The Head, as a knight rode out of the gates of the castle and watched Merric and Ana from a distance as they walked past. Deciding that the two youths were not up to anything suspicious and were no threat to his lands, the knight retreated back into his castle.

Wildflowers were growing in the meadows, and before long the ground beneath their feet seemed to be covered in a multicoloured patchwork blanket. The closer they got to the forest, and the river that lay beyond, the more full of life the land seemed to get. Merric could scarcely believe that he had woken up in the cold, harsh mountains that morning, as he was now surrounded by bluebells and foxgloves and all manner of flowers that he did not know the names of, and rabbits could be seen frolicking around in the grass. Merric pulled off his cloak and rolled it up, tying it to his pack. The weather was markedly different down here in the lowlands by the river, compared to how it had been in the exposed highlands and the inhospitable mountains they had been travelling through for the past few days. Were it not for the trees ahead of him that were beginning to turn a reddish brown, and the snow topping the mountain peaks beyond, he could almost have believed that it was still summer.

They reached the forest and walked between the trees that were covered with moss. The trees of the East Wood were spread out, and they could still see the sky above them. Plenty of sunlight drifted down between the leaves, casting a golden glow across the mossy ground. Some of the leaves had already fallen and they crunched under Merric's feet as he walked. It must have rained recently, as the fresh smell of damp earth reached his nose. Not for the first time since they had left Rosewood, Merric felt like he and Ana were out for a stroll together through a beautiful, peaceful woods. Except of course for the fact that Ana was walking a few paces ahead of Merric and only spoke to him rarely.

All sorts of wildlife skittered through the forest. Squirrels and rabbits peered at them curiously before scurrying off, and at one point a deer ambled across the trail that Merric and Ana were following, completely at ease and unworried by the two humans.

'Do you hear that?' Merric asked, coming to a stop after an hour of walking through the trees.

Ana stopped and listened. She, too, could hear the sound of rushing water.

'The river must be close,' she said.

Merric had not been sure what to expect, but when they reached the Rush it was nothing like the river he had seen further to the south around Bridge Ford. The river was much narrower here, perhaps narrow enough that he could have had a shouted conversation with someone on the opposite bank. But here the Rush tumbled along violently, barrelling down from the mountains. The water resembled little more than frothing white foam as it pounded over boulders and cascaded down waterfalls. It may have been narrower up here in the north, Merric knew that anyone foolish enough to try and cross the river over these thundering rapids would be drowned or dashed against the rocks within seconds.

When they reached the riverbank, Merric and Ana turned south. Adkyn had told them that the crossing was a ford, which could be found on a brief stretch of river which was much calmer than the rest, so this is what they had to look out for. A trail, possibly made by the passage of animals over the years, hugged close to the eastern bank of the river in the shade of the trees, and they followed this, their eyes automatically scanning the trees on the other side of the river.

Perhaps it was just because of the stories that Merric had heard growing up giving him an unfair opinion of it, but he could completely understand why some called the forest on the western bank of the Rush the Haunted Wood. It was dark and eerie looking, especially in comparison to the bright, airy forest they were walking through on their own side of the river. Nothing moved in those far trees, as though nothing at all lived there. Adkyn's insistence that the forest was the heart of the Mother's domain in the world did little to reassure Merric or change his opinion of it.

Always at the front of his mind was the knowledge that the opposite side of the river was beyond the border of The Head, and with a chill he recalled the last time he had left the relative safety of his own dukedom. That land on the far bank was The Hinterland, which was not part of any of the dukedoms but fell under the direct control of the king. Far from being reassured by this fact, it made Merric even more nervous. A Monfort army was currently encamped in The Hinterland, across the river from Bridge Ford, and that all but confirmed the fact that the king had sided with Lord Aric. Once across the river, it was likely

347

that they would be in just as much danger as if they were in The Southstones itself.

The mist and spray that hung above the churning water clung to Merric and Ana's clothes. The trail along which they walked continued to follow closely beside the riverbank, but the land rose and fell constantly. At some points the thundering river was by their feet, while at other times the Rush had crashed down into a deep ravine far below. They were heading generally downhill, as the river flowed from the mountains down towards the sea that lay many miles away. There were times when the trail descended so steeply that they had to cling on to branches of nearby trees to help themselves safely negotiate the slope.

They did not speak as they walked, partly because the river was loud and any conversation would have needed to be shouted. This gave Merric lots of time to think. He just could not shake the idea that they were being watched from the western bank, but whenever he looked in that direction he could see nothing. Part of him thought it must be his own paranoid imagination. And yet, if the Monforts did indeed know about this crossing then surely they would not leave it unguarded.

Ana began to get a little ahead of Merric. She found it easier to negotiate the uneven trail and seemed as eager as he was to find the crossing. Though whether it was her desire to reach The Dale, or an excitement to be in the forest that Adkyn had spoken so lovingly about, Merric could not tell. The river rounded a bend and he found Ana stood at the water's edge, her hands on her hips. Merric looked curiously around, to see what had made her stop, and saw that the river looked a little calmer here.

'I think this is the place,' Ana called over to him.

The water still looked fast flowing, but it was no longer churning into a white mass. Merric still did not fancy trying to wade across it, and looked nervously at the water. According to Adkyn the water was only knee-deep here, but it still looked strong enough to knock them off their feet. And just beyond this point the river disappeared over another waterfall. Merric knew it would spell certain death if they were to be swept over the edge.

'Do you think it's all safe to cross?' Merric asked, looking up and down the stretch of river.

'I can't tell,' Ana said. 'Adkyn seemed to suggest that only part of it is shallow enough to wade across.'

Merric looked dubiously at where the river disappeared over the waterfall, not wanting to guess how far it dropped.

'If we get it wrong…' he began, but did not finish.

'I know,' Ana said.

The riverbank here was wide and shingled. She went back into the trees and returned with a fallen branch. Merric watched as she carefully went right up to the water's edge and began poking the branch into the river at intervals, trying to see if she could find where it was shallow enough to cross. But the fast current snatched the branch out of her hands and it went bobbing off towards the waterfall.

'I guess we wait for Kasper then,' she said, frustrated.

Merric looked around at the shingle and the hardpacked earth ground around the trees, wondering if he could would be able see a sign of the passing of the Monfort soldiers that summer himself. If he could find that then that would show where they had been able to safely cross. But within minutes he gave up, accepting that he had no idea what he was looking for.

Disappointed, and eager to get across the river and continue on his journey, Merric had no choice but to wait. He plonked himself down onto the shingle and played absent-mindedly with a pebble that he tossed from hand to hand. Ana stayed on her feet, pacing up and down and looking into the trees on the far side.

More to pass the time than because of hunger, Merric took off his pack and ate some of the remaining food he had brought from the inn in Rosewood. He offered some to Ana, but she shook her head and took her own food out of her own pack. Merric sighed, wondering how long she would continue to punish him. He knew he deserved it, but it did not make it any more bearable.

To distract himself, Merric rose to his feet and wandered over to the edge of the waterfall. He was greeted by a spectacular sight. His stomach gave a lurch when he saw how far the waterfall fell before crashing into the plunge pool far below. The river continued to rumble south, cutting its way through a deep ravine and growing wider. A few miles away the East Wood ended, and Merric could see, in the far distance, the specks that were the towers of Bridge Ford.

He was startled by the sudden sound of cracking twigs, and he spun around. Kasper and Tomas appeared from between the trees. They looked as surprised to see Merric as he was to see them.

'Have you found it?' Tomas asked, amazed.

Merric nodded, and Ana came over and joined them.

'We think so,' he said. 'It's on this stretch, though we don't know exactly where.'

Kasper went over to the water's edge and looked up and down for a few minutes, before heading into the trees behind him.

'This is the place, alright,' he confirmed, his voice calling out.

They hurried over to him and he pointed to the hard-packed dirt, where they could just about make out the shape of footprints and hoofmarks. Merric had looked here himself earlier, but it had taken Kasper's keen eyes to spot what he had missed.

'How you see this stuff, I'll never know,' Tomas said, impressed.

'Well, it looks like we were right about the Monforts anyway,' Kasper said to Merric, 'they *did* find a way to cross. I'll be honest, a part of me wasn't expecting this crossing to really exist. Did you find Adkyn?'

Merric quickly explained about their meeting with the mountain man, and what Adkyn had told them about the forest across the river. He also told them how it was Ana who was to thank for getting him to tell them where the crossing was.

'And it's a good job you did,' Kasper admitted to her. 'We might have walked straight past this place. I never would have imagined the crossing being so close to a waterfall.'

They all turned and looked at it with some unease, watching as the river disappeared over into the abyss.

'So now that we've found it,' Tomas said, 'we'll have to warn Lady Sophya about this crossing.'

'And Lord Tymon, at Bridge Ford,' Merric added, ignoring the look of dislike that appeared on Kasper's face at the mention of his baron's name. 'He's the closest, after all.'

'Who will go?' Kasper asked.

Merric knew that it was time for one of them to bid farewell to the others, as there was no other way for them to notify Eagle Mount and Bridge Ford. And stopping the Monforts from using the crossing again was almost as important as them reaching The Dale. They all looked at each other for a few moments.

'I'll go,' Tomas said, at last.

'Are you sure?' Merric asked him.

Tomas nodded.

'You need Kasper to help you find your way to The Dale, and I know how important it is for Ana to reach the forest,' he said, looking across the river at the dark, eerie trees. 'And of course you need to be the one to speak to the Florins,' he added to Merric.

They all knew that it made sense, but they were sad to have to say goodbye to Tomas.

'I want to come with you,' he said, 'but I can do this. I *should* do this. It's what I can do for The Head.'

Merric smiled fondly at him. Tomas had been a loyal and dedicated servant, and a brave squire. It was now time for Tomas to start his own life, he knew, and not live in Merric's shadow. Especially now that Merric had lost the respect of so many folk in The Head, and Tomas had such a bright future ahead of him.

'Go to Bridge Ford first,' Merric advised. 'Tell them where the crossing is. I expect Lord Tymon will send some of his soldiers here to guard this spot on the eastern bank. And then once you've told Sophya then Sir Oskar and Sir Orsten will know what to do.'

'Don't worry,' Tomas said, straightening his back to show that he was read, 'I'll make sure everything is done properly. And what about you? What should I say about you? I know that Lady Sophya would want to hear about you. I bet she misses you.'

'That doesn't matter,' Merric said, with a lump in his throat. 'All that's important is that they send soldiers here, just in case the Monforts decide to invade. It seems quiet here now, but I bet it won't be if they decide to use this crossing again.'

Tomas nodded, before holding out his plump hand.

'Good luck, my lord,' he said, before correcting himself. 'Good luck, Merric.'

Merric shook Tomas' hand, and smiled down at his old servant. Unspoken words hung there between them. Tomas then turned and shook Kasper's hand, and Ana gave him a warm hug.

'Be careful, Tomas,' she said.

'And you,' he replied with a smile.

They broke apart and he breathed out slowly. He clasped his sword hilt in his hand with a fierce determination, and then turned and disappeared into the trees, heading back in the direction he had come.

Merric watched him go, with a tinge of sadness mingled with pride, before turning back to the river.

'This is it, then,' Ana said.

'No time like the present,' Merric agreed.

The three of them walked up to the water's edge, at the point where Kasper said the old footprints of the Monforts appeared from. They made sure the straps of their packs were tight and secure, before looking at the swift current and hoping that they were not about to make a big mistake. If there had been heavy rainfall up in the mountains recently then that might have made the water at the crossing deeper and stronger than usual, and they all had visions of being swept downstream and over the waterfall.

'I'll go first,' Merric said, steeling himself, but Kasper shook his head.

'Me first,' he said, and his tone told Merric that it was not up for debate.

The hunter took a deep breath as he glanced once more at the water surging past, before taking a step forward into the river. His boot was instantly buffeted by the power of the water, and he wobbled for a moment. Finding his balance, he took another step so that both of his feet were now in the river. Merric and Ana watched with bated breath. Kasper took a few more steps, his legs braced wide against the rush of water, and his arms outstretched.

'It's okay,' he said back to them, 'I think.'

He looked forwards again and took a few more steps. The water rose above his boots and up to his knees, but did not seem to be getting any deeper than that. Merric went into the river after him, gasping at how cold the water was around his legs. He took slow, high steps so that his feet cleared the water. He could feel the river smashing into his feet, trying to knock him over. It was an alarming sensation, but after a couple of minutes he had learned to compensate by leaning a little in the direction the water was flowing from. He glanced back and saw Ana in the river as well.

'Are you okay?' he called to her.

'Keep going!' she shouted back.

She waved him onwards, looking uncomfortable but with a grim determination on her face.

The river was littered with large boulders that were scattered along their route across the water, and Kasper was waiting up ahead beside one. When Merric reached him Kasper grabbed hold of his arm and pulled him into the shelter of the boulder, where the current of the water did not seem to be so strong. When Ana had joined them too, Kasper peered around the boulder.

'We're maybe a third of the way across,' he said, and Merric and Ana just nodded to show that they understood there was still a long way to go.

It was the most nerve-wracking and uncomfortable journey that Merric had ever been on. One false step and he would be washed away to almost certain death. They pushed onwards towards the next boulder, their feet freezing cold and numb. A few times Merric nearly lost his balance, and he had to plunge his hands into the water to keep himself from falling off his feet. He was shaking so hard from the icy water that he could barely think straight, and found it harder and harder to concentrate on where he was putting his feet.

They were almost halfway across the river when the first arrow appeared.

Merric heard it a split second before he saw it. It was a whistling sound just audible over the roaring of the river. He ducked down instinctively, feeling the seat of his breeches touch the water as he did so. A small gasp came from behind him, and in horror he turned and saw Ana clutch at her right arm. The arrow had struck her a glancing blow. She clapped her hand to her arm, but the arrow had knocked her off balance. She fell backwards into the water, the look of pain on her face giving way to panic.

'Kasper, help!' Merric shouted, before leaping after Ana.

She was being swept along by the river, and hindered by her wounded arm she was struggling to keep herself from being dunked under the surface. Merric half ran and half splashed after her, feeling the river forcing him downstream in her wake. She was quickly being dragged out of his reach. Merric ignored all the danger to himself and could only think about helping Ana. He dove forwards into the water. Immediately he felt the strong current take hold of him and whisk him forwards. His outstretched hand managed to grasp her wrist, but now he was being swept along with her. His free hand grappled about desperately, trying to find a handhold of some sort, but every stone he grabbed hold of on the riverbed just came loose in his hand. The waterfall loomed closer and closer, until they were just feet away from being swept to their deaths.

He felt his fingers close around a stone which remained rigidly in place, and he gripped on as tight as he could.

'Hold on!' he shouted to Ana, and while she held onto him with all her might Merric could feel her slipping.

'Let me go,' she said, her face pale from the wound on her arm. 'Save yourself!'

Her feet were dangling over the edge of the waterfall, her legs being battered by the river as it tumbled over.

'I'm not letting you go!' Merric cried, his teeth gritted.

The stone in his hand gave way, and he was swept once more towards the waterfall. Ana screamed when the riverbed beneath her vanished entirely and she tumbled over the edge. Merric felt himself begin to fall as well, and with one final, desperate grasp he felt his hand grab hold of the cliff of rock. The water cascading over the waterfall was pummelling him painfully, but he kept hold of both the rock and Ana's hand with all the strength he could muster.

He could hear a voice shouting his name, but the roar of the waterfall was deafening. He looked down and he and Ana locked eyes.

'Hold on!' he shouted again, and her grip tightened, clutching desperately onto him.

He knew it was useless though. He could feel his own hand slipping from the rock and knew he would not be able to hold on for much longer. They would both fall to their deaths. Ana's eyes looked down at the long drop, but Merric gave her arm a jerk.

'No!' he shouted, 'look at me! Don't look down!'

Now only his very fingertips were still holding onto the rock.

'Ana-' he began, not wanting to die with things being left unsaid..

But then he felt a hand take hold of his and heave him upwards. His head broke through the torrent of water thundering over edge, and he used his legs to help pull Ana up as well. Another pair of strong hands seized him under arms and helped heave him to safety. Merric looked around in surprise, and he saw Kasper pulling him up and away from the abyss. If the second pair of hands had belonged to Kasper then whose were the first? He looked down and saw that his hand was simply holding onto a rock protruding from the riverbed.

With Merric safe, Kasper reached down and heaved Ana upwards. She came over the edge of the waterfall, coughing and spluttering. Together, Merric and Kasper managed to pull her into the shelter of one of the boulders that littered the river. With her safe for the moment, Merric grabbed the shoulder straps of her pack and yanked her towards him, embracing her tightly. They were both soaked to the skin. Ana let out a slight whimper and reluctantly pulled away from Merric's embrace. Her sleeve was red with blood, and her teeth were gritted against the pain and the cold. She clamped her hand against the wound on her arm.

'Kasper! She's hurt,' Merric said through his own chattering teeth.

He was trembling, though whether from the icy water or from shock he could not say.

Kasper glanced their way, his longbow in his hands and an arrow notched on the string. With Merric and Ana out of immediate danger, he had turned his attention back at their attackers. Another couple of arrows came shooting out from the trees on the western bank. One plunged harmlessly into the water and the other clacked against the boulder and went spinning over their heads. Merric ducked just in time, and watched as Kasper shot an arrow in the direction of their attackers.

'If we don't get rid of them then we'll all be hurt, or worse,' Kasper said, looking back over his shoulder at Merric and Ana again.

'I'll be fine,' Ana said looking up at Merric through her sodden hair that was plastered across her face.

'Stay here,' Merric said to her.

He drew Hopebearer, making sure that Ana was sheltered from the arrows and the worst of the raging current. Squatting beside Kasper he peered around the boulder, but could not see any sign of their attackers.

'I don't see them,' he said.

'I think there's four of them,' Kasper replied.

Something suddenly caught his eye and he notched another arrow, adjusting his aim slightly. The soaking bowstring twanged and the arrow shot towards the treeline on the western bank, and they were rewarded with a cry of pain.

'Three of them,' Kasper corrected himself.

Another few arrows came their way, and Kasper ducked, snarling. Merric glanced around their cover again, and saw another boulder a little further across the river.

'I'm going to run for it,' he said.

He half expected Kasper to try and stop him, but the hunter only nodded grimly. Merric took a steadying breath and hurried as fast as he could through the knee-deep water, expecting an arrow to strike him at any moment. The river tugged at his feet but he kept on splashing through the water, no longer noticing the cold. He ducked into the shelter of the next boulder. Kasper and the unseen enemy continued to trade arrows, and Merric used their distraction to continue further across the river, hiding once more behind another boulder.

He had drawn the attention of the enemy now, and arrow after arrow splintered against the stone of his hiding spot. Kasper was making his way across the river after Merric, shooting more arrows at the western bank as he moved. Merric risked another glance around the boulder and could make out the shapes of the archers in the trees that were now just fifty feet away from him. They were just shadows in the gloom of the forest, but he knew that he would not need many guesses to work out what uniform they wore.

Two of the enemy archers were a bit further north of the ford, and the last one was stood alone in the trees straight ahead of Merric, beside the waterfall. Merric looked back at Kasper and, catching his attention, pointed at himself and then at the lone enemy archer. Kasper understood, and stood again, letting off another arrow towards the two enemies to the north.

Merric charged out from behind the last boulder, feeling a sense of relief when his feet found dry land on the western bank of the Rush. He could see the lone archer hurriedly notch an arrow and aim it at him, but the rushed shot went wide. Merric ran towards him, water dripping from *Hopebearer's* blade. The archer dropped his longbow and yanked a short sword from its scabbard. Merric darted between the trees and he could see, as expected, the symbol of the Monfort family stitched onto the chest of the man's jerkin. With a roar of determination Merric brought his sword swinging down towards the archer. His blow knocked straight through the archer's own sword, but the man dodged aside to avoid the blade. Merric swung back with a reverse swing and smashed the hilt of *Hopebearer* into the side of the archer's head. He went down like a sack of potatoes, knocked out cold.

Looking round, Merric caught sight of the other two archers. One of them had already fallen to another of Kasper's arrows. The hunter had now also reached the western bank of the river, and had another arrow pointed directly at the single remaining archer. The soldier, who had the symbol of the king stitched onto his own breast, looked between Kasper and Merric and knew that he was defeated. He dropped his longbow and raised his hands.

'I yield!' he cried.

'Watch him!' Merric called to Kasper, who nodded.

Taking no time to savour the victory, Merric splashed back into the river, wading over to where Ana was waiting. She smiled when she saw him safe.

'Did you get them?' she asked.

'We got them,' Merric said, relieved to find her still conscious.

He carefully pulled Ana to her feet and draped her arm around his shoulder. Struggling against the force of the water he slowly helped her towards the western bank.

'You saved me,' she said simply, as though she did not quite believe it.

'It was about time I returned the favour,' Merric replied with a smile. 'Besides, Kasper saved us both.'

He chose not to mention the mysterious hand who had first grabbed him. Thinking about Adkyn's similar experience in this very spot, and Merric's own previous rescue in the Willowbank outside Oaktyn, he decided that could wait for some other time.

Kasper had taken the captive archer over to where the Monfort soldier that Merric had knocked out was laying. He had rummaged around in the prisoners' small camp and found a length of rope, which he used to tie both men to a tree.

'Did you see their uniforms?' Kasper called over as he tied the final knot, when Merric and Ana approached.

Merric nodded.

'Monfort men and king's men, fighting together. Just like we feared,' he said.

'Are you okay?' Kasper asked Ana, eyeing her arm.

'It's not as bad as it looks,' she said bravely, trying to ignore the pain in her arm. But despite her words, Kasper took a strip of cloth and bound it around her the injury anyway.

Merric looked around at the trees that bordered the western bank of the river. Everything felt different to how it had been on the other side, and not just because the woods here looked less welcoming. They had only travelled the width of the river, but to Merric it felt like they had crossed halfway around the world.

'Well,' he said, looking around at the others, 'we've left The Head.'

The others seemed as unsettled by their new surroundings as he did. He, at least, had left his home dukedom before, even if it was only for his disastrous attempt at rescuing Sir Sebastien. For Kasper and Ana it was their first time ever leaving The Head, and it had certainly not been an easy crossing. Neither looked particularly comfortable at the knowledge that they were now in enemy territory.

'Let's get away from the river,' Kasper said, taking charge. 'These archers were probably just the scouts, told to keep a lookout at the ford. They might have a camp nearby, and who knows how many more of them there are.'

He retrieved as many arrows as he could find and refilled his quiver, and Merric sheathed *Hopebearer* again. He was chilled to the bone and desired nothing more than to rest and dry out his clothes, but he knew that Kasper was right. They could not spend a minute longer here on the riverbank, where more enemies could be loitering nearby. The Haunted Wood, or the Old Forest as Adkyn had named it, did not look like an inviting place, but at least they would be able to hide themselves within the dense forest and avoid any more soldiers who meant them harm.

'Can you walk?' Merric asked Ana as they made to set off into the forest.

'Of course I can,' she said defiantly, not wanting them to think her weak, but she also did not complain when Merric helped her along, her arm still draped around his shoulder.

The Head was behind them now, and only the unknown was ahead.

* * *

A pair of hidden eyes watched as Merric disappeared into the trees, along with the hunter and the girl. The figure, watching from afar, had chosen not to help when the fight had begun, deciding that he would be of better use if he remained out of sight. The time for him to do his part would soon come.

CHAPTER SEVENTEEN

The Haunted Wood

Sophya stepped out of the Grand Priory and into the drizzle that was falling over Eaglestone. Sir Orsten and Sir Oskar joined her, and they set off quickly across the square towards the gates of the castle. They were accompanied by half a dozen Eagle Guard, who had been newly recruited from among the finest knights in The Head to replace those who had been lost.

The rain was soaking Sophya's clothes, but she made every effort to look as though this did not bother her. Before, she would have hitched up her skirts and hurried to get out of the rain as quickly as possible and stop her precious hair from getting too wet. But she was a duchess now, and as such she had to keep up appearances.

Sir Oskar and Sir Orsten walked beside her in silence. They knew that Sophya was cross with them, and neither of them liked the fact that they had let her down. When she had discovered Merric's empty bedchamber and found the letter addressed to her, Sophya had been sick with worry. She worried still. Not because she was now the ruler of The Head, but because she was anxious at the thought of Merric being out there somewhere, all alone and possibly in danger. What if he did something foolish, or else had an accident, or got lost? Sir Oskar and Sir Orsten had led the search parties themselves, but despite looking for days they had found no sign of him. They had tried to make Sophya feel better by reassuring her that Merric had looked after himself well enough that summer.

'He wasn't alone then though, was he,' she had snapped back, her worry getting the better of her.

It was then that she had discovered that Tomas had now disappeared as well, and after a little investigating she found out that Ana was also missing. She could only assume that they had gone off to look for their friend themselves, and she hoped that they would be more successful than Sir Oskar and Sir Orsten had been.

But she had not been able to dwell on her worry for Merric though. He had left her with The Head to run, and at a very dangerous time as well. Fortunately, the Oakheart twins had done a better job of supporting her in this new role than they had done at finding Merric. She was not ready to forgive them for this failing quite yet, and they were fully aware of it.

Up ahead, a crowd had formed in the square. Sophya looked at them curiously. Usually, folk were keen to get out of the rain, but here they were standing around with no apparent interest in seeking shelter. Whatever was going on? She veered away from the gate of Eagle Mount and headed instead towards this gathering. Seeing her approach, the crowd parted with bows and curtseys. She was soon able to catch a glimpse of the four men standing at the centre of the mass of townsfolk. Her mouth opened slightly in surprise.

Sir Orsten drew his sword, and the Eagle Guard did the same.

'No, stop,' Sir Oskar said, calming his brother.

The four men were clearly Monfort soldiers, that much Sophya could tell. But the symbol of the black marching knight had been removed from their jerkins, and the men gave no sign of being a threat.

One of the soldiers, a bearded man, dropped to a knee.

'My lady,' he said. 'We didn't mean to cause no alarm.'

'Why are you here?' she asked stiffly, the memories of her time as an unknowing prisoner of the Monforts still fresh in her mind.

'We've got some information,' the bearded man said. 'Something we thought you might want to know.'

Half an hour later, the four Monfort deserters were stood in the Grand Hall, and Sophya was sat in the chair on the raised dais which had previously been occupied by her father and then Merric. Despite the protests of one of her handmaids, who had been waiting just inside the castle keep, Sophya had refused to go to her bedchamber and change into a dry dress. She sensed that what these men had to say was more important than making herself look more presentable. She had been right. The bearded soldier had just finished telling her and the Oakheart twins about their surprise meeting with Merric, and informing them about what the ex-duke was now planning to do.

Sophya's initial reaction had been relief at the thought that Merric was safe. But then the meaning of the soldier's words hit her.

'He's going to The Dale?' she said, looking in alarm at Sir Oskar and Sir Orsten.

'It certainly seems so, my lady,' Sir Oskar agreed.

'But I thought we agreed that it was too dangerous to attempt to reach The Dale, after Sir Sebastien's failed attempt,' Sophya said. 'And now Lord Tymon has sent us word that there is a Monfort army waiting on the western bank of the Rush! There's no way Merric could get past them, not unless he can turn himself invisible or something.'

She knew that her cousin was clever, but no one was *that* clever.

'I fear that he has no concerns for his own safety,' Sir Orsten said. 'If he feels that securing an alliance with The Dale will make up for what happened at Bridge Ford, then I do not think that anything would let him give up in his attempt.'

Sophya once again wished that the Oakheart twins had been able to find Merric when he had first run away. Then he would be here at the castle, safe, and not trying something so dangerous.

She took a couple of deep breaths, not wanting her worry for her cousin to show. She straightened her back, hoping she looked like her father had done in the face of worrying news.

'We will pray to the Mother to protect him,' she said.

'Please, my lady,' one of the other ex-Monfort soldiers piped up.

Sophya looked at him, and she saw him blush slightly. In times past, Sophya had loved having this effect on young men like him. In fact, she and her handmaids used to spend hours every day making sure that she turned knights' heads wherever she went. But she knew that Merric was not the only one who had been forced to grow up in the time since her father, mother and brother had died. Since Rayden Monfort, she no longer had any interest in chasing after boys like she used to. That had led to a dark time in her life, and she had no desire to see it repeated. And besides, she had far more important things to worry about now.

'What is it?' she asked the young soldier, eager for any news which may help her to remove her fears that Merric was walking into mortal peril.

'There might be another way to cross the river,' he said.

He told them about the stories he had heard, and that he had told Merric of them too. He explained that Merric had been determined to find this crossing, and use that as a back route into The Dale, avoiding the Monfort army waiting on The Head's doorstep.

The Oakheart twins looked at each other, and then Sir Orsten took a step to leave.

'I will go after him at once,' he said. 'If I can find him then I might be able to help him.'

'No, brother,' Sir Oskar said, holding out a hand to stop him. 'If he has found this crossing then he will be long gone by now. He is out of our reach, and beyond our help.'

Sir Orsten looked back at Sophya, who gave a reluctant nod.

'Merric has his friends with him, and I know they'll do all they can to keep him safe. Thank you,' she said, turning back to the four soldiers. 'It means a great deal to us that you travelled here to bring us this news. You are welcome to stay and call The Head your home.'

When the soldiers had nodded their thanks and left, Sir Oskar and Sir Orsten approached Sophya.

She bit her lip.

'Do you believe what that soldier said, about there being another way across the river? I've always believed the crossing at Bridge Ford is the only way over the Rush.'

'As have I,' Sir Oskar agreed. 'But if there is another route one can take then this might be our best chance of getting word to Lord Godfrei in The Dale. We must put our trust in Merric.'

Sophya nodded, thoughtfully. Her mind drifted away from Eagle Mount as she wondered where her cousin was now. Was he still safe? Had he found his way across the river? Were his friends still with him? And did he have the courage to do what needed to be done to give The Head a fighting chance in the war that must surely soon be upon them?

* * *

The forest was unlike any that Merric had ever seen before. The air felt warm and stuffy, and there was no breeze at all between the crooked old trunks. The leaves hung limply from the branches, as still and unmoving as the gnarled trees themselves. The sun and the sky above were completely hidden beyond the forest canopy, but Kasper led them between the trees in the direction that he thought, and hoped, was west.

It felt like a very ancient forest, and an unnatural one. The twisted trunks and reaching branches of the trees were like the hunched bodies of stooped old men, dappled in shades of green and grey. The very air felt almost alive, and Merric could feel the hairs on the back of his neck prickling. On the map in his study in Eagle Mount, Merric had known it as the Haunted Wood, but there were some who called it Tricksters Forest, and Adkyn had called it the Old Forest. To Merric, all the names seemed appropriate.

They walked as quickly as they could across the mossy, uneven ground, but Merric knew that he and Ana were slowing them down. Her arm had stopped bleeding, but she looked exhausted by the journey through the half-light of the forest. Merric had already slung her pack and crossbow over his own shoulder, and now he too was growing weary with every step. When he suggested to Kasper that they stop for a rest, the hunter shook his head with an uneasy expression.

'I don't like it in these woods,' he confessed. 'We should not stay here a moment longer than we need to.'

And so they continued on, Kasper with his longbow in his hands and an arrow notched ready on the string. He peered around cautiously, but no danger appeared. Nothing moved at all in the gloom beneath the trees, except for the three of them. If anything, this appeared to unsettle Kasper even more. Merric followed him as best he could, still supporting Ana. Her arm was draped over his shoulders and his hand was gripping her tightly around her waist. A day ago she would have pushed aside such a touch, but either her injury and weakened state, or else the fact that Merric had saved her from tumbling down the waterfall, was softening her attitude towards him. She welcomed the help.

While the forest was deathly still, a constant cacophony of sounds surrounded them. The roaring of the Rush had disappeared when they had delved into the woods, being muffled unnaturally by the trees. But now, all around them, they could hear the croaks of frogs that they could not see and the chirping of crickets, as well as other calls and cries of creatures that Merric did not recognise.

The ground was mossy beneath their feet, but at times it gave way, without warning, to bogs which they had no choice but to walk through, their feet disappearing beneath the thick, green water. It did not have the usual stagnant smell of bog-water though, and carried the same sweet, scent that seemed to fill the whole forest. It reminded Merric of something he had smelt once before, but he could not think where.

After a while of walking in silence through the eerie forest, Kasper stopped suddenly. Merric, not concentrating, nearly walked into the back of him.

'What is it?' he asked.

Kasper was sniffing at the air. Curious, Merric did the same and noticed the faint hint of the smell of woodsmoke through the sweet scent of the forest.

'Is it a fire?' Merric wondered, peering around the trees and seeing nothing.

'This way,' Kasper said, lifting his longbow slightly as he stepped carefully towards the smell.

Merric followed, loosening *Hopebearer* in the scabbard at his hip. Ana released her arm from around his shoulders, shaking her head when he looked back at her with an outstretched hand.

'I'm okay,' she promised, 'you go ahead.'

Hesitating for a moment, he went after Kasper. After a couple of minutes they discovered a small encampment. A fire had been made between the trees, and while the flames had been extinguished the charred and blackened wood still smoked steadily, which rose lazily and drifted in a grey cloud around the trees with no breeze to blow it away.

Merric took an alarmed step backwards when he saw the bodies. At least half a dozen men were lying dead on the ground around the campfire. Some looked as though they had been killed while sitting on the logs that had been their seats, while others appeared to have attempted to flee, only to be cut down before they had made it a handful of steps from the camp. Merric did not need to ask Kasper who the men were. Despite the blood he could clearly make out their uniforms. The black marching knight of the Monforts and the crown of the king were visible on their chests.

'They didn't even have a chance to draw their weapons,' Merric said with a shake of his head, seeing that the men's swords were still in their scabbards and spears and longbows were leaning against the surrounding trees where they had been left.

Kasper walked into the midst of the encampment, careful not to step on any of the bodies. He lowered his longbow and looked around at the devastation.

'It looks like they were caught unawares,' he said.

'Who could have done this?' Merric asked.

He of course had no love for the men who served Lord Aric, but the sight of the slaughter made him feel uneasy. There was something unnatural about it all.

'There's no sign of anyone,' Kasper said, squatting and looking around for footprints. 'I can only see six sets of tracks, all belonging to the victims.'

'He doesn't leave any footprints,' Ana said.

Merric turned at the sound of her voice. He had not heard Ana arrive at the encampment. She was looking around the scene with the same unease that Merric felt.

'Who?' Kasper asked, looking up at her.

'The Green Knight,' she said.

Merric scoffed and shook his head, turning away, but Kasper kept looking at her.

'That's just a story,' he said to her.

'Perhaps,' Ana said, wincing slightly as she reached out to a tree to steady herself. 'But all stories are based on truths, to some extent.'

She did not seem discouraged by the look of doubt on Merric's face.

'I have always believed that the Mother can be found somewhere in the world,' Ana said. 'She doesn't just watch over us from the heavens, but lives among us.'

'You're talking about the Lady of the Lake?' Kasper asked her, still watching her closely.

'Adkyn told us that this forest is the heart of the Mother's realm in the world. If that's true then She lives here, somewhere, and so her loyal protector and guardian would be here too. The Green Knight swore to defend the Mother's honour, and these men defiled Her.'

'How?' Kasper asked, his eyes narrowed.

The hunter was not particularly religious, but he was unsettled by this forest and was willing to concede to her knowledge.

'If this forest is Her home, then to chop trees and make a fire is a most terrible of crimes.'

Kasper looked around at the fire and nodded thoughtfully.

Merric glanced down uneasily at the bodies of the dead men. He did not really believe in the Mother, or the Lady of the Lake and the Green Knight. But, if they did exist, and they had killed these soldiers, then what would happen to the three of them? Kasper seemed to be sharing his thoughts.

'We should get moving,' he said.

Kasper and Ana were more than happy to agree to this. It was a disturbing scene, and they had no wish to stay there. But first, Kasper squatted down beside the dead soldiers' packs.

'Best see if they have anything of use.'

He rummaged around in the packs, pulling out stale loaves of bread and some cheese wrapped in a cloth. Putting them in his own pack he straightened up, and gestured for them to follow him.

Merric went to help Ana, but she waved him off.

'I can manage,' she said, and gave him a smile.

They walked for what Merric assumed was a few more hours, but he could not accurately have guessed exactly how much time had passed. There were no landmarks to identify the length of their journey, and the pale green light that filtered down through the trees did not seem to change, no matter how long they walked for.

'Surely the sun should be setting by now,' Merric said.

'Maybe,' Kasper said, looking upwards as though trying to see the sun for himself.

Frowning, Merric fell back a little and walked beside Ana.

'Let me take my pack,' she said, looking across at Merric who was continuing to struggle under the weight of both of their baggage.

'I can manage,' Merric lied.

Ana tutted at his bravado and pulled her pack off his shoulder.

'Your arm,' Merric protested.

'It's feeling a lot better,' Ana said.

When Merric did not believe her, she proved it by swinging the arm around. She even rolled up her sleeve and

Merric was amazed to see that the injury was already beginning to heal over. She appeared less astonished by the speed at which her body was recovering than Merric was. She seemed to understand this unnatural place better than any of them.

They reached a glittering stream which meandered across their route. Kasper crossed first, hopping from stone to stone and reaching the opposite bank without getting his feet wet. Ana went next, the colour starting to return to her face as her arm healed, and she made the crossing look far easier than someone who had been so recently injured should have. When Merric reached the others as well they pressed on through the trees, though he kept on glancing curiously at Ana and marvelling at her quick recovery.

Kasper kept them walking at a relentless pace, only reluctantly allowing them to come to a stop, finally, when Merric almost stumbled and fell in his exhaustion. He consented to them having a short break, and Merric and Ana collapsed gratefully onto the soft mossy ground. Kasper himself stayed on his feet and was glancing back the way they came, looking anxious to be on the move again.

'What is it?' Merric asked him wearily, spotting the hunter's behaviour.

'Probably nothing,' Kasper muttered. 'I just can't shake a feeling that we're being followed.'

Merric raised his eyebrows and looked back behind them. Nothing was stirring there at all.

'I can't see anything,' he offered.

Kasper shook his head.

'I know,' he said. 'It's just a feeling, I can't explain it.'

Kasper only allowed them a few minutes of rest, and then they set off again in the same direction they had been walking ever since they entered the forest. How Kasper knew they were still heading west, with no view of the sky above to guide him, Merric could never know, but he trusted the hunter's judgement. The trees gave no sign of thinning, and at times they had to squeeze between the twisted trunks, brushing aside sticky cobwebs and creeping vines to make a path. And yet still the sun gave no sign of setting, no matter how long they walked for. The warm, oppressive, stuffy air continued to press in all around them, and the forest was draped in the never-ending green hazy light.

Eventually, just as the monotony of the forest was beginning to frustrate Merric, they caught sight of a glow up ahead somewhere in the trees. Merric thought eagerly of a clearing, and assumed this was the source of the brightness. He longed for a sight of the sun and sky above him and a breath of cool air on his face after the humidity of the forest. But as they grew closer, the brightness looked less like it was from sunlight and more like it was an unnatural white glow. It began to get so bright that they could barely look directly towards it, and it caused the trees ahead of them to resemble nothing more than silhouettes against the piercing glow.

'Let's go around,' Kasper said, looking uneasily at the unnatural light.

Merric agreed, not wanting to get any closer. But Ana pushed past them both, walking straight towards the glow.

'Ana!' Merric hissed, wondering why he was keeping his voice down.

She ignored him and continued walking straight towards the light, as though she were a moth drawn to it. Kasper and Merric glanced at each other, before hurrying after her. Merric pushed past trees as he ran after Ana, blundering blindly towards the bright glow, and emerged suddenly beside a wide pool.

He drew up short, his gasp caught in his throat. It was larger than a pond but was too small to be considered a lake. The surface of the water was silent and still, and seemed to be glowing as though reflecting moonlight. But when Merric looked upwards he could see that the trees were arched together like a dome, and even here the sky was completely hidden from sight. The roots of the trees were reaching towards the water, and everything was bathed in the pale light which seemed to be coming from the depths of the pool itself.

Ana was kneeling at the water's edge, and Merric hurried up beside her.

'Don't touch the water,' he urged her, though he did not know why he assumed that would be an unwise thing to do.

'This is it,' Ana said, looking excitedly up at Merric.

The pool was reflected in her eyes, and the glow gave her an ethereal look.

'This is what Adkyn spoke of,' she continued, gazing in wonder at the pool. 'This is the heart of the Mother's realm. This is where all life here started.'

Merric glanced nervously at the pool. He saw no beautiful woman rising out of the water's depths as the tales of the Lady of the Lake told, nor any sign of Her knightly protector, but the unnatural lake gave him a deeply uncomfortable feeling.

'Let's go,' Merric said, trying to keep the nerves from his voice, and he reached for Ana's uninjured arm.

'Just a minute,' Ana said, and she bowed her head in prayer.

Kasper had arrived beside Merric, and he too looked troubled by the sight of the pool.

'Let's give her a moment,' he said, steering Merric away by the elbow.

'But-' Merric struggled, as Kasper guided him away from Ana.

'This is important to her,' Kasper muttered, when he came to a stop just beyond the trees.

They waited there, out of sight of the pool which was emitting the ghostly light.

'I didn't like that place,' Merric said, giving a shudder.

'Nor did I,' Kasper agreed, 'but we're not supposed to. This is for Ana, not us.'

He did not say anything more, and after a couple of minutes Ana returned to them, a humble smile on her face. Merric had wanted to ask her what had happened by the pool, or if she had heard anything in response to her prayers, but he somehow knew that it would be a foolish thing to ask. If he had learned anything growing up it was that religion was a very personal thing.

They left the glowing pool behind them and continued on their way. If nothing else, their arrival at that sacred place had broken up the repetitiveness of the journey through the seemingly endless forest. Before long, Merric stopped being curious about the way that the forest did not seem to grow light and dark with the passing of the sun and the moon, and he just began to accept it. In fact, lots of things seemed to stop bothering him the longer they walked. The smells and sounds of the forest began to feel normal to him, and even Kasper's concern that they were being followed stopped feeling like something to worry about.

Despite there being food in their packs they kept walking without stopping to eat, feeling no desire for food or drink. Merric hardly seemed to notice anything as they walked. His mind was as relaxed and calm as it had ever been. There were times when he was not even sure if he was awake or asleep on his feet. Reality and dreams seemed to blur together. At one point, Merric thought he could see the glowing eyes of fae forest creatures watching them pass from behind the trees, but when he blinked and looked again they were gone.

'Did you just see…' he asked Ana, tapping her on her shoulder.

'Yes, I did,' Ana said with a smile before he had finished, her voice almost lazy.

Merric kept peering around as they walked, and again he saw the eyes watching them. This time, though, they did not disappear when he looked more closely. He blinked, and they blinked back.

'It's not real,' Merric said, confidently, turning away from them. 'I'm just tired. I'm imagining things.'

Fireflies danced around the trees, adding their own light to the strange green twilight that filled the whole forest. Merric watched them, mesmerised, feeling his legs plodding onwards of their own accord. Even Kasper, who had been walking with his longbow in his hands, was starting to look more relaxed and content. He eventually slung the longbow over his shoulder, no longer feeling like he needed it close at hand.

'Are we lost?' Merric asked Kasper, who stubbornly shook his head.

'No, we just keep going west,' he said.

'But which way is west?' Merric muttered, finding himself laughing for some reason.

Kasper stopped in his tracks, scratching his head.

'You know what? I don't actually know,' he admitted.

'We're lost,' Merric said wisely to Ana, as though he alone knew it.

'I'm getting tired,' Ana yawned, and as soon as she said this Merric felt his own eyes beginning to close too.

'We should stop, just for a little while,' Merric said, and this time Kasper did not object.

'Just for a little while,' he agreed.

They stopped right where they were and collapsed onto the ground, leaning against trees and closing their eyes gratefully. Almost immediately Merric felt sleep wash over him, and nothing had ever felt more welcome in his entire life.

Merric dreamed that they were walking through the forest still. In his dream, the creatures he had seen watching them from behind the trees came right up to them. The woodland sprites were strange little creatures, standing no taller than Merric's knee. They looked like they were made from the trees themselves, with rattles in their small, wooden hands that clinked as they walked. Their glowing eyes were all different shades of yellow and green and pink, and they chittered curiously up at Merric, Kasper and Ana. Their little voices almost sounded like windchimes, like songs that echoed around the trees.

At first, Merric had been scared of the little creatures, but he quickly learned that they meant them no harm.

They danced around them, singing their strange little songs, and were soon joined by other fae creatures. Fawns emerged nervously from behind the trees, looking fearfully at the humans walking through their forest. The fawns almost resembled normal folk, except horns grew from beneath their curly hair and their legs resembled those of a goats. Soon, even the most cautious of the fawns had grown accustomed to Merric and the others, and they joined in with the song being sung by the small woodland sprites. One or two of the fawns even produced panpipes and added their music to the air.

The dream grew stranger still when a clip-clopping announced the arrival of a herd of centaurs, who appeared out of the twilight gloom. The heads, arms and naked torsos of beautiful men and women were merged with the bodies and legs of horses of every colour. They gently reached down with their strong arms and hoisted Merric, Ana and Kasper onto their backs. Merric rode on the back of a female centaur whose long auburn hair cascaded down to her waist, and she smiled back at him as she carried him along, giving him a chance to rest his weary feet.

The procession trotted and danced its way through the trees. The centaurs led the way and were followed by the panpipe-playing fawns and the singing woodland sprites. Like some strange carnival procession they made their way through the forest, until with a sudden flourish the music ended and the centaurs came to a halt. Merric looked ahead and saw that the trees were thinning. Beyond them, rocky mountains could be seen rising up. Merric and the others were almost sad to say goodbye to their new friends. The centaurs plucked their passengers from their backs and placed them gently onto the ground. They bowed their graceful heads and turned around, trotting back into the heart of the forest again. The fawns and the woodland sprites went with them, still dancing and playing their mischievous music. The sound faded, and eventually they disappeared from both sight and sound as the gloom of the forest swallowed them up.

CHAPTER EIGHTEEN

An unforeseen meeting

Merric awoke slowly, stretching his arms and feeling surprisingly well rested. He felt like he had enjoyed the best sleep he had experienced in a long time. Kasper and Ana were stirring as well, rubbing the sleep from their eyes.

The air around them was no longer the usual green-tinged twilight that they had been used to during their journey through the forest, and the light instead resembled the last dark before the arrival of dawn. There was a slight pink to the sky to Merric's right, marking the first signs of a new day's sunrise, and it took a moment for him to realise what he was seeing. He could see the sky again, for the first time in what seemed like ages.

He glanced around and saw that the trees grew much thinner here than they did where they had stopped to sleep. Not only could Merric see the sky, but he could see the land beyond the trees as well. Up ahead of them, through the breaks in the canopy of leaves, he could make out mountains beyond the border of the forest. With a look of disbelief appearing on his face, Merric spun around and looked back into the depths of the forest. Was he imagining it, or could he still hear the faint sound of panpipes?

He shook his head, as though to remove such thoughts from his mind. It had just been a dream, brought on by that strange forest. But when he glanced around at Kasper and Ana he saw that they both had confused expressions on their faces too, as though they were having similar thoughts to him.

'I guess we had walked further before stopping than we thought,' Kasper offered, and Merric eagerly jumped on this explanation.

'We've reached the other side of the forest without realising it,' he agreed.

'I'm starving,' Ana added.

They all were, and after eating nothing during their journey through the forest they now tucked in eagerly to the food they had in their packs.

'How long do you reckon we were in there?' Ana asked, looking back into the trees.

Based on how hungry he was, Merric guessed it could even have been as much as several days. That forest had played curious tricks on their minds, and he doubted they would ever know for sure what had happened to them during their journey through the trees. They wolfed down the food, and drank deeply from the water of a stream that was trickling nearby. Eager to be away from that strange place, Merric turned to Kasper.

'How far do you think it is to The Dale now?' he asked him.

Kasper pointed at the mountains ahead of them that they could see through the thinning trees.

'That way is north,' he said. 'Those mountains must mark the beginning of The Dale.'

Merric concentrated his mind on the vast map back in Eagle Mount.

'The Great North Road leads up from The Hinterland,' he said. 'It heads right through the mountains and into The Dale itself. It should be a little west of here.'

'Let's just hope that we find the way still open to us,' Kasper said. 'I'd rather not find the road barred and have to climb over the mountains instead.'

Glancing up at the snowy peaks ahead of them, Merric and Ana quietly agreed.

They packed up their things and made to leave. As they did so they heard the cracking of twigs behind them. They all spun around, looking back into the gloom of the forest. It was not the sound of hooves that Merric had heard in his dream, but rather the heavy tread of boots.

'Who is that?' Ana said.

Merric thought back to what Kasper had said about his suspicions that someone, or something, was following them. They all stood there for a moment, peering into the trees.

'Let's not wait to find out,' Kasper said at last.

They set off, walking northwards and leaving the forest and the sound of footsteps behind them. Merric and Kasper were glad to be away from the trees, but Ana turned back more than once to look back at the forest, as though unable to say goodbye to it.

The land beyond the Haunted Wood was a sloping grassland covered in wildflowers. It led uphill towards the first low mountains of the Silver Peaks that marked the border of The Dale. The sun had risen, casting its morning light across the hillside. The air felt chilly after the stuffiness of the forest, and their breath rose in a mist in front of their faces. Merric could not help himself from glancing backwards from time to time, looking back down the hill towards the forest that seemed to stretch for miles. He could not see any sign of anyone following them. He wondered if, like so many other things during their time in the forest, he had simply imagined the sound of footsteps.

They were aiming for a gap between two low mountains ahead of them, which they reasoned would give their best chance of reaching the Great North Road. From Merric's memory of the map, the Pembrook river carved its way through the Silver Peaks. Once they had entered the mountains they should be able to follow the river westward until they found the road. It sounded simple enough in his head, and he hoped it would prove to be no more difficult than that in reality. The going would be hard, but Merric preferred that option rather than going back into the Haunted Wood and trying to find the Great North Road further south. When he mentioned this to Kasper, the hunter quite agreed.

'And it's not just that forest that I'd rather avoid,' Kasper added. 'The further south we join up with the road the more likely we are to bump into Monfort patrols.'

As they neared the mountains the grass beneath their feet turned to rock, and the hike became more difficult. Merric thought nervously of the wolves they had run into on their journey to find Adkyn, and he worried about a similar encounter here. Fortunately, Kasper's longbow gave Merric some reassurance. Birds circled overhead, but they saw little sign of life apart from them. They rested for an hour when the sun was at its highest point, but they had eaten all of their food that morning and so had nothing to have for their midday meal. Regretting getting carried away at breakfast, Merric and the others got back to their feet and continued walking uphill. The mountains loomed overhead, and they kept on heading towards the wooded gap between the two nearest ones.

They entered the trees with some apprehension, but Merric was relieved to find that they were quite different to the gnarled old trunks of the Haunted Forest. He almost found the sight of the normal pine trees, standing straight like soldiers, reassuring and regular. His mood was further cheered when Kasper, spotting movement ahead of them, unslung his longbow and dashed off. He returned, a couple of minutes later, grinning.

'Got us some dinner for tonight,' he said, cheerfully.

They walked for an hour longer, feeling fallen pine needles beneath their feet. Merric was starting to relax after their odd adventures in the Haunted Wood, and was feeling oddly safe beneath the trees. He stooped down and plucked up a pinecone from the ground. He heaved it as far as he could, and it disappeared into the trees.

'Pathetic,' Ana mocked, and picked one up herself.

Even with her previously injured arm, which had healed remarkably quickly, her throw easily outranged his. Kasper could only smirk and shake his head, amused, as Merric and Ana kept on hunting around for the choicest pinecones and trying to outdo each other as they launched them as far as they could. Sometimes, Kasper forgot just how young his two youthful friends were.

The trees ended as suddenly as they had started. They discovered that they had passed between the two mountains, and were greeted by a spectacular sight. They were surrounded on all sides by snow-topped peaks of an unimaginable scale. Previously only seeing them from afar, Merric could never have imagined just how big the mountains really were. They rose higher and higher as they stretched off into the distance, marking the natural border of The Dale. Merric had also not been prepared for the sight of the Pembrook river. Their way ahead was barred by a wide ravine, cut through the mountains over thousands of years. Cautiously approaching the edge of the ravine they could see the pale blue water of the river below. Ana stood right at the edge, peering downwards, but Merric, with a sick feeling in his stomach, reached out and pulled her back from the precipice.

The river flowed east, disappearing round a bend to the east as the ravine meandered between the mountains like a blue ribbon, and Merric knew that somewhere over there the Pembrook joined with the Rush. To the west, somewhere, the Great North Road crossed the river, and that was where they must now head.

Just as they were about to set off, there came the sound of someone else emerging out of the trees behind them, and a voice called out.

'Look how far you have come,' the voice said.

Merric spun around, pulling his sword from his scabbard. Kasper and Ana suddenly had their own weapons in their hands too.

A figure was stood facing them. He was casually tossing a stone up and down and catching it with one hand. The figure was no more than a silhouette with the sun behind him, and Merric could not make out his face. But there was something familiar about his accent. The figure took a few steps forward, out of the blinding sunlight, and Merric gasped when he finally recognised him.

'Seb!' he cried, relief flooding through him.

Sir Sebastien grinned back at Merric, his arms outstretched as though to confirm that it was, indeed, him. He was still wearing his armour, and did not seem to have suffered too badly at his captors' hands.

'I can't believe it! You're alive!' Merric exclaimed.

He hurried a few steps closer to his friend, before pausing and sheathing *Hopebearer*.

'Sorry,' he laughed, pointing at the sword, 'an old habit.'

'Completely understandable,' Sir Sebastien chuckled. 'You have been having quite an adventure!'

'How did you find me? How did you escape?' Merric said, shaking his head in disbelief at seeing his friend alive and well.

'Merric,' Ana warned.

Unlike Merric, she had noticed that Sir Sebastien had his own sword in his hand.

'Ah! You must be Ana?' Sir Sebastien said, ignoring Merric's question and looking at her. 'I have heard so much about you.'

Ana did not answer him. Merric was so pleased to see Sir Sebastien that he had not noticed that she and Kasper had not lowered their weapons.

'Merric, get back,' Kasper said, his longbow aimed at the Ouestorian. 'Get away from him.'

'And who is this?' Sir Sebastien crooned. 'You do enjoy the company of *common* folk, don't you, Merric?'

Merric frowned at Sir Sebastien, wondering why his friend was being like this. Then, at long last, he finally noticed the sword.

'Seb, what's going on?' he said, starting to feel uneasy. 'How did you escape the Monforts?'

It was the second time he had asked the question, and was growing concerned that Sir Sebastien was not answering it.

The Ouestorian knight just laughed again. It was the same happy laugh he had used when the two of them had spent time together at Eagle Mount, but now it sent chills through Merric.

'Escaped?' he laughed. 'That's a good one, *mon duc.*'

He said the last two words in a mocking tone. Merric took a few steps away from his friend. Sir Sebastien lifted his sword and rested it over his shoulder in a casual manner, still tossing the stone up and down with his other hand. The blade glistened in the sunlight, and Merric recognised it as being the same sword that he had given the knight when he had set off on his journey.

'I see that since I failed to make it to The Dale, you have decided to come yourself,' Sir Sebastien said. 'But I am curious, did you do that out of a sense of duty, or out of a sense of shame?'

Merric just stared at him.

'You see,' Sir Sebastien said, a smirk playing across his face, 'I saw what you did when you rode out from

Bridge Ford in your valiant effort to rescue me. Tell me, how does it feel, knowing you got all those men killed?'

Merric could only mouth wordlessly at him, trying to process what Sir Sebastien was saying.

'They did not need to die,' the Ouestorian said with a sigh. 'If you had only handed yourself over to the Monforts, then they would live still. You were all they wanted.'

As quick as a flash, Sir Sebastien darted forward and grabbed hold of Merric. He gripped him tightly, one of his forearms pinning Merric's neck against his armoured chest. He looked at Kasper and Ana, as though daring one of them to try and shoot him, and risk hitting Merric instead.

'You are coming with me,' Sir Sebastien whispered into Merric's ear, before glancing back at the other two. 'Do not try anything stupid. Our young friend here is required at The Citadel. I am sure you would not want to keep Lord Aric waiting any longer.'

Merric felt himself turning purple as his windpipe was being constricted. He gasped for breath. He could only look on, helplessly, as Kasper and Ana continued to aim at Sir Sebastien, looks of desperation and horror on their faces. Merric suddenly felt a tug as the Ouestorian began to drag him back towards the trees.

With a twang, Ana shot her crossbow. Sir Sebastien jerked his head to the side and the bolt just missed him, hitting a tree trunk with a thud and remaining there, quivering. With a snarl, the Ouestorian kicked Merric to the ground and then hurled the stone that he still held in his hand hard towards Kasper. It struck the archer cleanly on the forehead before Kasper could release his arrow. He crumpled to the ground, unconscious.

Merric clawed at his painful throat, gasping for breath as he laid on the rocky ground. With him out of the fight for a moment, and Kasper knocked out cold, Sir Sebastien focused on taking out Ana next. She hurrying to reload her crossbow, but the Ouestorian was charging at her, his sword raised. She took a couple of steps away from him but could go no further because of the ravine at her back. Sir Sebastien swung his sword at her and she ducked, letting the blade sing over her head and cutting nothing but air. He brought his sword round again with a savage backstroke, and Ana just managed to raise her crossbow in time. His blade bit deep into the wood, sending splinters flying. He attacked a third time, and Ana blocked it again. But this time the crossbow split in two. Both halves flew out of her hands and tumbled through the air down towards the river far below. The faint sound of a splash rose up to meet them. The colour had drained from her face, but Ana gritted her teeth in determination as she awaited Sir Sebastien's killing blow.

Merric slowly rose to his hands and knees, still struggling to breathe. He tried to draw *Hopebearer* but he could only half unsheathe it from his position on all fours. Ana dodged another of Sir Sebastien's attacks, and seeing her there, defenceless and moments from death, gave Merric a surge of much needed strength.

'No!' he cried, rising to his feet and finally managing to draw his sword.

He stumbled over to Sir Sebastien, gasping for breath and ignoring the blotches that marred his vision caused by his near-suffocation. Hearing his shout, the Ouestorian turned and watched him approach.

'No, Merric,' he said calmly.

He beat aside Merric's sword, almost playfully. Merric mustered all of his energy and kept swinging *Hopebearer* at Sir Sebastien, trying desperately to remember everything that the Ouestorian himself had taught him. He was not going to let anyone else die for him, not after what had happened to the Eagle Guard.

'You will not stop me,' Sir Sebastien jeered as he parried Merric's attacks. 'Rayden Monfort failed, and his scarred henchman failed. I will not!'

'Fight back!' Merric demanded, but the Ouestorian just laughed.

Merric continued to have his blows parried away, but his sword finally managed to find an opening in Sir Sebastien's lazy defences. *Hopebearer* cut into the Ouestorian's arm, finding a gap between the knight's armour.

Sir Sebastien seethed at the pain, his eyes now showing anger rather than amusement. He brought his fist back and punched Merric hard across the head with the hilt of the sword. Merric reeled backwards and stumbled, dazed. Sir Sebastien growled in satisfaction, seeing Merric sprawled on the ground again. He turned around to finish off Ana, who still stood defencelessly with her back to the ravine.

His sword came hissing down towards her. As quick as a flash, Ana reached over her shoulder and into her quiver, tugging out one of her crossbow bolts. She seized hold of Sir Sebastien's sword hand so that his attack went wide, and brought her other hand forward.

Sir Sebastien screamed when the crossbow bolt pierced his eye. He reeled backwards, clawing at it, before turning his one good eye at Ana. With a bellow of pain and rage he lunged towards her.

She flung herself to one side and Sir Sebastien missed her. He wobbled there for a moment, his arms grasping at thin air. With a dreadful scream he toppled over the edge of the ravine. His cry of terror faded and disappeared as he fell to the watery death that awaited him below.

CHAPTER NINETEEN

Sir Henri the Handsome

They crouched down behind the thistle bushes that grew along the ridge, looking down onto the road in the valley below. There was no sign of movement, neither to the south, where the road snaked around clusters of pine trees as it led out of the mountains and into The Hinterland, nor to the north, where it crossed over the river and wound its way higher up into the mountains.

'It looks quiet enough,' Ana said.

A couple of hours earlier, still reeling from the desperate struggle, Ana and Merric had roused Kasper from his unconscious state with a splash of water to his face. Apart from the nasty lump on his forehead from where the thrown stone had struck him, not to mention a splitting headache, he seemed to have suffered no lasting damage from the attack. After making sure that Kasper was okay, Merric had slumped back, stunned by the shock of his friend's sudden reappearance, not to mention what Sir

Sebastien had then tried to do. With Kasper distracted by the throbbing pain in his head, and Merric's mind trying to make sense of what had just happened, Ana herself had taken the lead.

She had led them west, following the edge of the ravine with the river flowing below them. By the late afternoon they had reached the edge of the valley, along which the Great North Road weaved its way through the Silver Peaks on its way to The Dale.

As they crouched behind the bushes, peering down at the road, Kasper had to agree with Ana's assumption.

'Yeah,' he said, 'I think you're right. It looks quiet. We should probably make a run for it, though. If there are any Monfort men hiding down there then they'll definitely try to stop us crossing the river. Once we're on the other side we'll be safe. They wouldn't dare cross into The Dale themselves.'

They all looked across at the river. The road sloped down to the riverbank and forded the shallow water, before rising up again on the other side. It was an unremarkable border, separating The Dale from The Hinterland. In fact, unwary travellers who were not paying attention could easily cross into The Dale without even realising it. It was not as grand or imposing an entrance to the dukedom as Bridge Ford was, but The Dale had always stayed out of the squabbles between dukes that had marred High Realm's history, and as such they had clearly felt that walls and gates were not necessary to guard their borders.

'Are you ready, Kasper?' Ana said, turning and looking at him.

Kasper was fingering the lump on his head, but his hand dropped away when he felt her eyes on him.

'Ready when you are,' he assured her. 'But I'll be happier when this wretched aching goes away.'

Ana glanced across at Merric, who had been silent ever since Sir Sebastien had fallen into the ravine. He gave her a nod to show that he, too, was ready.

They rose from their vantage point and hurried quickly down the side of the ridge towards the road. The ground under their feet was a mixture of loose stone and tufts of highland grass, and their descent caused a small avalanche of pebbles to tumble down alongside them towards the road below.

They reached the road, and a quick glance around told them that their clumsy decent had not triggered a sudden appearance of Monfort soldiers who had been waiting in ambush. Breathing a sigh of relief, they never-the-less set off along the road at a fast pace, heading north towards the ford and the relative safety of The Dale that lay beyond.

As they hurried along the road, Ana kept on glancing across at Merric. He tried to reassure her by throwing her a casual smile to show that he was okay. She half smiled back, but did not look altogether convinced.

In truth, Merric did not feel okay at all. His mind was still reeling at the sudden appearance of Sir Sebastien.

Seeing his friend had been shock enough, as he had half convinced himself that Sir Sebastien had been killed by the Monforts when Merric had failed to rescue him. The fact that the Ouestorian was not only alive but had also tried to kill Ana and Kasper was more than Merric could comprehend. What had caused his friend to suddenly try to do something like that?

But despite his confusion about Sir Sebastien's behaviour, all Merric could think about now was his friend's face as he had fallen down into the ravine. Merric knew that the look of terror and hatred on Sir Sebastien's face would haunt his dreams for weeks to come. It had been nothing like the laughing, friendly face of the man who had been his close companion back when Merric had been Duke of The Head. And that troubled him more than anything else.

'I'm sorry,' Ana said, glancing once more at Merric.

He did not know whether she meant that she was sorry that Sir Sebastien was not the man Merric had thought he was, or that she was sorry that she had been forced to kill him.

'You had no choice,' he said, deciding that she meant the latter. 'It was him or us.'

Ana smiled gratefully at him. Deciding that it might be safe to discuss the matter, she continued.

'He was trying to take you, wasn't he.'

Merric nodded slowly.

'Maybe that was part of the arrangement for being released from the Monforts' dungeons?' he suggested. 'Maybe he was let go in return for taking me to them.'

'No,' Ana said, firmly. 'The man you knew would never have agreed to something like that. He was your friend!'

Merric felt slightly uncomfortable hearing her defend Sir Sebastien in a way that he knew the Ouestorian would never have defended her. He hoped she was right though. He did not want to believe that Sir Sebastien would betray him just to save himself. He thought desperately for another explanation for the Ouestorian's actions, but could think of none.

They reached the river and splashed across the cold mountain water. It could not have been more different to the ford they had used to cross the Rush a few days earlier. The Pembrook river was wide but gentle and slow moving, with the water only just covering their feet. It was icy cold but crystal clear, and Merric squatted and scooped some of the water into his mouth with cupped hands. It was wonderfully refreshing. Despite how cold it was he even rubbed some of it onto his face to help perk himself up.

When they reached the northern bank of the river, Merric paused and looked around. They had done it. They had reached the dukedom of the Florin family, and were one step closer to securing the alliance between them and The Head. For the first time since he had set off from Eagle Mount, Merric felt a glimmer of hope inside.

He looked up at the mountains that towered over them on both sides, bright in the afternoon sunshine that shone down through breaks in the white clouds. He could see hawks and other birds circling high in the sky, but other than that there was no one to witness Merric, Ana and Kasper's arrival in The Dale. Up ahead the road meandered around the peaks, rising higher and higher through the mountain pass that was the only route through the Silver Peaks and into the dukedom of the Florins. In the worst winters it was said that the route through the mountains was entirely impassable because of the snow drifts that would form there, but fortunately they were still a couple of months away from such worries. Far ahead, in the distance, the crests of the highest mountains disappeared into the clouds, their snow-topped summits hidden from view.

Kasper and Ana walked straight past Merric as he stood there, looking about and marvelling at the mountains that were unlike anything he had ever seen. Even the Storm Mountains in the north of The Head, where they had met Adkyn, would have been dwarfed by the Silver Peaks. Realising he had been left behind, Merric hurried up the road after the others. What little conversation passed between the three of them soon fizzled out as the road became steeper as it climbed through the mountains. They soon did not have any energy left to waste on words.

The air grew colder as the sun sank out of sight behind the mountains to the west, casting chilly shadows across the road. There was very little plant life growing up here, with only the occasional thicket of wiry bushes breaking up the endless grey of the rocks. There were no trees lining the road nor clinging to the edge of the mountainsides, and Merric thought with mounting apprehension about the cold night they could expect if they camped somewhere with no wood available for a fire.

The road curved widely to the right, beneath a sheer cliff of rock which towered overhead. In front of them the road continued to rise, illuminated in the setting sun which shone through a gap in the mountains. In the orange glow that drenched the scene ahead of them, Merric spied a lone figure standing on the road, as though waiting for them. He was sat atop a horse in the middle of the road, and while he was too far away to make out clearly, Merric could tell that the figure was looking down the road at them, watching their approach.

'Look!' Merric said.

'Who do you think he is?' Ana asked.

Kasper went to pull his longbow from his shoulder. Their run-in with the hostile Sir Sebastien had clearly put him on edge. But Merric stopped him.

'Let's keep going,' he suggested. 'If he's from The Dale then he might be a friend to us.'

Kasper looked apprehensive, not wanting to trust a stranger met here in an unfamiliar land, but he let go of his longbow and decided to trust Merric's judgement this time.

They kept walking up the road, looking nervously at the waiting figure. As they neared him they could see that he was a knight. His armour glinted in the evening light, and his orange surcoat seemed to positively blaze in the setting sun. He was wearing his helmet as though ready for battle, but he was sat in a relaxed posture in his saddle. His sword was in its sheath and his shield was slung over his back. He did not seem to be a threat to them. Merric kept his hand far from the hilt of *Hopebearer* as he walked towards the knight, wanting to show that they, too, were not looking for a fight.

'Greetings,' the knight called out, slightly muffled through his helmet, when they were just a stone's throw away.

Merric, Ana and Kasper came to a halt. Now that they were close they could make out the symbol of a dark green tower on the knight's orange surcoat.

'We're friends,' Merric called back.

The knight dismounted and walked his horse down the road towards them. When he reached them he stopped and patted his horse on the neck.

'Of that, I have no doubt,' the knight said, his helmeted head looking at each of them in turn. 'My wardens have been watching you ever since you crossed the Pembrook, and they sent word to me of your approach. If you had ill intentions towards The Dale then they would not have let you come this far.'

'Your wardens?' Merric asked, not understanding.

He had not seen anyone since they had arrived at the Great North Road, and he had certainly not had any idea that they were being watched.

The knight gave a slight wave of his hand and Merric sensed movement out of the corner of his eye. Kasper started in alarm and went for his longbow again when he saw the dozen or so figures stir in the mountains around them. They were clad in cloaks of grey and brown wool, which all but camouflaged them perfectly against the mountainside. Each clutched a longbow of their own and had long, wild hair that blew about their faces in the mountain wind. The men looked at ease, and Kasper slowly released his grip on his longbow.

'They've been watching us?' he asked, looking around at them as though disappointed that he had not seen them before. 'They have done well to hide themselves from my keen eyes. I usually miss very little.'

'I would be disappointed if you *had* spotted them, for it is their job to be hidden from view,' the knight laughed. 'My name is Sir Henri Irons. I am the Sentinel of the Pass, charged by Lord Godfrei Florin to watch over the entrance to The Dale. My men and I are proud to say that no one enters our dukedom without our knowledge.'

'How do you know we're friends?' Merric asked, not feeling entirely comforted by the sight of the archers that surrounded the heights around him. He knew that, if Sir Henri willed it, the three of them would be riddled with arrows before Merric would even have had a chance to take a single step.

'We have heard rumours that there are armies amassing in The Hinterland,' Sir Henri said. 'The banners of the Monforts and the king have been seen, and so we have been extra vigilant on our borders, on the lookout for trespassers with ill will towards our dukedom. But you are no Monforts, I can tell that much for certain. I confess that I am curious though. Who are you? You do not get many folk travelling abroad these days.'

Merric paused for a moment, but he saw no reason to hide the truth from Sir Henri. After all, he was here to seek the aid of The Dale, and if he could not trust them then it would be a wasted journey.

'We're from The Head,' he said. 'We're travelling to Bluewall Castle, to seek an audience with Lord Godfrei Florin.'

The knight's helmeted head tilted to one side, considering Merric.

'How did you get past the Monforts?' he asked, curiously. 'I hear the army of Sir Axyl Monfort, Lord Aric's nephew, is encamped outside Bridge Ford and is barring all travel to and from The Head.'

'It's a long story,' Merric said, smiling wearily.

Sir Henri did not press the matter, and looked in turn at Kasper and Ana as though studying them too.

'Are you envoys of Lord Merric Jacelyn?' he asked.

Merric hesitated, glancing at Ana, who nodded.

'I am Merric Jacelyn,' he said.

Sir Henri stared at him for a moment before raising his hands and lifting off his helmet, revealing a head of shoulder-length red hair. He was a young knight, perhaps around the same age Tristan had been, and only a few years older than Merric himself. He was clean shaven, and had a birthmark on the side of his face like a wine stain. Sir Henri seemed to notice Merric's eyes flicker towards the birthmark, and his face reddened slightly.

'You are certainly an unexpected visitor to The Dale, my lord,' Sir Henri said to Merric, seeming unable to look him directly in the eyes now that he had removed his helmet. 'It will take you at least another day to cross the mountains, and you will not find any comfort sleeping on the side of the road. I insist that you accept my hospitality and shelter at my castle for this night. It is not far.'

The prospect of a roof to sleep under was a desirable one, so they went gladly with Sir Henri as he led them further up the Great North Road. The wardens blended once more into the mountainside and disappeared from sight, ready to continue their watching of the border. Merric and the others walked up the road for another hour before Merric spied Sir Henri's castle. It was a simple fortress, just a single tower circled by a wall. It sat beside the road on a shoulder of rock that extended out from the mountainside. It looked like a desolate, lonely place to live, but light was blazing from the windows that were dotted around the circular tower, and Merric relished the idea of a little comfort.

'Welcome to Valley Gate,' Sir Henri said. 'It is the castle of the Sentinel of the Pass, and has been my home for the past two years.'

The gates were pulled open at their approach by a pair of wardens, and up close Merric could see that they were all small men, light of foot and well-used to the mountains that they called home. They seemed to possess keen eyes, and Merric was not surprised that their gaze missed nothing in these mountains.

Once inside the walls, another man took Sir Henri's horse and the knight led the three of them through a doorway and into the tower. The chamber beyond was circular, and seemed to be the garrison's armoury. Barrels packed full of arrows filled much of the space, and a few more of the wardens were sat around repairing the feather fletchings on some of them, or else sharpening the steel arrowheads on a grindstone. A wooden staircase stood at one side of the room and Sir Henri took them upstairs, past what appeared to be a kitchen and up another flight, which led to the hall of the simple castle. An empty fireplace stood in a niche in the circular wall, while a table sat in the middle of the floor. Torches in brackets illuminated tapestries that were draped across the stone walls, which Merric assumed were Sir Henri's attempt to make the cold, barren castle feel a little more like home.

A boy, also dressed in orange with the dark green tower symbol on his chest, emerged up the stairs behind them and stared curiously at the visitors. He went to the hearth and lit a fire, and soon the draughty hall was filled with a pleasant warmth and the sound of crackling flames.

'Thank you Luc,' Sir Henri said to the boy, who disappeared back down the stairs. 'He is my squire,' he explained to Merric. 'I do not think he will ever forgive me for leaving the family castle of Hearth Home and coming here to this desolate place instead.'

While Kasper and Ana sank gratefully onto chairs and warmed their hands by the fire, Merric wandered around the walls inspecting the tapestries. He could not claim to be an expert in art, but the tapestries were beautiful and seemed to chart the history and exploits of a noble family. He assumed it was Sir Henri's own family. He had not heard of the Irons family before, but judging by the depictions on the tapestries he assumed they had a great and chivalrous history.

As he circled the wall, looking with interest at the tapestries, he reached a window and paused. The sun had almost completely set now, but there was still enough light to show that the castle of Valley Gate offered a spectacular view of the road as it headed south out of The Dale and towards The Hinterland. There was no chance that anyone could enter the dukedom without the knowledge of the Sentinel of the Pass, nor without his permission.

'I regret that I cannot offer the surroundings that one such as yourself deserves, my lord,' Sir Henri apologised to Merric. 'We are not suited to guests here at Valley Gate. We have no servants, and little in the way of luxuries. It is only myself, my squire Luc and two dozen wardens that live here. We have supplies of food and firewood delivered to us by wagon once every fortnight, but apart from that we are on our own out here.'

'The shelter of your roof is more than enough hospitality for us,' Merric assured him. 'You are kind to take us in.'

'My lord, it is not a matter of kindness, but rather a matter of duty,' Sir Henri said, bowing his head.

Merric knew there was no point in keeping the truth from the knight.

'There's no need to call me "my lord",' he said, 'I am Duke of The Head no longer.'

Sir Henri looked at him in puzzlement, not understanding.

Reluctantly, Merric explained to him how his rash and reckless actions had led to so many good knights being killed. He told him that he had stepped down from being duke, leaving his cousin, Sophya, to rule instead. He expected Sir Henri to judge him, or to look down on him at the very least, but the knight looked at Merric in something that resembled sympathy and understanding.

'The pressures of leadership are many, and are a daunting prospect,' he said kindly. 'I am the eldest son of

414

the Baron of Hearth Home, and it would therefore one day fall to me to rule the barony when he passes away. But my younger brother is far more suited to being a lord than I ever would be. So, I gave up my inheritance and instead offered myself to Lord Godfrei, to serve as Sentinel of the Pass. It is an honourable position, but not one sought after by many young knights in The Dale, as such a responsibility takes one far away from the social circles of the dukedom's nobility. But, as you can probably tell,' he added, indicating his face, 'I have never been one to enjoy jousts and feasts and mixing with the young lords and ladies of The Dale. I have never been one to seek attention of others. "Henri the Handsome", they call me sarcastically, though I do not think they are intentionally being unkind. This lifestyle, out here in the mountains, suits me perfectly.'

Sir Henri was stood beside the fire as he spoke, his hands clasped behind his back and looking slightly uncomfortable. Merric did not know what to say in response to that, and he felt a pang of sympathy for the knight. He saw no reason why someone's appearance should alter how others see them, but he knew that it was an unfortunate truth that not everyone felt that way.

Luc emerged up the stairs from the floor below once more, carrying a tray of cold chicken and bread and a flagon of wine. He set it all down onto the table.

'Ahh, excellent!' Sir Henri said, turning and smiling at the three of them. 'Please, I would be honoured if you would join me for supper.'

They gladly tucked into the food, but Merric was eager to continue his conversation with Sir Henri. He had quickly grown fond of the knight, who seemed kind and genuine.

'What manner of man is Lord Godfrei?' Merric asked him, preparing himself for when he would come face to face with the Duke of The Dale.

Sir Henri chewed slowly and thought carefully about his answer. He swallowed his food and hesitated before speaking.

'I was too young to remember our previous duke,' he began, avoiding answering the question directly, 'but by all accounts Lord Baldwyn Florin had been a strict but fair ruler. He was well respected by the folk of The Dale, not unlike Lord Roberd Jacelyn was in The Head,' he said, bowing his head respectfully at the three of them. 'He was the kind of duke that folk could not help but be inspired by, and even in his older years he led the army of The Dale into battle himself.'

Merric knew that Lord Baldwyn, who had been Lady Cathreen's own father, had himself led the charge of his knights at the Battle of King's Keep. While he had died that day, Lord Roberd had always said that it had been Lord Baldwyn's courage that had won the battle.

Unfortunately the glory had, unjustly, gone to Lord Aric Monfort instead.

'His son, Lord Godfrei Florin, is a kind-hearted leader,' Sir Henri continued, choosing his words carefully. 'No one can doubt his love for The Dale, nor his devotion to the folk here.' Sir Henri paused for a moment. 'But I fear that he does not possess his father's courage. He himself knows this flaw better than anyone else. But,' he added, 'it is unfair to compare oneself to one's father.'

'What happened when the news of Lady Cathreen's death came to The Dale?' Merric asked.

'We received the message directly from the king. It was a shock to us all, I can tell you that much. Even here in The Dale the Jacelyn family is held in high esteem.'

'Did the king try and pin the blame on Merric?' Ana asked.

'Oh, certainly,' Sir Henri said, with a slight grimace on his blemished face. 'But none here believed such nonsense of course. We all know that the Monforts are the guilty ones, not you. I am in no doubt that everyone in the whole realm, apart from perhaps the king himself who is blinded to it, is fully aware of just how eager Lord Aric and his family are for power. He came here you know, around a year ago. I try not to build a negative opinion of anyone, but I fear that Lord Aric and his son, Sir Rayden, did little to warm themselves to me when I greeted them on their entry to The Dale. I would never normally wish ill will on anyone, but I believe that you did the realm a favour when you killed Sir Rayden in battle,' he said, looking at Merric.

Merric smiled awkwardly in response to the praise, as he always did.

'What about Lord Godfrei?' Kasper asked. 'Did he believe the king when he put the blame on Merric?'

'No, I think he knew that the Monforts themselves were likely responsible for the murder of his sister and her family, but he chose not to act.'

'Why not?' Merric said. 'Would he not have wanted to have justice for his sister's murder? I would have thought that even the fact that a fellow duke had been murdered would be enough to spur him into action, regardless of the fact that his sister had been a victim also.'

Sir Henri let out a sad, humourless laugh.

'I thought I had given you enough of an insight into Lord Godfrei,' he said. 'He may mourn his sister's passing, but he loves The Dale, and will do anything to keep the folk who live here safe. He will not speak out against Lord Aric for fear of invoking the wrath of the Monforts, or the wrath of the king himself for that matter.'

Merric looked back down at his plate, feeling his heart sinking. Was their journey going to have been a wasted effort? If Lord Godfrei had no desire for war, then Merric did not know how he would be able to change his mind. Kasper, who had finished eating, looked at Sir Henri.

'And what about everyone else?' he asked. 'Are they ready for war?'

Sir Henri sat back in his chair, taking a moment before answering.

'Most of the common folk here would not have been able to even tell you the name of The Head's duke. They will not have ever heard of the Jacelyn family. They long for rain for their crops, warmth in the winter and health for their children. It matters little to them about the games being played by the nobility of High Realm, or who rules dukedoms that they will never visit. But I tell you this: all of us here in The Dale have a strong sense of honour and justice, from lowly farmer to the duke himself. We look out for each other, and have no time for bullies and tyrants. If Lord Godfrei declared the Monforts as enemies of The Dale then lord, knight and common folk alike would gladly take up arms. But therein lies the problem. If you desire Lord Godfrei to strike up some kind of alliance with The Head then I fear he will not listen. I am sorry to say it, but I would not want you to continue your journey to Bluewall Castle without knowing the truth.'

'We cannot fight the Monforts alone,' Merric said, dejectedly. 'Especially if the king has given Aric the support of his own army as well. We in The Head would stand no chance against them, even if we put a sword into the hand of every man, woman and child.'

'You plead to the wrong man,' Sir Henri said apologetically to him. 'If we had the chance then we would gladly join your cause, but we cannot do so without the permission of Lord Godfrei.'

Sir Henri looked at their disappointed faces, and gave them a fortifying smile.

'By all means, continue your journey to Bluewall Castle,' he said. 'Sleep here tonight, I insist. Tomorrow I will take you north and out of the mountains myself. Together we will travel to Lord Godfrei, and we will see if I can be proven wrong.'

* * *

'You've found the crossing?' Sophya exclaimed, stunned.

Tomas had arrived back at Eagle Mount just as most in the castle were thinking about heading to their beds for the night. Sophya had been preparing to go to sleep herself when Sir Oskar had knocked hurriedly on the door to her bedchamber.

'Apologies, my lady,' he had said, bowing his head and averting his eyes when her handmaid had opened the chamber door, revealing Sophya in nothing more than a petticoat and corset.

She had brushed aside his mumbled apologies, and when Sir Oskar had told him of Tomas' return she had dashed downstairs immediately, pausing only briefly to allow her handmaid to drape a silken gown over her shoulders. Arriving in the Grand Hall and finding Tomas stood there, she had swooped down on him and given him a tight hug. Tomas had been a little alarmed by this gesture of affection, but had patted her awkwardly on the back.

Once he had assured Sophya that Merric was safe, he had told her about them finding the hidden crossing over the Rush, and that Merric, Ana and Kasper were going to continue on their way to The Dale. He was a little surprised to learn that Sophya already knew of Merric's intentions, not knowing that the four deserters from the Monfort army had decided to come this way.

'Sir Oskar,' Sophya said, turning to look at the knight who had accompanied her down to the Grand Hall. 'We must send soldiers there at once.'

'I quite agree, my lady. If young Tomas is right, and Lord Aric knows of this secret way into The Head, then we must guard it. It is no use for us to defend the crossing at Bridge Ford if they can just use this other route to get behind us. My brother is already mustering soldiers in the courtyard, and they await your orders to set off this very night.'

'It's already sorted,' Tomas piped up. 'I went first to Bridge Ford, to let them know. Lord Tymon has already sent fifty men, and some of his best knights, to prepare defences at the crossing.'

Sir Oskar nodded approvingly, and smiled at Tomas.

'You have done well, lad,' he said, before turning to Sophya. 'My lady, it sounds like Lord Tymon has matters in hand. I will inform my brother to let the boys get back to their beds.'

'Myk,' Sophya said, motioning to the castle steward who had been loitering in the corner. 'Make sure that Tomas' bedchamber is prepared for him. You must be exhausted from your journey!'

'Thank you, my lady,' Tomas said, before hesitating. 'I'm not sure what I'm supposed to do now. Merric asked me to go to Bridge Ford, and then come here, and I've done that.'

Sir Oskar put a hand on Tomas' shoulder.

'We shall find a use for you,' he said with a smile.

'Thank you for bringing us this news, Tomas,' Sophya said, as Myk led him from the Grand Hall.

Sophya sat down and looked thoughtful. The moonlight streaming in through the huge glass window bathed her in a purple light.

'Is everything okay, my lady?' Sir Oskar asked.

'What do you think his chances are?'

Sir Oskar raised his eyebrows and breathed out slowly.

'I will not lie to you; it is a dangerous road that Merric is travelling. But the Haunted Wood is a rarely-trodden path. He is more likely to avoid detection taking that route than he would be travelling the main road.'

'What can we do to help him?'

'Nothing has changed, I regret to say,' Sir Oskar said. 'The Monfort army blocks our route out of The

Head, and even if we took our own army across this hidden ford then we would be exposed on the wrong side of the river. We would be outnumbered, and butchered. We cannot take action against Lord Aric until the numbers are a little more even. We must put our hopes on Merric, and pray to the Mother that he is able to recruit Lord Godfrei to our cause.'

CHAPTER TWENTY

The Lord of Bluewall Castle

The journey north out of the Silver Peaks was much quicker than the previous day's trek up into the mountains. Not only was it mostly downhill, but it was also made easier by the horses that Sir Henri had loaned Merric, Kasper and Ana from the small stable in Valley Gate. Merric could not help feeling a stab of sadness at the loss of his own horse following his disastrous crossing of the river at Bridge Ford, and he wondered where Nosy was now. Wherever he was, and whoever had him now, Merric hoped he was being well looked after.

Sir Henri rode with them, leading the way along the Great North Road as it snaked between the tallest peaks. When they reached the far side of the great mountain range they were given a spectacular view of the land of The Dale ahead of them, like a map laid out at their feet. It looked impossibly green after the endless grey of the Silver Peaks. They left the mountains behind them as the road delved down into the countryside beyond, and the sights of the villages and farms and fields reminded Merric greatly of the land around Eagle Mount where he had grown up. It was a beautiful land, and he could understand why Lord Godfrei wanted to keep it that way.

Folk waved cheerily at them as they passed through villages and rode past farms, and other travellers on the road greeted them pleasantly. They did not know Merric and his companions, but the green tower emblazoned on Sir Henri's surcoat were easily recognised. Everyone in The Dale had heard of the great Irons family, and knew that Lord Ricard Irons' eldest son was the current Sentinel of the Pass. The knight kept his helmet on as they rode, despite there being no danger, and Merric knew that this was because Sir Henri did not like showing his face if he could help it. To the folk they passed, though, this just made their border protector look even more heroic and mysterious.

They made quick progress as they rode across The Dale. There were smiling folk wherever Merric looked. Children played, farmers chatted happily while they worked, and proud singing could be heard from inside priories that they passed. The folk of The Dale knew peace, and Merric could not help but feel guilty. After all, he was riding to appeal to Lord Godfrei Florin to join in a war that might tear apart the lives of these happy folk.

Their journey across The Dale would take them more than one day, so they stopped and ate at a tavern and slept beneath the stars when night fell. Merric felt sure that Sir Henri would have been a welcome guest at any of the castles they saw on their journey, but he had quickly learned that the knight was keen to keep his distance from other nobles in The Dale. Even when they stopped to eat, Sir Henri preferred to wait outside and tend to the horses while the others had gone into the tavern to eat their fill. He had even declined Ana's offer to bring food out to him, preferring to keep his helmet in place until they had left the tavern behind.

Merric wondered what had caused this lack of confidence in Sir Henri, and if it really was just because of the blemish on his face. It made Merric sad to think of it. Sir Henri was a valiant knight, and had given his life over to protecting The Dale from his lonely castle up in the mountains. He wished there was something he could say that would change how Sir Henri felt about himself, but he knew that they had only just met, and nothing he could say would be able to change things.

On the second afternoon since leaving Valley Gate they crested a rise and Bluewall Castle appeared before them. The castle was sat on an island in the middle of a river, with the water flowing around it on all sides. It was a grand castle, with its tall walls built from grey stone and its graceful towers rising into the sky, their likenesses reflected in the water of the river as it drifted lazily past. It was perhaps slightly smaller than Eagle Mount, but Bluewall Castle more than made up for that with its splendour.

They rode along the Great North Road, looking up in wonder at the home of the Florin family as they drew closer. The banner of the Florins flapped majestically from every tower, with the symbol of a silver dragon dancing across a field of red. The folk of The Dale were proud of the fact that their land had never been ravaged by war, and as such over the generations the Florins had made the castle more and more decorative rather than defensive. Carved dragons looked down from every part of the castle, and great arched windows were cut into the walls where other castles would have narrow arrow slits.

A small town had grown up on the eastern bank of the river, separated from the castle on its central island by a wide drawbridge which looked like it had not needed to be raised in hundreds of years. As Merric and the others passed through the small town and clip-clopped onto the drawbridge, he could see that the castle gates ahead of them were just as richly engraved and carved as the gates of the Grand Priory in Eaglestone. It was one thing seeing this on a building dedicated to the Mother, but something else entirely seeing it on a castle. In the light of the pleasant autumn afternoon, the sunshine glistening on the blue river was reflected onto the grey stone of the walls, mirroring the dancing pattern of the water. Merric realised this must have been what had given the castle its name.

The Florin soldiers standing guard in the gateway gave Merric, Ana and Kasper a curious look, but bowed their heads at Sir Henri and let them pass through. The courtyard beyond was spotlessly clean and just as grand as the outside walls of the castle. The grooms who hurried forwards to take their horses did so with well-practiced ease. It was all a little unsettling to Merric. There was something about the lived-in and homely feeling of Eagle Mount that made it feel pleasant and welcoming. Everything here at Bluewall Castle was perhaps just a bit too polished for his liking. He wondered whether it had been like this in Lord Baldwyn Florin's time as well, or if it was just his son's doing.

Sir Henri, who must have visited the castle many times and so knew his way around, led Merric and the others up into the keep and up a broad flight of steps, which was framed on both sides by extravagantly carved statues and huge tapestries. Most of them seemed to portray beautiful vistas of the dukedom's countryside and famous events from the history of the Florin family.

'Soon after Lord Baldwyn's death at the Battle of King's Keep, a tapestry was made showing his glorious charge,' Sir Henri said to Merric. 'It hung in that space there. But it did not take long before Lord Godfrei had it removed.'

'Why?' Merric asked.

'Some believe it is too painful a memory for the duke,' Sir Henri offered. 'But some think that Lord

Godfrei simply does not like to be reminded of his father's greatness.'

A harassed-looking figure came striding down the steps towards them, and Sir Henri bent down to whisper in Merric's ear.

'This is Lord Godfrei's steward,' he muttered. 'Nothing happens here without his say so.'

'Sir Henri,' the steward said by way of greeting, stopping a few steps above them. 'This is most unexpected. Is all well at the mountain pass?'

'I beg Lord Godfrei's forgiveness for coming down from my post at Valley Gate,' Sir Henri said, 'but I escort important visitors to our dukedom. They beg an audience with his lordship.'

The steward raised his eyebrows doubtfully as he surveyed Merric, Ana and Kasper. They certainly did not look like important visitors.

'And may I ask who you are?' he said, impatiently.

'My name is Merric Jacelyn,' Merric began.

The steward's eyebrows rose a little further. Clearly the steward was required to know all important folk in High Realm, and as such he was familiar with Merric's name.

'The Duke of The Head?' he asked, looking incredulously at Merric's grubby and travel-stained clothes.

Merric decided it was not the right time to correct the steward, so just nodded.

'I urgently require a word with Lord Godfrei,' he said.

'I see, my lord,' the steward said, bowing at the waist. 'If you will wait up here then I will inform his lordship of your arrival.'

He turned and led them up the stairs, his back straight and his hands clasped neatly behind him. Merric and his companions waited outside a large pair of doors, which he assumed led into the main hall of the castle, while the steward disappeared through them.

He returned only a few moments later, and when the doors opened Merric automatically made to step forwards. The steward, however, held up a hand.

'Alas, Lord Godfrei offers his sincerest apologies,' he said. 'Most regrettably he is too busy presently to receive you.'

'What?' Merric said, dumbfounded. 'He's too *busy?*'

'As I am sure you can understand, running the dukedom is an arduous job, my lord,' the steward said, tactfully.

'But this is really important!' Merric insisted, fully aware of how childish he sounded.

The steward clearly thought he did too, as his smile vanished along with his patience.

'Lord Godfrei is a busy man,' he said, his voice curt. 'I suggest you find lodgings in the town and we will find you when Lord Godfrei has a moment to spare.'

'We've come all the way from The Head! You have no idea what we've gone through to get here!'

'Lord Godfrei has given the order that you are to be forcefully removed from the castle, if you will not leave voluntarily.'

'But-' Merric protested, but he was cut off by Kasper who put a hand on his shoulder.

'Come on, let's go,' Kasper growled.

Merric had no choice but to allow himself to be steered back down the stairs and out of the castle keep. The steward watched them leave with his arms folded.

'We need to speak to Lord Godfrei!' Merric complained, once out of his earshot.

'I know!' Kasper said. 'But starting an argument with the one man who can get you in front of him isn't going to help, is it?'

Ana had frustration on her face as well, but Sir Henri confessed that he had half expected such a cold welcome.

'My family has a house in the town,' he said by way of consolation. 'It will be empty apart from the matron who keeps the house in order. We can wait there.'

'And how long will Lord Godfrei keep us waiting?' Merric asked, furiously.

Sir Henri shook his head sadly.

'If he fears you are here to plead with him to draw swords against the Monforts then he may keep you waiting indefinitely. Like I said, he has no desire for war.'

Merric was feeling so disappointed and angry at this reception, after they had travelled all this way to get here, to pay any attention as they retrieved their horses from the castle grooms and walked back over the drawbridge and into the town. He was seething, furious at Lord Godfrei and furious at the steward who had seemed to enjoy delivering the rejection. He was only vaguely aware that Sir Henri had led them off the main street of the town, and taken them through a gateway and into the courtyard of his family's house.

It was a two-storey building, surrounding the courtyard on three sides. Behind them, on the fourth side of the courtyard, a wall stretched between the wings of the house, with the gateway that led out onto the street beyond. A dog ran across the courtyard to greet them, but other than that the house seemed deserted. Most of the window shutters were latched shut, and no smoke came from the chimney. They climbed down from their horses and Sir Henri tied their reins to hitching rings on the wall.

'Hullo, who's there?' came a husky old voice.

A plump old woman wearing an apron and bonnet emerged out of a doorway, and she smiled broadly when she saw Sir Henri.

'Oh it's you, Henri! Whatever brings you here, my love?'

The knight pulled his helmet off, and allowed the old woman to plant a kiss on his cheek.

'Isn't he the most handsome young man you've ever seen?' she said, beaming around at Merric, Ana and Kasper. 'I remember when he was just a baby. And now look at him, a dashing knight!'

Turning almost as red as his birthmark, Sir Henri introduced each of them to the squat elderly woman.

'And this is Penny,' he said, indicating the matron.

She smiled motherly at them all and ushered them inside the house.

'I had no idea you were going to be here,' she said frantically to Sir Henri, as she hurried to straighten chairs and sweep a few specks of dust from the floor. 'It must have been a year since your last visit? I saw your father a few weeks ago, when he had business with the duke, and he said he hadn't received so much as a letter from you in months. Naughty boy! I wasn't expecting to be joined by anyone else from the family until the spring. Your father is planning on spending the winter months at Hearth Home.'

'We will not be here for long,' Sir Henri said, apologising for inconveniencing her. 'We are awaiting an audience with Lord Godfrei. I hope we are not too much trouble for you?'

'Not at all, not at all! Well, you'll have to have a good meal while you wait,' she insisted, and bustled off in the direction of the kitchens.

Sir Henri gestured for Merric, Ana and Kasper to make themselves comfortable in the hall of the house, and they sank into chairs that sat around a cold fireplace. There was a bark, and the dog that they had seen in the courtyard came in, yapping happily, and bounded right up to Sir Henri.

'It's good to see you too, George,' he said, reaching down to stroke the dog, who rolled over and allowed her belly to be rubbed.

While the others relaxed, Merric found that he could not rest. He got back to his feet almost immediately, and began pacing up and down. They could not afford to waste time like this. He imagined what might be happening in The Head right now. Had Tomas managed to raise the alarm about the crossing over the Rush? Had they sent soldiers there to guard it, in case the Monforts planned to cross it again? The Monfort army could invade at any point, and Merric hated the feeling of just sitting idly, waiting for something bad to happen.

'Rest,' Sir Henri reassured him. 'You are safe within these walls.'

'It's not my safety that I'm thinking about,' Merric said, continuing to pace.

'We've come this far,' Ana said to him, 'I suppose we can wait a little longer.'

'Lord Godfrei likely just needs some time to think about what he will say to you, as I am certain he will know why you have come,' Sir Henri said.

This did nothing to calm Merric.

'Give him more time to think up an excuse, you mean?' he said.

Sir Henri just looked at Merric sympathetically.

'He is the duke,' he said, simply. 'If he is not willing to join the fight then there is little else we can do.'

Merric sat down in the chair once more and looked into the empty fireplace, which after a while Kasper knelt down and lit. Even the merry crackling of the flames did little to cheer Merric's mood. Sir Henri talked to Kasper, asking him about his village and his family. Ana was knelt on a fur rug that was spread across the floor, playing with George the dog who had taken an immediate liking to her. Merric just sat, brooding, and glancing up at the door every few minutes as though expecting to see a messenger from Lord Godfrei, summoning him back to Bluewall Castle.

The delicious smell of baking pie drifted from the direction of the kitchens, and they ate heartily, before drifting back to the seats by the fire. Kasper soon fell asleep, his head tipped back and his mouth open slightly as he snored. The others sat in silence, listening to the hypnotic sounds of the fire in the hearth and waiting in bated breath for a knock at the door. But no knock came, and Merric started to accept that he would not be summoned back to the castle that evening. As night well and truly fell, Penny showed the guests to bedchambers, and Merric eventually fell asleep.

The next morning, when he first awoke, it took him a moment to remember why he was feeling so anxious. But then the same familiar feeling of frustration and anticipation coursed through him. After a breakfast feast laid out by Penny, who seemed overjoyed at having houseguests once more, Kasper retreated into the courtyard where he had found an archery butt. He whiled away the morning shooting arrow after arrow into the target, hitting it dead centre every time. Sir Henri, grooming the horses, watched him with an impressed eye. Perhaps he desired to recruit Kasper to join his wardens up in Valley Gate.

Ana timidly approached Merric, who had snapped irritably at everyone that morning, with George at her heels.

'Let's go for a walk,' she suggested.

Merric opened his mouth to turn down the offer, but then changed his mind. There was little to be gained by staring at the door all day. If the summons came from the castle then Sir Henri or Kasper would come and find him. They therefore left through the gate in the courtyard and went out into the street. George ran off ahead, her tail wagging in excitement. Not knowing their way around the town, Merric and Ana just followed the dog, who was stopping every now and again to sniff at some curious new scent and yap happily at passers-by.

The street on which Sir Henri's family's home was positioned ran alongside the river. Buildings lined the left side of the road, while to the right small fishing boats were tied up along the dock. There was the sound of general hubbub as the townsfolk and fishermen went about their lives, paying little attention to the two youths. They walked past the drawbridge leading into the castle, and Merric could not help looking through the gates at the home of the Florins beyond. He wondered what Lord Godfrei was thinking and doing at that very moment.

George the dog continued to lead them down the road. The town came to an end but the road continued to head west, hugging the riverbank as it went. They had soon left both the town and the castle behind. The fields they walked beside were bordered with wooden fences, and George wriggled under one of them to bound joyfully after a flock of birds which took to the skies in alarm. Merric and Ana kept on walking, watching the happy dog with smiles on their faces.

The road veered to the right and crossed over the river on a humped back bridge made of stone. The land ahead of them rose and fell gently, covered in a patchwork of fields that had not yet been harvested of their crops ahead of the winter. It was warmer up here in The Dale, and the cold months were still a way off. George leaped and bounded through the tall plants, her head and flopping ears visible now and again as she sprang gleefully across the fields. They walked back along the other side of the river, the castle once again getting closer as they approached it from the other bank. When they drew level with it they came across a grove of willow trees growing at the river's edge, directly across from the town.

They sat down in the shade of the trees. There was still some warmth in the sun, and the shade was a welcome break. George came and laid next to them, panting heavily with her tongue lolling out. She lay peering into the river, watching the tiny fish swimming in the shallows, her tail wagging lazily from side to side.

'I know this probably isn't the right time,' Ana said, looking across at Merric with one eye closed against the glare of the bright sun, 'but I suppose it's the first time we've really had a moment to stop and think.'

Merric glanced back at her, tearing his eyes and mind away from Bluewall Castle that sat on its island right in front of them.

'I don't want to lose you as a friend,' she continued, looking down at the reed she had plucked and was now playing with absent-mindedly in her hands.

'Ana, you're not going to,' Merric said, shifting himself around so that he was sat facing her. 'That's never been what I wanted. To be honest, I don't really know what I wanted when I said those things to you.'

'You were worried about Sir Sebastien,' she said, offering Merric a reason for his behaviour.

Merric swallowed, as he found it painful to think about Sir Sebastien after what had happened in the mountains.

'I was,' he admitted. 'But that wasn't an excuse. I shouldn't have said what I said. I don't even think I believed what I said. '

'And what *do* you believe?' Ana asked, trying to sound casual.

Merric thought long and hard, frowning at the castle but not really looking at it.

'I don't know what the future will bring,' Merric admitted. 'But I don't want you to not be there with me.'

Ana reached across and took a hold of his hand.

'I will always be here,' she said. 'Don't ever think that I won't be.'

Merric gave her hand a squeeze and smiled at her, and she smiled back. He could not help but notice how pretty she looked, with the dappled sunlight on her blonde hair.

'It's been a really difficult time,' she said. 'But we'll get through it, somehow.'

They returned to the house later that afternoon, but one glance at Kasper told Merric that no message had come for him while he was gone. Trying not to let his disappointment show, he gave Penny a friendly greeting and Sir Henri showed him to the house's library.

'Kasper told me that you enjoy reading,' the knight said.

It was of course much smaller than the library at Eagle Mount, but after a few minutes of browsing the shelves Merric discovered several volumes that he had

439

never heard of before. He took a couple down and retreated into a chair in the corner and began pouring over them. He was so engrossed in the reading that he had barely noticed how dark it had become until Penny came in and lit a candle, to help him see.

'Has there been a message from Lord Godfrei?' he asked, surprised that the day was already nearly over.

'No, sorry my love,' she replied.

Dinner that evening was a rich stew, and Merric joined in the conversation this time. While he was still frustrated by the complete silence from Lord Godfrei, his talk with Ana had given Merric a much-needed pick-me-up. She had been his best friend for years, and the distance between them over the past weeks had left a hole in his heart. It was much easier to feel positive about the rest of the drama that was unfolding across the realm when he had Ana back on his side.

Just when they had finished eating they heard a knocking on the gate outside. They all looked at each other, and Merric jumped eagerly to his feet as Sir Henri went out into the courtyard to see who was calling. They could hear muttered conversation, and Merric waited with mounting anticipation. But when Sir Henri brought the visitor into the house Merric could see immediately that it was not the castle steward.

'Lord Merric,' the man said in a gruff voice, nodding his head in greeting.

He was shorter than Merric, and his cloak was stretched taught over his large belly. He lowered his hood to reveal a ruddy face and a balding head. His nose looked broken, and Merric could see numerous scars on the man's face which showed that he was a veteran of many battles.

'My name is Halstaff,' the newcomer growled.

Merric looked quizzically at Sir Henri, who elaborated.

'Halstaff is Lord's Counsel to Lord Godfrei,' he explained.

'Oh!' Merric said, looking back at the man. 'Erm, it's a pleasure to meet you.'

'I know why you're here,' Halstaff said, nodding his thanks at Penny as the matron brought him a cup of wine, which he gulped down in one go. 'Forget what you've been told. Lord Godfrei has no intention of granting you an audience. He's hoping you eventually give up and return back to The Head.'

'How can he?' Ana exclaimed. 'How can he be so against getting revenge on those who murdered his sister?'

Halstaff shrugged.

'Your young duke here killed Sir Rayden. As far as Lord Godfrei is concerned, revenge has been had. An eye for an eye and all that.'

'But what about Aric?' Merric said. 'Rayden was only following his father's orders. And now as far as we know the Monforts are trying to take control of The Head again.

They've already tried to kill me once and capture me twice.'

'Do you think I don't already know that?' Halstaff said impatiently, raising a hand in frustration. 'I have been trying to talk sense into Lord Godfrei for weeks, but I am sure Sir Henri has given you a pretty good idea of the character of our duke. Lord Godfrei is a good man, and I would follow him to the death if he would but command it, but he is as likely to march us to war as he is to ride off into the sunset on the dragon that is emblazoned on his banners.'

'So he sent you here to tell me to go home, is that it?' Merric said, accusingly.

'Lord Godfrei has no idea that I am here,' Halstaff growled, 'and he would name me Lord's Counsel no longer if he ever found out about this betrayal. He would not appreciate me going behind his back, but I cannot sit idle any longer. Now look, tomorrow he is holding court, and anyone who wishes can have a chance for an audience with him, to speak to him directly.'

Of course, Merric realised, Lord Godfrei could deny him an appointment until the end of time, but no ruler could ever turn away a petitioner at his court. Especially when there were crowds of other petitioners there to witness it. Merric expected he would be the first ever duke, or former duke, to join a line of petitioners waiting their time to speak and be heard. But he was not too proud to do such a thing.

'If you make your appeal to Lord Godfrei in front of the folk of The Dale then he will find it much harder to refuse to help you,' Halstaff said. 'If he does, he might find that he has a riot on his hands. The folk here are ready to take action, and you will be the spark that ignites the fire.'

'Thank you!' Merric said, as Halstaff tugged his hood back up and made to step outside again.

'Do not mention this to anyone, any of you,' the man warned. 'Lord Godfrei must never find out that I was here.'

'We won't say a word,' Merric promised. 'How can I thank you?'

Halstaff paused, halfway out of the door, and looked back at Merric.

'Do not mess this up, that's how,' he said.

* * *

The next day, Merric, Ana, Kasper and Sir Henri joined the throngs of folk making their way across the drawbridge and into Bluewall Castle. They followed the crowd as they passed through the courtyard and into the keep, climbing the broad staircase with the statues and tapestries looking down at them. The doors that had been closed on Merric's last visit now stood wide open, flanked by two Florin soldiers in their pristine uniforms and the symbol of the silver dragon on their chests. As Merric entered Lord Godfrei's hall with everyone else, he could not help but look around in awe.

Huge arched windows ran all around the walls, giving spectacular views of the lands around the castle. Sunlight streamed in, illuminating the Florin banners that hung from the high, vaulted ceiling far above. The pillars that supported the ceiling were even more intricately carved than the castle gates were outside, and Merric and the others stood close to one of these as the crowd gathered around the hall, looking up towards their duke.

Lord Godfrei sat on a raised dais, similar to how Merric had done at Eagle Mount when he himself had carried out his court sessions. To either side of Lord Godfrei were more men. One was the steward who had refused Merric entry previously, and he stood with a scroll of parchment in his hands, studying it closely and taking little notice of the crowd. Halstaff, the Lord's Counsel, was stood directly at Lord Godfrei's side, leaning close and holding whispered conversation with him. But when he straightened up he caught Merric's eye, and gave a tiny, almost imperceptible, nod. Two younger men stood at the duke's other side, richly dressed and proud-looking. They shared Lady Cathreen's blonde hair and prominent cheek bones, and Merric supposed these must be Lord Godfrei's sons.

Behind the duke stood twenty or so knights, all wearing the symbols of their own families on their surcoats. It created a colourful backdrop to the huge hall.

At first, Merric had assumed that these were the Florin equivalent of the Eagle Guard, but then he noticed that they were all chatting to each other and laughing at jests, in a way that disciplined bodyguards never would. He supposed that in The Dale it was customary for young knights, eager for fame and glory, to live at Bluewall Castle and be ready in case their duke ever had need for their services. Despite the helmet that hid his face, Merric could tell that Sir Henri was glancing at these knights uneasily. Merric wondered if some of them had been those who had called him "Henri the Handsome" in the past, and who he had been trying to distance himself from when he had taken up the post of Sentinel of the Pass.

Merric turned his attention to Lord Godfrei himself. The Duke of The Dale was a handsome man of middling years, sat proudly and straight-backed in his ornately carved chair. He had the same blond hair as his sons, except his short beard was turning to grey. He steepled his fingers thoughtfully as he looked around at the waiting petitioners.

The court session began, and Merric waited while petitioner after petitioner spoke and was heard. Lord Godfrei seemed like a fair man, and he gave each person his full attention before speaking in response. It became quickly evident to Merric that Sir Henri had been right. It was clear that Lord Godfrei's priority was the wellbeing of the folk of his dukedom, and when he spoke it seemed to be with genuine care and kindness. Merric neared the front of the queue that had formed, and he felt butterflies in his stomach. This was his one chance to secure the aid of The Dale, and if he failed it would likely spell doom for The Head, and possibly even for the whole realm. He could feel the pressure mounting. He was glad for the presence of Ana, Kasper and Sir Henri who stood around him, and he felt reassured by their closeness.

The petitioner in front of Merric was a farmer, appealing for a small loan from the duke to help see him through the winter months, which was granted. And then Merric himself was stood before Lord Godfrei.

The duke took one glance at Merric, and then at Sir Henri who was stood beside him, and seemed to realise at once who Merric was. He rose to his feet, his friendly manner vanishing at once.

'No,' he said, pointing behind Merric at the doors that led out of the hall. 'This court is for folk of The Dale only. You are not welcome here.'

The gathered petitioners, Florin soldiers, knights and nobles all looked round curiously, wondering who it was that Lord Florin was speaking to, and who had caused the blood to drain from their duke's face.

'My lord, he must be allowed to speak,' Halstaff countered, stepping forward. His loud voice, forged on the battlefield, boomed out across the hall.

'I will not hear him,' Lord Godfrei insisted.

'Is this the welcome that guests to The Dale can expect to receive?' Halstaff asked, determined that Merric would not miss his opportunity.

'He is no guest of mine,' Lord Godfrei said.

He was unnerved that Halstaff was not taking his side, and looked suspiciously at him.

'Who are you?' one of Lord Godfrei's sons demanded of Merric, his brow furrowed in confusion as he considered his father's unfriendly welcome.

'My name is Merric Jacelyn,' Merric said.

There was a sudden outburst of muttering all around him from those in the gathered crowd who recognised the Jacelyn name. Even the assortment of knights at the back of the raised dais were speaking to each other with interest, looking curiously at Merric. Some of them had also spotted Sir Henri stood beside him, wearing his helmet, and amused smiles played across their faces as they remembered him. He shifted uncomfortably beside Merric, trying to ignore them.

'The Duke of The Head?' Lord Godfrei's son said, bowing his head slightly. 'You are most welcome here, my lord!'

'No, he is *not* welcome here at all, Colman,' Lord Godfrei shot at his son, before turning back to Merric. 'I knew this day would come, and I am prepared for it. I am the Duke of The Dale, and I will not be dictated to by The Head.'

'I am no dictator, my lord,' Merric assured him. 'But I come before you seeking your help.' He spoke as loudly and clearly as he could, to make sure that everyone gathered in the hall could hear him. 'I have come from The Head to appeal to you on bended knee. War will soon be coming to our land, and it's my plea that you lend us the support of The Dale.'

The muttering around the hall grew in intensity. Some of the folk looked nervous, but the greater number seemed excited. They looked up at Lord Godfrei in anticipation. Sir Colman and his brother glanced at each other, before also turning to face their father with eager expectation. Lord Godfrei's eyes were darting around the huge hall in panic, but he appeared determined to stand his ground.

'If The Head is soon to be at war with the Monforts then it is of your own doing, and The Dale will have no part in it,' he said, as though that settled the matter.

'Our own doing?' Merric repeated. 'The Monforts came to Eagle Mount and murdered Lord Roberd and his family, and tried to claim The Head for themselves. We did nothing to deserve that.'

'There are some,' Lord Godfrei retorted, 'who believe that it was you, young man, who committed the murders yourself.'

'Father, please!' Sir Colman demanded, outraged. 'You forget yourself. None of us here believe those

Monfort lies. And you are speaking to a fellow duke. You must treat him with measured respect.'

Lord Godfrei looked to be in no mood to be lectured to by his son. He opened his mouth to argue back, but Merric spoke first, wanting to be completely truthful.

'I no longer call myself Duke of The Head,' he said. 'The rule of the dukedom has now been passed to Sophya Jacelyn, Lord Roberd's daughter and my cousin.'

'You are no longer the duke?' Halstaff growled, his eyes narrowed at Merric as though wanting to tell him that he would have appreciated that information the previous evening.

'The title fell to me as Lord Roberd's eldest male relative, but I was undeserving of it,' Merric said, honestly. 'I have much to learn, I admit it, and my foolishness has caused much pain. But I still serve The Head, and I have travelled a long way to stand here before you.'

'Then it is a wasted journey,' Lord Godfrei said.

Merric felt a rising frustration, but he kept such feelings at bay. Now was not the time for his adolescent rage and hot-headedness. In the past that had only caused trouble. Now was the time to act like a Jacelyn.

'We have both lost loved ones at the hands of the Monforts,' Merric said, with a calm compassion in his voice. 'They murdered your sister, Lady Cathreen, when they took Eagle Mount. She was a daughter of The Dale. Do you not want vengeance for her?'

Lord Godfrei had expected Merric to make this appeal, and had his response ready.

'As I hear it, you slew Lord Aric's son yourself,' he said. 'If he is indeed the one who robbed my beloved sister of her life then I believe that vengeance has already been had. The murderer is dead.'

'Rayden was acting on his father's orders,' Merric countered. 'The fight will not be over until Aric himself has answered for his crimes. We might have foiled his plot of taking The Head for himself, but he will try again. And we can be certain that he will use force next time. He already has an army outside our border, and it won't be long until every man that Aric commands will be ready to join them. He will tear this realm in two in order to get what he wants, and he does not care how many folk must die before he gets it. And once he's done with us, who is to say that he will not come for The Dale next?'

'But we here have no quarrel with The Southstones,' Lord Godfrei said, almost with a sense of pleading in his voice, willing for everyone listening to understand his reasons.

'And neither did we,' Merric pointed out. 'But that did not stop Aric from almost wiping out the Jacelyn family in one single night.'

Lord Godfrei looked at his two sons, and Merric imagined that he was picturing losing them to knives in the night, and how it would feel to suffer as the Jacelyns had suffered. But then he shook his head, and Merric knew why. Going to war with the Monforts was just as likely to lead to the deaths of those he held dear.'

'There are dark days ahead of us,' Merric admitted. 'I would never pretend that there won't be more suffering before things get better, but as nobles of High Realm we have a duty to fight for those who cannot defend themselves. If Aric invades The Head then it will be our common folk who suffer the most. Our fields will become battlefields. Families and children will learn about war with their own eyes. And innocent folk will be killed trying to halt the Monforts' greed.'

Merric sensed that some of the fight was leaving Lord Godfrei, and that he was beginning to understand. Though whether it was Merric's words that was doing it, or if it was the eyes of all the folk in Bluewall Castle's hall looking at him, Merric did not know.

But then he saw Lord Godfrei steel himself, and sit up a little straighter.

'No,' he said. 'We are proud of the relationship we have shared with the Monforts for countless generations. And I see no reason to throw that all away.'

'Your relationship with The Head is just as strong,' Merric said, feeling dispirited and willing Lord Godfrei to see reason. 'The Head and The Dale have stood side by side since the first days of High Realm, and that relationship only got stronger with the marriage of your sister to Lord Roberd. Your father knew it would help bring our families together.'

451

'My father,' Lord Godfrei scoffed, as though he had been waiting to see when mention of Lord Baldwyn would be brought into the conversation. 'You wish it were he who sat here now, do you not? You wish he still ruled The Dale, and not me? You believe he would come to your aid? He was always one for heroics, my father, and we know where that got him.'

'I don't appeal to the memory of Lord Baldwyn, my lord, I appeal to you. Without your help, The Head will stand no chance,' Merric insisted.

He could feel desperation flooding through him. He could not go back to The Head empty-handed. Lord Godfrei rose to his feet, his temper flaring finally.

'I will not order my own folk to their deaths to fight *your* battles for you,' he said. 'Death is all that awaits you should you go to war with The Southstones and the king. You must seek to resolve your quarrel with Lord Aric with words, not with swords.'

'We only know of one way to satisfy Aric without war, and that's with us surrendering The Head to his rule. You would allow our folk to live beneath the Monforts' tyranny?' Merric asked.

'If that is what it takes to avoid bloodshed, then yes!'

There was a ripple of unhappy sounds from across the hall. Lord Godfrei heard it, and he glanced around at the crowd in surprise. He looked as though he had expected the folk to be grateful for his desire to keep them safe, but was shocked to observe that they disapproved.

452

'Is that what you would do?' Merric demanded, also noticing the crowd's reaction. 'If the Monfort armies were stood waiting beyond your own borders? Would you allow them to seize The Dale for themselves? And allow the Monforts to rule your folk?'

'Never!' barked Sir Colman Florin, and others around the hall took up the same determined shout. 'We would not give them a moment's peace if they thought to try and rule us here.'

'War is coming,' Merric insisted. 'It may even be marching on The Head as we speak. You have kept me waiting, not granting me an audience, and that has wasted time that we just do not have! The black knight banner of the Monforts has flown from the towers of Eagle Mount once before, and I won't allow it to happen again.'

All heads turned towards Lord Godfrei, and Merric could see the troubled look in his eyes. Had the circumstances been different he may even have felt some sympathy towards the duke. He was doing all he could to keep his dukedom, and the folk who lived there, safe. He could not be criticised for wanting to do that. But the time for safe decisions was behind them, and bold action was needed. To defy the Monforts was now the best way to keep the folk of High Realm safe in the long term. Merric willed Lord Godfrei to understand that.

Sir Henri stepped forward, and reached up to remove his helmet. When he shook his long red hair free there was a collective murmuring from the folk stood around them when they saw his marked face. Some of the knights behind Lord Godfrei whispered to each other at the sight of him. Sir Henri ignored them all, his eyes only on his duke.

'My lord,' he said, bowing his head. 'I am honoured to serve you as Sentinel of the Pass, and will gladly continue to do so until death or old age prevent me.'

He looked nervous to be standing there, with his face for everyone to see. But he paused for a moment, and when he spoke again his voice was steady and as powerful as it had ever been when spoken from behind the protection of his helmet.

'We in The Dale are a proud people, and are honoured to serve the great house of Florin. Everyone from lowly farmer to honourable knight,' he continued, indicating the knights gathered behind their duke, who stopped their whispering at once at the recognition Sir Henri was giving them, 'all share the same pride in calling The Dale home. But we are also proud to be from High Realm, and Lord Aric Monfort and his family are threatening to tear the realm apart in their quest for power. We cannot abandon The Head in their time of true need.'

The assembled common folk, knights and lords all roared their approval, and looked eagerly up at their duke.

'We are ready,' Sir Henri continued, shouting to be heard over the noise. 'We are ready for a war. We cannot hide behind our mountains, oblivious to what is going on in the realm beyond our borders. We will not stand idle while other good folk bleed.'

The hall rang with cheering and punching of fists in the air. The knights on the dais drew their swords and raised them high, as did Sir Colman and his brother.

'For The Dale!' came the cries from the crowd.

'For The Head!

'For High Realm!'

Lord Godfrei seemed to slump slightly in his seat, glancing at Halstaff as though silently appealing for help.

They had done it, Merric thought. Together, he and Sir Henri had done it, surely. How could Lord Godfrei turn away from their appeals now?

The doors at the back of the hall opened, and there was a disturbance as someone pushed their way through the crowd in their attempt to reach the front. Merric and the others turned their heads to see who this new arrival was. Halstaff, on the raised dais beside his duke, caught sight of them and ordered the crowd to clear a path. A man came into view, his clothes shabby and a grey cloak draped over his shoulders. He looked exhausted, and his jaw was covered in course stubble. His eyes had bags beneath them, as though he had not slept in days, but he looked alert none-the-less. Recognising him as one of his wardens, Sir Henri went over to the man and had a hurried conversation with him. Lord Godfrei watched them with mounting concern.

Sir Henri's eyes widened as he spoke to the warden, and after a few more moments he turned and addressed Lord Godfrei.

'My duke!' he called urgently. 'A Monfort army has appeared on the Great North Road, marching towards our border.'

There was a further outbreak of urgent talk among the crowd, and Halstaff had to bellow to make himself heard.

'SILENCE!' he roared.

All eyes turned to Lord Godfrei, whose eyes were closed as though deep in thought.

'What reason do the Monforts have for marching this way?' Ana whispered to Merric. 'I thought The Head was their target.'

'It is still, I bet,' Merric replied. 'Maybe Aric has somehow found out that I've reached The Dale, and wants to discourage Lord Godfrei from joining forces with us. They can't invade The Head while they've got the worry of the Florins attacking them from behind.'

Merric knew that they had arrived at a critical moment. Lord Godfrei was still thinking, and it would be a matter of moments before he made the decision that would seal the fate of all. Would he allow the Monforts to threaten him into obedience, or would he answer their aggression with aggression of his own?

'My lord,' Merric said, seizing the opportunity to speak one last time, 'the time has come for you to decide.

Will The Dale allow this Monfort army to walk freely into its lands, bullying you into submission? Or will The Dale stand against them, and show that they will not be intimidated?'

Halstaff leant in close and whispered in Lord Godfrei's ear. Eventually the duke nodded reluctantly, and rose to his feet. He closed his eyes for a moment, as though marshalling all of his courage.

'As I have said before, we have no quarrel with The Southstones,' Lord Godfrei said to the whole hall, before looking at Merric.

Merric held his breath, and he felt Ana take hold of his hand behind his back.

'But our friends in The Head know from experience that this does not mean that our folk will be safe. We will reply to this Monfort aggression in kind,' Lord Godfrei concluded.

Merric looked across at Sir Henri, and then at Ana and Kasper, who were grinning back at him. He could scarce believe it.

'We will assemble the Florin army,' Lord Godfrei continued. 'We will march to Valley Gate, and make sure that this Monfort army does not try and take a single step into The Dale.'

There was an eruption of cheering, which almost drowned out Lord Godfrei's words. There was elation amongst the crowd who packed out the castle's main hall. Lord Godfrei himself was pale, as though hardly daring to believe that he had come to that decision, though the corners of his mouth were twitching in the faintest hint of a smile at the sight and sound of the proud cheering that filled the hall.

He raised his hands for silence, and it took a few moments for order to return.

'Our army will march to Valley Gate,' he repeated. 'The sight of our strength in arms will be enough to deter the Monforts from attempting to cross through the mountain pass, and we will send them back to The Southstones with their tails between their legs. And then,' he said, looking back at Merric, 'we will revisit the conversation regarding an alliance between our dukedoms. If Lord Aric does not cease in his attempts to take control of The Head, and it turns to war, then we will stand beside you.'

More cheers echoed around the hall, and this time no one tried to stop them. It had been a long time since the walls of Bluewall Castle had rung to the sound of such fierce pride.

'Father, I beg the honour of leading the army,' Sir Colman said, stepping towards him.

His brother, Sir Conrad, likewise dropped to a knee beside him.

'As do I.'

'No, my sons,' Lord Godfrei said. 'Halstaff will command the army.'

Sir Colman and Sir Conrad Florin looked disappointed. While Halstaff was a veteran of many wars, they knew that in truth their father merely did not want to risk his sons' lives, despite his confidence that the Monforts would be sent back out of the mountains at the merest sight of the Florin army.

Halstaff had already hopped down from the dais and was pacing towards Merric on his stout legs. All around him there was uproar as folk bumped into each other in their eagerness to act on the back of their duke's words. Soldiers were hurrying to their barracks to prepare to leave, and knights were calling for squires to prepare their horses. Common folk and merchants were talking animatedly about the exciting news.

'Good work, lad,' Halstaff growled to Merric. 'And you, too, Sir Henri. Aric could not have chosen a better time to send his men this way.'

'I'm not sure that we'd have been able to convince Lord Godfrei if that hadn't happened,' Merric admitted.

But it did not matter. The Dale was marching to war.

And if this Monfort army marching towards them could be stopped before it had a chance to trap the Florins inside their own dukedom, then there was a chance that maybe, just maybe, The Head and The Dale would, together, have a chance.

CHAPTER TWENTY-ONE

The mustering of The Dale

Bluewall Castle was a sudden hive of activity. The crowd of petitioners in the hall were herded out of the castle, and Merric and the others went with them. The courtyard was a mad rush of soldiers hurrying back and forth, pulling on armour and calling out to each other excitedly. Halstaff marched among them, barking orders and telling them to wipe the grins off their faces.

'You're professionals, so act like it!' he said.

The town beyond the drawbridge was just as abuzz with activity as the castle was. The Florin soldiers who garrisoned the castle were nowhere near enough men to be called even a small army, so Halstaff had given the command for the volunteer levies to be called. There was much excitement and shouting as the men of the town removed their blacksmith's aprons and fisherman's gloves, and were instead pulling on padded jerkins and old helmets that had been in storage, awaiting a day like this when they would be needed. Spears were pulled from the rafters of homes and shields were taken down from walls where they had been little more than decorations for years.

Sir Henri took Merric, Ana and Kasper back to his home, where Penny was watching the hustle and bustle outside from an upstairs window.

'I am afraid our stay here is being cut short,' Sir Henri said to her, as the others hurried to pack up their few belongings.

'I shall ready your horses,' she said breathlessly, hitching up her skirts and hurrying out into the courtyard with a speed that was surprising for her age. George the dog yapped excitedly at the sudden activity that filled the house.

'Merric, would you come here a moment?' Sir Henri called from a chamber at the back of the house.

When Merric reached him, his pack on his back and *Hopebearer* belted at his waist, the knight was waiting for him and holding out an old shield. Merric took it from him and examined the faded image that was painted onto the wood. The symbol of the green tower of the Irons family could just be made out.

'I hope you do not mind carrying my family symbol into battle?' Sir Henri said.

'I would be honoured!' Merric said, grateful to Sir Henri for everything he had done.

The shield was heavy, but he slung it onto his back and felt a reassurance by the weight. He knew he would need it if a battle was going to happen.

'And take this too,' Sir Henri said, handing Merric a helmet.

It was a simple domed helmet with a guard that extended down to protect the nose. It was similar to those that the Jacelyn soldiers wore. Sir Henri passed one each to Ana and Kasper too, who had just joined them having completed their own packing. Kasper politely turned down the offered helmet.

'I won't be able to aim straight with that thing on,' he said.

Ana, though, accepted hers gratefully and slung it from her pack. She also spotted a crossbow mounted on the wall, and Sir Henri gladly handed it to her. She seemed thrilled to have a replacement for her own crossbow which had been lost in the fight with Sir Sebastien. Ready to go, they all went out into the courtyard, where Penny bid them farewell.

'You keep them safe, now,' she said to Sir Henri, as the four of them mounted their horses.

They waved at the kindly old matron and rode out through the gate and into the street. Halstaff was leaving Bluewall Castle at the same time, clad in plain steel armour and leading the Florin soldiers over the drawbridge. A drummer was beating the march, and the sound would have been foreboding had it not been for the cheers from the town that greeted the appearance of the soldiers marching in perfect step in their spotless uniforms. The street was filled with the men and older boys who made up the volunteer levy. They were not soldiers, and had received only simple training in preparation for this moment, but each was eager to serve their dukedom for a short while. They hugged their wives and parents and children, promising that they would be home again safe and sound before they knew it.

'We just need to show these Monfort boys not to mess with us,' said one bright-faced youth to his mother, grinning from beneath a helmet slightly too large for him.

The crowd parted to let Halstaff and the Florin soldiers march past, before the levy volunteers joined onto the end of the procession. They contrasted starkly from the ordered march of the professional Florin soldiers, but their enthusiasm more than made up for that. Sir Henri, Merric, Ana and Kasper trotted after them on their horses and made their way to the front of the column, to where Halstaff rode.

'Will you allow us to join you?' Sir Henri asked Halstaff. 'I have been away from Valley Gate too long as it is.'

Halstaff nodded at them all and they fell into step with the rest of the small army. The grizzled Lord's Counsel led the column out of the town. Folk continued to cheer and weep as they left, throwing hastily picked flowers into their midst. Wives and mothers called final, teary farewells to their loved ones, and children ran alongside the marching men for half a mile, laughing and cheering, until one of the levy volunteer soldiers broke ranks and chased them off.

'Back you go, little scamps!' he said in his most fearsome voice. 'Aint no place in an army for you!'

His companions laughed at him.

'Oh, you're so terrifying, Franc!' one said.

'Save something for the Monforts!' teased another.

They numbered no more than four hundred men, and could hardly be called an army, and yet they marched in high spirits. The levy soldiers sang and laughed and joked, and Halstaff did not order them to stop. Their enthusiasm was welcome, and if there was a battle at the end of the march then the singing would stop soon enough. Better to let the men enjoy themselves while they still could.

They had been on the road for a little over an hour when they heard the sound of hoofbeats galloping after them. Merric turned and saw two men in the red surcoats of the Florin family racing after them, with a dozen more knights behind them.

'Halt!' Halstaff ordered when he, too, noticed them.

The soldiers and levy volunteers came to a stop, and turned and watched as the riders caught up with them.

'Sirs,' Halstaff greeted them when they had reined in beside them. 'I thought your father had commanded you to remain at Bluewall Castle.'

'Pay no heed to our father,' Sir Colman Florin said, struggling to curb his horse which was skittering around in excitement. He and his brother had both donned their armour, and looked eager to be involved if swords were to be drawn. 'I will be damned if no Florin did their part in seeing the Monfort rogues off.'

'If our father wishes to stop us, then he will need to come himself,' Sir Conrad agreed.

Both of their faces shone with a boyish excitement. Behind them, the rest of the knights looked just as enthusiastic, in a way that only impetuous young men, eager for fame and glory, could. A couple of them nodded their helmeted heads at Sir Henri, clearly impressed by what the Sentinel of the Pass had said back at Bluewall Castle.

'Very well,' Halstaff said. 'We have no time to lose, and must march directly to the mountain pass. I hope that our numbers will swell from the villages and castles that we'll pass on the way. However, unless they are fools, I expect the Monforts will have more than just a token force with them.'

He lowered his voice a little, so that the nearby soldiers would not overhear him.

'Despite our duke's confidence, I fear that this Monfort host will not turn away at the mere sight of us,' he said. 'And we will undoubtedly be outnumbered.'

'Then let us even the odds a little,' Sir Colman said from atop his pacing horse. 'Come, brother. If Old

Halstaff takes the main road to Valley Gate then let us ride south. We will take the longer route, and gather knights and men from the southern lands of The Dale.'

'Try not to kill all the Monforts before we join you,' Sir Conrad said, and together they turned and galloped off in a cloud of dust. The other knights rode off behind them, whooping and exclaiming at the joy of it all.

The levy volunteers, who had not overheard the conversation, cheered at the sight of their duke's sons riding so majestically. Being a part of the army was proving to be just as splendid as they had imagined it would be.

'Alright now, you lot,' Halstaff barked. 'That's enough of that noise. Forward, march!'

Encouraged by the brothers' unwillingness to sit idle as their father had requested, the small army continued to march along the road. Word must have spread far and wide from Bluewall Castle that The Dale was marching to face off the Monfort intruders, because in every village they passed more levy volunteers joined their ranks, eager to be a part of this glorious undertaking. Some did not even have proper weapons, and joined the swelling force with farm tools at their shoulders. Ever since Lady Cathreen had been murdered, the folk of The Dale had been itching to show that they would not allow the Monforts to get away with it. They had long been restrained by Lord Godfrei's determination to avoid any danger to his dukedom, but now that the army of Bluewall Castle had been unleashed, it was time for them to do their part.

Out of nearby castles came knights with handfuls of their own soldiers, and they too joined Halstaff's growing army. By the time the sun set on that first day they had grown from a few hundred to nearly two thousand men. The silver dragon symbol of the Florins, that was emblazoned on the soldiers' shields, was soon outnumbered by the symbols of a dozen other noble families of The Dale who had joined their cause. As the day came to a close they were even greeted by a baron and his son, along with fifty soldiers with the symbol of a leaping fox on their own shields.

'It is good to see you, old friend,' the baron said, an elderly man with a white beard, shaking hands with Halstaff.

'Lord Reynald, you are a welcome sight,' Halstaff replied.

The elderly lord turned and looked at Merric.

'I know your face, young sir,' Lord Reynald said, frowning with concentration and trying to remember where from.

Merric gave his name, and Lord Reynald put a grandfatherly hand on his shoulder.

'Of course! My sympathies for your loss,' he said with a shake of his head. 'The Jacelyns were a fine family, a fine family! Excellent hosts to us this summer just past. We attended the joust, my son and I. That is where I recognise you from, no doubt!'

'I was unhorsed by Sir Tristan Jacelyn,' Lord Reynald's middle-aged son said. 'He was a splendid knight. I say, forgive my rudeness! I have yet to introduce myself. My name is Sir Regan Fox of Fox Hall. My father is Baron of Foxtyn,' he said, pointing into the distance to where the town no doubt lay.

The army camped beside the road that night, and Merric found himself surrounded by an ocean of campfires. All around him came the sound of voices talking and laughing in anticipation of what was to come. To many of them it was a great adventure, and they were already looking forward to telling their children and grandchildren about their time in the army, when they had answered The Dale's call to serve their dukedom with pride. Many of them had not travelled more than a few miles from their homes in their entire lives, and now they were marching on behalf of their duke to fend off invaders to their dukedom. They bragged with each other about who was going to slay the most Monforts. The older men among them, who had fought in the war against the Ouestorians all those years ago, were more restrained. They had experienced battle first-hand, and knew that the songs often left many details out. From somewhere, out in the darkness, someone struck up a tune on a fiddle, and others joined in singing the song with gusto.

Halstaff was in a tent that had been set up for him and, along with Lord Reynald and the knights who had joined them, he was discussing the plans for the following day. Sir Henri had gone with them, but Merric, Ana and Kasper had built themselves a campfire and were sat close to it, enjoying the warmth from the flames. None of them were experts in battle, despite Merric having read on the subject many times, and they knew they could offer little help to the experienced knights in the discussing of battleplans.

The three of them did not speak much. Merric knew that, like himself, Kasper and Ana were anticipating what would happen the next day. Would the Monforts be discouraged from venturing further into The Dale, as Lord Godfrei had hoped? Were they expecting to find a timid land where the folk would not dare resist them, and therefore would seeing an army opposing their advance be enough to stop them in their tracks? Or would that not stop them? Were their orders to restrain The Dale from siding with The Head at any cost? Was Halstaff's small army going to be forced into a battle, as the grizzled Lord's Counsel had anticipated they would? The looming threat of battle filled Merric with icy nerves. The Florins entering into the war with the Monforts was what he had wanted, and was the reason why he had travelled all this way, but the thought of being on the eve of a battle made him feel more scared than he would have ever admitted.

It was true that he had been in a battle before, at Eagle Mount, but that had been the result of his attempt to rescue Sophya. He had never expected it to become a battle, but it had snowballed until it had become a full-scale fight for survival. And it had become one in which they had only just managed to win. The thought of taking part in a battle the next day was a much more terrifying prospect. That summer, at Eagle Mount, Merric had found no time to think about what he was doing, and there was certainly no time to become scared. But now it was the waiting, and the anticipation, that was the worst part.

If the rest of the army felt the same fear as Merric then they did not let it show. The camp slowly quietened as one by one the soldiers fell asleep, but Merric did not find that sleep came easily to him. He lay awake and watched the inky black sky slowly lighten above him, as the sun began to rise in the west.

When dawn came and Halstaff and the knights barked orders for the men to rise, eat a quick breakfast and prepare to march, Merric did not know whether he had managed to sleep at all. One look at Ana and Kasper told him that they had probably experienced similar restless nights. Kasper yawned and rubbed his hand over his face, before giving himself a light slap to help perk himself up ready for the day ahead. Ana rummaged around in her bag and pulled out some cold chicken that Penny had passed her when they left the Irons family's house. The three of them ate quickly, before stamping out the smouldering remains of their campfire and walking over to where their horses had been picketed along with those of the knights and lords who rode with them.

The army was on the move again before the sun had fully risen, and Merric knew that Halstaff was determined to reach the mountains and force back the Monforts before they penetrated too far. They marched all day without rest, and even the most enthusiastic of the levy soldiers had begun to complain about their feet hurting and that the pace being set by their commander was too fast. There was less singing now, and the soldiers were shifting their spears from shoulder to shoulder to help ease the pain of their aching muscles.

The road began to rise when they reached the foothills of the Silver Peaks, and Merric noticed a further change to the mood of the army as they began to climb. Faces grew more serious and nervous, and the levy volunteers were looking at the experienced Florin and Fox soldiers for reassurance and guidance as the threat of battle drew ever closer. Noticing this slight drop in morale among his troops, Halstaff stopped his horse on the side of the road and watched as the army marched past. He called out encouragement and reassuring words, telling them that The Dale is proud of them and that they could expect to receive a glorious welcome when they returned home in a few days' time, as heroes.

They were in the mountains proper now, and for most of the men it was the first time they had been here. After the fertile lands of The Dale, the barren, rocky, unwelcome landscape of the Silver Peaks was a shock to them. They had spent their lives thinking of the mountain range as being the backdrop to their homeland, beautiful with the sun shining off its peaks. But once up in the Silver Peaks themselves, and surrounded by the titanic mountains, they could see that it was a much harsher place than it looked from far away. Dark clouds were forming overhead and a chill wind was blowing up the mountain pass, completing the ominous picture.

As the afternoon wore on, Merric spied a pillar of black smoke drifting into the sky, further up in the mountains. The word quickly spread throughout the army as others spotted it too, and soon all were gazing ahead at the smoke, muttering nervously to each other. Sir Henri seemed especially concerned, riding at the front of the column with his helmeted head staring towards the distant smoke, as though willing the army to march faster. An hour later there was no mistaking the source of the pillar of smoke. It was coming from the direction of Valley Gate, and if the castle was burning then it could only mean one thing.

When they had entered the mountains, Halstaff had taken the precaution of sending scouts ahead of the army to see what lay further up the road. A couple of hours after the smoke was first spotted, the scouts returned. They came hurrying back down the road towards the army, stopping before Halstaff and struggling to catch their breath.

'Report,' Halstaff barked impatiently.

'The Monforts have reached Valley Gate,' they replied, urgently. 'They have put it to the torch, and are marching this way.'

'How many?' Halstaff demanded.

'Five thousand, at least,' one of the scouts said.

Merric turned to Sir Henri, to try and offer some words of comfort to the knight about the loss of his castle, and to express a hope that his squire and wardens had been able to escape. But before he could say a word to him, Halstaff had turned his horse and bellowed out at the army.

'Forward march, double time!'

The army jogged forwards, and the air was filled with the sound of jangling armour and boots stamping on the rocky ground. They rounded a corner in the road and reached a point where the mountain pass opened out into a wider valley. It was the perfect place for them to wait for the Monfort invaders. It was here that the army of The Dale would make its stand.

'Halt!' Halstaff ordered.

He shouted commands and the knights moved among their men, organising them. It took a while to position the levy soldiers, who had little knowledge of standing in formations, but within minutes they formed a line across the width of the valley. They stood in several ranks, with spearmen in front and archers behind. Merric sat on his horse behind the wall of soldiers with Kasper and Ana, feeling his heart beating unnaturally quickly. The valley ahead of them was flat for perhaps half a mile, before rising up again into the peaks, and the road disappeared from view as it rounded a shoulder of mountain. There was no sight of the Monforts, but Halstaff was confident that they were not far away. The knights moved up and down the line, offering words of encouragement.

'Steady men! Steady!'

'You are men of The Dale, do your dukedom proud!'

Kasper unslung his longbow and tested the tautness of the string. Then, with nothing else to do to occupy his hands, he began drumming his fingers on the arrows he carried in the quiver at his waist.

'Are you wishing you'd stayed in Little Harrow now?' Merric said to him in a poor attempt at humour.

'Do you wish you'd stayed in Eagle Mount?' Kasper retorted, and Merric forced himself to grin, despite his nerves.

He looked the other way and Ana nodded back at him, a faint smile of encouragement on her face. She had put on the helmet that Sir Henri had lent her, and braided her hair beneath it to stop it from getting in her way. Merric could not help but look at the long blonde hair as it cascaded out from under the helmet. He wanted nothing more than to reach out and stroke it between his fingers and give Ana a kiss, but he knew it was not the right time for such things. She may never have described herself as

474

beautiful, but there, in that moment, Merric had never seen anyone more beautiful in his whole life.

The mountains loomed overhead, like spectators at a joust. The peaks were looking down into the mountain pass below, where, between the steep rocky sides of the valley, the army of The Dale waited.

Merric heard the Monfort army long before he saw it. The very ground seemed to tremble at the sound of the marching feet coming down the mountain pass towards them. Some of the younger levy soldiers took a half step backwards, but were kept in check by their fellows who were stood around them. The heavy booming of marching feet and drums continued to pound in their ears as it echoed between the mountains, and the sound filled Merric with dread. He felt like he could feel the sound in his very bones. Halstaff was sat on his horse in front of the army, his back to them. He had adopted a casual pose, looking up the mountain pass with an armoured fist resting on his hip. but Merric knew that even the grim war veteran had to be unnerved by the sound of the approaching Monfort army.

After seeing the smoke from Valley Gate, Merric knew now that the Monforts were here to fight. They meant to draw swords against The Dale, if that was what it took to discourage them from interfering with their business with The Head. They would not turn back when they found their path blocked by this army of The Dale, especially when Halstaff's force was outnumbered. That meant that a battle would need to be fought. Everyone stood waiting in the valley knew it, and Merric wondered how many of them would still live when the day ended. The Monfort army was not even in sight yet, but already their presence was terrifying. He would not blame them if Halstaff's men turned tail and fled back down the Great North Road and returned to their homes, especially the levy soldiers who had received little more than basic instructions in how to use the weapons they now carried. Would their determination to avenge Lady Cathreen, and their desire to serve their dukedom, still exist when they saw the enemy for the first time?

But instead of turning and running, a lone voice began to sing.

> *From the Silver Peaks,*
> *To the crystal river.*
> *From the green meadows,*
> *To the lakes a-glimmer.*
> *Our hearts are iron,*
> *Our hopes are legion,*
> *We are men of The Dale.*

More voices joined in, and more. Soon, almost the entire army was singing. Again and again they sung the same seven lines, and the men stood closest to Merric seemed to visibly grow in courage before his eyes with each repetition of the words. No one took a step backwards, and men even began thrusting their spears into the air to punctuate the words. Merric did not know whether it was the words of the song, or if it was the brave voices that were singing it, but it gave him heart. He was glad that Ana and Kasper were with him. Whatever happened, they would be together.

And then the enemy appeared.

They emerged around the corner of the road up ahead, led by several figures on horseback. As the head of the Monfort army marched down into the valley, more and more men appeared further up the road. Their numbers seemed never ending, like a snake of soldiers uncoiling itself as they marched down towards where Merric and the army of The Dale stood waiting for them.

The Monfort army formed up in the valley opposite where Halstaff's force was assembled. Merric and the others could only watch in mounting trepidation as the Monfort army completed deploying, their numbers easily outnumbering Halstaff's army two to one. Merric breathed out slowly, looking at the army arrayed before them. Most wore the white of the Monforts, and the black marching knight flew from half a dozen banners flapping over their heads.

The two armies stood there, facing each other, one vastly outnumbered by the other, until a pair of horsemen detached themselves from the Monfort army and trotted forwards towards the centre of the valley that was soon to become a battlefield.

'Merric!' Halstaff called across to him.

Merric took a deep breath and walked his horse through the ranks of Florin soldiers in front of him, who made a gap to let him pass. He, Halstaff, Lord Reynald and Sir Henri rode out to meet the two Monfort men, and came to a halt halfway between the two armies.

The leader of the Monfort army was a knight with shortly cropped hair and a neat beard. He wore a surcoat with the symbol of the Monfort family embroidered on the chest, and he sat arrogantly on his large black horse. His face bore a family resemblance to Aric and Rayden, and Merric assumed he was a relation. He then turned his attention to the second man, and he almost choked when he saw who it was.

Sir Sebastien sat casually in his saddle, smirking back at him. He wore a patch over the eye that had been pierced by Ana's crossbow bolt, and the same side of his face was a gruesome red ruin of unhealed wounds, no doubt caused by his fall into the ravine that had somehow failed to kill him. Merric could not help but stare at the grisly damage to his old friend's face. Nothing remained of the kind-faced, handsome knight. If the ghastly wounds were painful then Sir Sebastien gave no indication of it. He sat there beside the Monfort knight, continuing to smirk at Merric.

'I am Sir Axyl Monfort,' the leader of the enemy army said, drawing Merric's attention away from the horribly disfigured face of Sir Sebastien. 'I am the nephew of Lord Aric Monfort, Duke of The Southstones, Sword of the South and Defender of the Realm.'

Halstaff wrinkled his nose slightly in dislike, but returned the pleasantries.

'Halstaff, Lord's Counsel to Lord Godfrei Florin,' he introduced himself gruffly.

Sir Axyl looked at Merric, Lord Reynald and Sir Henri who were stood waiting behind Halstaff, with humour etched on his face.

'Is this the best that you have?' he laughed. 'An old man, an ugly knight and this…boy?'

'That is him, Sir Axyl,' Sir Sebastien said, nodding with a grin at Merric.

Sir Axyl looked at Merric with renewed interest.

'You are the Jacelyn boy? Excellent, I shall kill two birds with one stone this day,' he chuckled.

Halstaff stared back at Sir Axyl, unsmiling.

'You will withdraw your army back beyond our borders,' he said. 'And you will carry word to Lord Aric that The Dale is closed to him.'

'No, I do not think I will accept your request,' Sir Axyl said, sounding almost bored. 'I will instead make you a counteroffer. You and your paltry army will return to your homes and your duke will allow us to take up residence in Bluewall Castle. Just to make sure that the Florins do not do anything foolish while we finish our matters with The Head.'

'Never,' Halstaff said resolutely. 'You will not take one more step further into The Dale, and if you try to fight us then you, sir, will never see your beloved Southstones again.'

'Oh, and one more thing,' Sir Axyl said, unconcerned by Halstaff's threat. 'You will give us *him*.'

He pointed at Merric.

'You will give us him,' Sir Axyl repeated, 'along with our other demands. If you refuse, then I assure you that every single one of you will die here today.'

- CHAPTER TWENTY-TWO -

The turncoat confronted

With neither Halstaff nor Sir Axyl Monfort willing to bow to the other's demands, they bid each other a cold farewell and turned to go back to their own armies. Sir Sebastien threw Merric a grin before turning his horse, but Merric avoided his gaze. He galloped back to the Florin army along with Halstaff, Lord Reynald and Sir Henri. The waiting soldiers looked at them in anticipation, wanting to know how the discussion had gone. Halstaff reined in his horse in front of the soldiers, while the other three took up their original positions behind the army.

Merric rode up to where Ana and Kasper waited, and they looked expectantly at him.

'We fight then?' Ana asked.

Merric just nodded.

'They were never going to turn around and run back home with their tails between their legs,' Kasper said gruffly, eyeing up the Monfort army almost in annoyance more than anything else. 'Let's hope I live through this, so that Maryl will be able to kill me when I get back home.'

Ana grinned at his jest, but her eyes betrayed that she did not find the situation amusing in the slightest. She looked around the valley, toying absent-mindedly with the amulet around her neck. Merric could tell what she was thinking. She was wondering how a blacksmith's daughter from Eaglestone had ended up here, on a battlefield in The Dale. Merric hoped that the Mother, if she truly existed, would look out for Ana this day. He wondered if he should tell her and Kasper that Sir Sebastien was still alive, and was now stood shoulder to shoulder with their enemy, but he could not find the words.

'Prepare for battle!' Halstaff roared.

Knowing that the time had come, and that there was no chance of a peaceful resolution, some of the soldiers closed their eyes and mouthed a hurried prayer to the Mother. Others gritted their teeth in determination, testing the sharpness of their weapons and giving themselves some private encouragement for the fight to come.

Merric looked towards Halstaff, wondering what would happen next. Who would make the first move? The Monforts, or themselves? Merric had read enough about battles of ages past to know that if you were outnumbered then it was best to let the enemy come to you. Halstaff seemed to think so too, as he sat still on his horse, watching the enemy through experienced eyes.

There was a shout from the distant enemy army, and the Monforts began marching forwards. At the same time, as though their advance had been the signal, the sky overhead began to grow darker as grey clouds rolled in.

'And just to top things off, it's about to rain,' Kasper said, as though such a thing really mattered when they were on the verge of battle.

Merric watched the Monfort army march closer. Horsemen at their centre carried long lances and wore heavy armour, while foot soldiers to either side were beating their swords and axes against their white shields, as though to taunt the Florin army who were waiting for them. Behind them, Merric could spy rows upon rows of archers, who were ready to rain death down upon Halstaff's army.

There was another barked order just as the enemy entered into longbow range, and the Monfort army halted. The younger and less experienced of the levy soldiers in the Florin army glanced around anxiously, expecting at any moment for the enemy to charge directly at them. Some of them visibly shook, struggling to hold their spears straight. Older soldiers gave them words of encouragement, both out of kindness and also out of a selfish desire of not wanting to be standing next to someone who would be too scared to fight.

There was movement among the now-stationary Monfort army. Kasper, recognising it for what it was, let out a sudden shout of warning to the soldiers within earshot.

'Arrows!' he bellowed.

As if on his signal, a wave of arrows suddenly shot up from the distant enemy archers and soared towards the Florin army in a high arc. Kasper's shout had been just in time. The soldiers nearest to them had ducked and raised their shields to protect themselves from the lethal projectiles. The sound of arrows thudding against wood filled the air as they struck the shields all across the Florin army. But despite the shouts of warning, not all of the soldiers were able to raise their shields in time. Some of the arrows found their mark, and Merric flinched when he heard the cries of pain from some of the men as they were struck.

Another volley of arrows was already arcing towards them from the Monforts, and some of these, too, struck down men from The Dale. The Florin archers at the back of their own army notched arrows to their bowstrings, in readiness to shoot back, but they paused at a shouted order from their commander.

'Hold!' came Halstaff's shout. 'Do not shoot!'

Stood a few paces ahead of the rest of the army, Halstaff made an inviting target for the enemy archers. He reluctantly dismounted and handed the reins of his horse to his squire. Now, he was pacing up and down in front of the Florin soldiers, his head bare and his heavy halberd gripped in both hands. He appeared completely unconcerned about the arrows landing all around him.

'Hold!' he repeated. 'Save your arrows for when they attack!'

The Florin archers could only stand idle and watch, distraught, as their fellow men from The Dale fell beneath the Monfort arrows. But they trusted Halstaff, and so obeyed the order not to shoot back. They gritted their teeth and prayed under their breath for an opportunity to return death to their enemies.

And still the arrows continued to fall upon Halstaff's army. The distant enemy archers now seemed to be aiming at the mounted figures, assuming them to be their leaders. Arrows began to land around Merric, Ana and Kasper.

'Get down from your horses,' Merric said, dismounting from his own. 'They're making us a target.'

Sir Regan Fox, further down the line, had been thrown from his horse when the animal had been panicked by an arrow that had narrowly missed it. And further beyond Sir Regan, Merric could see a squire urgently shaking the body of a fallen knight who was riddled with arrows, but the knight did not stir.

The inexperienced levy soldiers from the towns and villages of The Dale were cowering in terror beneath their shields, sheltering as best they could from the arrow storm as the Monfort archers continued to relentlessly send wave upon wave of arrows at the Florin army. Some of them even began to edge backwards, desperate to get away from the steel-pointed death. Merric knew that the battle so far must be a long way from the glorious adventure they had imagined it would be.

Sir Henri, still bravely sat on his horse, had seen the terrified men beginning to step backwards, and he galloped over to them.

'Steady men!' he cried. 'Hold fast!'

Seeing the knight towering over them on his horse, fearless of the death raining down from above, helped to steel the resolve of the levy soldiers. They planted their feet and forced themselves to stand still.

All of a sudden, the arrows stopped. The soldiers lowered their shields cautiously and peered out at the Monfort army. Some, fearful that the Monforts were lulling them into a false sense of security, continued to hide beneath their shields in case more arrows were suddenly sent their way. Those who did lower their shields, and looked out across the battlefield, were greeted with an extraordinary sight. The ground before them was littered with arrows, as thick as grass growing from a meadow. There were many dead and wounded men among the army, but there was no time to move the injured to the rear, as the reason for the sudden halt in arrows became clear. The Monfort horsemen at the centre of their army had begun walking forwards.

'Here they come, boys!' Merric heard Lord Reynald Fox call to the soldiers he had brought with him from Fox Hall.

The horsemen sped up to a trot, the hooves of their horses kicking up loose stones from the rocky floor of the valley. Their wickedly sharp lances caught the light menacingly. Rain began to fall from the grey clouds at that moment, but no one paid any attention to the drops plinking onto their helmets.

'Make ready!' Halstaff roared, raising his halberd so that all could see him.

The Florin archers at last raised their longbows over the heads of their fellow soldiers in front of them, and waited for the order.

'Loose!'

Others echoed Halstaff's order, and with a ripple of twanging bow strings the Florin archers let fly. A hundred arrows shot forward towards the advancing Monfort horsemen. The Florin soldiers let out a cheer of revenge as many of the arrows found their mark. Some of the enemy horsemen fell from their saddles, pierced by the arrows. But their armour was thick, and many more arrows clanged harmlessly off the steel plates.

'Draw!' shouted a serjeant of archers, and his men once more pulled back their bowstrings and aimed at the approaching horsemen.

'Loose!'

More Monfort men fell, but by now the horsemen had broken into a full gallop. Their lances were aiming at the line of Florin soldiers in front of them that made up the centre of the army of The Dale.

'Form shield wall!' shouted Halstaff.

The well-trained Florin soldiers pressed close to each other and overlapped their shields. They formed a solid wall with their spears thrust over the top, making a formidable obstacle for any horseman to try and break.

The Florin archers managed one final volley of arrows before the horsemen struck home. Some of the horses shied away from the soldiers' spears, but others drove straight into the shield wall. Spears were thrust, lances snapped and men cried out in pain. The shield wall crumpled beneath the weight of horsemen bearing down on them, but they held. Halstaff himself waded into the fray, swinging his halberd in vicious arcs that cut Monfort men from their saddles. The Florin soldiers surged forward, inspired by their leader and overcoming the initial shock of the charge. They stepped over the dead and fought the horsemen with grim determination.

'Men of Fox Hall!' Lord Reynald called. 'Charge!'

The elderly Baron of Foxtyn led his men into the flank of the faltering Monfort horsemen. Being attacked on two sides was too much for the Monfort men, and after a desperate fight the survivors turned their horses and galloped away. Some of the levy soldiers cheered the success of the professional Florin and Fox soldiers at the centre of their line, but the small victory had been won at a cost. Many lay dead, including old Lord Reynald himself.

There was little time to celebrate or mourn the dead. Beyond the retreating horsemen the bulk of the Monfort army was advancing. They marched to the beat of drums and jeered at their own fleeing horsemen. But the horsemen had done their job. By their sacrifice they had weakened the centre of the Florin army.

'Reform the line!' Halstaff shouted, seeing the new approaching danger.

The Florin and Fox soldiers resumed their original positions, leaving their dead behind. Some of the Fox soldiers were in tears at the death of their baron. From his position on the left of the army, Merric could not see Sir Regan, Lord Reynald's son, but he supposed that he was with his men. He was the new Baron of Foxtyn now.

Whereas the Monfort horsemen had galloped into the Florin army at full speed, their discipline giving way to excitement and eagerness, the enemy foot soldiers instead marched at a more orderly pace. The levy soldiers in front of Merric raised their shields and readied their spears as they watched their enemy approach. Old men and boys were visibly shaking, and Merric could only imagine the fear they were feeling.

'Steady! Steady!' Sir Henri called out, riding up and down behind them.

Merric could make out the faces of the Monfort soldiers beneath their helmets now. They looked confident. They knew how much they outnumbered the Florin army, and victory was all but assured. They were already imagining the glory they would receive from Lord Aric when they returned home to The Southstones. They would be heroes. All they needed to do was beat aside this small army from The Dale who stood in their way.

The two armies came together in a crash of spears and swords. All along the length of the Florin army the Monfort soldiers were attacking, swinging their weapons viciously at their outnumbered opponents. The lack of experience of the levy soldiers who made up more than half of the Florin army was showing, and they lunged and swiped clumsily with their spears, which were parried aside easily by their professional opponents. The Monfort soldiers fought back with well-practiced ease, and took no pity on their less-experienced enemy. A huge Monfort soldier, with a terrifying two-handed axe, waded through the Florin army in front of Merric, cutting down his enemies mercilessly with roars of bloodthirsty laughter.

The levy soldiers shied away from him, cowering from his brutal attacks. A gap was forming in the Florin line where they were giving way before their terrifying opponent. Merric did not stop to think. Leaving Kasper and Ana where they stood, he wrenched *Hopebearer* from its scabbard and charged forward.

'Merric!' Ana called after him, but he ignored her. If they did not plug the gap then the Monforts would pour through the opening and be behind the Florin army. And then it would be all over.

Sir Henri had clearly seen the danger as well, and had the same idea. With a blur of orange he galloped past Merric and charged into the mass of Monfort soldiers. His horse crashed into the big Monfort man with the axe and sent him sprawling, his axe spinning away and disappearing out of sight. A handful of levy soldiers, seeing Sir Henri's courage, leapt forward onto the prone giant of a man and got their revenge on the monster who had killed many of their friends. Merric charged in behind Sir Henri, and saw a snarling Monfort soldier turn to face him. Before the man could even raise his weapon, Merric had swung *Hopebearer* at his head. The sword crashed against the man's helmet and he fell to the ground with a grunt. Merric did not know whether he was dead or simply dazed, but he had no time to worry about that. Already, another Monfort soldier was lunging at him, and he just managed to dodge the attack, using the shield that Sir Henri had lent him to push the man away.

Sir Henri was yelling incoherently as he pushed back the wave of Monforts who had forced a path through the levy soldiers. Enemy soldiers crowded in around him, and a pair of them managed to pull the knight down from his horse. But Sir Henri was quickly back on his feet, and he was just as deadly even when not on horseback. He punished the Monfort soldiers dearly for their attempt to kill him. He continued to press onwards, and Merric went with him, doing his best to stay out of the way of the knight and his swinging sword. A levy soldier, well past his prime and with a head of thick grey hair, was laying pinned on the ground by the foot of a Monfort soldier who was about to strike down with the point of his sword.

'No!' Merric shouted, lunging forwards and feeling a jarring in his arm as his sword struck home.

He reached down and pulled the levy soldier back to his feet. The old man panted a hurried thanks, before wading back into the fight himself. Men closed in on all sides, and Merric could barely tell who was friend and who was foe in the tight press. They were all so closely packed together that he could hardly breathe, let alone swing his sword. Merric kept his eyes on Sir Henri who still fought on, and pushed with his shield against the press of bodies to keep himself from being crushed. He felt something clang off the top of his head, and was thankful for the heavy, uncomfortable helmet.

He heard fresh shouts behind him. Struggling to turn his head, Merric saw a press of soldiers with the silver dragon on their shields entering the fray. Reinforcements had come, and were plugging the gap in the Florin line.

'Sir Henri!' Merric shouted above the din of battle.

The knight turned and saw the newly arrived reinforcements, and gave Merric a nod. His job done, Sir Henri waded back through the press, his sword dancing through the air as he continued to fight off Monfort enemies. He seized Merric and the two of them struggled back through the Florin soldiers who were eagerly pressing forward, emerging safely behind them at last.

'Excellent work, Sir Henri!' the serjeant leading the reinforcements called, before getting stuck into the fight himself.

Merric put his hands on his knees, trying to catch his breath, but Sir Henri pulled him back upright.

'That has bought us some time,' Sir Henri said, 'but the line will not hold.'

He was looking along the length of the Florin army where the sheer numbers of the Monfort attackers was slowly pushing them backwards. The men of The Dale were fighting back with a grim determination, but it was not enough. The line was faltering, and Sir Henri knew it would only be moments before the Florin army would flee.

Halstaff had clearly seen the same thing. His gruff voice came bellowing out of the middle of a fierce fight happening at the centre of the army.

'Retreat!'

His order was echoed all across the Florin army, and the men, both professional soldiers and levy soldiers alike, began stepping backwards slowly. They did not turn and flee, but walked backwards in good order, continuing their desperate fight with the Monforts. Their enemy did not let up, and kept on battering brutally at the retreating Florin men. Here and there the Monfort men were managing to break through and create gaps in the army of The Dale.

Merric heard the hammering of approaching footsteps on the rain-washed rocky ground at the last possible moment. He span around and saw a Monfort soldier who had managed to break through the Florin line. His axe was raised as he ran, ready to deal Merric a killing blow. But before he could bring his axe down he grunted in pain and fell to the ground, both an arrow and a crossbow bolt in his back. Merric looked beyond where the man had been standing, and he could see Ana and Kasper perched on one of the huge boulders that littered the valley floor. Seeing Merric safe, they turned their attention back to the seething mass of Monfort soldiers beyond the Florin men, and sent more arrows and crossbow bolts their way.

The Florin retreat grew quicker as more of their number fell, and the survivors were unable to hold back the Monfort tide. With a jolt of alarm, Merric realised that within seconds the Florin line would be pushed back past the boulder on top of which Kasper and Ana were crouched, shooting down at the enemy.

They would be cut off.

Leaving Sir Henri to oversee the retreat of the Florin soldiers on this flank, Merric ran to the far left of the army to where Kasper and Ana's boulder stood.

'Get down!' he called urgently up to them. 'Down!'

But already the Florin soldiers had been pushed back, and by the time Ana and Kasper became aware of the danger their boulder was already surrounded by enemies. The Monfort men only just seemed to realise that they were up there, and they began throwing spears at the pair, jeering wildly at them.

Merric ran towards them, shouldering aside the closest Monfort soldier and cutting down the next with his sword. Distracted by Merric's sudden appearance, the soldiers ceased their attempts to harm Ana and Kasper and turned to face him instead. Seeing him in danger, Kasper shot another two arrows at the Monfort soldiers who were now approaching Merric, before he then followed Ana in clambering down from the boulder. One of the enemy soldiers, seeing them descend from their perch, and wanting revenge for the damage their arrows and crossbow bolts had been causing, turned and slashed his sword at Ana. She managed to deflect it away with the crossbow, and with a yell she swung the heavy wooden weapon back at the soldier and struck him across the jaw. He collapsed, unconscious, and Kasper grabbed Ana's arm.

'Come on!' he shouted to her.

Seeing them safely down from the boulder, Merric turned to run with them back towards the relative safety of the Florin army, but then a spear tip came out of nowhere. He dove to one side to avoid the wicked blade. He rolled back to his feet, overbalancing slightly from the unfamiliar weight of the helmet and shield, and found his way after Ana and Kasper blocked by more Monfort men who had appeared. Seeing his plight, Kasper sent another arrow sailing at the enemy soldiers. But it was no good. More and more Monfort soldiers surrounded Merric, and he turned and looked past them, catching Kasper's eyes.

'Go!' he shouted. 'Get her out of here!'

He could see Ana screaming, straining against Kasper to try and get back to Merric. Kasper's own eyes were swimming with horrified tears, but he knew it was useless. Yet more Monfort men were running towards where they stood, and Kasper had no choice but to hoist the still screaming Ana onto his shoulder and turn and run back towards the Florin army which was still retreating further back down the valley. Halstaff was going to make a final stand at the place where the valley narrowed and where they would better be able to defend themselves against the merciless Monfort attack.

Merric turned and looked around at the enemy soldiers surrounding him. They were not attacking, but held their weapons in their hands as though daring him to try and fight his way free. They grinned horribly with their blackened and broken teeth. And then Sir Sebastien appeared, walking between them to stand in front of Merric.

The Ouestorian looked at Merric, his chain mail and sword flecked with wet blood. The blood was not his, and Merric dreaded to think how many men of The Dale had fallen beneath his sword. He was not wearing his helmet, preferring to let everyone see the maimed side of his face. He flicked the wrist holding his sword, letting the blood splatter onto the wet rocks at his feet.

'Not so pretty now, am I?' he laughed when he saw the look on Merric's face.

'You serve the Monforts now then?' Merric said, *Hopebearer* pointed at his old friend.

Sir Sebastien continued to chuckle, and the sound was horrible against the distant background noise of steel clashing and men crying in pain from the fight that had moved further down the valley.

'I have always served the Monforts,' he corrected Merric. 'You were just too foolish to see it, *mon duc*. You were more than willing to trust me, and to spill your heart out to me.'

The words stung, but Merric did not allow anger to overcome him.

'Stop this madness,' he urged. 'It's not too late.'

Sir Sebastien jeered at him.

'I am surprised you did not catch on to me sooner. Those Oakheart twins always suspected something about me, but you were so easily convinced that I was your friend. You would never listen to their warnings.'

Merric looked around at the ring of Monfort soldiers who were encircling them. There was no way he would be able to escape. He looked back at Sir Sebastien, scared and sad that it had come to this. He raised *Hopebearer*, ready to fight.

Sir Sebastien simply tutted at the gesture.

'I am not going to fight you. Because if I fight you, then I will kill you. And that is not what Lord Aric wants.'

'Is that so?' Merric said, buying himself time to try and think. 'And what *does* Aric want?'

'I have told you many times. He wants *you*, alive. That is why he sent me to The Head. He wanted me to capture you and bring you back to him.' Sir Sebastien began circling Merric, relishing being able to reveal to

Merric just how foolish and blind he had been. 'But I was wondering how I would be able to do it. You were too well protected for me to try and kidnap. Then I decided the best way would be to first gain your trust. But how? I would be a stranger after all, and surely the great Duke of The Head would never trust a stranger, let alone a Ouestorian stranger. And then the perfect opportunity presented itself. That imbecile, the rogue with the scarred face, who had been on the run ever since Rayden lost Eagle Mount, still thought that Lord Aric wanted you dead. The idiot. He made an attempt on your life in the street. I could not allow him to kill you, as that went against what my master now wanted. I stopped him, and in doing so I also managed to win your trust. How very fortunate for me.'

Sir Sebastien's words were cutting deeply into Merric. How had he been so blind? How could he have ignored everyone's warnings? They had seen through the Ouestorian's charming smile and wit, but not Merric.

'I doubt that Lord Aric will miss his old henchman's service,' Sir Sebastien said in an offhand way. 'A wild dog like that can be a useful ally, it is true, but he has outlived his purpose. Now that Lord Aric has me as his loyal servant, he has no need for him. He can rot in the dungeons of Eagle Mount for all Lord Aric cares.'

The battle continued to rage in the distance. The Monfort archers advanced behind their fellow soldiers who were pushing the Florins back, sending more arrows raining down onto the helpless defenders, but Sir Sebastien

498

and the dozen Monfort soldiers with him had no interest in joining the pursuit of the defeated Florins. They had an even greater prize in front of them.

'I would never have been able to take you from The Head,' Sir Sebastien continued, thoughtfully. 'Even if your hands and feet were bound I would not have succeeded. I would surely be seen, and the game would be up. And besides, everyone was keeping much too close an eye on me in the castle. Some suspected my intentions. I confess it was very annoying.'

Merric did not want to listen to any more words, but Sir Sebastien kept on talking.

'But then you gave me the perfect opportunity. You sent me to The Dale to act as your envoy. That was a foolish mistake, and I thank you for it. I left The Head and rode straight to Lord Aric's men who were waiting in The Hinterland. At first, Sir Axyl was annoyed that I had not brought you with me, but then I told him of my plan. He approved. He ordered one of his men to send word to you that I had been captured, and that you were to come and release me. Now, I will be honest. Even I was not certain that you would be stupid enough to fall for my plan, so imagine my delight when I saw you come riding so gallantly across the river with your beloved Eagle Guard! Well, you know how the rest went.'

'You killed all those good men,' Merric said, 'just to try and capture me?'

'Ah now,' Sir Sebastien said, raising a finger. 'It may have been my plan, but let us be honest. It was you who caused their deaths. Your stupidity is responsible for all those *good men* dying.'

'Why are you doing this?' Merric said, wanting to understand the knight's cruelty. 'What reason do you have for serving Aric?'

'*Mon duc*,' Sir Sebastien laughed, 'I may not have been completely truthful to you. I did not leave beautiful Ouestoria out of choice. I was banished, you see. Some there, my father among them, did not like who I had become, or what my vision was for our kingdom. They thought I was too extreme, just because I wanted to return Ouestoria to its old ways. They saw me as a threat to the peace, and so I was cast out. I dream of returning there one day, with an army. I will take the crown of Ouestoria for myself, and leave any who oppose me dead at my feet. My father will be the first to die.'

Sir Sebastien laughed again, a manic, greedy laugh.

'And let me guess,' Merric said, 'Aric told you that he would help you take Ouestoria, if you first helped him take control of High Realm?'

'You are cleverer than you seem! Lord Aric is a traditional man,' Sir Sebastian said, his laughter fading to be replaced by an admiring look that passed over his face. 'He hates the way High Realm has become, its softness. We are kindred spirits in our views of how our kingdoms should be. He says he will be honoured to help me return Ouestoria to her days of glory.'

'Don't you see that he is just using you?' Merric said. 'Aric does not care about anyone else. He will use you to do his dirty work, and then discard you like he discarded his son, and Lord Warner Camoren, and the scarred knight.'

He willed Sir Sebastien to understand. The Ouestorian had caused many good folk to die, but there did not need to be more blood on his hands.

'He's just using you,' Merric said again. 'Stop this. Don't make me fight you.'

He raised *Hopebearer* a little higher, but a flash of annoyance passed over Sir Sebastien's face. His own sword darted forward, knocking Merric's blade back down again.

'I said no!' Sir Sebastien said, anger etching itself on his ruined face. 'And save your lies. With Lord Aric's help I will be king of Ouestoria, and then I can turn my back on this wretched kingdom and never have to step foot here again.'

'You said before that you loved High Realm,' Merric said. 'Another lie?'

'Tell me,' Sir Sebastien said. 'If you were banished from your home, would you love the backwater you were forced to live in? I hate this land, and I hate those that live here even more. My ancestors killed the knights of High Realm in battle, and I could not be prouder of that.'

'And now you're killing the folk of High Realm too,' Merric said, looking at the blood-soaked sword in Sir Sebastian's hand. The same sword that he, Merric, had given him as a gift. How blind he had been.

'These are not the first I have killed,' Sir Sebastien said casually, looking out at the bodies strewn across the battlefield. 'I was not ready to act when I first arrived in The Head. I was biding my time before journeying to Eaglestone, as it would look suspicious if I arrived immediately after Rayden was defeated. But I was not going to sit idly as I hid out in the woods. I took great pleasure in what I did.'

A sudden realisation hit Merric.

'The murders near Porby,' he gasped. 'They were you? I thought it was-'

'Lord Aric's scarred friend?' Sir Sebastien finished for him, amused. 'Yes, he seems the type, does he not? I must say, his sudden appearance and his foolish attempt to take your life became very convenient for me.'

Merric had indeed believed that the scarred knight, who had led the raid all those years ago when Merric's parents had died, and who had helped Rayden murder Tristan and the other Jacelyns, was the monster who had committed those ghastly murders near the village of Porby. He could not imagine the handsome Sir Sebastien doing such horrific acts. He looked into the face of his old friend, at the face which had lost its good looks long before it had taken the plummet down the ravine.

502

'I could have just stolen the food, of course,' Sir Sebastien continued, smiling fondly at the recollection, as though he was remembering a favourite childhood memory, 'but where is the fun in that? I have a talent for killing, you see, but such skills need to be practiced. Much like a sword needing a whet stone to stay sharp and not lose its edge.'

'You're more of a monster than the scarred knight ever could be,' Merric told him.

'Well, fortunately for you, you are one that I cannot kill. I have my orders.'

Merric knew that it was hopeless. Sir Sebastien was beyond redemption. There was nothing Merric could do to stop him from continuing with his misguided ambitions. But Merric was certain of one thing. He would not allow himself to be captured and taken to Lord Aric, to likely suffer a fate worse than death. Not if he could help it. And if he could stop Sir Sebastien then perhaps it would save more lives in the future.

Striking quickly, he heaved *Hopebearer* back up again and swung it with all of his might at his old friend. Sir Sebastien looked a little surprised at the sudden attack, but brought his own blood-stained sword up and deflected the attack away. Merric continued to swing his sword, trying to find an opening. But each time he thought he had gotten past Sir Sebastien's defences, the Ouestorian's sword appeared and blocked Merric's blade.

'I have taught you well,' Sir Sebastien noted, with a smirk across his ruined face. 'But not well enough.'

With a final sweep of his sword, the Ouestorian parried another of Merric's attacks so hard that *Hopebearer* was knocked from Merric's hands. With a nod from Sir Sebastien, a pair of Monfort soldiers dashed forwards and seized hold of Merric's arms. They pinned him there, holding him tightly.

'That's better,' Sir Sebastien said, seeing Merric restrained. 'Enough of that nonsense.'

He picked up *Hopebearer* and examined it.

'I have always admired this sword,' he said, turning it over in his hands.

'You'll never be worthy of carrying it,' Merric said.

'Then I will melt it down,' Sir Sebastien said in an offhand way, tossing the blade onto the ground again where it landed with a clang. 'Trinkets like that are of no concern to me. Not when you, boy, are what I really want. You will never know how this battle ends, nor the fate of your friends. Come, we ride to The Citadel, where Lord Aric awaits you.'

'Are you going to tell me *why* Aric wants me?' Merric demanded.

Sir Sebastien slapped him hard across the cheek.

'You will address him as *Lord* Aric,' he hissed. 'You may have cast aside your title but do not assume that others are as unworthy of being a duke as you are.'

Merric felt the fight leaving him. It was hopeless. He did not want to be taken alive, but the soldiers holding his arms were gripping so tightly that he could not move an inch. His shoulders sagging, Merric looked away to the north. The Florins were still fighting desperately, but it was a lost cause. He could see Halstaff in the front rank, his halberd rising and falling defiantly as he fought on. There was a flash of orange which could only be Sir Henri, still heroically trying to inspire the soldiers. Merric could not see Kasper and Ana, and he hoped they had managed to reach safety. He wished that he could see them one last time.

'Take him,' Sir Sebastien said.

The two soldiers holding Merric's arms began to haul him away when they heard the sudden braying of war horns. Merric heard it too. The sound echoed off the mountains all around them, and they looked around in confusion, trying to find the source of the sudden sound. The horns sounded again, and the Monfort soldiers were looking unnerved.

Further up the valley there was sudden movement, as the squires and servants at the rear of the Monfort army began running away from something that Merric could not see. There were panicked shouts, as the war horns sounded a third time. And now there was another sound too. The heavy drumming of hooves.

Around the bend of the valley there appeared horsemen. Hundreds of horsemen. They were riding knee

505

to knee as they surged along the valley, charging towards the rear of the Monfort army. A dozen different banners flapped over their heads, and at the front rode Lord Godfrei's sons, Sir Colman and Sir Conrad, the silver dragon of the Florins glittering on their shields. They were followed by what appeared to be all the nobility of The Dale. Hundreds of knights galloped alongside them, barrelling towards the back of the Monforts who had caused Halstaff's beleaguered army so much suffering.

They broke into a full charge, each man willing his horse to go faster and faster. They cheered and bellowed and screamed with defiance as they levelled their lances at their foes.

The Monfort army further down the valley, who had been on the verge of breaking the heavily outnumbered army of The Dale, turned to face this new threat. They were panicking at the sight of all these heavily armed horsemen galloping towards their rear. They had never imagined danger coming from behind, but the folk of The Dale knew the Silver Peaks well, and knew of all the narrow goat paths and hidden trails that led through the mountains.

Monfort knights tried to organise their soldiers to defend against the unexpected attack. Spearmen cowered behind their shields, while archers shot arrows towards the knights of The Dale. A few found their mark, but not enough to make any difference. Encouraged by the sudden arrival of Sir Colman and Sir Conrad, Halstaff's soldiers fought back with renewed vigour. They had been on the back foot all day, but now, with the Monfort army trapped between themselves and the newly arrived knights, they went onto the attack.

Merric, Sir Sebastien and the dozen Monfort soldiers were stood directly in the path of the horsemen led by Lord Godfrei's sons. Sir Sebastien began to yell a hurried order to rally his men to face this new threat, but it was too late. The wall of horses was just seconds away from overrunning them, and the eager knights showed no sign of stopping.

Shrugging off the hands that were holding onto him, Merric leapt up and grabbed hold of the side of the boulder on which Kasper and Ana had been sheltering previously. He scrambled up as the horsemen galloped right at them. He held on for dear life, while beneath him a wave of horses thundered past, crashing into the Monfort men who were utterly defenceless. Merric glanced back and saw, for a short moment, Sir Sebastien looking back at him with his ruined face, before he disappeared beneath the hooves of Sir Colman and Sir Conrad Florin's horses.

The knights of The Dale galloped down the valley, their swords rising and falling and their lances thrusting at the Monfort soldiers who were entirely at their mercy. Those who did not throw down their weapons and give up were cut down where they stood. Spurred on by the sudden rescue, the survivors of Halstaff's army ran forward, yelling for the surrender of the enemy who had, until moments ago, been on the verge of securing victory. Sir Axyl

Monfort, the leader of the enemy army, led a clutch of his soldiers in a desperate attempt to escape being trapped by the two armies. Sir Colman and his brother led the pursuit themselves, yelling in victory. Merric watched as Lord Aric's nephew, seeing there was no escape, reluctantly threw down his sword, admitting defeat. The remaining Monfort soldiers followed his lead and likewise gave themselves up. The battle was over.

Seeing the knights of The Dale and the survivors of Halstaff's army stripping the Monfort survivors of their weapons, Merric hopped down from the boulder, feeling slightly shaky on his legs. He walked over to where *Hopebearer* had been dropped. The sword had escaped being trampled and shattered beneath the horses' hooves, but the same could not be said of Sir Sebastien. Merric found the Ouestorian lying broken on the ground, and his body was unrecognisable from the handsome friend he had known back in Eagle Mount. Merric looked down at the horrid sight, feeling a sense of pity for the man who had manipulated him and betrayed him. Sir Sebastien was dead. Merric did not know whether he would have been able to bring himself to kill him, but in the end it had not mattered. The Ouestorian had been as hungry for power as Lord Aric was, and in the end that had led to his death.

Turning away from Sir Sebastien's body, Merric hurried back to where the survivors of Halstaff's army were stood. Merric could not believe how few of the army were still alive. He guessed that maybe as much as half their number had been killed. Those who remained looked exhausted and filthy and many carried injuries. They all looked to be in shock at having survived the battle, when defeat had seemed so certain. Merric ran over to them, scanning the faces as he drew closer, looking desperately for Ana and Kasper. With a huge burst of relief he found them stood with Sir Henri, whose orange surcoat was now stained almost entirely red with blood.

They were gathered around the body of Halstaff. He was dead, surrounded by countless Monfort men who he had killed. He had fallen as he would have wanted; gloriously, in battle, leading his men.

Ana looked up and saw Merric approaching. She gasped and ran over to him, wrapping her arms around him.

'Thank goodness you're safe,' Merric said gratefully, closing his eyes.

Ana did not reply, and just hugged him as though she never wanted to let go again.

'You are proving a tough one to kill,' Kasper said, the relief clear on his face as he clapped Merric on the back.

Sir Colman and Sir Conrad reined in their horses beside them, having seen the Monfort prisoners secured. Sir Henri and Lord Regan Fox, the new Baron of Foxtyn, joined them.

'Our apologies for our tardiness,' Sir Colman said. 'We were almost too late for the battle.'

'You are truly a sight for sore eyes,' Sir Henri said, bowing his head at Lord Godfrei's sons.

'The day is won,' Merric said, looking up at the two Florin knights. 'But many folk of The Dale have lost their lives.'

'We knew the risks,' Lord Regan Fox said. 'Every man here, my father included, was happy to lay down their lives for the protection of The Dale. Do not mourn their deaths, but honour them.'

'I fear this is just the beginning,' Sir Henri said. 'Lord Aric will not allow us to live in peace after our victory today'

'Of that I have no doubt,' Sir Colman said, smiling down at him from his horse. 'It is as you feared, young Merric. There is no question that war has arrived in High Realm, and I do not think that Lord Aric and the king will rest until they have their victory.'

'But one thing has changed,' Sir Henri said, putting a hand on Merric's shoulder.

'What's that?' Merric asked.

'The Head will not stand alone.'

Epilogue

Tomas hurried up the steps that led into the cavernous entrance hall of Eagle Mount's keep, the message clutched in his hand. He apologised to a pair of knights as he brushed past them in his urgency, and a servant let out a cry of alarm as she was almost bowled over while carrying a basket of freshly laundered clothes.

Recognising him, the two Jacelyn soldiers standing by the doors that led into the Grand Hall pushed them open, granting him entry. Tomas ran through the doorway, hurrying as fast as he could up the vast chamber. Up ahead, the enormous stained glass window depicting Jace and his giant eagle, Haerophon, loomed overhead. The glow from the setting sun was shining through the colourful glass, sending shards of bright light all across the walls and floor.

His feet pounded noisily on the flagstones, echoing all the way up to the high ceiling. Lady Sophya Jacelyn, Duchess of The Head, looked up at him, surprised by his sudden arrival. She was sat on the stone chair that Tomas had previously seen occupied by Merric and Lord Roberd, but he could not deny how well it suited her. She was surrounded by Sir Oskar and Sir Orsten Oakheart, as well as elderly Arch Prior Simeon, with whom she had been deep in conversation before Tomas' appearance.

'Tomas!' she exclaimed. 'I was not expecting to see you again tonight. I thought you were finished with your duties for the evening?'

Tomas bent over double, trying to catch his breath. He was still not used to the weight of the chain mail and the surcoat that he wore. He had been given both by Sophya on his return to Eagle Mount, in gratitude for everything he had done. Sophya had also given the Oakheart twins direction that they should complete his training and see him to his knighthood as soon as he was ready.

'I'm sorry for intruding, my lady,' Tomas said, puffing heavily from the run. 'I was heading into Eaglestone when a messenger arrived from Lord Tymon Conway.'

Sophya looked anxiously at the letter in Tomas' hand.

'From Bridge Ford?' she asked, uneasily.

She feared the worst. Ever since the Monfort army had appeared across the river they had been expecting Lord Aric to make his move. Sir Oskar took the letter from Tomas, his own face showing the same concern. He opened it and read quickly, his eyes furiously moving from side to side.

'What does it say?' Sophya asked. 'Has it begun? Has Lord Aric begun his invasion?'

'Quite the opposite, my lady,' Sir Oskar said, looking up from the letter. 'Lord Tymon writes that the Monfort army encamped across the Rush has gone. He has sent out scouts across the river, and they report that Sir Axyl Monfort has marched his army north, towards the Silver Peaks.'

'They attack The Dale?' Sir Orsten said, looking puzzled. 'Why suddenly change strategy?'

'Merric,' Sophya muttered, feeling a smile form on her face.

'Merric? You think he has reached Bluewall Castle?' Sir Oskar said, his spirits visibly lifting.

Tomas felt a twinge of hope course through him. He had been worried sick about Merric, Ana and Kasper ever since he had left them.

'The Monforts must know that he has reached The Dale at the very least,' Sophya said. 'That's why they've marched their army in that direction. They must know that Merric is getting the Florins to help us, and are trying to discourage them.'

'It gives us some breathing room, at the very least,' Sir Oskar said, glancing back down at the letter. 'The army that Sir Axyl Monfort led was only a fraction of the soldiers that the Monforts have to command, of course, but it is welcome that they are no longer camped on our borders. And if this news means that The Dale has joined us…'

'What are your orders, my lady?' Sir Orsten asked Sophya.

She stood and looked back at the window and the likeness of her distant ancestor made from the coloured glass. Her expression was impossible to read. But after a moment, she turned back to them all, a determined look on her face.

'Send word to every castle in The Head. To every baron, every lord and every knight. Tell them to muster every soldier they have, and call out their levies.'

Tomas felt a tingling through his entire body. A look of fierce pride passed over Sir Oskar's face, while his brother clenched his fists in enthusiastic anticipation.

'The time has come,' Sophya said. 'We will cross the river and take this fight to Lord Aric himself. And The Southstones will forever regret ever drawing their swords against us.'

Because The Head was marching to war.

Acknowledgements

When I finished writing *Hopebearer*, I had a clear idea of the journey that I wanted Merric to take next. However, much like in Merric's own adventure, the experience of writing this has not been a smooth journey. And so, there are a lot of people I want to thank for helping me to reach this point.

I would like to thank Christopher Badcock for his continued support while I wrote *Vagabond*. He has been an invaluable companion to me, much like Tomas has been to Merric. Thank you, Chris, for being my sounding board and letting me bounce ideas off you.

Thank you to my test readers for being brutally honest and helping me to forge the story that I wanted to tell. In no particular order, thank you George, Josh, Rob, Laura, Chris, Rebecca and Bob.

When I wrote *Hopebearer*, I gave my thanks to Laura May for her sacrifice as I disappeared into the world of High Realm for hours at a time. My gratitude for her support, patience and encouragement is just as strong now as it was then, but I am now honoured to call her Laura Wright.

My mother and father have been my biggest supporters in the two years since *Hopebearer* was completed, and I am proud to dedicate this second book to them.

And thank you to everyone who has supported me as a new author. Your words of encouragement and praise, and your enthusiasm for the world of High Realm, means a tremendous amount to me and has helped keep me going.

Now, it is time for me to crack on with the third and final part of The High Realm Chronicles. I am as excited as you are to see how this tale ends.